The Illegal

a novel by

John Mort

Southeast Missouri State University Press • 2013

The Illegal by John Mort

Copyright 2013: John Mort

Softcover: $15.00
ISBN: 978-0-9883103-46

First published in 2013 by
Southeast Missouri State University Press
One University Plaza, MS 2650
Cape Girardeau, MO 63701
www6.semo.edu / universitypress

Cover: Liz Lester Design

My thanks to Marianne Smith, for her insights into the Spanish language; to Terry Farish, Lenore Carroll, Lauren Miller, Catherine Browder, and Charles Hammer, for their careful, professional attention; and to my wife, Patricia, and son, Nathan, for their patience and guidance.

How shall we sing the Lord's song in a strange land?
Psalms 137: 4

I. Mexico

- 1 -

La Evangelista

Lieutenant Mario Oliveros stood guard. But because Captain Tejón and he were the only officers, "guard" meant little more than to take turns sleeping by the radio. It wasn't as though the company were in combat. They were enduring the last night of a three-week drug interdiction along a dammed portion of the Rio Grande called Lake Amistad, and had found nothing to interdict.

Sleep was impossible anyhow. Even at midnight the temperature was 37 degrees C—about 100 in the American system—and if he lay down inside the Tacoma pickup bed, he was hotter still. Twenty meters below, camped along the shore, the men could at least take a swim. All through the night, Mario listened to splashes and muffled laughter, as soldiers threw themselves into the tepid water.

Up on the cliff, Mario stripped to boxer shorts and t-shirt, and periodically dropped his feet into a bucket of water. He wet a towel, draped it around his neck, and read by flashlight his various science magazines, and then from a paperback of *Don Quixote*. Three weeks was a long time in the Coahuilan desert, and he was low on batteries and going through his magazines for the third time.

He called a communications check at 0300—to see if the radio worked, ascertain if any of the men were awake, and demonstrate that *he* was awake. He thought he caught a breeze in the Tacoma bed, backed hopefully toward the cliff's edge and that great gulp of air hanging over the water. Anyhow, the temperature had dropped to a chilly 92, and Mario lay back. He may have slept for several minutes. Or he hung over the abyss of sleep, and just as he was about to plunge into oblivion, found himself jerking backward from a dream. A woman had cried, "Help!"

He sat up with a gasp. Oh, these nights were hell. With his towel he wiped the sweat from his eyes, then miserably stood and staggered to the cliff's edge, where he urinated toward space, and never heard his urine fall. Where the water lay was a patch of absolute blackness, sparkling at faraway points from reflected stars, as if the sky had been turned upside-down. Ashore, he could make out the less-black peaks of soldiers' tents, and sandbars less black still, and then more pockets of blackness denoting massive basalt boulders. He heard willows faintly rustling. A big bird took flight, invisible wings thumping. A fetid, fishy odor rose, spiced with juniper, and he visualized his mother, stirring pickles in a crock with a big mahogany spoon. Momentarily, as if the world had ended, there was no sound.

Try to focus, he told himself. He had dreamed of a voice crying help. Not just a voice, but a woman's voice. No ghoulish female afterimage haunted him; how did he know he'd heard a woman? He stood utterly still, listening. An owl hooted.

Now he understood. He'd heard "Help," not "Ayúdame." His English was excellent, but he didn't dream in it.

He pulled on his trousers and boots, swallowed two salt tablets, and clipped a canteen to his belt. Every flashlight was weakened from his endless reading, but stars abounded, and in the army you grew accustomed to flailing about in the dark. And the woman couldn't be far away.

If such a woman exists, Señor Quixote.

He walked in the gravelly open places, wary of rattlesnakes, dodging clumps of ocotillo with its thin, spiny arms. The cliffs rising from the American side were greenish, almost phosphorescent in the starlight, and suggested coolness. But though he moved slowly, soon he was soaked in sweat, and sat for a moment on the cliff's edge, looking far down on the dark water. Mosquitoes found him, and he broke open his last packet of Te-Amo cigars simply to generate smoke.

The desert was a lovely place, no doubt, if you were a snake or a jackass.

Looking back, he could still make out the dark Tacoma, and

beyond it Tejón's starlit tent between the battered Nissan Pathfinder and the company's pride and joy, a four-year-old,   diesel-guzzling Humvee. Granted, his was a fool's errand anyhow, but good military procedure might be to walk at just this distance from the camp, describing a semi-circle back to the cliffs again. The dry air was tricky, but he didn't believe a voice carried any farther.

Only fifty meters ahead was the mesa, too small to have a name, that they'd used as a guide-on three days before. It was a sheer, nearly featureless up-thrust of rock, and cast a long shadow. Mario had a hunch about the mesa, and stepped across the shadow-line, almost into a patch of prickly pear. He knelt to listen.

He heard a sigh, something scraping, a rustling of stones.

"¿Hola?" he called.

Two reddish eyes bobbed straight up, down, and charged him. Involuntarily, he lifted his rifle, and the eyes veered away.

"¡Mierda!" he cried, falling backward.

It was only a deer. It leaped from the shadow and among the cacti, white rump brushing the Milky Way. Something had flushed it.

"¿Señora?" he whispered. Then, louder, "Anyone!"

He heard a groan. Excited but still mindful of snakes, he shuffled across the loose rock and sand toward the sound. Now he flicked on his weak light, cutting across what at first seemed like a pile of rags but slowly resolved into the form of a woman, sitting with legs outstretched and wide apart, and her head hung low.

He'd heard tales of drug smugglers using women for decoys, though none he'd encountered were so clever. And in the heat, smugglers had been lying low.

She lifted her head. "Are you the army?"

Because she spoke in English, he said, "Yes, ma'am." He held a hand to her cheek. It was clammy, hot like his own, and yet she wasn't sweating.

"No soldier will hurt me."

"I won't hurt you," he said. He held the canteen to her lips, and she tried to grab it from him.

"Easy," he said. He tore off a side of his cigar packet, laid it on a stone, and crushed two salt tablets with the butt end of his pocket knife. Gently, he pulled up her head.

"God is with the soldiers," the woman said. And, whispering hoarsely, "Oh, *thank* you, Jesus."

He brought the cardboard to her lips in a crude funnel. "This will taste bad."

She opened her mouth like a good child, but began coughing. He handed her the canteen and this time allowed her several long swallows. Then he pulled it back, took a swallow himself, and poured the rest over her head.

She gasped and shook her hair violently.

"Can you walk, Señora? It's a short distance to our camp." He took her hand and pulled her up.

"I saw your trucks from the mountain. I knew if I—" She held out her arms like a supplicant to a faith healer, and took one step. He hurried to her side before she could fall, and grabbed up an oversized leather bag—her purse—that must have weighed ten pounds. How in God's name had this woman survived?

"Thank you," she said, striving for a proper tone, but her words broke apart into a rough whisper.

They stepped past the shadow-line; she leaned on him heavily. In the starlight he thought she was a good-looking woman, though she was Mexican rather than gringa, and thus her English was puzzling. However, the feel of her dress was synthetic and expensive, like nothing a Mexican woman would wear, at least not deep in the country, not in the villages. She faltered, and sat quickly on a boulder.

"How far did you walk?"

"I don't know," she whispered. "Ignacio crashed the car—I was sleeping on the back seat. Do you have any more water—what's your name?"

He told her.

"I'm Maribel Garza. I almost made it, didn't I?"

"You did make it. You're American?"

"I was born in Oaxaca. My husband, he was from Dallas, a missionary. Do you have more water?"

"At the camp. Can you walk a little farther?"

"Oh." She stood, but couldn't move from the boulder. "I just—I just—"

If she'd been a soldier, he'd have thrown her over his shoulder in a fireman's carry. And perhaps that would have been wise for Maribel as well, but somehow such an action was too

rude for his sensibilities. He picked her up in his arms like ac-
tors do in movies, staggering, the heavy purse banging against
his kidneys. She laid her head against his chest as though she
were sleeping, and said nothing. He caught an odor like ripe
mangos.

He had not two hundred meters to go, but being so long in
the desert, without even one night of proper sleep, had taxed
him more that he realized. Soon his arms ached, but he didn't
want to set her down again. This one and only night, he was
Don Quixote.

He meant to be. To be pure. To uphold the Mexican Consti-
tution. But he hadn't been with a woman for months, and now
he had one in his arms. He wouldn't see her after tonight. She
seemed to be God-crazy. But with sweat pouring off him and
his arms in such pain they began to cramp, he felt an erection
grow. He tried to shift her higher so she wouldn't feel it, but
could barely hang onto her as it was. *Dios mio,* he thought.

As his erection withered and he marched on, he wondered
if the woman were real. She was a fabulous Mexican ghost, appearing to the hapless campesino as in some old folktale. She
was the delirious result of sleeplessness, another trial in purgatory, a military penance. Sweat pooled at his belt and trickled
down inside his trousers, and he plodded on, in sight of the
vehicles now, his legs working at a far remove from his over-
heated brain.

At last he eased her to her feet and bent with his hands on
his knees, panting. "We are there, Señora."

"Ignacio's *dead,*" she said.

The men called Captain Luis Tejón "Napoleon" because he
was short, loud, and treacherous. Trusting Mario, they used the
nickname in his presence, and he seldom corrected them. In
fact, to their list he might have added "vain" and "greedy."

Not lecherous, though, or cruel to animals. Sometimes late
at night Mario played mental games such as naming cities in Jalisco, his home state; counting his sexual encounters, beginning
with that Gomez girl's aggressive and unprovoked kiss in the
second grade; and listing Tejón's good points. He sent money to
his mother in Chihuahua. He'd been observed attending mass.

It was hard to think of anything more, but Tejón was far
from the worst commander he could have drawn. Mario feared
he was average.

Suffice it that he dreaded waking Tejón, but the woman was a significant development, and the eastern sky grew bright. She required medical attention. They'd need to do something about her car and the dead guide, or driver, or missionary, or whatever he was. The sooner all this was accomplished, the sooner they could return to Ciudad Acuña, the men could begin their leave, and Mario could get some sleep.

"You left your post, Lieutenant?"

This was Tejón's response to Mario's account. The captain was like Mario's father in this respect—he'd listen to a long narration that in response called for praise and even astonishment, and instead point out a character flaw. The technique had had some effect in his first year with Tejón, but after three years it was only a ritual that Mario doubted even Tejón took seriously.

Mario's sigh was a ritual, too. "I was never out of sight of camp, Señor."

Tejón, behind his tent urinating, groaned. "Jesucristo, Mario, this heat!"

"The army, Señor. They put you in the desert in summer, the mountains in winter."

Tejón dipped his hands in a basin and slicked back his thin hair. "I heard it will reach 50 today. Too hot even for drug- runners. Where's our coffee, Lieutenant?"

Coffee, in such heat? "I'll make it now. I thought you would want to know—"

Surprisingly, the captain smiled. "You went and played the hero on me, Mario."

"You would have done the same."

"Oh, not me, Mario, not me." Tejón rubbed his chin, perhaps debating a shave, then donned his glasses and tucked in his shirt. "Not exactly garrison soldiers, are we, Lieutenant?"

"In these conditions—"

"But we do our best with those conditions, don't we, Lieutenant? You did well."

"Thank you, Señor."

"Despite leaving your post. Well, I'll talk to this . . . holy sister."

"I don't believe she's a *nun*, Captain."

"This—this—*evangelista*." Sucking in his gut, Tejón strode to the Tacoma's tailgate, where Maribel had lain back on Mario's sleeping mat.

Mario started coffee on the propane stove and warmed black beans from a can on the second burner. Their store-bought tortillas were gone, but he remembered a can of pineapple he'd been saving for a late night break. He found bowls for the beans, washed two cups and two spoons, but Maribel would have to eat the pineapple from the can. He took everything around to the tailgate on a worn TV tray.

Tejón, tracing Maribel's route on a topographic map he'd spread out, looked up irritably, and then leaned back with amusement.

"Mario," Maribel said softly. She'd done some work with the pan of water he'd given her, scrubbing her face and arms. She'd treated her cuts and combed some of the snarls from her long hair. She had a wide-eyed, exotic look, both European and Indian. He thought she might be forty.

She turned up the can to let the chunks of fruit fall into her mouth, and moaned as the pineapple syrup slid over her teeth.

"Eat the beans, too, Señora," Mario said. "They aren't much, but they'll give you some strength."

"Lieutenant," Tejón said, holding up the map. "Put together a detail. You can take the Humvee—"

"Because it has a winch," he murmured.

"Sí. If her car won't start, you can tow it. And take the GPS. You'll need to call in coordinates to the judiciales."

No one liked dealing with the judiciales—the state police. Technically, the army superseded them, but often the opposite seemed true. And they were thugs. They were well-equipped thugs, with fancy boats for running down drug dealers and, some said, running drugs themselves. How else could they afford their fancy boats?

"If I call them, Señor, they may not come until next week. If I call you, and you inform the colonel, and the colonel calls Ramirez—"

Tejón chuckled. "He's a smart lieutenant, don't you think, Señora?"

Maribel nodded trustingly, as she shoveled in beans.

"He's so smart he reads books with his flashlight. We can't find a working flashlight in all the camp because Mario likes to read his books."

Maribel offered Mario a gentle look. But her speech seemed distant: "I don't care about the car."

"I'm afraid it's the dead man who's the problem. *I* believe your story, the lieutenant believes your story—"

"My clothes," she said. "I don't care."

"But the judiciales can be difficult. May I examine your bag, Senora?"

When she didn't object, Tejón rummaged in the purse, producing a passport which he studied for an instant, and then an envelope full of crisp American twenties. He flipped them with his broad thumb.

"A Mexican woman, now an American citizen, who suddenly wants to drive around in Mexico. It's dangerous, if nothing else—"

"I began to realize that, and that's why I hired Ignacio," Maribel said. "My mother died. That's why it was so sudden."

"And your husband—"

"I am a widow."

"I'm sorry, Señora," Mario put in. "What a time you've had."

Tejón raised a hand to silence him. "I'm grieved to hear of your mother's death, but this is almost four thousand dollars, Señora."

"It's hard to find an ATM. Checks are awkward. You can't always use a credit card. I had to pay Ignacio; and then we were going to visit his church, where I planned to make a donation." She began to cry. "Ignacio was a good Christian man."

"And now you don't have to pay him."

"¡Señor!" Mario said. "She's about to collapse!"

Tejón gave him a warning look. "I believe you are leading a detail, Lieutenant."

"Sí." Mario yanked the radio from behind Maribel and took a few steps toward the cliff. Her wide eyes followed him.

"I find it odd that your driver would suddenly veer into the desert."

She was a long moment answering. "He said he knew a shortcut."

"Only smugglers come this way. Occasionally, we catch a coyote with his pollos."

Maribel closed her eyes.

Tejón tucked the envelope into his shirt pocket. "I'll hold this money. It will be returned to you, of course, but there may be medical expenses. It will cost something to tow the car, the body must be disposed of—"

"No soldier will hurt me," Maribel said.

"Of course not, Señora. We honor all women."

"God will protect me. God is with the *soldiers.*"

Tejón looked accusingly at Mario, who shrugged.

"I'm sorry to ask these questions, Señora," Tejón went on. "Someone must, but I see how tired you are. I'll start the engine, so that the air runs, and you can tilt back in the seat and sleep a little. We'll have you at the hospital by ten."

"I don't need—"

"Yes, you do."

And then he guided Maribel toward the Pathfinder, slowly and deferentially, as if she were the aged mother he sent money to.

Even in the Humvee the going was tough. They had to veer from the smooth rock along the cliff when a chasm, choked with cacti and juniper, opened beneath them, and along their detour the sharp outcroppings of rock were often too formidable even for the Humvee's oversized wheels and four-wheel drive. But by 1100 hours, from a high point, they spied the car, sitting at the lip of an abandoned limestone quarry. A faintly outlined road stretched beyond, connecting with a gravel state highway that both the army and the judiciales used.

Mario passed his binoculars to César, the recruit just out of high school in Piedras Negras, to give the kid an opportunity to be right. "What kind of car?"

"It's a Cadillac," César said gravely. "Maybe three years old. Nice."

"It's beyond belief that she drove it all the way to Oaxaca," said Sergeant Francisco, whom Mario chose for details whenever he could. Once a street kid in Mexico City, Francisco was forever grateful to the army simply for a place to exist, and Mario relied on him. In fact, he was the nearest Mario came to having a friend.

Mario called the coordinates to Tejón on the company cell phone, adjusting the latitude slightly in an estimate of how much farther south the Cadillac was, though simply saying "the old quarry" was probably sufficient direction. Tejón agreed that the Cadillac might tempt the notoriously slow judiciales into something akin to efficiency. If so, they had a shorter distance to travel, and a better route. But it would take them an hour to organize, and Mario calculated he'd arrive before them.

Tejón told him to winch the Cadillac immediately to the Humvee, staking a claim, and Mario wondered if the captain intended to impound the Cadillac indefinitely. Maribel would go home in resignation, grateful for her life, and the car could be sold. Even that, Mario thought, was preferable to handing the keys to the judiciales.

"They'll maintain it's a crime scene, and make trouble."

"To hell with them," Tejón said. "It's our car."

"I understand, Señor."

Following the jagged ridgeline of the low mountains, he ground out their way to flat land, where he managed forty kilometers an hour, dodging yellowish huisache thickets and yucca with dead stalks tall as trees. It was a rough ride, and the two enlisted men clutched at whatever they could find to avoid banging their heads.

Francisco chuckled at Mario's haste. "Noble of you, Lieutenant, to carry the poor evangelista through the terrible heat."

Mario smiled and dropped his speed. "I saw my duty clearly before me."

"That's exactly right," said César seriously. "We serve the people of Mexico."

Mario turned north onto the quarry road, covered with tiny red flowers but otherwise smooth. He was doing eighty kph, and kicking up a contrail of dust, when he spied the car. He pointed the Humvee up a gravelly bank, then backed near enough that they could unwind the winch.

The temperature, he noted resignedly, had risen to 115.

They examined the Cadillac in wonder. Its front wheels had vaulted up, and stood barely touching ground, almost pawing at the air. Something underneath had caught on a hunk of rock, or the car would have plunged into the quarry at nearly a 70 degree angle.

"What a fool this driver was," Francisco said. "Too stupid for a coyote, that's certain. If he were not a driver for the religious woman, I'd say he was drunk."

"Couldn't see, perhaps. You take a wrong turn, you keep thinking it's the right one, ¿sí o no? It's a pretty good road; he was going too fast. No sign to tell him he's about to run off a cliff. A fool, like you say, but I can understand how it happened."

The car was closed in on either side with hillocks of crushed rock. César slid along the driver's side, and stared through the window at the dead man.

Francisco shoveled sand and gravel from beneath the rear bumper, and crawled under. "The stabilizer bars are broken!" he said. "Wait; only one of them. The other caught on the rock, and stopped the car. *Instantly.* No wonder our friend is dead."

"How many miles, César?"

The recruit kept staring. "What?"

"On the car. How many miles?"

"I'll have to open the *door*—"

Francisco pulled himself from beneath. "I say shoot it and put it out of its misery, Lieutenant. The oil pan isn't leaking but it's crushed, and I don't believe the crankshaft will turn over. The steering's all messed up. I couldn't see everything, but I believe the entire front end is bent."

"Can we tow it?"

"Sí." Francisco shrugged. "We can yank it out and winch up the front. But if I were the American lady, I might not want to haul it to Cadillac in Del Rio. She'll have to deal with the police on both sides, and the border patrol. Stabilizer bars, new ball joints, new tie rods, exhaust system—that will cost a fortune over there."

"Parts?"

"For parts it's valuable. The body looks fine. Fancy stereo. Tires. Maybe the wheels. Radiator. Glass all around. And the seats are leather. It was a fine car."

César returned, looking pale. "Sixty-four thousand miles. He *stinks.*"

Mario nodded and handed him the binoculars. "Get yourself some water, and climb that rock," he said, pointing to a crumbling bluff. "Watch for the judiciales."

Francisco eyed the kid bemusedly, then turned. "Shall we tow it, Señor?"

"Wait."

Mario slid along the driver's side and opened the door. The keys were in the ignition and he could read the indicators on the dash, but not enough power remained to run down the windows. And César was right about the stench. Flies were absent, but the temperature in the closed car must have climbed above 150 degrees F, and the driver was hardly recognizable as a human being. You could see the gash where his head had struck the wheel, blackened around its edges now, slushy. His eyes, frozen open, seemed not horrified but deeply sad.

The expression didn't reflect the instant of his death, however. Heat had loosened the skin around his eyes, causing his blackening face to sag downward. He looked like a melting wax figure.

Mario took a deep breath and then ducked his head inside as if diving. He rolled the driver to the side, and found his billfold. The man was from Ciudad Acuña, so the judiciales would probably make an effort to contact his family. More troubling, he had eleven hundred dollars—and a few pesos. This was his salary, probably, but the amount was enough to suggest he was a smuggler. If you wanted to build a circumstantial case, and make enough trouble for a rich American woman that she had to hire lawyers and pay exorbitant fees to exonerate herself, it was enough. *What were you doing so far from the main road, Señora? Are you running drugs, Señora?*

He'd have to give something to his men to insure their complicity. He'd hold onto the balance in case he saw the evangelista again; otherwise, when several months had passed, he'd give the money to the dead man's family.

He hoped his deeds matched his good intentions. And he hoped he wasn't being too clever. He returned the pesos, and two hundred, drew another breath, and slid the billfold back into the man's trousers. He straightened the poor fellow to his former position, gave the interior a hard glance, and as he closed the door, slapped at a fly. Looking through the window, he saw a dozen more on the dead man's sagging face. Dios mio, they were quick.

He retrieved a bottle of water from the Humvee and joined his men on the bluff. They'd found buckets to sit on from the tin quarry shack and a spot of shade under a gnarled juniper.

Francisco handed him a smashed cellphone.

"What is this?"

"Why the evangelista had to walk. What's the verdict, Lieutenant? Do we tow it?"

"We give it to the police."

Squinting, Mario studied the haze to the south, where he thought he saw rising dust. He took off his cap and poured water on his head. He reached for his last three Te-Amos, lit one, and offered the other two.

The boy shook his head emphatically in what seemed like

moral revulsion. Francisco lit his, took a long draw, and contemplated the smoke. "Why do you smoke this brand, Lieutenant?"

"I think I was fourteen, it was when I worked at the big hotel. I saw Clint Eastwood in *For a Few Dollars More.*"

Young César spoke up nervously. "Clint Eastwood smoked *Te-Amos*?"

"It's hard to say. But I couldn't afford habanos."

Silently, he handed them each one hundred dollars, and held up a third hundred so they could see, before tucking it into his shirt pocket with the rest of the dead man's money. "He had five hundred," Mario said.

"Why not take it all?" César said. He stalked a few meters away and looked off south through the binoculars. "The money belongs to his family, Señor."

"True," Francisco said. "But if we found them and gave them the money, the judiciales would hear of it. Or Napoleon would. Let's say we give it to Napoleon in the first place."

César nodded. "He'd keep it for himself."

"Two hundred is just enough for the judiciales not to be suspicious. They'll turn a fair profit with parts. They'll deliver the body to the undertaker and contact the family, maybe even give them a little something."

Mario rose, and now could make out a flash of red through the dust.

César looked thoughtful. "If they keep the car, they have done an illegal thing, and won't bother the evangelista," he said. "It's like she paid them."

Francisco smiled. "See why the lieutenant is the lieutenant?"

"Smart!"

"We'll find out how smart I am," said Mario. He eyed them both. "We dug under the car to see if it could be towed. All we want is the woman's luggage. We didn't examine the body. And, of course, I didn't give you any gringo money."

Francisco backed the Humvee off the road, but kept the engine running so that César could lie down in cool air. The heat made him nauseous. Then Francisco took a position at the grill with his rifle shouldered—a nice touch, Mario thought.

He stood in the middle of the road to greet the judiciales—two men, peering from behind tinted glass. They drove a black Cadillac Escalade, one of the new, surprisingly powerful hybrids. It was hardly as versatile as a Humvee, but faster, and maybe even more macho.

"A Cadillac convention," Francisco called out.

The captain's name was Pérez. Mario had observed him in the cafés down by the tourist bazaars in Ciudad Acuña, often consorting with the city police, or anyhow with their pretty office workers. As the Escalade idled he wrote, or pretended to write, on a clipboard, allowing Mario to cook a moment longer. At last he dismounted along with his sergeant, who exchanged a word with Francisco; they were drinking pals.

Before the captain could speak, Mario saluted him—unnecessarily, but he wanted to establish deference. Pérez returned the salute and said, "You've examined the body?"

"No, Captain. We arrived only minutes ahead of you, and anyhow it's a police matter. We secured the area and dug under the bumper to see where our cable would go, should you want us to tow the vehicle."

With a bandanna, Peréz daubed the sweat from around his reddish eyes. He had a thin face, a thin moustache, but a lot of hair, and perhaps women found him good-looking. His uniform was standard-issue, but starched, and Mario thought how ragged he must look by contrast. Good duty, those cafés.

"Gracias, but I believe we can manage," Peréz said. He shook Mario's hand. "A Cadillac with Texas plates in the middle of nowhere. Look suspicious to you, Lieutenant?"

"That's for the police to decide, but in my opinion, this was a stupid accident. The driver thought he was taking a shortcut and drove too fast. That car must be worth something, eh?"

"I believe it might be. Well, I'm glad the army and the police could cooperate in this unfortunate matter, Lieutenant. . . ."

"Oliveros."

"Have I seen you in the city?"

"Sí, sometimes they allow us a brief rest. Mostly, we are out there. . . " Mario motioned vaguely to the north.

"In hell, you mean. Have you ever known it to be so hot?"

"I think it's this global warming they talk about on the television."

"Who can say?" Pérez nodded to his sergeant, who stepped toward the Cadillac. "Can you get around us all right, or should I move the vehicle?"

"We're fine. I appreciate your prompt attention, Captain; my men are anxious for a nice long shower."

"And for other things, my guess is. Here." He handed

Mario a card. "We could have a drink sometime. In the interest of army and police relations."

"I'll look forward to it, Señor." Mario studied the card, a bit taken aback. Pérez was a politician, it seemed. Remarkable, and perhaps he'd call the man and study his manner with pretty clerks, at least if they were on speaking terms after the captain discovered the condition of the car. "I have one request, Captain. I wonder if you could open the trunk, so that we can take the missionary lady's luggage to the hospital."

Again, Pérez wiped the sweat from his eyes. They both watched as the sergeant opened the car door to retrieve the keys. "She's an evangelista?"

"A kindly, older lady who recently lost her mother."

The sergeant walked toward them, holding his nose.

Pérez laughed. "Something smells here, Oliveros, besides the dead man."

"Why don't we examine her luggage?"

The suitcases contained only those lightweight synthetic garments such as all the female turistas wore, and underwear, and other womanly things that the sergeant held up with a certain reserve. Pérez motioned for him to open a cardboard box, but it was filled with New Testaments en español.

"No drogas," Mario put in. "No anything. Sometimes, we are too cynical, eh?"

"Possibly my attitude has been influenced by drug smugglers, who even last night were shooting at me."

"I know what you mean." Mario nodded to Francisco, who took the driver's seat. "The family will be informed, Captain?"

"Obviously."

"And the car—"

"Will be taken care of."

This time Pérez was ahead of him with his salute. Mario smiled and climbed into the Humvee with his men, and Francisco pointed them toward Ciudad Acuña. They rode several kilometers before Francisco said, "A brave and selfless public servant, that Pérez."

"Handsome, too."

"As I watched you deal with him, a philosophical question occurred to me."

"I enjoy those."

"I know. It's this: if the evangelista had been a fat priest, would you still have carried him?"

Mario laughed. He was no Don Quixote, but he'd done as right by the woman, and his men, as one could in the desert heat.

"That's more of a religious question," he said.

- 2 -

Las Palmas

Mario and his detail arrived at their "temporary" home, a motel called Las Palmas, at nearly the same time as the body of the company. He felt obliged to stand with the men for moments more, even though inside himself he was screaming for privacy. And to escape the heat: it was 3 P.M., and 50 degrees C—or 122, north of the Rio Grande.

Las Palmas had been built twenty years before for the soon-to-wither American tourist trade—the place still boasted three dried-out royal palms and a peeling Triple-A decal. New barracks for the battalion were under construction, but they'd been under construction for five years. So far, dishonest contractors and whimsical army funding had resulted merely in slabs of concrete overgrown with weeds. Thieves had run off with the copper plumbing, leaving only plastic drain pipes like saguaros, listing prayerfully toward the sky.

Mario stood the men in haphazard formation in a spot of shade, as one by one they secured their gear to the Humvee, which would be locked for several days. Under no circumstances were they to cross the border, he told them, and by the way, the girls downtown are unclean. Beware of strangers with promises of easy money; the army has its eyes everywhere, and knows when you go astray. This last advice was in reality a caution against desertion. Enlisted men were paid so little that he could count on one a month being recruited by smugglers. Any soldier in the company could have delivered the same speech, having heard it a hundred times—except perhaps young César, who stared at Mario with grave innocence.

Tejón, newly shaved, wearing a fresh uniform rather than civilian clothes, came out of the office with keys and pay envelopes. With a yelp, the men dispersed by the pool that had never had any water in it. However, the air conditioning was still reliable, and the television offered two pornographic channels, one of them free. The men would shower, change to their cruising clothes, and make individual or tribal pilgrimages, seeking liquor, sex, and religion.

Tejón handed Mario his pay and glanced at his fancy watch.

"You are still official, Captain. If I can be of any help—"

Tejón slapped his back; his hand clung to Mario's fatigue shirt like hot tar. "Maybe not this time, mi amigo. You can help by resting, and keeping an eye on our fine young men. Don't let them wander too far."

"Something is happening?"

"Something is always happening, Lieutenant, in the army of Mexico!"

"Sí." Mario tried not to show his irritation. "What of the woman, Señor?"

"Still at the hospital, I think. I will check on her." The captain flipped up his sunglasses and smiled almost mockingly. "You are in love?"

Mario laughed.

"Well, she couldn't stop talking about *you*. I returned her money, by the way."

"The right thing to do, Señor. She—she could have been your sister."

"Not *my* sister, poor woman. But as the widow of a general—"

"General!"

"They met in her village, a beautiful and touching story. As I say, a military man, even if he was a gringo."

"I thought he was a missionary."

"A righteous general, let us say. Truly, a man of distinction."

"I understand," Mario said, although he didn't. "And the dead fellow?"

Tejón dropped his sunglasses in place, perhaps to mask a flare of anger. "Mario, why did you let the police keep her car? You *know* she won't see it again."

"Good only for parts, Señor." Mario shrugged. "But valuable enough to keep them happy."

"Ah." Tejón cocked his head thoughtfully and gave a short laugh. "I have a clever lieutenant in my command. The driver was only a guide, as your sweetheart said. He wanted her to speak at his church, and afterwards she would distribute Bibles, and presumably make a donation. I never met anyone like her."

"¿Señor?"

"Who told the absolute truth. We called some people—all that she said was true."

Mario smiled. "Down to no soldier would hurt her."

"We should all have such faith. Why don't you find a pretty girl tonight, mi amigo?"

Mario couldn't find words.

"Not like that one, no, no. She's nice-looking, but you would probably have to fall to your knees and convert. And she called her people in el norte; she may already be gone. A girl other than a rich evangelista, Mario. But whom you can fill with fire in due course."

Mario smiled. He found himself almost liking his captain. "I'm tired, Señor."

"Sí," Tejón said, nodding. "In this heat, we all grow tired."

His room smelled like sickness and was hotter than the inside of a Cadillac left in the sun, but he turned on the air conditioner, and with a sigh and something like a death rattle, it began converting hot air to cool. Sweating profusely, he pawed in his duffel bag for clean boxer shorts, then brushed his teeth, shaved, and stepped into the shower. The water ran hot for a moment, then began to cool, cooling him as well, and washing away three weeks of grime. He toweled down, treated his cuts and insect bites with a stinging ointment, and checked the thermostat. It read 86 in Fahrenheit. A miracle!

He collapsed on the bed, pushing his long legs under the sheets, which were wrinkled but reasonably clean. He pulled three pillows under his head and hit the remote.

Fighting was reported north of the border. Well, a skirmish. An Arizona Congressman claimed that Columbus, New Mexico—where Pancho Villa had staged his raid in 1916—had become a Mexican army garrison. An official from Mexico City countered with a story just as far-fetched. He said the renegades were crazy people who called themselves "Cíbolistas."

The Cíbolistas were trying to establish a sort of utopia in

central or northern New Mexico, near where Coronado had looked for his seven cities of gold. Daring crimes appealed to them, the official said, as a means of raising money and attracting followers, but in any case the Cíbolistas were Mexican Americans, rather than Mexicans. "*Many* American citizens have brown skin," she said—almost smugly.

"Nonsense," said the Congressman. He had very good information that the renegades were regular Mexican army. No doubt some of them were deserters. But all ran drugs, dashing in and out of remote places on their ATVs.

"You don't believe the Cíbolistas are real?" asked a young woman, a reporter for CNN en español.

The Congressman shrugged and smiled, maybe because the reporter was pretty. "Who knows?" he said. "Mexico never got over losing Texas."

He'd regret saying that, Mario thought. Mexican TV would run it endlessly—American TV, too, though perhaps in el norte the Congressman preached to the choir. Yes, the gringos had stolen Texas, and then New Mexico and California, with trumped-up wars and forced treaties. But surely no one thought Mexico was going to war with the United States over so much parched land. Mexico had plenty of that already.

But Mario agreed with the Congressman that the Cíbolistas were probably a romantic invention. It was *all* about drugs, as the Congressman said. The cartels were trying to punch into New Mexico and Texas, vast, unpopulated areas that couldn't be secured. Things were bad enough that his men worried they'd be redeployed. So far little Acuña remained quiet, but there was bloody work to be had in Reynosa and Juarez. Kidnappings. Beheadings. Worst of all, you couldn't trust that the man next to you hadn't been corrupted. They wouldn't escape it much longer.

They'd escape it tonight. He flipped through channels, found no movie worth watching, little in Spanish, and most of that those incessant talk shows, at last settling on the Texas Rangers and turning the English low. Nothing was more lulling than a ball game: you became a little involved and, before you knew it, were waking from a sound nap.

The phone rang, yanking him from nothingness. "¿Sí? ¿Hola?"

The voice was tentative, almost shy. "Lieutenant, can I talk to you?"

"This evening, César, will that be satisfactory?"

"Sí, Señor."

The boy sounded desperate, and Mario's job as executive officer was to play father confessor, but he doubted César's problems were so profound they couldn't be put off for a few hours.

The temperature inside had fallen to 80 degrees F. He stepped naked to the curtains, shivering gratefully. Peeking out, he noted the numbers on the bank thermometer: 47/115. Ah, he thought. A cold wave.

The courtyard was deserted. One or two of the men might be secluded in their rooms, but most were in the cantinas and wouldn't return until ten or so, to drink and play cards through the night. He went down to the lobby, where the bored clerk was watching an old Tin Tan movie. Fortunately, the computer was free.

June 8
Mario,

My son, thank you for wiring the money. Do not short yourself, however. We've had plenty of rain and the garden is wonderful. I wish you could see it. I tried to count and I believe we have seventy-five watermelons! Salvio has made a cart for your old motorcycle and he will take them to market. We think they are worth five or even ten pesos each!

So few turistas have come this year that they laid some people off at the hotel. But I'm such a good cook they can't do without me!

Well, I hope you are well and finding ways to hide from the heat. It must be a terrible place, that long river. I never heard a good thing about it. Please stay out of danger and don't forget to pray. Pray to the Virgin and to the Father and you will be rewarded with happiness.

Your loving mother,
Doracita

Mario laughed cruelly. He held a vague belief in God, but had seen small evidence of the old fellow's sympathy for Mexicans, and the world at large seemed determined on turning itself into hell. These were the last days, perhaps. That's what his mother would have said.

Mama,

We are taking a break in Ciudad Acuña. It has been very hot even for the desert, but the air conditioning in my luxurious room is excellent. It's only twenty-six in there, can you believe it?

We have been working hard apprehending smugglers and indocumentados. I don't like the work much and dream of the day when I have enough money to buy a farm, possibly in the state of Sonora where they raise tomatoes in greenhouses and sell them to the norteamericanos. Perhaps you'd want to come and live with me when you've tired of working in the hotel. Even so, I have three years remaining of my commission, so I'm not going anywhere for a while.

What do you hear of Alicia? I think of her now and then.

Do not worry about the money, Mama. The army pays me very well and I expect any day to learn of my promotion to first lieutenant. How I wish I had one of those watermelons!

Mario

He had no other messages. He hadn't heard from Alicia in almost a year and supposed she'd given up on him. He missed her, but it hadn't been a happy love affair. She was an accountant for the hotel where his mother worked, twenty-nine, and wanted to get married. What's more, she wanted him to quit the army and take over her family's business.

"You can't just *quit* the army," he said. "And what would I do?"

"You could run our resort now that Papa is growing old. You speak such good English!"

"My English is all right, but my bank account is anemic."

"Papa will help us."

He thought hard about her proposal. He was a fair carpenter, and could fix up and expand the resort without spending much. If a profit were possible, he supposed he could cater to the whims of rich gringos as well as anyone. Testing her, he suggested instead that they find some land and grow vegetables.

"Like your father," Alicia said.

He shrugged. "Modernize. Buy a tractor and more land."

"Your father was a nice man, but everybody said he couldn't

change with the times. Even before the gringos came along with their not-so-free trade, all you did on the farm was work, work, work, trying to make two or three acres feed a family. I'm not a campesino, Mario; I'm a modern woman. I don't want to grub in the soil."

She was right. And unlike most of the men he'd grown up with, including his father, he saw the virtue in having a smart woman at your side, and listening to her.

But he wanted to be a farmer. Perhaps his desire was a directive from the grave: *succeed, son, where I have failed.* The gringos had sabotaged the market for corn, but other crops could be planted. He'd find a way.

He shut off the computer and plunged into the heat, which, at six P.M., still hovered at 42/110. Clinging to the shadows of buildings, he walked a slow kilometer to a supermercado, where he bought oranges and a tin of saltines, as well as canned fruit, pudding, soup, and tuna for their next sojourn into the desert. He bought an American popular science magazine with a cover story about rising sea levels, even though he'd have preferred to find it in Spanish. All of the Mexican magazines concerned the activities of singers and soap opera stars. The newspapers seemed only to report murders—and horoscopes.

He wanted cheese for his crackers, but it had sold out.

"¿Hielo?" he asked the clerk, without hope.

The girl smiled flirtatiously. "Sí."

How long since he'd had ice? Dios mio, he'd have to run to his room to keep it from melting. He ducked back into the store for mango and pineapple juice, a lime, and Cuban rum. The world had not quite given up on ice. It was something to celebrate.

Tomorrow he'd read the American magazine, repair his gear, and take the Tacoma to headquarters for resupply. Batteries! He'd buy fifty of them! And he'd drop by the bank to wire his mother five hundred pesos, and deposit another five hundred in his minuscule savings. He'd petition Tejón once more about the promotion. Maybe the two of them could talk to the colonel.

But tonight he had hielo, and was going to get extremely drunk, and watch stupid American television. A movie from the 1970s, maybe, full of car chases and voluptuous, comic-book

29

women. Like a kid, he broke into a run, carrying his plastic food sacks in one hand, the chunk of ice, wrapped in butcher paper, in the other. Within a block the paper was damp; in two blocks it was dripping.

And then he saw Maribel, sitting on a shaded concrete bench. She was bruised and Band-Aided, and still wore her ragged dress from the desert, but she'd applied makeup and combed her hair to her shoulders. Down the wall behind her drooped violet and red bougainvillea, framing her like some village girl arrived at last in the merciless city. He stared at her unconsciously, as if she were an animal on display, until she pulled at her hair, and looked away.

"I thought you'd gone, Señora."

She pulled her hair again as she looked up at him. "I think I was . . . out of my mind."

"You were under terrible stress. Do you realize you walked almost ten kilometers?"

"I don't remember it, Mario. If you knew me, if you had any idea who I am, you—oh, I don't know what to say. I just trust in the Lord and praise Him. But you saved my life. I couldn't leave without properly thanking you."

He reached for his billfold and took out the seven hundred dollars, which he'd separated from his pay with a paper clip. "This belonged to the dead man, Señora. I'm sorry some of it's gone; I thought it better that my men have it than the judiciales. You make little bribes through the day. That's how things work along the border."

"I'll wire some money to Ignacio's family." She dropped the seven hundred into her big purse and, smiling, pointed at his ice. "You're dripping, soldier."

"And you won't see your car again. To repair it would have required—"

"No hope for the car. Your gracious captain explained."

"He—"

"Dropped me off downtown and pointed toward the bridge. And then I saw you walking." She held his eyes for an instant. "Mario, do you have my luggage?"

"Of course!" He walked beside her, clutching the ice to his stomach when it threatened to burst through the paper, glancing down at her nervous smile. The grimy dress did her no justice, he thought, though she was pretty enough. Pretty wasn't quite the word. She was mature, dignified, and the events of the day had dragged her low. Her eyes saddened and grew sympathetic, as he stared.

He secured the suitcase and box from the Humvee, and they stood awkwardly in the hammering sun. Water dripped from his ice, as if from his belly, and made a puddle between them. "May I come to your room, Mario?"

"Señora—"

She talked quickly, as if trying to convince herself. "My friends won't be here for several hours. I could cross, I could get a room, but I thought we could—"

Was she propositioning him? Were American women so forward as that? He stared until she averted her eyes. "Of course, you are welcome, Señora."

"Such a gentleman," she said, and flashed a smile.

Perhaps he was. They marched past the motel clerk, who didn't so much as lift his eyes, and at last the cold air of his room hit them. Maribel slumped against the wall and whispered, "Oh thank you, Jesus!"

He might have laughed at her, if to do so were not impolite and if he were not seduced by his own obsession. Trembling with desire, he dropped the ice block into a pan and chipped some of it with his pocket knife. "Would you care for a drink, Señora?"

"Call me Maribel. *Please.*" She eyed his rum with an affected neutrality. "I think only water, but with some of that wonderful ice. You know, in el norte, they have ice everywhere. Mario . . . would you mind if I took a shower?"

He splashed in mango juice and took his first long drink. "Of course not, Maribel."

"And then . . . do you think I could have some of your tuna? And the crackers? Such good crackers in Mexico."

He shrugged. "I wish I had something better to offer."

"You weren't expecting company," she said, smiling wearily and closing the door.

No, he thought. I was expecting oblivion. He drank, imagining Maribel's naked body while she showered. He pressed the cold rum to his forehead, feeling excited and miserable.

She emerged with a towel wrapped around her hair, her brown face almost rosy from steam. Her rumpled pink housecoat lent her a relaxed, middle-aged aura. She was *at home,* he thought, though the notion was absurd. She made quick work of her tuna and crackers, and sat opposite him, licking her fingers then leaning back to savor her ice water. She crossed her legs, which were shapely but also muscular; she stretched out her feet and wriggled her toes in the cool air.

"Except for you, Mario, I could have died." She looked at him with the sincerity of a child. "If there's ever anything, *anything* I can do for you—"

It wasn't the rum in his blood; he hadn't had enough of it. He thought she was beckoning to him with her strong brown legs. He thought they were two lonely souls, not particularly compatible, who faced the end of the world together. He kissed her.

She tucked her legs under and shrank in the chair. "*No.*"

He grabbed her shoulders, kissed her neck.

"No, I can't. Mario, *please.*"

Her religion, he thought; that was why. But it was also true that unlike most of his men, or Captain Pérez the budding politician, he had no luck with women. He was a soldier in a second-rate army and had no luck at all. Unlike Don Quixote, he couldn't pretend otherwise.

He held his glass to the light and tried to speak without emotion. "Tomorrow you will reach the Promised Land."

"It's Dallas, which is a long way from Heaven." She smiled sweetly. "However, there's ice any time you want."

He didn't reply.

"You'd fit right in. You speak excellent English." She held up his magazine. "Read it, too!"

He dropped in more ice cubes, and poured another splash of rum. He wasn't attracted to her, and she had imposed. He wanted her to leave. He wanted to drink until he passed out in his cool cocoon—give him one night, at least! Still she remained, naked under that frumpy housecoat. He strained for civility. "You are . . . Zapoteco?"

"Mizteco. And German. And Baptist." She laughed, but then stared at him intently. "Are you a Christian, Mario?"

He had never hated religion so much. "My mother is Catholic."

Maribel smiled almost wistfully. "You are good to your mother?"

"I try. But tell me, so far south in Oaxaca, how did you meet the American general?"

She took a deep breath. "They came to build us a church on the mountainside. From his own church, the men's group in Dallas—the prayer warriors, he called them."

"And you—"

"I was twenty-six, teaching in the school. So long ago! He was a *good* man, Mario, but so unhappy. Like you."

He recognized her "like you" as the prelude to what evangelicos called "witnessing." Still, that she could so quickly divine his misery was alarming. He sighed. "How did your husband die?"

"In Iraq. His third deployment. He was going to resign his commission." She stood, and now her face was determined. "I must leave. I'm so sorry about—"

"Hush, Señora," he said, pitying her, as he pitied himself. "I'm glad for your company."

"And you *smile* like that! I led you on, sitting there in my housecoat. Oh, Mario, you—it's hard to explain—you just shut down. As a woman. I haven't—in years, I haven't even—well, you're alone. There's always work. You just shut *down.*"

With his unhappy eyes cast low, he noted a burn mark, two centimeters square, inside her thigh. And still, she spoke: "I trusted you, instinctively I trusted you, and I wasn't trying to—honestly, I didn't mean—"

He raised a hand for her to stop, and she disappeared into the bathroom. She emerged again with a stiff smile, but he grabbed the suitcases, announcing he'd walk her to the bridge. She thought he was a gentleman, after all.

Now she wore a pale red, ribbony cotton dress that dipped generously over her breasts. She must have bought it down south. In fact, she resembled one of those fast-fading tarts that accompanied soldiers—and gringos—in border towns, but of course she didn't know that. And he felt a fleeting joy in pretense. He strolled with his fine lady down the hot, oily streets, and the predators in the shadows, smoking cigarettes, panting, dared nothing because he was a soldier.

Far north in air-conditioned Dallas, she'd wear the sexy dress on Independence Day and tell her female friends of her adventures in the mother country, of the miracle in the desert. Her strength had given out—*oh sisters! God brings us trials!* But she kept faith—*oh Lord, take me if that is your will!* And God sent an angel of mercy.

Me, Mario thought. *What a man!*

He pulled her to him, and they kissed, and now she pressed hard against him. His penis stirred, and he thought, how foolish we are. Why not make love on a hot night, even with a stranger, especially with a stranger, when only grief awaits you in the morning?

"Lost," she said.

"Maribel?"

"We're all lost and gone astray." She dropped her head on his shoulder. "Oh, Mario, lay all your burdens upon *Him.*"

She tore away and turned toward the bridge, as if playing a scene in a movie. But then she dug in her purse and scribbled something.

"My number in Dallas."

He shrugged, but she pushed the scrap of paper into his shirt pocket.

"You never know," she said.

- 3 -

The Rio Grande

In the morning he sat over coffee and toast at Ramon's Café, trying as an act of discipline to read the article about sea levels, but his head still buzzed from rum.

On the radio the Arkansas country singer, Randy DePaul, began his plaintive ballad, entitled "Alicia." No, it was "Felicia," a song about a Texas cowboy who'd fallen in love with a Mexican girl working in the onion fields of Uvalde. The border patrol picked her up and drove her across the bridge at El Paso, where the lovers kissed goodbye. A Latina Mario had never heard of sang Spanish verses, and afterward DePaul twanged his way through the English. An accordion wailed, and then a steel guitar. The song was a hit on both sides of the border, and Mario left the café humming the damn thing.

He ran his errands, taking the Tacoma to headquarters for rations, five hundred rounds of ammunition, repellant, toilet paper, and hand soap, and checking for new directives from Mexico City. He spied Captain Pérez leaning on a post in front of the city police building, immaculate in the heat, his cap pulled low and eyes hidden behind sunglasses. Mario saluted the captain, thinking that he might agree they'd struck an acceptable bargain in the desert, even if the captain hadn't known he was striking it. Pérez didn't stir.

When in the afternoon he returned to Las Palmas, he found Tejón supervising several of the men as they attached a battered aluminum outboard—the kind favored by local fisherman—to a hitch on the Humvee. He'd brought up the boat with the Pathfinder, but apparently the cargo required a more powerful engine.

"Lieutenant," Tejón said, smiling broadly, but with his eyes masked behind dark glasses precisely the style of the police captain's. "You've been doing the army's business."

"As have you, Señor," Mario said, pointing to the boat. The cargo was covered tightly with a tarp, and he feared what it was. "Has our mission changed?"

"Yes, yes, we go out tonight. We go *now*."

"The men are due another day's rest, Señor."

Tejón's sweaty face rippled with exasperation. "Sí, Lieutenant. Convey my apologies. Tell them their day will be returned to them, and that additionally they will be rewarded a full week's pay."

"And what shall I tell them of our mission, Señor?"

Tejón grunted as he clamped down the hitch. "Lieutenant Oliveros, what is the first thing every soldier must do?"

"Obey orders, Señor."

"Bueno, Lieutenant. You have a magnificent future in the Mexican army." Tejón pointed toward the long row of rooms. "Adelante."

Head bowed grimly, Mario marched forward and rapped on every door. One man couldn't be found, but the others, whether sleepy or high, were not so disgruntled. A week's pay made a fine inducement.

He still had to deal with young César. Mario knocked, and knocked again, and at last heard a moaning. "Open up!" he commanded, but no one answered, and Mario returned to the office for a master key. When he pushed open the door, it scudded over an encrusted puddle of what might have been soup, and the odor of urine was overpowering. The boy lay drawn up on his bed, crying, naked except for his army-issue boxer shorts.

"You never came!"

Mario grimaced. They shouldn't let them in so young. "César, what's wrong?"

Sobbing, César lifted a trembling hand over his groin. "It *hurts*."

Mario suppressed a laugh. "You have been with las putas. When we were in Piedras Negras? Yes, three weeks ago."

"Mi madre—"

"I won't inform your mother, César. Get in uniform. Now! Why didn't you tell me this yesterday?"

"I *tried*—"

True, Mario thought. *I ignored him.*

By now Tejón had the little convoy pointed toward the street. Most of the men crowded dazedly into the air-conditioned Pathfinder—or, if they had been slow in reporting, into the Tacoma's bed. Tejón appeared to have reserved the Humvee for Mario and himself.

César, walking with obvious discomfort and holding back his tears, inspired sarcastic applause from the men. Mario raised a hand to cut it off.

Tejón motioned impatiently to the back seat of the Humvee and tapped the face of his watch. César crawled in. Mario took the wheel, turning south toward the highway, and then northwest, awaiting the captain's directions. The bank clock read 49/119 at 5:17. Another four months of this heat, Mario thought.

At a bump César cried out dramatically.

"We could drop him at the clinic," Mario said.

"He could have gone himself. I cannot be concerned with this soldier's . . . chilito." Tejón turned in the seat. "Sit up, young man! Master your pain!"

"Captain, what good will this man be to us—"

"He must learn his lesson, Lieutenant." Tejón smiled. "Young soldier, I assure you, your chilito will not fall off. Tomorrow we'll take you to the clinic. But perhaps next time you will think more profoundly on where you put it, sí o no?"

"Sí, Señor," César whimpered.

"Louder!"

"¡Sí, Señor!"

"Bueno. Always remember, young man, I am your captain. I'll take care of you." Tejón settled back. "As I take care of you, eh, Lieutenant?"

Still slightly hung over, Mario narrowed his eyes at the glaring road. After saying goodbye to Maribel, he drank until he passed out. Maybe it was fortunate they came to the city so seldom. "Where are we going, Señor?" he said at last.

"Cañon del caballo, do you know it?"

"The dry gorge without horses. I saw some burros there once."

"Call it cañon del burro, then. There's a road down to the water."

Mario glanced at the rearview mirror. The boat rode well. "Las drogas, captain? We've never done that."

Tejón tipped back his sunglasses, rubbed his eyes, and dropped the glasses in place again. "It's not what it seems."

"It seems dangerous."

Tejón sighed. "We are helping our brothers, the city police. We are even helping the judiciales."

"There is no helping the judiciales, Señor."

"You will follow orders, Lieutenant Oliveros."

"Sí, Señor." He took a gamble. "And my promotion?"

Tejon smiled benevolently and reached below the seat for a briefcase. He popped it open with a flourish and held up the folded papers so Mario could glance at them. "You sign them in the morning, I take them to the colonel, you pick up your bars. Another one thousand pesos, not so bad, eh? Of course, you must agree to work for me for an additional six years."

Mario swallowed.

"Just kidding!" He patted Mario's arm. "Relax, mi amigo. Tonight we'll all get rich. Your captain will take care of you, am I right, César?"

"Right, Señor!" César said, mastering his pain.

Mario forced a smile. How did you write your mother about drugs? Well, you mentioned the promotion, gave her another two hundred pesos, and marched on. Drugs would be smuggled, alcaldes would be kidnapped, and heads would be severed, whether or not he was part of it. He hunched over the wheel, at last cracking the window and lighting a cigar. It tasted bad and he cast it away. *Drugs.* What could he do? Turn Tejón over to his superiors? They all expected a cut.

He drove along the cliffs, then inland to skirt a minor canyon. He crossed a high rock bridge, then slowed to a crawl through a plain of stones. Mario knew the captain wanted him at point because he was a good driver, but the trailer presented a problem with its small wheels, and several times soldiers had to dismount from the Pathfinder to lift and push.

As they neared the water, the desert floor changed from gravel to sand, and the boat wheels sank to their hubs. But here the Humvee, with its powerful diesel, bludgeoned through, until finally Mario saw the outlines of mountains on the American side, and a pale half moon hanging over Lake Amistad. They drove west along the cliffs until the lake had narrowed to no more than a kilometer wide, and you could see the ever-   diminishing Rio Grande, winding into the sun like a trickle of blood.

Darkness fell as Mario found the short, steep road. Tejón vaulted from the Humvee and down to the shore, barking orders. The men shouted and cursed the heat, as they removed a camouflage of boards and sagebrush from a concrete ramp. Francisco let fly a dozen rounds when he spied a rattlesnake.

"No! No! ¡Silencio!" screamed Tejón.

Mario backed slowly down the grade, setting the brake as the men undid the hitch, and lowered the boat down the ramp. The boat pitched heavily, riding low.

Francisco appeared, his face basking in the last flickers of sunlight. "What is our Napoleon up to?"

"He says he'll make you rich, Francisco."

"This money is coming to me so fast I can't spend it all. I must request leave to see my broker. Are you sure our Napoleon knows what he's doing?"

"Francisco, I'm not sure."

"Lieutenant! César! We must hurry!" Tejón hissed.

Slinging their rifles, Mario and César waded out and pulled back the tarp as Tejón loosened it. The boat was piled high with bales of marijuana.

No one was surprised.

"Leave us one, Captain!" came from the shore.

"One is worth ten of you. And what did I say? No lights!"

"We're not even here," Francisco called out.

"Could we not bring Sergeant Francisco?" Mario asked, his voice dropping low. "The boy is so young. And sick."

"I'm a soldier!" César insisted, and crawled high upon the load, and held his rifle importantly.

"¡Bueno!" Tejón said, turning in the prow, studying the black horizon. He needed only to stuff his hand inside his shirt, thought Mario. "Guide us, Lieutenant. Between those mountains!"

Mario opened the throttle full, but the boat was overloaded, the four-stroke Yamaha overburdened, and their progress slow in the heavy air. Running without lights, they chugged into the open water, while the company receded to shadows, and then couldn't be seen. An hour passed in the darkness, and it didn't seem that the Yankee mountains had drawn nearer. For a while

Mario guided on a fire ravaging the brush along a hillside and smelled the acrid smoke, until the fire, too, was behind them. At last the GPS device matched the numbers Tejón had given him, and Mario cut the laboring little engine.

They waited. They drifted, and twice Mario and César paddled the awkward craft to regain their coordinates. The odor of gasoline slowly dissipated; the tepid breeze brought the faint smell of sulphur from stagnant lagoons.

The half moon disappeared behind clouds. The stars, shining through haze, were few and distant. Clouds of mosquitoes found them, and César proved the only one thoughtful enough to have brought repellant. Tejón passed back two lukewarm Coronas. Mario's uniform had soaked through with sweat, and he thought, *If I dove deep, the water would be cool.*

After a time—thirty minutes, according to Mario's watch, but it seemed as though days had passed—Tejón had to talk. "Compadres, we took in a very bad man today."

"A very bad man," whispered César.

"These are *his* drugs. You didn't know that I am a liaison to the city police, Lieutenant? *First* Lieutenant?"

Mario blinked, but all was blackness. They'd arrived in no man's land. The GPS device, offering only numbers and cartoon water, was useless.

"And this bad man, we had him in the jail, and I said, *I* will take his drugs, *I* will make the delivery just exactly as he would have done. And the smugglers will sail right into the hands of the American Border Patrol."

"The Americans!"

"We'll call them at the appointed hour. They're waiting over there." He motioned vaguely toward el norte. "They'll have their drugs and their smugglers. Mexico will be rid of them, and we'll have the *money,* Mario! We must share with the police, of course."

"And headquarters?"

"With them also. Even so, Lieutenant—"

"What of the judiciales?"

"Indeed." Tejón laughed. "What of them?"

César shrieked in pain.

"¡Silencio!" cried Tejón.

"Ay—eee. . ." César slipped off the mountain of marijuana, dropping his boots on the gunwale and causing the boat to teeter dangerously low. Mario could hear him gritting his teeth as he urinated, and then sucking in sobs. As César crawled again to his high perch, Tejón flashed a red light, waited half a minute, and did it again. "2300 hours," he whispered. "Time!"

Four red blinks returned, startlingly near, and then something black slithered out of the blackness. They heard voices, low and indistinct as if from far across the water, and a narrow beam of light swept over them.

"¡Amigos! ¡Amigos!" cried Tejón.

"You're the army!"

They *could* have worn civilian clothes, Mario thought. The smugglers had probably sat studying them from the darkness, divining the stupidity of their prey.

"We're the army, sí," said stupid Napoleon. "Bareiro, he is so sick, but he has *friends* in the army! The city police—"

"You are the police?"

"No, no. Bareiro, he *sends* us. No tricks, he is a sick man. He says—your birthday is tomorrow. He says—your wife is in El Paso. She is American; her name is Car-o-line. You have three children. You—"

"Tell that fucker to shut up," came a gringo voice, a devil in the darkness. "He brays like a fuckin' donkey."

"He's all wrong," said the first voice.

"He's the man got the dope, an' all he wants is his money. What do we care how they squabble with themselves? Let's load this crap an' get outta here."

"It's a trap."

"Manny, they cain't trail this boat; it don't make no noise. They cain't find it on their fuckin' radar, and you yourself don't know where I'm takin' it."

"We will deal with you, Señor," said the first voice, and his body materialized on the prow. He was dressed in black, with a black baseball cap pulled low. With an oar he guided the black boat next to them, placed a foot on the gunwale, and began accepting bales from Mario and César. He passed them into the darkness to the invisible gringo.

"Lotta shit," the gringo said.

Several packages returned, wrapped in brown paper. Tejón opened one.

"Satisfactory, Señor?"

"Sí," said Tejón. "Bareiro will be pleased with the night's work."

"We'll talk to Bareiro," the man in black said. "If it's not all as you say, someone will visit you one day soon."

"Ay—eee. . . ," moaned César.

"¡Silencio!" shouted Tejón.

It seemed then that something more should happen, but the black boat vanished. The marijuana was gone, Tejón held his money, but it all had gone by too quickly to process. Mario stood in a half-crouch, disoriented, and thought he heard a motor whir—not a gasoline engine, but an electric motor. Was this possible—a boat so sleek and fast, powered only by batteries?

"Well!" Tejón said.   .

Once again they were flooded with light: the little captain, the recruit, and Mario. But it was not the smugglers, whom Mario believed no one could find, but a patrol boat riding high. Mario couldn't see beyond the glare, but he knew where the machine gun stood; he knew this powerful, high-riding boat. He thought he heard the voice of Captain Pérez. He would dream that he had, and encounter the man's flaring red eyes in the brilliant light of nightmares, but for now he couldn't be sure. He was sure only that these were the judiciales, and that they had been waiting.

They would talk to the American Border Patrol. *They* would take the credit. Most important, they'd keep the money.

Stupid Napoleon—vain and greedy!

A bullhorn crackled: "Smugglers!"

Mario crouched by the little engine and drew up his rifle. He hadn't any cover, unless it was the lake itself.

"We are the army!" Tejón screamed. "¡Ejército mexicano!"

"You're *not* the army. You're smugglers."

"Sí, sí, we are the army!"

A dozen rounds burst out. César, he of perpetual pain, slumped over, never again to shame his saintly mother. Again the machine gun rattled, and Mario shot through his clip as well, aiming into the glare, but dying Napoleon turned, his face writhing in sorrow, and veered into Mario's aim. Tejón took a dozen rounds from two directions, shielding Mario, but before he died, puzzlement crossed his face, why his clever lieutenant, for whom he had secured a promotion, shot him down.

Involuntarily, Mario stepped forward, but stumbled over César. He slumped off the side as though shot, but then kicked the bottom of the boat, and dove. He pierced the warm water until he reached a cold, black place. He hadn't been shot.

He surfaced by the outboard, gasping once, clamping his jaw shut, forcing himself to breathe quietly. The boat swayed as a policeman stepped aboard. Grasping a hook, Mario quickly paddled just beneath a gunwale, even as the man pulled the starter rope, and the propeller spun.

He hung on for several kilometers as the mountains drew near and the lake narrowed sharply. North, and then northwest. They split the difference between Mexico and the United States, until at last the boat turned and Mario saw lights on the southern shore.

He understood how this would be represented. The judiciales came to the aid of brave Mexican soldiers, outnumbered and outgunned, fighting smugglers to the death on the Rio Grande. Sadly, they were too late. Sadly, one of the bodies was unaccounted for, but presumed dead like the other heroes.

It didn't matter what the soldiers in his own unit said. It didn't matter what the colonel said. They weren't witnesses. Better to chime in with the official story than to acknowledge they'd been smuggling drugs.

Dead, an allowance would come to Mario's mother. Possibly, a first lieutenant's allowance. Alive, back again in Ciudad Acuña, if somehow he could reach the place, he'd still be dead. First, an embarrassment, then dead.

—Your captain . . . está muerto. Why are *you* alive?

—The judiciales attacked us.

—Really, Lieutenant? Why would they do that?

—They wanted the money. The money for las drogas.

—We have talked to the judiciales. They say you deal in drugs. They say, after you shot your commanding officer, you tried to escape with the money to el norte, where you keep a woman.

He let go the boat. He swam, a dead man in the black water in the black night. He was a strong swimmer. He'd learned to swim long ago, when he brought out boats for the turistas, and swam back to shore.

The river disappeared, choked with river cane. He swam through a fearsome place, all weeds and silt, where viscous water dragged down his arms but he couldn't stand, where if he sank he'd drown in mud. He clawed his way from willow to willow and hung panting, so weary he didn't know his name.

The Rio Grande became a river again where the Pecos entered, and the current overwhelmed him. He washed up on a narrow piece of Mexico at the base of cliffs, and slogged through wet sand, disturbing frogs and owls and bats. He crawled onto a dry log and tried to rest, but mosquitoes attacked him.

At last he cleared the Pecos and his path grew easier, the Rio Grande a narrow stream now, deep in a dark canyon. The half moon emerged from behind the clouds and showed him pools, sand bars, and rotting logjams from times of high water.

He reached a place with cliffs rising both on the south and the north, but where he could climb. It was a hard place, with nothing for anyone. The army had never ventured so far. But he couldn't go home, unless he wished to wander as a deserter. In the United States he was illegal, but in Mexico he was dead.

He'd found the paper with her number in the morning and almost thrown it away. But it was in his billfold now. He'd saved it whimsically, not because of the number, not because there was anything magical about the missionary woman, but because of what she'd written.

"Buena suerte, Mario."

Luck!

He grasped roots and jutting rocks, jamming his feet wherever he could. He hung forty feet above the canyon floor and pulled himself to a dark cavity that might have been a cave. He thought he heard a rattlesnake, but listened again and heard nothing. His hands were wet and he tried to dry them on his shirt, but the wetness was blood from digging at clay. He lay on his back, eyes closed, and breathed deliberately.

He was from Boca de Tomatlán, a lush, watery place on the Pacific coast, south of Puerto Vallarta, in the state of Jalisco. He grew up quick as a banana plant on a fertile slope where his mother and father raised pigs and corn and vegetables. The life was warm and pleasant but money was short, even for schooling. And yet he was a studious, serious boy, reading Cervantes and Calderon and the poems of Lorca and Neruda. His favorite story was One Hundred Years of Solitude. *Boca de Tomatlán seemed like Macondo now, a place of unreliable memories, of dreams. If you journeyed there, it disappeared.*

He worked for the grand hotel, driving the water taxi, guiding the rich gringa women and their fat husbands out into Banderas Bay to spot whales. He learned to smile and make jokes and his tips were excellent. His English, everyone said, was remarkable.

—Good morning, sir. My name is Mario Oliveros.

He bought a Honda motor scooter. It was the finest thing he'd ever owned, and impressed a young woman named Alicia. But then his sister needed an operation, and he joined the army to help pay for it.

And he was so smart, and so conscientious, and spoke such careful English, that the army paid his way to the great capital, where they trained him to be an officer.

Mario leaned on his elbow, licking his cracked lips. He should have drunk his fill in the river, but couldn't hazard climbing down again. He tested his weight on the shelf above him and hoisted himself up. All the strength left his arms, and he lay again, exhausted. He rose, and the shelf broke under his foot; he grabbed a juniper root as pieces of the rock flew into the darkness and splashed below.

One more pull, and he stood on a plain of smooth rock, broken here and there with clumps of prickly pear. Was he mistaken? Delirious in this Godforsaken place? He saw lights far ahead.

II. Dallas

- 4 -

The Biggest Little Town in the World

His watch read four A.M., meaning that he had not quite two hours before people stirred. It was the best time to attack an enemy. And the best time to steal: criminals everywhere had finished their night's work; the police dozed.

He estimated hardly twenty houses in the town—too small for a constable. Still, someone might have trouble sleeping, and Mario knew from watching the news that every gringo owned a gun. So he crept along in shadows of junipers and mesquites— just as in Mexico, almost no shade trees grew. No vegetable gardens to raid, either; at most, people had done some landscaping around beds of cacti, and their backyards were the desert. The houses could have been in Coahuilla: tin roofs tipped up on cinder blocks.

Who lived here, Latinos or gringos? Behind several houses were gigantic diesel trucks, gleaming with chrome. Were Latinos in this country rich enough for such fancy rigs? He had no way to know, but of more interest, in front of the only house with a shade tree, stood one of those green-and-white panel trucks the American Border Patrol favored. Under the tree was a plastic wading pool for children.

Keeping his eye on the front window, Mario crept near. He'd have lapped from the pool like a dog but spotted a garden hose, shut off at the nozzle rather than wherever the spigot was. He opened the nozzle and sucked greedily, as if the alkaline water were Coca-Cola. The water began to run cold, and he sprayed his hair and face and hands. He was bruised, cut, and sore. He almost couldn't get to his feet, and fought the temptation to lie under the tree and sleep. No doubt the border patrolman, stepping out to greet the day, would find his presence amusing.

A dog barked from several houses away. From out in the desert, a coyote answered. Nervously, Mario turned onto the street again. His watch read 4:10.

Several gravel streets converged on a wide paved area with a post office and a rambling frame structure that looked like a frontier fort. A sign announced Judge Roy Bean's courthouse—the eccentric, hanging judge, at least as Mario remembered Paul Newman's portrayal. Another ramshackle building announced itself as the "opera house" Bean had erected for his idol, Lilly Langtry. Both looked easy to break into, but the visitor center, a modern structure, seemed the best place to find water, food, and American money.

Dropping again into shadows, Mario moved to the rear of the building and spotted a metal door and a small window without bars. That two by four lying next to the wall could be used on the window. If he set off an alarm, in such a tiny town at such an improbable hour, he'd have fifteen minutes before anyone came, possibly longer. Two cameras were mounted up high; did he care? His shadowy image might lead to something if the police concluded that they were looking at a Mexican in uniform, rather than a rat that hadn't quite drowned. After that, one competent American officer would have to connect with one competent Mexican. What were the odds of that?

He laughed maniacally, took a step forward, and the door opened. He staggered back, dumbfounded, and dropped flat in the gravel. He hadn't time to find a shadow.

"You don't care about me," said a short, plump woman of perhaps twenty. At first Mario thought she was crazy, a schizophrenic talking to herself in the wee hours, but then he saw she wore one of those hands-free phones such as the tourists brought along to Ciudad Acuña. She propped open the door with the board he'd almost picked up, disappeared momentarily, then rolled out a gigantic plastic garbage can. "I could die and you wouldn't even come to my funeral," she said, dragging the can toward the dumpster one hundred feet away.

Mario slipped through the door. He followed an aisle, with boxes to either side of him, that ran into the public area, where he spied displays in glass cases, racks of literature, and a half-round service desk. He couldn't see an entry point and rolled over the desk, then crouched. He found the cash register, opened several desk drawers looking for a key, settled for a bent screwdriver. He paused. Attacking the register with a screwdriver would be noisy.

"You can be sweet," the woman said, banging her way through the back door. "I know it's early. *Of course* you need your sleep, sweetheart."

He lay on the floor under the computer by a woman's shoes and socks. The owner of the shoes had also stashed cigarettes and a lighter down low; Mario slipped the lighter into his pocket.

The young woman came directly toward the service desk, talking all the while. She seemed harmless, but he didn't want to frighten her—or be discovered. Her hand reached over the counter next to the computer, grabbed a tissue, and she blew her nose. "I would," she said. "You know I would. But you'll be gone so long. How will I ever get to Corpus?"

She banged her way into one of the restrooms. He rose, glanced again at the cash register, and then on the counter spotted a plastic jar with a grainy photograph taped to it. "Save Cindy," the jar said. "Find a cure." The jar was jammed full of paper money and coins.

He didn't want to steal from incurable Cindy, but surely, the museum had some Mexican visitors. His money might seem unusual, but not suspicious. He extracted an American ten and twenty, and dropped in his damp pesos.

The museum had little for sale. But an open door led into an employee room, where he found a rack of Western shirts of the sort Roy Bean might have worn, and on a shelf above the rack was a felt Stetson that fit. He couldn't find trousers, so he'd remain half-army, half-cowboy for a while.

He heard the swipe of a mop in the restroom. On the floor he found a six-pack of bottled water; and in the refrigerator were crackers and several packages of beef jerky. A plastic container held something resembling cake, but it had turned green. He heard the janitor again, and backed away.

He retrieved sunglasses from a lost and found box; and as he returned to the service counter grabbed a map of the great state of Texas. Then he stood by the back door, watching from the shadows as the young woman came to the counter again, and reached for another tissue. "I love you," she said. "Do you love me?"

His watch read 5:02.

Two hours later his weariness and the rising heat of the new day put him in a state near delirium, so that when he saw a couch fifty meters off the road, he thought he was dreaming. But the couch failed to dissolve when he touched it, and somehow he mustered the strength to drag it into a thicket of mesquites. "I'm all right," he announced to the burning sky. "I'm fine." He lay back, eating jerky and drinking bottled water, and fell asleep. He slept for ten hours, despite the flies that bit him, and his raging dreams of bottomless water and faces twisted in anger. He woke to the westering sun, brought up a hand to wipe away sweat, and something yanked at his boot. He sat in disbelief. A wild hog had fastened on his toe.

"¡Mierda! No!" he screamed. Involuntarily, he reached for his rifle, but of course he didn't have one. He tried to yank back his foot, but the hog, a great boar covered with shaggy, mud-matted black hair, wouldn't let go. He shook Mario's boot from side to side, and bit down.

"Ay!" Mario cried. Leaning forward, he managed to strike the boar with his fist, but the animal was unfazed. He felt along the ground, found a rock the size of a grapefruit, and brought it down on the boar's snout. Grunting, the boar let go and backed off a few steps. It studied Mario dispassionately.

"You devil! I'm not food!"

As if it understood, the boar grunted and moved a distance away, where it rooted in a heap of cans. Mario unstrung his boot, pulled it off gingerly, then removed the bloody sock. A chunk of his little toe hung loose.

The boar lifted his head, sniffing.

"Don't come near! I'll—" Using his pocketknife—with his wallet, his watch, and himself, all that had survived the river— he quickly cut away the dangling flesh, though nausea came on all the same. He poured half a bottle of his precious water over the cut. Then he knifed off part of his trouser leg and wound it tightly around the mutilated toe.

The boar remained too near for Mario's satisfaction, and he gathered several stones and threw them. The boar jumped slightly when hit in the ribs, and eyed Mario with his black eyes. At last he moved away, leaving the acrid odor of burnt oil and decayed flesh—but no, that came from the couch itself.

Mario rose, the odor still clung to his skin, and he understood at last that he'd camped below a landfill—a magnet to wild hogs and myriad other varmints. To the boar he was only a species of stinking garbage.

He crawled up the great spillway of trash, reaching the apex of a truck incline. He could see Mexican mountains to the south, and little Langtry between those mountains and the four-lane highway that rolled eastward to San Antonio and dropped into the harshest of deserts going west. He knew the highway festered with agents. More usefully, he spied the canyon of the Pecos approximately ten kilometers east. He could travel that way if he had to, if he couldn't find water.

From a mound of construction trash he extracted a bent piece of galvanized pipe to use as a cane—or club, if he encountered the boar again. His nose led him to a box of rotting vegetables thrown out by some grocery. He found withered carrots which were edible once he'd scraped them, two limp turnips, and a head of lettuce with rotting outside leaves, but he cut those away and ate the center. He sat on a bucket, sweating, and ate the turnips, then allowed himself two more strips of jerky and a long swallow of water.

His toe throbbed, and he unwound the bloody cloth gingerly, then cut more strips from his trousers. He formed a pad over what remained of his toe, wound it tightly, tied it off. Then he cut the toe out of his boot and carefully slipped it on again. What a ridiculous wound, but it hurt, and could prove infectious.

According to his map, the road meandered toward a town called Ozona—two hundred kilometers north of the Rio Grande, which Mario hoped was beyond the border patrol's range of interest. In the fever of the day, as he lay cooking on the couch, he'd calculated he might walk the distance in three nights, at most four. With his injured foot, even ten kilometers was a tall order. That hog! If he were a religious man, he'd have thought the beast was a punishment from God. He shook his fist at the gibbous moon. "What more can you do to me?" he shouted.

The road was white limestone—dusty, glaring, hot under his feet as the sun set, and then ghostly in the moonlight. Over winter it had been graded, but it remained rough because of ribs of solid rock that a blade skipped over. The road's roughness perhaps explained why he encountered no traffic, and he surmised he'd blundered upon a route that no illegals followed. He could bear the temperature, the relentless flies rested, but soon he had to sit and lift his throbbing foot onto a rock. He held the map to the moon and saw that the road meandered over to the Pecos in eighty kilometers, but he couldn't manage it. He'd have to join the river now, and find a place to hide until his toe healed.

He kept on the road until it forded a dry wash that ran northeast. He surprised two steers which gave him hopes for water, but in another three kilometers he'd found none, and then the wash disappeared, leaving a low mountain before him. He drank the last of his water, ate more jerky, and climbed the mountain, digging into the soft slope with his pipe, trying to put all the pressure on his uninjured foot. In a juniper grove he surprised three white-tailed deer that bounded ahead of him, streaking like mercury in the moonlight, and again he mourned the loss of his rifle.

He reached a plain of agave and prickly pear, seemingly growing out of solid rock. He sliced a chunk of agave and sucked on it, bringing to mind a memory of buying pulque, fermented agave, in some dry little town north of Monterey. The soldiers split five liters among them and grew jolly and wise. Laughing, shrieking in pain from his throbbing toe, Mario carefully sliced off a prickly pear paddle, trod on it to break off the needles, and peeled it. He ate it slowly with the last of his jerky. Now he was thirsty, but he thought he heard the Pecos.

Weaving and dodging, he discovered pathways through the prickly pear and limped slowly eastward. Despite his caution, he backed into needles from time to time and yowled at the moon. Needles stung one arm and pierced low on a thigh, and he reached involuntarily to yank them out and beat at his flesh. He visualized a pair of needle nose pliers his hand had hovered over at the museum; how he needed them now!

At last he looked down on the Pecos, wide and glistening, and bound with high cliffs like the Rio Grande. The going was easier at the cliff's edge, and two kilometers northward he found a break where a tiny creek pushed through. He sat on a tower of limestone and gravel, mustering the resolve to descend. More deer rustled below him and trotted toward the river, never looking up. The deer gave him an idea, but for the moment all he needed was water, and in another several hours, shelter from the sun. He eased forward on the slope, reaching out with his legs for anchors. Shortly, the gravel under him loosened, grew fluid, and for the last several meters he slid wildly, jamming his hurt toe.

"Dios! Dios!" he screamed. "Oh, *kill* me!"

When the pain subsided, he followed a shaft of moonlight out to the river, leaning heavily on his pipe. A flat rock shelf, without vegetation or a beach, extended directly to the water, and he fell prone and drank his fill. The water was warm, slightly brackish, but clear, and he ducked his head under, then took off his boots and washed his feet. The stub of toe had swollen to twice its normal size. He washed out his socks and slipped his boots over his bare feet, then sat pulling prickly pear needles from his legs.

Above the valley floor stood a grove of junipers and above that, an outcropping of mesquites. Too tired to worry about rattlers, he bulled his way into the junipers and found a flat place, then limped down to the valley floor again and cut willow branches for a bed. He used his Stetson, already smashed beyond repair, for a pillow and propped his stub of a toe on a rock. Birds sang, announcing the dawn.

He writhed in the heat. He feared another hog might emerge and finish off his foot. Half-awake, dreaming, it made sense to work a sock over the toe again and slip a Judge Roy Bean shopping bag over that. He woke and the toe had worked itself bare, a hideous, purplish thing large as his steel pipe. He couldn't touch it without screaming.

He sat up dripping sweat and entered into conversation with a melon-sized rock that had the face of Luis Tejón. "You're not dead!"

"We're both dead, Lieutenant."

"What is this place, then?"

"It's hot enough for hell, but I think it must be purgatory."

The big rock was *not* Tejón. It didn't even look like him.

"I put you in for promotion," the rock said.

"What good will that do if I'm dead?"

"That's between you and God."

God! *God?* "Why do you treat me this way?" he cried out to God. "What did I do?"

At dusk he lugged the Tejón-rock above the draw that led to the Pecos and waited. His toe covered over the moon and was amazing to contemplate. And he had arrived at a profound truth: If he didn't believe in God, then he couldn't assign blame to the old geezer. What a fool I've been, Mario thought, as he lifted high the rock and let it fall on the third little doe.

The doe dropped, struggled once to rise, and lay quivering. The other two skittered away in the darkness, hooves clicking on the rock, and stood at the river's edge, coughing. Mario slid to the valley floor and cut the doe's throat, then dragged her toward the water, away from the torrent of blood. He sliced open her abdomen and severed her intestines. He threw them in the Pecos, and still, from one hundred meters away, the two does stared with their foreign eyes.

He couldn't saw through bones with his knife but managed to skin the doe around the neck and slowly work her hide free. He cut away the bluish outer membrane, the fat, and then set to slicing off long strips of muscle. He placed stones in a circle and hurried back into the valley for firewood, gathering prickly pear paddles, too.

His thumb shook on the lighter wheel. Why hadn't he searched for matches? What if the lighter was out of fuel? But it lit, his mesquite twigs crackled and drew strength, and soon he had a bold fire. He sat back, a feeling of control returning to him. A man needed that feeling, he realized, for sanity.

He propped up mesquite sticks to roast some of his strips and lay others to dry on a flat stone a little removed from the heat. He pulled off his bloody Judge Roy Bean shirt and his ragged Mexican army trousers, and jumped into the river. Down several feet, the water stabbed him with cold and revived memories of a pure spring upland of Boca de Tomatlán. He used to go there on Sundays, and read books, and dream.

He ate venison and roasted cactus. Even without salt it made a fine meal. And if there were good food to eat and water to drink, how could this valley be purgatory? It was simply a forgotten place at the raw end of a country he didn't know.

He stored his dried venison in an improvised springhouse— the source of the creek, running out of a cave. Exploring up and down the Pecos, he found boards and constructed a rude bed, and slept soundly by the water's cool flow. Toward evening as the mosquitoes rose, he built a fire at the mouth of the cave. Fire discouraged rattlesnakes. It warmed his venison and toasted his cactus.

He could not have said how many days had passed when the sun disappeared. It abandoned the earth to an eerie half-light, and wind rose from the west. The wind blew for days, carrying grit, ashes from some faraway fire, and chaff from the desert floor. It gusted at what he estimated to be sixty miles per hour, and he couldn't stand. He couldn't build a fire. He lay in his cave in a near coma, listening to the eternal scratching and screaming a few feet before him. He recalled the passages in *One Hundred Years of Solitude* in which the citizens of Macondo came down with insomnia, and then forgetfulness, and had to go about labeling coffee pots and knives, to know what they were for. He dreamed he was in a cage deep in the mountain, that wild men would devour him.

He woke to a pack rat making off with a chunk of his venison. He chased it into the cave until he was covered with mud. He staggered out of the cave, blinking because the sun had returned. His toe was healing, and he walked without a limp.

Gathering firewood at a snag on the Pecos, he found nylon tent rope and fishing line, and slowly, making many mistakes, fabricated a fish trap, lashing together dry ocotillo strips. He baited the trap with venison. Every morning he brought up several perch and catfish, and once a beautiful striped bass.

One morning as he strode out to check his trap, two canoes appeared, filled with cheery young people wearing expensive sports clothing, chatting over the water about the rapids ahead and the caves with Indian pictographs. Rather than scurry for cover, Mario stood watching them, and waved. They waved back.

"Wild man," a pretty girl called. He looked down at his clothes, and felt his growth of beard.

Odd how comforting it had become, burrowing into the cool cave at night, filling his days with whittling and gathering firewood and drying fish. He watched an eagle fly between the canyon walls and plunge for a rabbit. He studied a mountain lion as it stalked a deer on the cliff above, almost jaunty, the definition of stealth, and with such a fluid motion it seemed more like a well-oiled machine than an animal.

He missed cigars. He missed reading. He wasn't so sure about human beings, but without them about you, you ceased to exist.

He'd camped three weeks in his valley, and his toe had

healed to a tough stub without a nail, and no longer compromised walking. He was fit. His fish and venison had given him strength, and he'd enjoyed a dozen nights of cool, dreamless sleep. But staying was becoming a kind of cowardice.

In another three days, he turned his fish trap into a bucket and packed it with dried perch, cactus strips, and water. He followed the river north until he found the white road again. On his second night of travel, he slipped inside a tool shed behind a silent ranch house, where he found a pair of dirty jeans lying across an electric welder. The jeans were baggy, but his fatigues had turned to shreds.

Farther north, he discovered a weedy vegetable garden with ripe tomatoes. He wolfed down a dozen to quench his thirst and would have eaten more were it not for two eager beagles that came sniffing, then began to bay. A porch light snapped on at the house, and Mario ran down the road.

Near dawn of his third night of walking, he reached the summit of a bare mountain. Flat and gently rolling dry land, broken up with yellowish patches of huisache, stretched toward the lights of a city not far away. How might he enter? At night, surely, to scout for the border patrol. He scanned the dark horizon for a place to sleep through the day.

Headlights popped into view at the far end of what he now understood to be a cultivated field, and he heard the rasp of a diesel. The truck stopped, turned around, and began slowly backing toward him, even as an old school bus followed. The bus's gasoline engine wheezed and faltered as the driver turned off the grade and onto the field.

He watched as the silhouettes of workers filed from the bus, grabbed picking bags, and trudged northward toward the truck. Inspired, Mario walked directly toward the bus, where the driver and the man Mario had deduced was the foreman talked. He stood politely, head lowered, as he'd seen braceros do in old films.

The foreman turned slowly. "You lost, Pancho?"

"I had to relieve myself."

The foreman stared at Mario in the half-light and threw him a picking bag. "Well, get on out there, then."

The men stretched between six rows of cantaloupes, bending over in the strengthening light. They all were Mexicans. Twenty-two melons filled a bag, though you didn't need to count. You lifted the bag up to the man on the truck. He dumped the melons and handed the bag back. Simple as that.

Except that the pace was set by an old man—the others called him Eduardo—who never smiled, never spoke, but simply kept picking. The rows were half a kilometer long, and because of the old man, you couldn't stop.

At the end of the run, the truck was only half full, but it took some time for the foreman to maneuver it to the next set of rows. The men drank from two water coolers, ate melons, and smoked cigarettes. Several of them wet towels and tied them around their necks, or made cowls under their hats. Eduardo took a long drink and sat on his haunches, slowly unwrapping a stick of gum.

"Hey, cowboy, where'd you find that hat?" asked a young man who looked enough like César that for an instant Mario was disoriented. He took off the filthy Stetson.

"It was a fine hat once," he said, smiling.

Eduardo slowly rose. The crew made another mindless march behind the truck and drank water again, until they had picked six rows and filled the truck. Another truck arrived, but it was lunch-time. Mario grabbed a cantaloupe and flopped down under a mesquite. The friendly kid joined him, pulling a white bread sandwich, a candy bar, and some taco chips from a plastic sack.

"You illegal?" the kid asked.

Mario stared hard.

The kid stuck out a hand. "I'm Roger Hernandez."

"I'm Mario," Mario said, wondering how a Latino could be named Roger. But though the kid's skin was brown, he behaved like a gringo. Possibly, he couldn't speak Spanish.

"I didn't mean anything by that. Old Eduardo is illegal, and he's lived here about a million years. My *dad* was illegal."

"No longer?"

"Naw, my mom's American."

What a puzzle all this was. "Your father's . . . profession?"

"Oil and gas. It's goin' along pretty good, but I couldn't get on this year."

"Ah," Mario said, not truly understanding. "Tell me, Roger. Are we near the town of Ozona?"

Roger laughed. "What, you just wandered out of the desert? It's about ten miles."

"Ozona, is it. . . " For an instant Mario's English deserted him."¿Una ciudad grande?"

Roger laughed. "Biggest little town in the world! Nothin' to *do,* though."

"And you, Roger. You are regularly employed in farming?"

"I'm goin' to Texas Tech this fall. This is just a summer job. Last year for it, too."

"Too dry?"

"Always dry. Too *hot.* These melons get scalded unless you just pour the water to 'em. They gotta go deeper an' deeper to find the aquifer, and it costs too much for what they can sell the melons. They can't afford to raise 'em, can't afford to truck 'em. No more work for Eduardo."

Mario smiled at the old man, taking a siesta under a juniper. "Does he ever speak?"

"Just works. You gonna stick around, Mario? We could do some stuff."

"I'm traveling to Dallas."

"Lucky *you.* How 'bout those Cowboys!"

"I enjoy Clint Eastwood," Mario said.

Roger threw him a bewildered stare, and maybe it was fortunate that it was time to resume work.

By six, Mario's muscles had grown so sore he had to grab the handrail to pull himself onto the bus. He'd thought his time in the wilderness had left him in good shape, but apparently not good enough for stoop labor. He watched Eduardo steadily cross the field, seemingly unfazed by the day. Something to be said for that, Mario thought. Doing one thing, even a humble thing, better than anyone else.

Miraculously, the bus was air-conditioned. Mario leaned his head against a window and fell instantly asleep, even as he cautioned himself to stay awake. He awoke to horns honking and the shuffling of men onto the city street. He joined the line to receive his pay, fighting the impulse to turn round and round, and marvel at the sights of this strange town.

The street was alarmingly wide. The traffic seemed well-regulated, but dangerously fast. He saw no prostitutes in the foyers of restaurants nor guards at bank doors. And every color seemed garish to Mario, used to oranges and greens and browns in different places.

Gradually, however, his senses adjusted, and he perceived

different versions of the same old things: bars, laundries, gas stations. He longed to visit the grocery. Beer. Fresh fruit. Cigars!

Across the street, a bus pulled in and passengers began disembarking. Everyone was Mexican. They all looked as weary as Mario felt.

Young Roger Hernandez leaned out the window of a Toyota Tacoma like the one in Mario's unit, except that Roger's was shiny and undented. What a country, where a mere boy could own such a fine truck. A pretty blonde rode beside him, disorienting Mario. He didn't disapprove, but nowhere in Mexico had he observed such combinations.

"See you tomorrow, Mario," Roger called out.

As Mario waved, his eyes caught the green and white of a border patrol truck, parked by a high concrete wall. An agent crossed to the bus and spot-checked identifications, waving many on with a smile and a pat. He, too, was Mexican, or like young Roger, a Latino who'd been born here. Mario fidgeted and cast his eyes about for escape routes.

"Social?" asked a gringa woman through a tiny window.

"Excuse me, I—"

"Social Security number."

"I—"

"Crew C?"

"Sí," he said.

"C as in 'sí,' or did you work on Crew C?"

Mario smiled. "The last."

"Bring your Social tomorrow or you don't work," the woman said. "$69.90."

"Gracias," he said, wondering if such a huge amount was a mistake, but others had made still more.

Across the street, the agent pulled a man aside. He motioned, and another officer, a gringa woman, left the panel truck and hurried up with handcuffs.

Ozona might be the biggest little town in the world, but it wouldn't be big enough. At first Mario wanted to run, but the officers were already occupied. He did the contrary thing. He walked slowly across the street and stepped to the terminal's small office.

Behind the clerk, a radio played "Felicia," confusing Mario. He felt wobbly inside and couldn't find words. Just a silly song, he told himself.

The clerk was a thin Latino with gray hair. He combed what was left of it straight back. "Tan triste," he said, smiling at Mario.

"Why doesn't he go after her? Why doesn't he go down in Mexico and marry her?"

"You missed a verse. See, he's on parole. He can't go after her, or they'll throw him in jail. They can *never* be together."

"Ah," Mario said. "Poetic. Señor, is there a bus to Dallas?"

"Not tonight, amigo."

"Where may I travel tonight?"

"San Angelo."

"Is San Angelo bigger than Ozona?"

The clerk laughed. "Ozona is the biggest little town in the world, Señor."

Mario forced a smile, all the while studying the green-and-white truck. "So I've heard."

The clerk eyed the truck, too. "I *think* . . . a man could get lost in San Angelo, Señor."

- 5 -

San Angelo

He stepped onto a concrete dock, through a deserted, dim lobby with a moldy smell, and fell on the wet sidewalk. Far above, a traffic light changed from green to yellow, and he seemed to be sinking, miles of water overhead, and the throb of propellers, and dead men floating face down. He turned on his elbow, watched the silvery stuff run off eaves and awnings and hit the oily puddles like automatic fire, and he was frightened. He thought, *rain*. He couldn't remember when he'd last seen rain; it seemed unnatural, and risky.

But he stood, and none among the homeless, huddled and shivering like pigeons under the station's long eaves, carried a rifle.

"Ya got a cigarette?" one asked, and Mario offered the old fellow a cigar and lit one himself. He stepped into the rain, turned up his head and tasted it, and slicked back his hair. He took off his broken boots and walked barefooted, glorying in the air the rain had washed clean, turning round and round in his fresh, awakened skin. He walked eastward through the city's canyons, all the remainder of the night, until he saw the sun, split by clouds, orange.

Across the Conchos River he found a park, where he sat beneath a picnic shelter among dripping pin oaks, smoking cigars and reading the San Angelo *Standard-Times* like some Martian man of leisure. Sunday, the paper announced, July 8. A month ago exactly, he'd died on the Rio Grande.

At mid-morning he followed the river between boarded-up backyards and under bridges, noting hiding places; he hadn't

enough money for a motel. The river flowed through an un-
developed area, and back into a poor part of town full of tire
shops, salvage yards, feed stores, and perpetual flea markets. A
grove of pines behind an abandoned factory showed promise,
and he took time to drag up boards and buckets and sheets of
black plastic such as were used in the melon fields for mulch.
The river delivered amazing amounts of junk: doors and windows, railroad ties and tree branches, dead animals, shopping
sacks, plastic bottles. He swatted a mosquito, thought of César
and Tejón, and reminded himself to buy repellant.

He crawled up to an exit lane off a four-lane highway and
stood, bewildered in the steaming grass, the bright sun. A
jacked-up, four-door, four-wheel drive, growling pickup truck
bore down on him, and he leaped past the curb. A redheaded
kid stuck his head out: "Asshole, get a job!"

Homeless, that's what people thought. At officer's school
he'd read a translation of *Down and Out in Paris and London,* in
which the Englishman George Orwell described his temporary
life as a bum. The experience offered at least one great lesson:
the world judges a man by his clothes.

Also, Mario thought, by the color of his skin, his swagger,
and the money he places on the counter. But clothes were a start.

Neon signs stretched to the horizon, all looking alike to him,
but at length he singled out a Walmart about a kilometer away,
and he trusted Walmart. He knew of several in the Mexico City
suburbs, and sometimes his mother and he took the bus to the
one in Puerto Vallarta.

"Hello, how are you today?" said a dignified old gentleman
at the door, startling Mario from the prolonged silence he'd
grown used to.

Mario extended a hand. "I am good, Señor. It is kind of you
to ask. How are you this fine Sunday morning?"

The old fellow withdrew his hand. "Oh, I'm awright, I
guess. Nice rain we had."

"It has come too late to help the corn, perhaps."

"Corn?" The old man seemed puzzled, but smiled anyhow.
"You have a wonderful day, now."

"Thank you, Señor, and the same to you. Could you direct
me to the clothing section for . . . for the men?"

"Straight ahead, on your left. You have a wonderful day,
now."

"And you as well, Señor. Have a wonderful day!" What a pleasant fellow, Mario thought, thinking better of himself as well.

In the bathroom he laid out his purchases: jeans, a marked-down polo shirt, running shoes, a toothbrush, toothpaste, a pair of socks, and a year's worth of razors because you couldn't buy only one. He threw away his Judge Roy Bean shirt, holding it up first to see if it might be salvaged; it was like a friend who'd gone bad. His boots also were beyond hope. He stepped into his new jeans but kept his grease-stained old ones, rolling them in a handy Walmart sack. He'd wash them in the river.

He created a lather with soap from the dispenser and set to work on his beard, carving out a thin moustache, then cutting it away as well, because he had no scissors with which to maintain it.

A man in a straw cowboy hat entered, shook out his penis, and sidled up to the urinal as if settling upon a horse. He glanced once at Mario, and his face filled with rage.

"Good morning to you, sir," Mario said.

"Jest passin' through?"

"Sí, I am a traveler."

"Well, this ain't the way, Pancho. It jest ain't the *way.*"

In Mexico, where plumbing was scarce, the gringo would have been out of line, but this was his country, filled with baños. Why not use them fully? Mario did not perfectly understand the point of propriety here. The gringo's manner angered him, but he kept hacking at his beard. "I am sorry if you are offended, sir."

"Offended! You think I'm *offended?*" The man pounded the flush knob and turned away. He kicked the trash can as he entered the store again, startling the old man who had been so friendly when Mario entered the store.

"Hola, Grandpa," Mario said, but the old man didn't recognize him. He seemed to be in pain. He entered a stall, and soon began to moan, and cry out to God.

"Do you need medical attention, Señor?" Mario asked, but the old man only gasped and went silent.

A spiritual, rather than a medical crisis, Mario surmised, but he left the bathroom puzzled. He'd need more than a polo shirt to impersonate these Americans.

He calculated that he could eat ten times at Wendy's with his remaining money. To augment his diet, he'd build a small fire in his camp and heat such things as bouillon and Ramen noodles.

He sat in Wendy's for several hours. The thermometer at the bank read 114 degrees Fahrenheit, but the one inside registered only 72. And apparently his gringo disguise was sufficient to convince several young women, who flirted with him. After so long in the wilderness, Mario found this pleasurable, but with only five days of eating ahead of him, pursuing young women seemed a luxury. Besides, these specimens were scarcely weaned and giggled incessantly.

The gringos ordered their food from an outdoor intercom, then drove around to pay for it, all to avoid walking. They were a big people. He observed several men who must have weighed 140 kilograms—that was . . . 300 pounds and more. He could barely comprehend what they ordered: triple cheeseburgers, massive quantities of fried potatoes, and sugar drinks by the liter. He thought they rather resembled pigs with their fat jowls, broad noses, and deep-set eyes. He chuckled. *American hairless pigs.*

Of course, Mexicans also ate too much, and in some towns you could find the gringo drive-up system. Fat Americans and fat Mexicans were much the same. Once you'd observed them to be fat, you didn't observe anything else. Not fair, he supposed. Like that cowboy at Walmart judging him because of his dirty clothes.

He noticed another pattern: as customers passed over their money, and as the workers returned change, coins sometimes dropped. Usually, pennies fell, but also nickels and dimes. Some customers tried to reach down, but they were too near the building to open their doors completely and couldn't squeeze their big bodies downward. Thus they drove on.

Toward midnight Mario returned, walking quickly up to the service windows of some thirty-seven Wendy's, McDonald's, Taco Bells, and the like, picking up pennies and dimes and sometimes quarters, moving onward as casually as a Mexican in an American disguise could manage. By five A.M. he had recovered less than four dollars and concluded the effort wasn't worth undertaking.

Many establishments had cameras. But whether they did or not, he couldn't go in and out of light, and walk up to pay station after pay station, without seeming suspicious. He had seen no evidence of the border patrol in San Angelo, but certainly the local police were deployed. If he was going to be apprehended, it should be for more than pocket change.

In another day, he discovered a large, indoor mall, outside of which a bank announced the temperature to be 118. Nothing stirred except cars, shrouded in bluish exhaust, currents of heat radiating upward from them. They lumbered down the sticky asphalt, and melted away like mirages.

Inside the mall, squads of old people marched fiercely, monitoring their hearts with little devices attached to their waists. Mario's bored countrymen looked on from restaurants and the counters of clothing stores. He followed the old folks into a zone of kiosks, but no melons were for sale, no tomatillos or pulque or cheese from Oaxaca—nothing but a variety of the junk tourists were offered in Ciudad Acuña. He sat in the food court, sparsely populated with old people taking a break from their march. Some purchased sandwiches and drinks, laid out books, writing materials, and medicine, and took up lodging. Not wanting to part with his change, Mario found an abandoned soft drink cup, washed it out, and sat with drinking water and an abandoned Louis L'Amour novel. The big clock said 3:30, and the heat would not break before six.

Toward dusk, in the Walmart parking lot, he approached a man with a twisted white beard and a grocery cart filled with cans. The existence of other homeless in San Angelo comforted him. If confronted by the police, he'd act crazy like most of them did.

"Where do you sell your cans, friend?"

The man drew back suspiciously, clutching his cart. "These is mine."

"There's plenty for all, yes? It must be this terrible heat, but I counted twenty as I walked up to you."

The bearded man relaxed and pointed almost in the direction of Mario's home in the pines. "Boss Carter buys them. On that old farm."

Mario recalled the place: towers of scrap metal surrounded by an impressive steel fence and with a lopsided frame house in the middle. A rough field behind might once have been cultivated, so perhaps that's what the bearded man meant by "farm." Mario had found out all he needed, but he enjoyed the bearded man, if only because he sensed a soul more desperate than his own. "How many cans make a . . . pound?"

"Twenty-nine. Less if you find the tall ones. Only what you really want is copper. They's a fortune in copper."

"And silver and gold, my friend."

The man smiled distantly.

"But no one fights over aluminum, eh?"

"You talk strange."

"I suppose I do." He laughed. "I am Mario."

"Ted," the man said.

"You patrol this area daily, Ted?"

"Jest Sundays. Under the bridge, where they drink and do their drugs, an' along the highway, that's all mine. An' I like that parkin' lot on the hill, by the Walmart, because all the cans roll down by theirselves an' there ain't no work to it."

"Very good, Ted," Mario said, and extended his hand. "I'll be sure to stay out of your territory."

Gathering cans at dawn, when sometimes the temperature plunged as low as 85, was best. He could walk the gutters without encountering heavy traffic, and he'd found several drinking places, best visited before cleaning crews turned their attention to parking lots. Certain dumpsters were productive, and car washes, and the alleys behind liquor stores. Along the city's River Walk was good, as well as the bins around old Fort Concho.

He tried to stay with his task until he'd earned ten dollars. Because the price per pound fluctuated, reaching ten dollars meant finding anywhere from three to five hundred cans. He placed gallon jugs of water along his routes and noted public buildings where he could take an air-conditioned break and use the restroom. In the parks, he doused himself with water and threw himself onto the grass, until his strength returned. Almost always, the heat forced him indoors short of his goal.

At a garage sale he found a bicycle with two side baskets for only ten dollars. He stayed cooler, eased his transport of cans, and covered more area. He rode slowly, eying gutters, trying to gather two cans per minute. Sometimes, he reached his goal by noon.

One day his receipts climbed to the astounding total of thirteen dollars, and on a lucky Sunday he found the fortune in copper Ted had been prospecting for: ripped-out plumbing in a dumpster; the cords to abandoned washing machines, stoves, and air conditioners; bits and pieces of electrical wire behind a construction site. He was exhausted, ten days of can hunting had netted less than one day in the cantaloupe field, but nonetheless he had saved fifty dollars.

If he could finish by noon, the boiling afternoons were almost pleasant. He read the newspaper at McDonald's, paperback Westerns at Wendy's and the mall's food court, and escaped the heat until 3:30, when he found refuge in a dollar-house theatre. He slept through most of the movies. A promenade down the entertaining aisles of Walmart completed his day.

The crew at Carter's Salvage began to call him by name. They all were uneducated Mexicans such as you'd find selling produce in any little Mexican town. They sent money home to their parents and wives, and thought the United States an extraordinary place where, if you saved every nickel, eventually you could buy a house made of bricks. Better, still, one day you could return home rich and build your brick house for all your friends to see. They were cooperative, competent men for whom the idea of happiness was almost irrelevant. You worked, you rested, and on Sundays perhaps you drank a little to soothe your muscles.

A Salvadoran named Roberto Figueroa kept apart from them. Roberto had finished high school, leaving him with a superior air; he ate lunch alone and made fun of the music the men played. He never said hello to Mario, but simply stared as if he were trying to figure out something. Not wanting enemies, Mario always greeted Roberto warmly and refused to take offense at his hostile ways. Salvadorans were to Mexicans, after all, as Mexicans were to Americans. Many were hotheads, and he supposed they had their reasons.

A thin-haired, perpetually scowling woman named Pauline kept books and ran the scales. None of the crew spoke much English, but because of Pauline they didn't need to. Sometimes, a fight broke out, usually between Roberto and one of the others, and then Boss Carter himself emerged from his sagging house and cursed until the fighting stopped.

To call Boss obese did him an injustice: fat flowed from under his chin in concentric circles, abruptly ceasing at his hips, giving the impression of a gigantic, wobbly pear. His legs had been amputated some years before, or he might have seemed round. The men speculated how one so fat could live even one more day, and if Boss Carter were late in appearing, they soon advanced theories: insulin shock, heart disease, or perhaps just an attack of gluttony.

Then the garage door lifted, and Boss roared out on his riding lawn mower. He'd converted the mower to hand controls and used it to patrol his empire.

Legends had arisen about Boss. He was a war hero. He'd been in prison. He'd had three wives, one of them a Mexican. But it was verifiably true that he'd raised cotton here, before San Angelo sprawled in his direction and the farm was zoned from existence. After that, Boss ran a drive-in movie—you could still make out some of the scaffolding—and after that, a swap meet. The swap meet had evolved, or devolved, into the scrap yard.

Boss had six children, the men claimed, all of whom despised him and awaited his death, so they could split his money. The men thought a *lot* of money existed, secreted away in the house and perhaps buried under the drive-in scaffolding.

Sometimes, a crony from Boss's storied past drove up to his ruined picket fence, and Boss emerged to offer personal service, driving the mower into the cavernous barn in search of a half-horse motor or shower assembly. He paid for cans and copper and brass, and sold rebar and angle iron, alternators and ignition switches and tail-light lenses, out of a wallet he kept chained to his belt. The wallet was so full of bills, it couldn't be closed.

One day as Boss paid Mario his $11.57, he said, "Come up to the house."

Puzzled, Mario followed after the mower and into the garage. He wondered if he should help Boss down from the mower, but the man had powerful arms and one intact, withered knee; "Fuck," he said, and "Well, fuck me *sideways*," as he dropped to his buttocks, flowing off the mower like an octopus. He swung along on his massive fists, knee dragging, trunk rocking like a bowling pin about to fall, until he reached a mechanic's creeper. His great body obscured the creeper completely, so that he appeared to levitate across the basement's concrete floor.

A high pile of boxes blocked the stairwell. No one had been up there for a long time.

In dark rooms behind were Boss's living quarters. A faint, barn-like odor came from them, but as far as Mario could tell, they were uncluttered, even neat. He surmised that the man had carefully planned this interview and turned in a great effort to make his rooms presentable.

Boss pulled himself into a massive, padded wheelchair and rolled behind a desk. The desk held a computer, reference books, and a stack of letters, most of them unopened. He motioned, and Mario sat deep in what was probably a salvaged chair. He studied a bowl of mints with a layer of dust across it.

The air-conditioning operated superbly, but nonetheless Boss wiped his face with a towel. He smiled but couldn't catch his breath. At last he nodded to the refrigerator. "Pour us some iced tea."

The refrigerator was full of medicines, herbal supplements, and liquid concoctions Mario couldn't guess the nature of, but he found the tea, ice, and then two tall glasses on a drain board.

Boss still panted. "Take . . . lemon?"

"No, sir."

"Mario, right? You speak damn good English."

"Thank you."

"Been watchin' you. That one's different, I said to myself. The others, hard-workin' men, but lucky if they been through the third grade. Only, look at *him*. Why the fuck is a man like that pickin' up beer cans? Got no *Social*, I said to myself."

Mario glanced nervously toward the garage door. "Sir—"

Boss brought up the wallet big as Texas and placed three one-hundred dollar bills on the table. "I *despise* Social Security. Don't pay *no* taxes if I can avoid it. An' there ain't no mother-fuckin' retirement plan at Carter's Salvage."

Mario stared at the billfold. "You are offering me work, Señor?"

"First Spanish word you've used. Fuckin'-ay, I need a foreman to watch over them jabberin' Mexicans. They like you, I can tell. Any man works as hard as you do, every goddam day, in this *unbelievable* heat, for ten lousy bucks—fuckin' Abe Lincoln, that's what he is. Three hunnert a week, that's *cash*, an' I'm givin' you a week's advance."

Mario nodded in amazement. "Yes, sir. Thank you, sir."

"What you think of this fightin' goin' on over in New Mexico?"

"I've not followed the news—"

"They called in the National Guard on them fuckin' cartels. Border's got en*tirely* outta hand." Boss meshed his fingers together and sat back in the wheelchair. "Don't get any ideas about that wallet."

"No, sir! But . . . you're asking for trouble. There are some men—"

"Yeah, it's stupid, but I done it in the old days, an' I try to carry on. They talk about it all over the county, Boss Carter's wallet. They also talk about *this.*" Boss reached under the desk and lifted up a double-barreled shotgun.

"Señor!"

Boss grinned. "Just acquaintin' you with my system, Mario."

He soon learned how to run the two scales—the drive-up for the trucks filled with scrap iron and the smaller one for sacks of cans and buckets of copper. Customers expressed their pleasure that they no longer had to deal with the insulting Salvadoran or the sour Pauline. In fact, most avoided dealing with Boss Carter, who quoted prices like an oracle and never budged. Mario held to Boss's pronouncements, but with a smile and the impression of regret.

Boss didn't kill time up at the house. He tracked metals prices on the Internet, and emerged periodically to direct Mario to load a truck with aluminum or steel or cast iron to take to the railyard, where it began its long journey to China or Brazil. It was this—the exact worth of metals and when to sell—that Mario had no feel for.

He knew how to move men and, with August near, negotiated a different schedule: five A.M. until one. "Until November, I think," he told Boss.

"We'll give her a try," Boss said. "They ain't worth piss in the afternoons, that's for sure."

Even Roberto said thanks.

Mario wondered if the fierce young man belonged to one of those fabled Salvadoran gangs. Branches proliferated throughout the Southwest, including Dallas. Roberto said he'd lived there for several years but otherwise remained silent how he'd come to work for Boss.

"Tell me about Dallas, Roberto," Mario asked.

"Oh, eet ees a beeg, beeg cit-tee," Roberto said, mimicking the cartoon character, Speedy Gonzalez. "Not for country boys."

Mario rolled his eyes. He'd told Roberto he came from a little town in the state of Jalisco. And as far as he was concerned, hailing from the country gave you an advantage, because you could adapt to anything. Barrio children learned nothing but street skills. "Do you know of a neighborhood in Dallas called Oak Cliff? I heard about it on the radio."

Roberto's eyes glistened with understanding. "Mexican town."

"And you don't like Mexicans."

"I rode atop the trains through Chiapas and Oaxaca. First it was the gangs, then the *army.*" Roberto scrutinized Mario's face, but Mario wasn't prepared to offer the details of his own journey.

"As if you could tell the difference," Roberto went on. "They stole my money, they stole my boots, they beat me and left me in an old barn to die."

"I'm sorry for that," Mario said. "I've heard how bad it is in the South. How was it in Jalisco?"

Roberto frowned. "Better, I have to admit. An old woman there gave me food and a few pesos."

"See? Mexicans are good people. *Me,* for instance."

Roberto spat, though only to keep from laughing. As Boss put it, he had a bad attitude. He acted as if he'd done better things in the past, and would in the future. At the same time, he was a hard, intelligent worker, and Mario granted him such status as he could. He made him the chief operator of Boss's forklift and designated him a driver of the trucks bound to the railyard. Roberto wasn't legal, but he had a Texas driver's license that seemed to pass inspection.

Boss set them to stripping copper from his hoard of air- conditioners, carefully stacked in a broad tower. Little was wrong with many of them; the gringos didn't even try to fix their Chinese machines. Mario asked if each of the men could take home one that functioned.

Boss looked skeptical. "That make 'em work harder?"

"Even more if we move our task into the barn, set up fans, and fill a cooler with your excellent iced tea."

"You'll have a union in here, Mario."

But this was teasing, because Boss liked him. More than that. He did favors for Mario as if he were trying to make up for something he hadn't done for someone else. He showed Mario another room in the barn, filled to the ceiling with portable re-frigerators and boxes of plumbing fixtures. Once, Boss said, he kept an office here, with a stool and shower.

"Came out here to get away from the wife," Boss said. "She couldn't stand me in the house. I couldn't stand *her* in the house. I had my friends, you know, an' we'd play a little cards, an' drink. Then I lost my legs."

"But you don't play poker with your toes!"

Boss laughed. "That's a good 'un, Mario. Naw, I got so I wasn't fit company." He dropped his eyes. "Even tried to kill myself once."

His eyes were moist, and Mario, surprised, looked away in order to spare the man. "I have always thought . . . a man should have that right."

"Maybe." Boss pointed vaguely at the stumps of his legs. "Fella gets in a state like this, life ain't but barely worth livin'. That's the God's truth."

"It's the disease. It wasn't your fault, Boss."

"Well, it shore was." He sighed. "First off, I fucked   ever-thing with a skirt. Eat? God Almighty. We'd barbecue a wild hog somebody shot, an' there'd be beans an' cornbread, an' we'd swill down beer like it was Kool-Aid. I'd have a sweet potata pie all to myself.

"An' I give everbody shit. My friends was as mean as I was, an' come to think of it, most a' them's in rest homes now, or daid. Had friends on the City Council in those days, the pigs. Well, they was just *pigs!* I ain't got no wife, an' I ain't got no friends, an' I ain't got no legs, an' fuck, yes, it's my fault." Boss swallowed hard. "Anyways, Mario. You can make yourself an apartment here. If you want."

"Thank you, Señor. Gracias. Gracias."

Mario spent several sweaty afternoons cleaning out the three rooms and all of a Sunday unclogging drains. He cut a hole in the wall for one of the restored air-conditioners. In another week he'd found a cot at a garage sale, a lamp, a cof-fee pot, a microwave. You could say this much for the United States: it was full of goods.

He couldn't relax but had to admit he'd come a long way from the Rio Grande. Even Roberto seemed friendlier, surpris-ing Mario one evening as he sat in the shade with his new copy of *Don Quixote* and a cigar. Roberto offered two tickets for a

Labor Day norteña concert. Mario could expect food, dancing, and fireworks.

"Labor Day is in May."

"Not in this country. And the *Mexicans* do whatever the Americans do."

Mario's anger flared. *"We* work. *They* work."

"As you say." Roberto lit a cigarette and spat. "Perhaps you will find a woman there."

This was a reference to Mario's conspicuous celibacy, and either insulting or helpful. He decided it was helpful. *"Two* tickets. Let's go together, Roberto."

Roberto motioned toward the dented, ten-year-old Toyota pickup he'd bought from Boss for $200. The other men said it was a piece of junk, but Roberto replaced the clutch and now drove all over town. "I won't be in San Angelo, amigo." He paused and looked quickly away. "Anyhow, I hate that damned accordion music."

Mario nodded his thanks. Roberto had a kind streak despite himself. And he looked forward to the event, even entertaining the quixotic notion that he'd bring a young woman back to his junkyard suites.

He quickly concluded that—just as in Mexico—holidays here were filled up with platitudes and bad food. The gringo mayor attempted to speak Spanish, and some eminent Latino spoke en inglés of the cooperation of all working people. Hard times, both men acknowledged, and many are out of work. Don't worry! This is the greatest country in the world, with the hardest working people. The American economy will come roaring back!

The music was lively, American country and western mixed with norteña, but failed to move him. The accordion wasn't prominent enough, in his opinion. And the drunken crowd, dancing by the sweltering river, seemed alien. *Alien.* Like many words in English, it was precise and yet suggestive. Always you were an alien. Always you were alienated.

As Roberto had predicted, beautiful girls abounded, but they were American girls who happened to be brown and too young. He found himself longing for Alicia. He needed a woman old and wise enough to understand that he'd played a bad hand honorably. He needed someone to whom he could pour out his heart and who'd encourage him to hope. He needed his mother.

He got out the faded sheet with Maribel's phone number and the words, *"Buena Suerte."*

Yes, he was lonely. But for a moment, when he lay back in the grass and the heavens burst in yellow and blue and green, he felt content. So many people were out of work, and yet *he* wasn't. He had money in his pockets. He ate well. He could afford cigars and paperback books. That was what this country offered, a chance to make an honest living, and it was much. Consider poor, corrupted Mexico, forever biting its tail from hunger. You could not court a woman, give over your life to a great cause, find peace within yourself, without first filling your belly.

He bought a lime paleta and watched the teenagers strut exactly as they would have at a Mexican disco, and he'd made all the effort he could. Not two months before, he reminded himself, he'd been scrounging for change in the Taco Bell parking lot.

He returned through the woods, thinking again of his mother. Someone had told him that you could send e-mails from the public library, but you needed a card. You could obtain a card if you showed them something that proved your address, such as a utility bill. He would devise a way to bill himself. Possibly, he could use one of Boss Carter's invoices.

He thought of the last time he'd been with Alicia, when she allowed him to strip away her blouse and bra, before shooing him into the night. Catholic girls often behaved like that, but Alicia was too old for teasing. She wanted him to give up his soul—to agree to take over her father's business—before she gave herself. Next day, he returned to Mexico City, and they didn't see each other again. And he'd come to think that this was for the best, but one of the girls at the concert looked like Alicia, and in the darkness, alone again, he chided himself for not approaching her. As he neared the salvage yard, he stopped walking, as if he might still return and seek out the nearly familiar face. He reached for a cigar.

As he struck his match, he knew something was wrong. He hurried forward, but couldn't pinpoint the problem until he'd unlocked the gate. The lights were out in Boss's house. He couldn't recall a time when it had been entirely dark. As he drew near, he saw that the garage was open, the door to the basement thrown wide.

He smelled death. On either side of the border, it smelled the same, and brought on an instinctive fear he'd never mastered. If you did master it, then you'd been in the army too long. Fighting to control his stomach, he flipped the light switch.

The floor wasn't level. That's why the stream of blood ran out almost to the stairs. Already it had congealed a little, and he could hear flies. Boss Carter lay in a corner as if flung there, though no man could have lifted him. His throat was slit like a butchered hog's. His face was white as pulque, except for a blackness about the eyes.

On the desk lay Boss's shotgun, broken, with shells scattered about on the floor. A bottle of whiskey had spilled as well, over sliced bread, roast beef, taco chips, and a store-bought cherry pie. Mario guessed that Boss heard something and tried to load the gun, but was too drunk. He forced himself to look at the bloody carcass again: the billfold and its chain were gone.

Roberto had done this. The two tickets constituted a ruse to take Mario off the property. Though he hadn't realized it, Mario had served as a sort of bodyguard for Boss.

In five hours the crew came to work, and Roberto's absence would pretty much cement his guilt. Still, the police needed to do their work, and as quickly as possible. *Have I touched anything*, Mario asked himself, *moved anything*?

No. Even so, if he fled, he'd become a prime suspect. And he'd established his presence in San Angelo sufficiently that people could identify him. This was the dilemma of being illegal—of being alien. You did nothing, and still you were a criminal. If he stayed, he'd be exonerated. But the police would turn him over to the border patrol, who'd transport him to Mexico.

He couldn't bring himself to use Boss's desk phone, and went out to the garage. He dialed 060, then recalled that they used 911 here. Yes, murder, he explained. Robbery, murder. He tried to give directions, but the woman knew where Carter's Salvage was.

"Remain where you are, sir."

"Sí."

He switched on the porch light and walked across the yard to open wide the gate. Then he went to the barn, threw his clothing and toiletries into a back pack, and rolled out his bicycle. As he turned into the darkness, he heard sirens.

- 6 -

Heavenly Nights

As he bicycled east, only the Fort Worth and Dallas newspapers were for sale. When a week had passed, it occurred to him to seek out a library, where he read through several issues of the San Angelo *Standard-Times*. But he found no bold headlines such as he'd imagined: "Police Name Suspect in Scrap Yard Murder" or "Killer Apprehended."

The day following the crime, a story ran about one Rupert Carter, found dead at an address on East Chadbourne. But this "Rupert" was described merely as the proprietor of a recycling business. His survivors were not named. And details of his death were omitted, which to Mario suggested that the police were holding their leads closely.

A follow-up story ran in the local section. It appeared five days after Boss's death and read as if readers were already well-acquainted with the details. An attorney estimated the value of the estate at seven million dollars but said that "certain difficulties" remained regarding the will. The coroner promised his report for the following Monday, but when Mario consulted Monday's paper, he found no follow-up.

One rainy night, as he lay under a bridge by a small fire, he dreamed of coming into the basement again. Boss opened his eyes and spoke with great fear, his words garbled. Boss might have said, "Can you clean up this mess?" Frantically, Mario searched for a towel and returned to apologize when he couldn't find one. Boss had died again, and it seemed like Mario's fault, because he'd failed to wipe up the blood.

He awoke, gasping, and reached for the rifle he didn't have.

He'd heard a cow, slopping through the muddy creek below. A truck rumbled overhead, shaking the pilings, and Mario knew he couldn't return to sleep.

Still, the sense that he was a fugitive began to fall away from him. He ate in Mexican restaurants in small towns and bought supplies from shops that in Mexico they called tiendas. Loafers populated such places. They couldn't find work, and he wondered if Dallas would be the same.

Sometimes, Mario forgot that the towns he passed through weren't Mexican. When he remembered, the sounds of casual Spanish brought him to tears.

In the black night he cried for his mother and chided himself for conduct more like César's than that of a true soldier. Four months had passed, and she would have finished her mourning and spent the death settlement from the army. Yes, for now, it was better to remain dead. One day he'd find a safe place and send her money again.

He climbed a long grade, coasted for many kilometers under a full moon, and time seemed suspended. Ahead, along the shining highway, armadillos sniffed and stumbled as though drunk.

He had *not* killed Boss, or César or Tejón. He *had* saved nearly twelve hundred dollars. The world was boiling away, but he had nothing to do with it, and only the summers were unendurable. Winters in Texas were gentle and long. With luck, he might still find his way.

Nearing Dallas at last, he bought a throwaway cellphone and punched in Maribel's number, then panicked and aborted the call. He'd commanded twenty-eight men. He'd killed a deer with a stone and gutted it with a puny pocket knife. He'd hiked one hundred miles through the Texas desert, but calling a strange woman was impossible. In Mexico you met a respectable woman at church, or a third party introduced you.

He had to call her. He couldn't survive without help.

He'd called a woman he didn't already know only once in his life, when he was a cadet. The academy was strict, but on Sundays they were released into the city for several hours of wandering free. They were encouraged to make religious observances and buy sentimental gifts for their mothers.

Mario always passed a florist's shop bordering the Zócalo, a fancy, indoor place where the most beautiful girl he'd ever seen worked. Though he never learned her name, the sound of her voice, her every graceful gesture, seemed perfect. And she threw him encouraging glances. Halfway through the semester, after much agonizing, he bought a single rose and left it on her counter with his name.

Afterwards when he passed, the girl's eyes were knowing, and sad. At last he called her shop. "I am Mario. I walk by your place of work, and your smile carries me through the week. I left you a rose."

"You are a soldier, Señor."

"Sí. But what of—?" What of love, he almost asked. What of the stars above, your beauty and gentle wisdom, our special, unspoken bond?

"Soldiers wander far, and make no money. I'm truly sorry."

He *had* wandered far and made little money—and now was without a country as well. Perhaps the girl had no romance about her, but she was wise. And he'd be wise not to invest too much hope in Maribel, but his desperation gave him no rest. Her number lent him an identity in this foreign place. As the countryside dropped behind and the traffic grew heavy, he tried again.

"Brighter Day Fellowship. Please listen to the following—"

He ended the call and bicycled into a cemetery, where he sat on a concrete bench and smoked a cigar. The cemetery retained rural trappings, a part of him noted, but now only a rusty wrought iron fence protected it from massive department stores and parking lots that went on like the sea. Forgotten, the cemetery became an island of peace.

He rode eastward past strip malls and neighborhoods walled off with high wooden fences. Once he'd calmed, and scolded himself for behaving like a teenager, Mario reasoned that only a few explanations were possible:

She'd transposed a digit.

She'd moved, and the number had been reassigned.

She'd made up a number. No, she'd left it voluntarily, pressing it on him. And she'd written with careful legibility. What was the answer?

Maribel was an evangelista. Brighter Day, apparently some variety of church, must be where she worked. He dismounted and walked slowly onward. The neighborhoods receded and he passed a great hospital; an ambulance shrieked past as he punched in the number. He pushed the bicycle with one hand, holding the phone to his ear with the other, just like a gringo.

"Brighter Day Fellowship. Join with us in your walk with Jesus!" The recording was of a man's voice, and so cloying Mario nearly hung up again. What a strange country!

Soothing music came on, and the voice resumed: "Please listen to the following list of options. Press one, hours of worship; two, today's Bible verse; three, Pastor Tom Malone's mini-sermon; four, child care at Brighter Day; five, our youth ministry; six, Bible study for men, women, and singles; seven, Latino outreach; eight, are you experiencing a spiritual crisis? Lose your job? Abuse at home? An unequal yoking? Stay on the line, and a counselor—"

Possibly he qualified for the last option, but it led only to another recording and an admonition to prayer. "Ay-eee!" he cried, and then a woman spoke:

"Praise the sweet name of Jesus! How may I help you today?"

All he could get out was, "Hola."

"Would you prefer our Spanish counselor, sir?"

"I—I want to speak to Maribel Garza."

"Do you have a wrong number, sir? This is the Brighter Day help line."

"She's an employee."

"Do you have her extension, sir?"

Any lie would do. "Her mother's sick, and I didn't know—"

"Certainly. Forgive me, sir." He heard the tapping of a keyboard, and a mindless hymn—"Oh Praise Him! Oh Praise Him!"—as the woman investigated. Then she spoke again: "There's no one here by that name, sir."

"Is this . . . Dallas?"

"Plano, sir."

"Is *Play*-no—" It was the Spanish word for "flat," loosely interpreted as a plain or flat place, pronounced "plah-no." The American pronunciation annoyed him—"not Dallas?"

"Sort of. Part of the Metroplex. Sir, I have an incoming call."

Now he stood on the overpass of a great highway. The traffic east, the traffic west, sped into the unknown. And he was about to lose this almost-friendly voice with its almost-genuine concern. "Is *Play*-no near to Oak Cliff?"

"Twenty-five miles north. Thank you, sir, and—"

"You have been gracious."
"Walk with Jesus!"

In Oak Cliff, Mario found a motel tucked between a dump for concrete wastes and a grove of wild pecans by a stagnant creek. The place was called Heavenly Nights and in late afternoon looked peaceful enough, and surely it was cheap. A short, disheveled man with "Cabrera" scrawled on his nametag asked Mario for his driver's license.

"I don't have one."

Cabrera nodded and glanced at the TV mounted high, where a Univision soap opera played. Mario looked, too. The actress was beautiful, though perhaps too old for her part. After a time Cabrera said, "¿Un otro I.D., Señor?"

"My papers are being forwarded . . . " Mario paused, then placed two twenties on the counter. "Is there not some other way to deal with this matter?"

Cabrera studied the twenties with large, tragic eyes. "Not a problem. It's only for your benefit we ask, in case something is lost."

"Ah, bueno."

"For a week it is 200 dollars." Cabrera pocketed the twenties as if he'd won a hand of poker, and Mario placed ten more twenties on the counter.

"Numero cuatro," Cabrera said, handing over the key. "A very fine room with cable television."

The exchange was almost gratifying. It told Mario much about the rules of living as an indocumentado in a city as large as Dallas. He still had 900 dollars, and could remain several weeks in this place and be able to eat, explore the city, and find new ways to make money.

"Señor," Cabrera called after him. "Do you need to work? Every morning, you can join a crew."

His spirits lifting, Mario turned to see Cabrera holding up a Social Security card enshrined in plastic. Cabrera dropped it onto the counter and worked off a smudge of grease with a paper towel. Mario reached for it.

Cabrera sighed. "Se renta, Señor."

Mario pulled out his billfold again, but hesitated.

Cabrera nodded. "Work is hard to find right now, Señor."

"Quanto?"

"Only twenty-five."

"For the week?"

Cabrera sighed again. "For one day only. It's a good number, my brother's. Unfortunately, he has been injured, he has a large family. . . "

Mario frowned and put down twenty-five dollars.

He found the room, spare but adequate, and washed out his clothes in the sink. The metal door had two deadbolts and a dramatic dent on its outside, which Mario took as a bad sign. He shaved, then walked down Jefferson into the heart of Oak Cliff, with its taquerias and supermarkets and liquor stores, half a dozen churches, and several second-hand stores. He bought food, a coffee pot, and a Little Leaguer's aluminum bat.

Someone pounded on his door precisely at SIX A.M., by which time Mario had had his coffee, a piece of bread, and an apple. He crawled into a pickup bed with eight other men, Latino, gringo, and black. Two, knowing each other, spoke quietly, but the rest were silent, and Mario understood. This was day labor, and his co-workers were variously hung over, schizophrenic, or both.

The driver stopped at McDonald's and some of the men bought coffee. Then they twisted about back streets, passing fine houses and the most expensive-seeming stores Mario had ever seen. Just at seven they reached a park with a stream running through it.

"What is this beautiful place?" he asked no one in particular.

The man next to him, grizzled and middle-aged, opened his eyes as if from deep sleep. "It's called Highland Park. It is dry everywhere in Texas. Farmers can't raise their crops, but in Highland Park they fill their pools and water their grass all the same."

"They can afford it, I suppose."

"The world will die of thirst, and they will water their pretty flowers." The man stuck out his hand. "I'm Raul Zamora."

Mario gave his name. "You talk like a rebel, Raul."

Raul frowned. "No, but I've been around this country. I know some things."

Raul and Mario drew the easy detail of bolting together prefabricated picnic tables. By noon they'd finished eight and carried them to various locations, marked with red exes in the lush grass, throughout the park.

Neither had brought lunch. They sat on one of the benches, smoking Mario's cigars. Raul was from Sonora, south of Hermosillo, where he'd grown up raising celery and bell peppers for the American market. Used to be, this time of year, the days were almost as hot as in Texas. But farmers went for outings up into the barrancas, where you could swim in pristine waters and shoot deer.

"You couldn't even take a car in the old days," Raul said. "We rode horses. Sometimes, we bought corn and fish from the Tarahumara."

"Utopia!" Mario laughed. "Every night, getting drunk on corn beer."

Raul wrinkled his nose. "You wouldn't want to drink it, my friend."

Mario lay back in the grass. It was probably more than 100, but a breeze blew up from the creek and the rustling of leaves in the great trees was pleasant to listen to. "What do you think, Raul?" he asked. "Is life better in this country?"

"Right now, you can't find work. And Texas is never the best place."

"Where, then?"

Raul laughed. "Cíbola."

Mario laughed, too. "I am looking for a *real* place."

"Iowa is good. In Arkansas I had a woman. If you're illegal, everywhere is the same. You just make enough to eat."

"Do you have a family, Raul?"

"I have a sister, but we're not speaking." He frowned. "No one else. You?"

"I worry about my mother."

A runner came through the trees, dressed in blue sweats and bright blue shoes. She was slender with fine muscles and sweated almost stylishly in the late October sun. Altogether she made a refined, confident, but not quite dismissive appearance. She smiled as she passed. "Hola" and "Good afternoon," they called to her, and turned to watch as she ran onward.

Raul laughed harshly. "You'll never get any of *that*, amigo."

Mario looked away. "I was only thinking—"

"It's clear what you were thinking, but they do not even *shit* in Highland Park."

Mario laughed again. He liked Raul.

"I'm serious. You know that wiggly white stuff, that cheese they make from soy beans? That's what they eat here."

"It's called tofu. I've never tried it."

"It's a food so pure, you don't shit it out. Everything is absorbed by the small gut. You don't believe me?" Raul swept a hand toward the running path. "Just look at that girl."

Mario could find no answer to this and was grateful when they resumed work. But he grew so hungry in the afternoon that even tofu would have sufficed, and at quitting time, when the pay envelopes were handed out, went immediately into McDonald's, despite his vow to eat only in his room.

There he discovered he'd earned only sixty dollars. His rent amounted to twenty-eight, and after the fee for a Social Security card only seven dollars remained. If he didn't work on weekends, he couldn't break even. And what if he fell sick?

He complained to Cabrera. "A man can't live on seven dollars."

Cabrera gave out his tragic sigh. "Some jobs pay more."

"Do you have such jobs?"

"Not me, amigo. All I can offer is the card."

In truth, some jobs were better. He cleared fifty dollars after three days with a mowing crew, and the company of the men, Mexicans and Guatemalans, was agreeable. After work they drank Budweisers with the foreman and told stories of coming to el norte. Unfortunately, mowing season ended early this year because of the drought. Full-time landscaping jobs had become just as rare. Construction? Good luck, amigo.

Miraculously, it rained, and he lay out a day. For a mere five dollars he borrowed the driver's license of Cabrera's fabled brother, gave the motel as an address, secured a library card, and requested the San Angelo *Standard-Times*. The librarian ushered him to a computer, but the paper's website seemed incomplete. He must go to the great downtown library across the Trinity River, the librarian informed him, and he hadn't enough time. Through the afternoon and evening he read a history of Texas, as the invaders recounted it, and a stack of popular science magazines.

Then he worked for three weeks south of downtown, unloading damaged freight from railroad cars that had derailed near the city of Canton. He joined a sullen crew of several races and languages, mostly winos seeking just enough money for a drunk. But Mario showed up daily, becoming the on-the-cheap supervisor: he knew how to get the work underway in the mornings and how to stack the salvage in the truck trailers. The true foreman, a chain-smoking black man named Abner, turned the work over to him, slipping him an extra twenty every evening.

For two days they carried out cans of green beans, and each man could take away a flat. Another day they unloaded toilet paper, packed in great boxes because each roll weighed so little. No man could lift a box by himself, but all were allowed what rolls they could fit into a garbage bag, and Mario managed one hundred. He bargained with Cabrera.

"I have a good supply already, and it's so cheap—"

"Ten dollars. It's very high quality."

"Too much! I will take five off your rent for the week. And I'm doing you a great favor."

"Gracias, Señor Cabrera. You're a generous man."

The damaged freight job ended with a car of whiskey, packed in three-quarter liter bottles, six to the case. Even undamaged cases had to be opened, inspected, and repacked, and though Abner provided good dollies and ramps, the work was back-breaking. Abner stayed near this time, for fear of organized theft, but when the job was done, he gave each man one unopened bottle. He drove Mario all the way to the motel and handed over a full case.

"That's 150 dollars, my good friend," Abner said. "If you don't drink it yourself."

"Thank you, Abner."

"If I have more work, I'll ask for you."

Despite the handicaps, Mario had saved two hundred dollars in three weeks, and he had the whiskey to sell. He left out one bottle and hid the remainder by standing on a chair and pushing up a ceiling tile.

His muscles ached from the week, but tomorrow was Sunday. Between the bed and the room's one chair, he made a comfortable place, and when the heater proved inadequate, wrapped himself in the bedspread. Imagine! Temperatures falling to 60!

Reading scientific articles remained one of his pleasures, and he wanted to learn more about climate change. But tonight he felt too weary to concentrate, and the whiskey, mixed with Coke, tasted better and better. And—the only one of Maribel's promises that had proved true—ice was plentiful at Heavenly Nights.

He turned on the TV to a Bruce Lee movie from the 1970s, dubbed in Spanish. On another channel he watched the report, which for a moment he couldn't tell was a movie or the news, about renegades who'd blown up a section of the international fence. Then they'd made a charge down the main street of Columbus, New Mexico, only a few miles to the north, and taken over the railroad depot. The journalist noted that this was the rebel group's second foray. The first time, they'd progressed as far as White Sands, where F-16s buzzed them and a company from Fort Bliss boxed them in.

Cíbolistas, the group called themselves.

The attack on Columbus repeated Pancho Villa's incursion of one hundred years before, and tourists had at first thought they were witnessing a re-enactment. The mood changed when a woman took a bullet from a perfectly modern weapon. Still, these silly Cíbolistas, these neo-Villistas, were easily routed by state police, and New Mexico officials expressed confidence that the entire "splinter group" had been rounded up.

"Drug runners from Juarez," was the characterization out of Mexico City. A spokeswoman for the president conveyed the profound regrets of the nation. "Mexicans are a free people," she said. "Apparently, some of them feel free to behave like fools. Make no mistake, we are winning this war."

Mario rose in agitation, sat in despair. What was he doing here? He should be fighting the cartels—or he should join them. He admired how they thumbed their noses at the God-damned Mexican army, not to mention the Americans. *Anything* would be preferable to the dangling, hopeless life he led.

No, not anything. Not trafficking in drugs. He'd watched two friends die when they tried it.

The whiskey took him over, and he pitied himself. Looking back, he realized that his long journey to Dallas had been endurable only because he held the goal of finding Maribel. He had not hoped for love. He needed a friend. At the least, she could have pointed him in a better direction than this awful motel.

Mingling with the canned laughter from the television, he heard norteña and mariachi music from passing cars, punctuated by deep, ominous basses and shouts and drunken laughter from the parking lot. The whiskey told him he'd find solace out among the Saturday night revelers.

He opened his door, and a girl fell into his arms. He staggered back, and she staggered forward. She stood up straight, and smiled flirtatiously. "Oh, Señor."

He stepped toward her, pushing out his hands as he might herd a farm animal, but she slipped to the side. "May I use your phone?"

"There's a phone at the office—"

She'd already sat in his chair, and punched in her number. "I need to call my sister," she said pitifully. "That Cabrera, he'll want money."

"Money to make a phone call?"

"He's a vulture."

True enough, but she quickly hung up the phone. And sat, her legs crossed, tattoos of flowers on both ankles, one shoe dangling on a toe. She had wide hips and thin breasts. Her face was pretty, but streaked with mascara and blush. She chewed vigorously on her gum, her eyes roved ceaselessly, and her crossed leg danced. She was *on* something, probably methamphetamine.

"I must ask you to leave."

She threw back her head, laughing. "A man so good- looking shouldn't be alone on a Saturday night."

Moments before, he'd thought the same thing.

She pointed to the bottle of whiskey, still two-thirds full. "Why not pour a drink for your guest, Señor? Why not be happy tonight?"

Grimacing, he stepped into the bathroom for a plastic glass and handed it to the girl with the bottle. He grabbed her arm and pulled her to her feet.

"Go," he said. "You can have the whiskey."

She slipped from him and fell backwards on the bed, holding the bottle upright through her fall. She spread her plump thighs and clapped them together. She gestured with one hand, mimicking masturbation.

"Why would you want to be *alone*, Señor, when you could be with a fine woman?" She hunched up on the bed and slid down her panties. "See? I am wet for you, handsome man! Fifty dollars, I'll stay the night."

"Get out!"

"Forty, because you gave me the whiskey."

Something snapped. He had worked at the worst of jobs

in a country he might never understand. Maribel had proved false. A trail of dead men lay behind him. Screaming, he picked up the Little Leaguer's baseball bat and smashed it on the bed. His anger, which surprised him in its intensity, quickly fled. But when he looked up at the girl, her manner had changed from whining supplication to horror.

"Don't hit me," she said, her eyes moving frantically. "Oh please, Señor, don't *hit* me."

"I wouldn't . . . hit you," he said, looking down on her as if from a great distance.

She fell to the floor, bawling and shrieking. She crawled forward, kissed his shoe, and pulled herself up his leg even as he tried to shake her free. She buried her face against his knees, and sobbed. "I'm sorry, Señor. Don't hit me, do I deserve that? I will do anything, anything for you, Señor, anything!"

"Jesuchristo," he muttered. Somehow, he pulled his leg free. She collapsed on the floor, and reluctantly, as if he'd been assigned responsibility for someone else's filthy child, he picked her up and dropped her on the bed. He pulled off her shoes and threw the bedspread over her. He found his jacket despite the chaos of the room and said, "Sleep if off, Señorita. The room is yours."

He chained his bike, the only thing she might conceivably sell, to the steel bed frame and walked into the darkness.

Crossing the green belt, he stood looking down on the Trinity River, which presumably flowed wide at times but now was barely a stream. Still, the air was better here. If you worked in Dallas for a while, you grew used to your eyes watering from fumes, your nose erupting in sneezes. Dallas hadn't worked out, and perhaps, while he still had some money, he should find a smaller town. What farm work was available in winter? What work of any sort?

He wandered among the skyscrapers. The homeless awoke seemingly in unison and staggered about in the cold, securing their meager belongings, seeking transfusions of coffee. He bought a sandwich at a convenience store and kept walking, not wanting to return before noon, by which time the girl surely would be gone.

He came upon a grand old cathedral called Guadalupe. Only in Mexico City had he seen such a fine church. At the door a priest greeted him in a kind tone and offered a program. The auditorium was massive and filled with Mexicans, or anyhow, Latinos. So many children! And all of them small, crawling, slobbering, crying, reaching out their fat arms to be carried by their plump mothers. Their mothers, their fathers, were young—much younger than Mario.

Where had they come from? Were they legal or illegal? They were, he guessed from their simple clothing, their beaten-down look, *poor*. He estimated a thousand in the congregation, listening, or not listening, to an energetic priest with a homily on *"La ley y la palabra."*

Toe the line, brother. Your reward is in Heaven.

Quickly tiring of the harangue, Mario stared up at the effigy of Christ, who in this mestizo incarnation seemed not merely to be suffering, but to have been violated, bloodied, a downtrodden idealist broken simply for speaking out. Mario was moved. This Christ might not be real, but he was correct.

He seriously contemplated the priest's exhortations to join in Wednesday night Catholic studies. He might discover how to secure documents and find a real job. He might find a real woman. Yes, he thought, and afterwards he'd contact his mother that he'd returned to the church. What harm such a lie, when he could never go home?

The ushers fanned out to gather the offering, and a bland-faced, deeply brown woman holding an infant nudged her husband, a short, wiry fellow with yellowed teeth, for something to give. Reluctantly, as if he were fighting pain, the man reached into his jeans and produced a crumpled dollar.

Depression hit Mario fully. To be so poor as that! He himself gave a dollar and escaped out the rear, even as the flock trudged forward for communion.

The poor man, he thought. *The poor woman.*

He was grateful that the girl had gone from his room. He could be alone again with his bicycle and the investment schemes offered on the TV. Beyond despair, he pushed up the ceiling tile and retrieved his whiskey. He drank until he slept. He woke and drank until he vomited. He went out for burritos and drank some more.

As if in a dream, Mario opened the door to Cabrera's pounding. The man peered into the room, attempted to enter, but Mario placed his arm across the threshold.

Cabrera seemed sad. "There has been a complaint."

"Sí," Mario said. "But complaining, what good does it do?"

"The young woman you were entertaining—"

"The puta?"

"Sí, she's only a whore, but she says you promised her one hundred dollars and didn't pay her. Then you threatened her with violence."

"This isn't true, Cabrera. I could almost say . . . she tried to rape me."

Cabrera came near to laughing. "I bring this to your attention only to help you. If she goes to the police—"

"How much will *you* take, Cabrera? Twenty percent? Fifty?"

Cabrera blinked his mournful eyes. "Señor, I can't have troublemakers here. I have a business to run. If I myself must go to the police, they will take this matter, this 'battering' as they call it, very seriously. I can't allow—"

"Cabrera, your business is whores and false papers. You won't go to the police."

"Señor, you wrong me. It's true; these girls are full of lies. Perhaps just fifty dollars and a bottle of that fine whiskey—"

Mario shut the door.

And drank. He surmised that five bottles of Kentucky whiskey might kill him several times over. He'd never been near to suicide, but he wouldn't mind dying today. Life was a miserable thing, where you worked without rest, and men cheated you, and love itself was a hopeless trap. The rich controlled everything except religion, which, with money, they had no need for. *Dios mio,* he thought, *I have no one, not even a sad, ignorant wife to give a dollar to.* No one but a nameless, teenaged whore.

He fell into a befuddled sleep, full of quickly moving, violent dreams. The whiskey woke him after midnight, and he stumbled into the bathroom to vomit, instead falling into dry heaves and sweating. He stared at himself in the mirror. *How did this happen?* he asked himself. *I am a soldier.*

He'd found his own army, disgruntled soldiers, drug punks who'd seen the light, whores and petty thieves and crazy people in home-made wheelchairs, and they'd go tilting at windmills all along the border, steal from the rich, distribute food and medicine to the poor, and meanwhile live a jolly life deep in the dry mountains. He'd grow a fierce moustache and carry a machete and satisfy fifty women. Yes!

He laughed, and sobbed, and poured the rest of his fine whiskey down the toilet.

- 7 -

The Air-Conditioning Business

On the muted television, programs changed like the seasons. He lay in bed not quite paralyzed, poison pounding in his blood. *Pounding.* He heard a woman's voice beyond the door, a man's—his mother, urging his father to speak more charitably of the priest; his father, complaining of the money she insisted on giving to that fat little wino.

—It's *my* money, which I work very hard for at the hotel.

—You would not *need* to work except for that greedy priest. And then you could help at home.

—Claudio, you lie to yourself. The time you could grow vegetables and expect to feed your family is long in the past. Mario knows this. Even little Silvio knows this.

—If I had more land!

—Then you would want a tractor and a pump to bring water up the mountain, and still you would not make enough.

Morning light sifted through the blinds, and Mario told himself to rise. The whore, Cabrera, Raul's theories of the upper class—none of it really mattered. He had to get hold of himself.

Down along the Trinity sprawled a dozen scrap yards where he might look for work. Somehow he'd master the problem of papers. Perhaps the Guadalupe priest could help. He'd *confess* to the priest. "My case is unusual," he'd say. "I did not choose to be illegal, but I cannot go to the authorities."

His joints ached, but he eased his feet to the floor and reeled to the bathroom. He put his hand against the wall, but his urine gushed without pain. He closed his eyes with no instinct to pray.

This time the pounding he heard was real. No doubt it was

Cabrera, wanting his rent. Lingering an instant to study his face, puffy and with a week's growth of beard, Mario thought, I couldn't be a lieutenant anymore. Not even for a drug boss. He chuckled at his midnight resolve to find himself a revolution. What was worth fighting for? Why not an army where you lie on the beach, eating pineapples? Fatalistically, almost cheerfully, he found his billfold and opened the door.

"You look like shit, man."

Mario brought a hand to his forehead, and closed his eyes. Roberto Figueroa, the murderer. Murderer of an unpleasant man who nonetheless had been kind to Mario and who despite all his blustering was helpless. Nothing good could explain why Roberto had tracked him here, and without speaking, Mario stepped carefully back. He assumed the martial arts crouch he'd learned in officers' school.

"Mario, it's me, su amigo. Roberto!"

Mario feinted with his left, and as Roberto stumbled in surprise, jabbed two fingers of his right hand into Roberto's eyes. When Roberto sank to his knees, screaming, Mario grabbed an arm and yanked it up his back. He lifted it to its breaking point. "You *killed* him."

"Boss killed *himself.*"

Mario knew what his eyes had seen. "He—"

"You saw the shotgun, ¿sí? But Boss couldn't pull the trigger. *That is what the police said!* He was drunk, he crawled over the floor, he. . . "

Mario released Roberto's arm as he tried to understand. "He cut his own throat?"

Roberto stood slowly, rubbing his arm, his face torn between relief and self-righteousness. "You and I, Mario, we have talked to the Devil late at night, but to be so sad inside as that!"

Mario fell back on the bed. "Boss had nothing to live for."

Roberto dropped into the chair by the phone. He carefully massaged his eyelids, then blinked rapidly. "His daughter came with a lawyer, and they shut down the place. They said the junk was worth—"

"Seven million, that's what I read," Mario said. "But what of his billfold? The one he carried on a chain? If it was not a robbery—"

"In the safe. Along with his will; that is why they knew he killed himself. He gave everyone money but his family. 'The aluminum is to be divided among the workers,' Boss said, and the lawyer told us to sell it. There's one thousand dollars for you if you go back—"

"The police—"

"Know you're illegal. But they're not looking for you." He shrugged. "Or any of us."

Mario lowered his head. "Boss was my friend."

In the bathroom, Roberto examined a cut on his chin and washed his eyes. "He wasn't my friend, but he was a fair man in his fashion. How could you think I killed a poor creature such as that?"

Mario sighed. His mouth tasted bad. "Forgive me, Roberto."

"I saw you on the street, and first I thought, just another homeless man. Then I recognized you and tried to call out, but you went down in the woods along the Trinity. It has taken me a week to find you." Roberto rose. "Let's eat. We'll go to Pancho's Buffet, it's cheap and very hot, like a certain Mexican I know."

Mario found his voice at last. He'd been near to suicide himself. Boss's death began to make some sense. "Sí," he said dully.

"And then we'll go to my place. If you promise not to attack me again, you can stay there. I have work for you."

Roberto—and now Mario—lived across the Trinity River in a decayed industrial area called Deep Ellum. Mario didn't quite understand the joke associated with the name, or at any rate couldn't find it humorous. Originally, the story went, Deep Ellum was called "Deep Elm," but Texans couldn't pronounce "elm" any way but "ell-um."

Roberto's place hid behind an office in a strip mall that contained a partnership of psychologists, a bridal and quinceañera store, an insurance agency that catered to Latinos, a Vietnamese nail parlor, a pawn shop, a sports bar, a liquor store, and a church called Agua de Vida.

Roberto had no mailbox, no apartment number. You came around to the back, walked up the steps of a loading dock, and pressed a buzzer if you didn't have a key. The door opened onto a great garage where living quarters, with one door and no windows, had been formed on the concrete. Roberto had hacked out a hole for an air-conditioner.

Inside stood a single, large room with cots against a wall. The amenities included a metal shower stall, a sink, and a stool with a plastic curtain around it. Along the walls were a refrigerator, a microwave, a TV with pirated cable, and some comfortable chairs.

If you walked around the garage bay, you'd soon stumble into Roberto's pallets of air-conditioners. Many came from Boss's operation and were in the process either of being fixed or junked for copper. After that you'd find a deep freezer, a lawn mower, plastic jugs of motor oil, a workbench with a vise and an assortment of tools, and janitorial supplies. Roberto worked as the custodian and unofficial maintenance man.

Or perhaps he was official, because a gray-haired gringo, always in the same cowboy hat, string tie, and red sports coat, came around the first of every month with a paycheck. Sometimes, the gringo lingered to crack jokes and talk business in a vague way. Once he brought a six-pack of Budweiser.

Roberto rescued him from the Heavenly Nights Motel, and Mario was grateful, but he didn't understand his new arrangement. Everything seemed legal and illegal at the same time. The apartment had no metering, for instance. Did Roberto steal his utilities, or were they part of his pay? In any case, Roberto had keys for the entire strip mall and shortly subcontracted with Mario to swab down bathrooms and refill dispensers, run the vacuum cleaner, and sweep and buff the tiled floor in the nail parlor.

One evening Roberto pulled inside the Toyota truck he'd bought from Boss. They replaced the dented fender, set up some fans, and through the night sanded and masked and primed. Just at dawn they sprayed the truck a royal blue.

"It's much improved," Mario said. "But I'm not sure it will impress the women."

Roberto shook his head. "I must look respectable in . . . el norte."

North Dallas, he meant, and the suburbs beyond, where the rich Christians lived. *Play-no.* Free hand, Roberto painted yellow lightning bolts on the Toyota's doors, and the words "Roberto's Electrical Service." The truck already boasted high racks for wire and conduit, bolted onto a camper shell.

"You're an electrician now?" Mario asked.

Roberto shrugged. "Sí. But in this country, they make you take a test for everything. It's to keep Latinos out, but I can string wires as well as anyone. I've worked with 220, even 440—and big motors!"

"You could work in Oak Cliff."

"The money is in el norte. It's not like the old days, when houses went up like mushrooms, but plenty of work remains if you know where to look, and electricians make the most because nobody understands what they do. They keep their own hours and never even sweat."

Roberto worked all night, sometimes, bringing back box after box of electrical wire—many sizes, differing lengths, some of it burnt looking. "You like movies, Mario?"

Roberto handed over a stack of DVDs and also a pouch full of knives, cutters, and strippers. "They want it clean. You know that from working for Boss Carter. You can sit here all day, amigo, stripping and stripping—and watch movies while you work!"

Mario didn't believe that all the copper Roberto brought him was the waste from construction sites, though that's what Roberto claimed. Boss himself had been none too saintly when it came to buying junk. And if you were illegal, you couldn't be completely honest, or you'd starve. You couldn't even work without committing what the gringos called identity theft.

Roberto's wages, though somewhat irregular, were generous, and Mario didn't have to worry about Social Security or taxes. In fact, he had almost no expenses, and his savings, which he kept in a cigar box under his cot, mounted quickly.

He rode his bicycle down the rough streets of the warehouse district, marveling that so much industry had been abandoned; attended movies during his solitary afternoons, working on his accent and trying to appreciate the differences between bawdy American humor and bawdy Mexican; and spent many hours at the great downtown library.

He read of American farming techniques. Take corn, for instance. The American varieties had been engineered through the manipulation of genes. Farmers planted patented seeds, and you couldn't save them or the big companies took you to court. Still, using these magical seeds, it was theoretically possible to raise seven hundred bushels an acre.

The drawback was water. They had tried the amazing corn in Kansas and Oklahoma where rainfall always fell short, and the big wells they drilled were sucking dry something called the Ogallala Aquifer. Some thought such farms would disappear and that this region, the High Plains, would return to range land. Others thought it would become a desert.

But because they planted such big plots—and because their government subsidized them—the Americans grew corn more cheaply than Mexican campesinos. And because of NAFTA, the gringos were free to dump their corn on the Mexican market.

Mario's father had raised a fine blue corn, saving seeds every year as *his* father had. The family used the corn for everything from tortillas to pig feed, and yet his father sold half his crop in the market, until the American corn drove prices so low, his father couldn't compete. The family began to live on his mother's wages from the hotel and Mario's from guiding tourists.

His father tried to start a business butchering hogs, but it was brutal work. He died from a stroke brought on by high blood pressure brought on, Mario thought, because he'd lost the means to support his family. What Mario hadn't perfectly understood was that American corn drove his father from business. Out of work, campesinos much like him had fled to the cities—and then to el norte. Ironically, the Americans had only themselves to blame for their woes along the border: their cheap corn and, of course, their drug habit.

If you waited long enough, however, everything changed and changed again. American corn became too valuable to dump on Mexican peasants. Prices jumped by half, poor land was pressed into production, because all the world was hungry—or needed fuel.

Prices fell yet again when banks ran out of money, and factories closed, and people couldn't buy corn or anything else. Now, with record drought and shortened yields, they had nowhere to go but up. *I'll buy a farm,* Mario thought, *and grow this magical Yankee maize. With my profits I'll invest in goats, and sell cheese. And maybe I'll plant peach trees, the nearest thing to a mango that grows in this climate.*

He'd marry a gringo, raise children, and happily disappear.

He began eating breakfast at a diner called Texas Toast because he enjoyed watching the waitress. Amanda moved from the kitchen to the tables with a precise grace, balancing plates down one arm while she pulled up a high chair with her free hand, reeling back on one foot—never dropping a plate—as she dodged a lumbering fat man. She reminded Mario of the deer he'd encountered in the desert.

She was graceful and, he fancied, innocent. He might talk to her about his farming fantasies or of his beautiful home in Boca de Tomatlán. In turn, perhaps she could teach him about this great flat place called Dallas.

He asked about the jewelry on her tongue, which he found disconcerting. "Did the piercings hurt?"

"Just for a while, you know. It kinda swells up."

"Do they impede your eating?"

The suggestion puzzled her. "Well . . . I can take them *out*."

She extended her tongue, and he bent closer to examine the two pieces, like small ball bearings, with great seriousness. "Piercing tongues was an Aztec ritual. What is your purpose?"

She smiled, and slowly her eyes turned flirtatious. Her voice dropped an octave and she waggled her tongue. "To give *pleasure*, of course."

She slipped away, giggling, and he was left to ponder what she meant, even as his penis stirred. Meeting her eyes across the busy tables, he thought of asking her to meet him after her shift, but didn't. He left her a generous tip and thought, *later*.

With the arrival of March, the feeble winter turned immediately to summer, and business took off. By February they'd fixed a number of Boss's air-conditioners, but Roberto had big new units, too, sealed in plastic or in heavy crates, that had arrived in the garage as if elves left them. And Roberto's inventory did not end with the garage: he had units tucked away in storage facilities in at least three locations.

Roberto knew *something* about wiring, but often their job was only delivery, sometimes to real electricians who paid in cash. Sometimes, they drew the hot job of pouring the slab that supported the unit. Roberto helped knock together the form, took a call on his cellphone, and left in his truck, leaving Mario to rake and trowel. Mario was agreeable, though the temperature was already over 100, and he wondered what the work would be like in July.

They ranged a two-hundred-mile radius, as far west as Fort Worth and almost to Oklahoma heading north, and he learned the layout of the city. No one walked. He'd require a vehicle if he wanted to be independent in this sprawling place. "I need a drivers license."

Roberto nodded. "You need a green card even more. Even

if it's illegal, everything that follows will *seem* legal. With your green card, you can do anything in this country."

Mario laughed. "Except vote, perhaps."

Roberto erupted. "What would you vote for? Nothing matters in the United States but money, Mario. How much you have; how much you can lend; how much you can borrow. Americans vote with *money*."

"Why do you hate them so much? They're like us, Roberto. And they didn't ask for us to come here."

"I don't hate them. Mexicans, either. One at a time, it's true, they're like us."

"Is it because they took the wrong side in your civil war?"

Roberto shrugged. "They took the side of money."

"Was your father one of the rebels?"

"He tried to stay out of it, but they killed him anyhow."

"The rebels or the government?"

He laughed. "What's the difference? Communists, capitalists, they're all pigs."

"But you went to high school."

"I went to school because of my mother. It was expensive, I wanted to quit, but she wouldn't let me. After the war, she worked sewing shirts, until they moved the factory to Vietnam where they will work for a crust of bread." He sighed. "That's my sad story, amigo. No sadder than yours."

They'd stopped in traffic on a bustling northern street. Without turning in his seat, Mario could count six banks. He said softly, "This philosophy of yours, Roberto. It won't help much when a policeman detains me. How do *I* secure a green card?"

"Your Christmas bonus," Roberto said, with a faint smile.

Sometimes, they went into the fine neighborhoods of el norte after dark, backed up to the brand-new slab of a brand-new house, and loaded an air-conditioner onto the Toyota. "They're trading this one in," Roberto would say. Or "It's defective." Once, under a midnight moon, they picked up a unit they'd delivered that morning. "They want a bigger one," Roberto explained. After they'd made several such night runs, Mario required no explanation.

Nothing mattered but money. It didn't matter how you got it, only that you had it.

And Mario's cigar box rapidly filled. He traded his stacks of ones for tens and twenties. He considered depositing some of the money into a bank account. He almost wired a sum to his mother—but balked. He didn't know how to explain that he wasn't dead.

Roberto bought a fine Chevrolet truck and painted his lightning strokes on the doors. And though Christmas was still months away, he gave Mario the drivers license of one Ernesto Polanco, whom Mario somewhat resembled. Cautiously, Mario drove the Toyota.

One hot Saturday afternoon, he took the graceful waitress, Amanda, to a film she wanted to see, featuring an aging American actress faced with finding love again when her husband took up with a younger woman. Grateful for the air-conditioning, Mario fell asleep. Then he watched the bright face of his companion, daubing at tears.

Afterwards, Amanda wanted to go to Walmart, his favorite store, and they cruised the aisles for more than an hour, discussing lawn mowers, curtains, shoes, appliances, cuts of beef—and, by a large cut-out of Randy Depaul with his guitar, a brand-new line of tee shirts and blue jeans. What an exemplary capitalist the man was, Mario thought, teaming with Walmart. All because of "Felicia" and unrequited love.

At last, contemplating purchases she couldn't afford, Amanda lay her head on his shoulder. She had selected nothing but a Chinese rolling pin. "You're so nice to me, Mario. I want to make you some cookies."

He thought then to buy flour and raisins, but Amanda preferred the cookie dough you found in the frozen section. At the last minute, she remembered she had no baking sheet or grease to coat it with.

Then they walked to the Toyota across what not so long ago had been open prairie, holding their recyclable sacks almost proudly in the bewilderingly egalitarian parking lot with its Mexicans, Indians, Africans, Chinese, punk white suburban kids, Ukrainians carrying Bibles, Pakistanis, fancy white women, down-at-the-heels divorced dads, and Englishmen. *I belong*, Mario thought.

Amanda rented an upstairs apartment in a sprawling, twenty-year-old complex where you could smell the spices of Indian cooking, and Mexican, and Vietnamese. On the landings women sat with their babies and stared at Amanda and Mario, but other apartments were shut tightly, blinds drawn,   air-conditioners pulsing mightily.

That's how I live, Mario thought, *hidden away.*

The door stood open. A squat Mexican woman, face damp, rose slowly and spoke softly to Amanda—"Too hot. Too hot"— as she motioned to the bedroom off the little kitchen. Nervously, Amanda fumbled with her purse.

"Let me pay, Amanda," Mario said.

"Diez," the Mexican woman said, eying Mario as if he were a scabby dog in the village street. He gave her the ten and said, "Gracias, Senora. Buenos tardes," in the kindest tone he could muster. He was the one with the money.

The woman waddled onto the landing and began her laborious journey down the steps, while Amanda emerged from the bedroom cradling her baby, which laid its sweaty head against her shoulder and moved its mouth, but seemed too weak to cry. She reached with her free arm to draw water in the kitchen sink. "I have to give him a bath, Mario. I'm sorry!"

"Don't you have air-conditioning? You can't live in Texas without—"

"It's broken. I called—"

It was perhaps three miles to the garage, and with his dubious license he stayed within the speed limit, but still he returned and installed the new unit, almost a duplicate, in ninety minutes.

He didn't ask about the baby's father. That Amanda had a baby seemed the natural order of things; that the father was absent seemed just as inevitable. Cool air funneled in from the gasping Texas night, the baby slept peacefully, and money was everything. He threw two hundred on the kitchen counter.

"For the electric bill," he said.

He made love to the graceful waitress, and afterwards they sat naked on her couch, he bending to kiss her cool, slender neck, she stroking his penis, as they watched *I Love Lucy* and ate warm chocolate chip cookies.

- 8 -

The Heist

"She'll be easy to get rid of."

This was Roberto's comment on Mario's acquisition of a girl-friend, so rude that he was rendered speechless. On the other hand, without quite admitting it, he'd had the same thought.

"What do you talk about with this girl?"

Amanda ran to the door and threw her arms around him. She tried to cook. He drove her to Walmart for baby clothes and diapers. When the baby was down, they made love, and sometimes he spent the night. Except when the baby woke, the love-making was pleasant, and afterwards he slept profoundly. In the morning he enjoyed watching her as she prepared for work, toweling her short hair, putting on makeup, brewing coffee. She moved quickly then, efficiently, and he took pleasure in her grace.

But she knew nothing about Mexico and didn't want to learn. She knew less about Dallas than he. He wondered if she'd ever read a book. She liked to watch the shopping channels and used credit cards to buy jewelry and wall decorations, diminutive tea sets and plastic clocks and even dolls. These bizarre items crowded the apartment's tiny mantle, her dresser, and a high shelf in her closet. They were "collectibles," she said, and would be worth a fortune one day.

The answer to Roberto's question was that Amanda and he had nothing to say to each other beyond "I will bring the truck around," and "We need some milk."

And yes, she'd be easy to get rid of, but six months passed, and still he hadn't formed the words.

Sometimes, he went along with Roberto to a club in Oak Cliff—or rather, the sprawling parking lot across from it. Inside, families dined and listened to the old men of a mariachi band; outside, less accomplished bands set up in truck beds or on nearby porches, and played norteña ballads or country and western with accordion riffs. Young women drifted by, but in small numbers, and mostly they were hostile. The parking lot was a men's gathering where you sat on tailgates, bobbing with the music, drinking.

Some men could drink twenty beers from quitting time to three in the morning, when they might sleep for an hour in their trucks before going to work again. Some did methamphetamine, too, buying from tough hombres who materialized out of the shadows like wraiths. Here was one place Mexican drugs ended up, Mario thought: killing Mexicans.

But, comparing notes, you sometimes learned about work. There was this, for instance:

"Did you talk to the Hondurans? They're buying beer for everyone."

"Where did they make so much money?"

"In the Panhandle. They cut up pigs in a factory."

"That's terrible work!"

"Sí, the lines move so fast that sometimes men are hurt, and the factory refuses to pay for their care. They say the men bring their injuries to work, or that they are on drugs. The Hondurans tried to organize, and the company turned them in for being illegal. So it happened that one of the bosses came home to a burned-down house."

"These men did this?" Mario asked.

The speaker shrugged. "They didn't say so. But the pig company gave them money to go away."

Mario laughed. "So if we behave like pigs, they will pay us? *Oink! Oink!*"

The men fell silent, judging him. Something almost violent rose in the air. Then everyone broke into laughter and made cries of *"Oink!"* More Budweisers were passed around.

Roberto found the gatherings valuable, drifting from group to group with questions about construction jobs, wages, and even politics. What was the possibility of federal amnesty?

"They couldn't exist one day without us," said a young

Mexican who kept turning about in the street light, so to display his gleaming muscles. "They will pardon us all."

"They might turn on us," Roberto said. "Cut us down with machine guns."

"You are thinking of Salvador, and that was a long time ago. Never in the United States."

"What if we are in the way? What if they want even the worst jobs for themselves? They could truck us out. Drop us in the desert. That's what they did during their Great Depression and again with the braceros when they didn't need them anymore."

Yes, you learned things in the parking lot. But after several weeks, Mario demurred. He didn't like beer that much and drugs not at all. He missed Amanda. "Do you want to drink yourself to death, Roberto? My head aches afterwards, and I want to sleep forever. What's the point? You all talk like revolutionaries."

"Maybe I *am* a revolutionary. Huh? What do you think about that, amigo? These men, these men who can't find work enough, these men who are always short on money, they only want what the gringos have."

"If they had it?"

Roberto laughed. "They'd turn into pigs!"

Such a life, Mario thought, laughing, too. Let others cheat and grasp. All he wanted was a farm in Arkansas, a sturdy house, and honest work to do. On his last party-night, he had some advice for his friend. "Roberto, we can't go on stealing air-conditioners."

Roberto surprised him. "No. The police will find us soon."

Amanda worked on Christmas, but on New Year's Day Mario offered to take her home to her parents. She smiled but shook her head.

He made a reservation at what he thought to be a fancy restaurant, "Old World Dining." He hoped this might atone for her bleak holidays, through which he'd been almost absent, but the place was full of blue-haired women on walkers, the food— even the meat—all tasted like pudding, and Amanda's baby bawled inconsolably.

Back at her apartment, she said, "You can sit *rat* there and watch football," by which she didn't mean soccer.

He told her he had work to do, but they both knew he was leaving her. He braced himself for protests, but she sat on the couch, looked away, and said nothing.

That afternoon he went with Roberto to a different sort of party, at a big house in Highland Park overlooking the park where Raul Zamora and he had bolted together picnic tables. They passed through a stone entryway—an imitation of a castle door—and then down a long hall into a bright, high-ceilinged room with windows all around.

A large oval carpet, brown and green and blood red, featured campesinos raising picks against a background of volcanoes. It seemed too fine a carpet to step on, and Mario walked around its edges on the polished oak, viewing bullfighters and Indian prints on Zapotec rugs. He grabbed a Dos Equis, avoiding the tequila because he didn't want to be drunk in so intimidating a place. He sat semi-hidden between a potted royal palm and a glass case filled with glum Mayan gods—illegal immigrants, he surmised, from Chitchén Itzá or Tikal.

Several gringos from the university moved easily about. They were probably professors except for the tough-looking fellow wearing an ear-ring and no socks, who was continuously on his cell phone. He, too, didn't belong here, or the reason he did was beyond Mario's understanding. A tall black woman, with short, graying hair, spoke energetically about the burdens of her race "in academia," but Mario couldn't grasp what she meant even when she shouted, which she began to do after two glasses of Chardonnay.

Mostly it was a crowd of well-dressed, second-generation Mexicans and Central Americans, teachers and social workers, accountants and priests and doctors. The talk shifted between English and Spanish."Guadalupe Arts," the group was called, celebrating Latino contributions to the Americas.

In a while he worked up the courage to go after food—wonderful, casual food such as he hadn't tasted since his days working at the hotel. Corn tortillas; four kinds of peppers; a salad of jicama, lettuce, and beans; Oaxacan cheese; and a pot of menudo. He discovered little street tacos with marinated beef tongue, and ate five of them. He dared to mix a rum and pineapple, and, almost content, settled again by the disapproving gods. He wished he could light a cigar.

The talk grew fluid, even joyous. It was educated talk of

books, Texas politics, TV shows, consumerism, joblessness, Catholicism—and a subject on which Mario could have spoken eloquently, the border. The border; always the border. Friends who couldn't make it north. Children lost to drugs and gangs.

He marveled at Roberto, weaving effortlessly among these well-mannered folks—well-mannered himself. Well-dressed, in his dark trousers and pressed brown shirt. He smiled and made confident, inoffensive jokes. For an old señora, he found a comfortable chair and went off to fill her plate. And to everyone, simply by listening, he gave the impression of bright-eyed intelligence, a serene judgment held in polite reserve.

He is a ladrón, Mario could have told them. He is a fraud. And yet he is also my friend and no more fraudulent than me. Mario looked about, wondering if half the people in this beautiful room were frauds, if the room itself was a species of lie. He mixed another pineapple rum.

Someone returning from Nuevo Laredo had brought along a piñata and tacked it up now before the bay window. A young Latina with long hair, wearing a red fiesta dress—a student, Mario guessed—skipped forward.

"Come on! Come on!" she urged, grabbing hands and laughing, but it was a sophisticated crowd, reluctant to show interest in such a childish diversion. "Roberto! Where is Roberto?" the woman cried, and in an instant Mario learned a great deal about his friend, as the grinning Roberto turned the woman around and blindfolded her. Rosa was his girl.

She swung the stick wildly, her slender ankles flashing under full skirts.

"Cold! Cold!"

"Ah, Rosa, you'll *never* hit it."

Rosa swung again, grazing the piñata. It swung wildly, but no candies fell.

"She has found her range."

This time Rosa hit the piñata squarely, but tripped on the elegant carpet, staggered, and fell into Mario's lap. Instinctively, he grabbed her shoulders, even as people scrambled for the candies.

Rosa pulled back her blindfold. She was not embarrassed, but merry. He wondered if her falling into his arms had been deliberate. Something in her quick black eyes reminded him of his dream girl on the Zócalo, but also of village girls, standing confidently alone, studying the army as it passed. If you were a soldier, you wanted a girl like that because she signified something. Grace, history, the life you'd never have. You'd always known her. She was a deep and immediate temptation.

Yes, he'd seen her before. The blend of European and Indian in her face—a gringo in every other way. She was a younger version of Maribel.

"You are a shy one, Roberto's friend," she said, so that only he could hear. Already she was rising, and he wanted to hold her and always keep her near.

"I'm not sure I belong here."

She laughed. "In this room or on this earth?"

And then she held out her arms to Roberto, who glanced over at Mario, not jealously but with pride. *Now you understand,* his eyes said.

He lifted Rosa high, so that she stood on the bay window's parapet, and walked back and forth. She had the crowd. The old men's eyes shone with memories and lust, and the women's filled, not with envy but sorrow for what might have been.

"¡Viva la revolución!" she cried, laughing, playful.

"¡Viva la revolución!" came a chorus.

"A revolution," Rosa went on almost teasingly. "In attitude. The Anglos—they are us. And we are *them.* We're all Americans, but Latinos live with terrible injustice, and we must teach our suburban friends. We will join hands in a great statement of solidarity at—where else?—your neighborhood Walmart. A peaceful protest, friends, a campaign of information where we join hands with our brothers and sisters—the illegals, their families—oh, and the *children!*"

"What business allows this?" The question came from a broad-shouldered man in a tie and coat. He had a military haircut, a thick, pock-marked face. He looked like a labor leader or the mayor of a border town. Or maybe a wheeler-dealer with a chain of restaurants. A man up from the ranks, touched by corruption, not entirely corrupt.

Rosa seemed less assured. "Ricardo, thank you for your input. Of course, we're not specifically targeting Walmart—"

"That's good. They had some problems with their contract help, their lawyers settled with the immigration lawyers—a long time ago. They claim to be squeaky clean. Who knows if they are? But drugs are everywhere, all you see on the TV are illegals, and *white* people are out of work. Oh, I tell you, the gringos are in no mood for trouble. You can bet they won't stand for college students in front of their stores, waving signs about César Chávez and, and—*Pancho Villa*."

This brought a laugh. Rosa laughed, too, as if revolution were good family fun, but quickly strove to regain the crowd's attention. "Thanks, Ricardo. Again, we aren't singling out Walmart. But what other place in America is so familiar? Where else does everyone, *everyone*, go to do business? And commerce— isn't that the heart of America?"

The man Rosa called Ricardo moved along the fancy food bar and filled a plate. Then he threaded through the crowd and headed for the door, where several men joined him. "Those idiots in New Mexico," hung on the air, coming from Ricardo or one of his friends, and the chatter of the crowd briefly ceased. Ricardo had the floor, but merely smiled and stepped out with his friends for a smoke on the green lawn, under the gnarly old live oaks.

Now Rosa wore an air of aggrievement. It was as though sensitivity had to contend with bad manners, beauty with baseness. Her voice grew soft, seductive. Mario was spellbound. Perhaps he was in love. A man would pretend, lie, steal, *kill* for such a woman.

"Our brothers and sisters—the illegals—you know how they're exploited. We want to remind our kind, white friends that the meals they eat, the houses they live in, wouldn't exist without Mexicans, without . . . Salvadorans and Guatemalans and Hondurans. ¿Sí ó no?"

"¡Sí!"

"Roberto, my love—"

If Roberto truly had won the love of beautiful Rosa, he was near to becoming an American. And yet Ricardo, with his rough assurance, had stolen Rosa's moment. Everyone feared idiots who could throw themselves against a wall of bullets, as seven of them had in Las Cruces, for baffling reasons. First, they'd held up a bank, crying, "Cíbola! Cíbola!" Then they streaked down city streets, finally crashing into a barricade. Only two of the seven escaped, though they were the ones with the money.

Of course, you couldn't be sure you were getting the real story—not from the police, or bank officials, or gringo reporters. But drugs didn't seem to be involved, which was alarming.

If it were only a matter of one cartel battling another, or even of cartels assaulting the police—well, that was capitalism, after all, run amok. But what about bank robbers with a cause? And what sort of cause? Some misty Shangri-La hiding among the peaks of the Sangre de Cristo?

Roberto smiled grandly and held high a map of Dallas, glued to a poster board and with myriad colored pushpins, each indicating a Walmart or Sam's Club. The plan was to demonstrate at every one of them on the same day, Rosa said. She'd invited labor leaders, a dozen mayors, and legislators from *both parties!* It ought to make national news.

"My sister works there," a woman called out.

"Absolutely," Rosa said. "Our sisters—"

"She's happy there. Now, some of these restaurants—"

Rosa sighed. "I didn't say that Walmart is the worst offender."

Roberto spoke for the first time. "But the *most*. Seventy-seven of them! They're everywhere."

"Yes! Yes!" cried Rosa's band of supporters, most of them young women, pretty and fierce.

And the crowd applauded. Maybe Rosa was nuts, but it was her house and her wonderful food, and they liked her.

She threw out her hands in triumph. "We'll be everywhere, too, my friends. Every Walmart. Everywhere!"

Roberto stalked in, wearing a dark leather jacket and a black shirt, and in a serious mood. "Let's go," he said.

So Mario drew on his pants and climbed into the Chevrolet truck, which had acquired a long trailer. All right, they were picking up something. Something that took two men to lift and couldn't stand the light of day.

"Are we in a movie, Roberto?"

Roberto drove cautiously, even stopping for a yellow light. "What do you mean?"

"You are dressed all in black, like a commando on Channel 49."

Roberto seemed offended. "In these clothes, I can't be seen at night."

Mario closed his eyes and fumbled about. "Where are you, Roberto? Where have you gone?"

Roberto didn't laugh. He stopped the truck along a dark

industrial street, between a partially demolished grain elevator and an abandoned, six-story factory made of bricks. The truck's lights caught several rats as they scurried around a dumpster.

Barbed wire stretched in a Y atop a chain-link fence. Still, the fence wasn't much of a barrier. You could crawl under it in several places along a rancid creek, bordered by oily bare dirt.

Roberto reached behind his seat for a canvas satchel and handed it across. "For you."

Inside the satchel were blocks of plastic explosive, blasting caps, det cord, fuse, a generator, and length of stranded wire. "This is from the American army!"

"This, too," Roberto said, passing over night-vision binoculars. Mario had used a similar pair along Lake Amistad.

"To your right, to your right," Roberto said. "Down. Do you see the tank?"

"Propane."

"Can you blow it up?"

"Of course." Mario took a breath. "But the entire building will burn."

"That's what I want. Fifteen minutes from now."

Mario laughed. "¿Viva la revolución?"

"A diversion."

Mario swallowed hard. "It's bad enough what I've done already, Roberto. Each time I steal, I tell myself it's a temporary thing. You're my friend, you saved me, but this is serious. They would put us away for life."

"I ask only because of your experience, Lieutenant."

"¿Lieutenant?"

"The police in San Angelo, they found out who you used to be. An army officer trying to run a drug deal, who got in a little over his head. They thought you were dead." He shrugged. "If you believe the Mexican police."

"I did nothing!"

"You must have done *something*, or you would have stayed in Mexico. But it's all right. It's not like I'm going to turn you over to the border patrol." Roberto reached for the door latch. "You can leave now, and believe me, I understand. I'll set the charge myself."

"Already you've made me an accessory!"

Roberto shrugged. "To many things, my friend."

"I want to be legal," Mario said. "To be honest. In this country—in this life—I go from one corruption to another." He sighed. "Why are you fighting the gringos?"

"I fight for a profession and to marry a good woman."

"Rosa! But—"

"She thinks I run a legitimate business. She thinks I have money, which she goes through like a drug. The woman doesn't stop to think, we must make signs. We must pay the printer for brochures. Transportation is involved, food, where even to go to the bathroom."

Mario began to understand. "The Walmarts? I thought that was just her. . ."

"Foolishness? That's the word I'd use." He sighed. "Rosa is younger than we are, amigo. She does not know how hard it is to live. The money has to come from somewhere, but she doesn't think that way. She reads books, she writes articles for magazines, but she doesn't understand about money. I have lied to her, Mario. I must make good."

One night, curious where the air-conditioners came from, Mario followed his friend into el norte, but Roberto didn't visit warehouses or construction sites. He drove to a community college, hidden from the great central highway, shrouded among pecans and pin oaks. Mario found the library, sat reading by a window where he could see the Chevrolet truck. Roberto emerged three hours later.

"I know a secret about you as well," Mario said. "You're going to school."

Roberto nodded. "To become an electrician, sí. I take the test next month."

Mario patted Roberto's shoulder. "You'll get your license, my friend. You'll be an electrician, and you'll marry Rosa. And the two of you can go to parties, and make love, and have children—and blow up the world if you want." He grasped the satchel. He found pliers and a small flashlight in the glove compartment. "But I can't do this anymore."

"No more, amigo." Roberto's voice broke. "I swear it."

Mario had used plastic explosives only once, clearing trees and rubble from a landslide three miles high, near Pico de Orizaba. You needed to observe certain precautions, but plastic, unlike dynamite, wasn't dangerous to handle.

He couldn't time the little generator, and so it was useless. Holding the flashlight in his teeth, he crimped a blasting cap onto the fuse, then duct-taped two blocks of explosive to the tank and pressed the cap into one of them with his thumbs. He taped over the entry point and measured fifteen feet of fuse by wrapping it from his hand to his elbow. Then he lit the fuse and walked quickly away, his heart thumping madly.

He crawled under the fence and brushed himself off. He could make out a tiny glow behind him. He walked across the street, counting his steps, a doomed man. In the truck again, he hung his head. "I'm a terrorist."

"How long?"

"Fifteen minutes, as you said." Mario glanced at his watch. "Fourteen."

Roberto eased the truck slowly away, and they drove four blocks south, the long trailer rattling behind them over the rough streets. Roberto spoke once on his cell phone, saying only, "Thursday," and "No, no. At the house."

They parked on a better-lighted street, in a neighborhood of old frame houses mixed with small businesses. Mario's watch read two A.M.

He felt the truck shake as the tank went up. He shook, too. Turning in the seat, he saw that the sky glowed in the direction from which they'd come. They waited two minutes, then five, until they heard sirens.

"There are many Latino firemen," Roberto observed.

"Policemen, too."

Roberto pulled into the parking lot opposite and backed the trailer to a loading dock. He pointed to cameras mounted high. He passed a ski mask and baseball cap to Mario, and a black sweatshirt that said, "Southern Methodist."

The door was unlocked, meaning to Mario that an employee was helping them. No alarm sounded, unless somewhere a silent alarm had been activated. Inside, they relied on street light, and in what seemed to be a break room, Roberto left open a refrigerator. As if he knew where to look, Roberto found two dollies, and then they carried out massive coils of wire, generators in crates, breaker boxes, gigantic motors made in China. They loaded welders, a conduit bender, drill presses, bench grinders, sets of drill bits and screwdrivers and wrenches, a belt sander, even a table saw.

They were finished in thirty minutes. To protect his inside man, Roberto pulled on gloves and disappeared into a dark corner, where he tripped the alarm. Then he pounded the back door lock and the jamb with a sledgehammer, leaving impressive dents on the door.

To their north, searchlights pierced a cloud of smoke, which had blocked off the sky. Sirens wailed so consistently, it was impossible to tell their direction, but on the street again, while they were stopped at a light, a police cruiser zipped past them in the opposite lane.

Involuntarily, Mario stretched out his foot for a gas pedal. "We cannot go far—"

For answer, Roberto turned onto a side street, cut the lights, and expertly backed the trailer up a driveway, hitting a remote in the process, not even pausing as the garage door rose. They unhitched the trailer, closed the door, and turned onto the street again.

Mario paced. Roberto sat at the table, drinking a beer. "It went well," he said at last, but as if uncertain.

"The policeman who passed us, will he think about it later? Identify the truck?"

Roberto shrugged. "He was going too fast to get the numbers, and anyhow they are stolen."

Mario laughed bitterly and turned on the television. "Too bad we are quitting, just when we were getting good at this."

"I thank you for going with me tonight, my friend," Roberto said. "We both made some real money. And I swear—I *swear*—it's over."

Mario pressed the numbers: the endless talent and variety shows, on Univision; old sitcoms everywhere, you could love Lucy any time of day, in English or Spanish; infomercials—programacíon pagada—on that worthless 55. Canned religion on 19, 34, and 47. Nothing truly local. Robot TV.

But Fox 4 had a reporter on the scene. "Cause of the fire?"

"At this point we don't know," said the chief, impressive in his helmet and sooty yellow bunker coat. "We'll have an arson team here at first light. But I want to say this: Two men were sleeping in that building."

"Homeless?"

"Yes, drug addicts, but they're dead. So if anybody out there saw something—I'm not saying that's what we've got here—but if this fire was deliberate—"

The reporter could scarcely contain her glee. "Murder!"

Roberto called out: "Mario—"

"*I* did it."

"Because I asked you, my friend. We were *both* there. Mario, they were drug addicts—"

Mario reached under his cot for his backpack, some shirts and underwear, thinking, *I am calm.* He almost forgot the cigar box, with its $11,000. He wanted to fling it at Roberto in a white rage. And yet, looking at his friend—the tough Salvadoran hanging his head in shame—his anger already was subsiding.

A crime, he thought, was like combat: precarious, volatile. In seconds an innocent man ruined himself. *He* had placed the charge, not Roberto. Guilt rushed like a drug into the remotest cells of his soul. He could never fix what he'd done. To carry a weapon on behalf of your government, that was one thing. Or to shoot a man in self-defense. But to kill helpless creatures in their sleep!

He threw the Toyota's keys onto the table. "We're finished."

Roberto was crying. "Mario—"

"You're almost a good man," he called back from the door. It made little sense even as he said it. In the dark garage, he tumbled over the vacuum cleaner. "You saved me," he said, and then he pushed open the outside door and breathed the poisonous Dallas air.

He couldn't have said where he walked, but at last found himself climbing the steps to Amanda's apartment. He brought up a fist to knock and hesitated. He sat on the landing, shivering and indecisive. It was five A.M.

Perhaps the smell of his cigar brought her out. She opened the door, leaned softly against it, and stood with one palm flat against her chest, holding her housecoat. He didn't rise, but ran a hand up her legs and let it rest between her warm thighs.

"I didn't want to wake you," he said.

"I was already up," she whispered. "I have to go to work. Mario—"

He took back his hands, turned, and buried his face against her stomach. She dropped a hand in his hair, and caressed his forehead. "Mario, I have a . . . guest."

"Yes," he said, standing, holding her close. What did he care, with everyone so near to death, who she slept with? Ah, poor girl, she weighed almost nothing. When she died, hardly one hundred pounds would be gone from the earth.

"Wait," she said, and slipped inside again, carefully closing the door behind her. In the meantime, he managed a small decision. He reached into the backpack and counted out $2000 from his stacks of twenties.

It didn't matter how you got it, only that you had it.

She opened the door again and handed him a tall travel cup. "Cream and two sugars," she said. "I remembered."

"You're a good person, Amanda."

"Oh, Mario." She kissed his cheek. "Where's your jacket? That nice jacket I bought you? It's freezin' out here."

He parted her coat, lifted the gown underneath, and caught her breasts in his hands. She pushed against him, and he dropped his hands to the small of her back, pulled her close, and kissed her. Then he grabbed the cup and dropped the money into her coat pocket. He went halfway down the stairs.

"Thank you for the coffee," he said.

"*Call* me."

Sunrise found him back in Oak Cliff, eating a quesadilla filled with honey, coming up slowly on the bus station. Wherever the first bus was bound, that's where he was going.

Then he met Raul Zamora, standing where the day-laborers gathered, looking much older than Mario remembered. Raul had lined up a week of work in Oklahoma, just north of Lake Texoma, building hog barns. "Good money, amigo," Raul said. "Come and join me."

Mario found the Social Security card of one Felix Moreno in his billfold. The gringo boss nodded, and Mario took a seat near the back, under a blower. The jobsite was one hundred miles to the north. He'd keep on going. He closed his eyes, but couldn't sleep.

- 9 -

The Two Rauls

He'd waited almost fifteen years, but good times had arrived for Raul Zamora.

Sometimes he entered the United States illegally, but more often as a guest worker: sugar beets in Idaho, melons in Colorado, tobacco in Missouri, lettuce in Arizona, and cotton in Texas. He returned to Mexico periodically to make furniture. Once he hired on with a shoe factory in Arkansas, several months before its own migration to Mexico. Somewhere, with the help of a girlfriend, Raul applied for his permanent residency.

Too old for stoop labor, he moved in with his sister in Fort Worth and worked in her Vietnamese husband's restaurant. The family reunion came to an end when Raul got into a fist fight with his new brother-in-law and was shown the door. That began Raul's long battle with an arthritic back and an American economy running short of jobs. He came near to homelessness.

Then the Vietnamese man died, and a few months after that, the sister, too. In due course, the court-appointed lawyer found Raul's green card, still in its official envelope, as part of his sister's estate. Her tiny house was his, too. He thought he'd soon be hired as a janitor with the Fort Worth school system, but for a while longer he had to scrounge cash where he could, if only to make house payments.

Raul showed Mario the beautiful green card—so simple a thing, to be so dear—and buttoned it with his other papers inside his heavy shirt. "At last I have my own bed," he said. "Though I have no one to share it with. How are things with you, my friend?"

"I've earned some money," Mario said. "But I'm not happy. I think I may not return to Dallas. I'd go home if I could."

Raul nodded understandingly but made no comment.

"What do you know of Tulsa?"

Raul shrugged. "It's just another town."

"You told me once, of all places, Arkansas is the best."

"Yes, you could go to the chicken country near Fort Smith. It's very green, and many Mexicans live there."

Ten miles into Oklahoma they turned onto Indian land and then into a vast, dusty woods. Mario couldn't see anything that resembled a farm. A high metal fence, broken only by the gravel road on which they traveled, marched through oaks and sycamores, still clinging to their leaves. At a gate, a guard walked the length of the bus and waved them on indifferently.

At last the trees yielded to a series of hills that had been scraped clear with bulldozers. Broken trees and boulders lay in piles, with rivulets cut by spring rains between them, dry now in winter, choked with weeds and red silt. They lumbered down the rutted road past sewage lagoons and the stubble of cornfields, toward a dense stand of junipers through which Mario could now and then catch the gleam of Lake Texoma. Here, on a slope, the new barn rose.

Through the morning, Raul and he mixed mortar for a crew of masons working off scaffolds. It was hard work, made even harder because of Raul's bad back. But the temperature wasn't much over fifty, and in his sleepless and grieving state, Mario found that the tasks of wielding a shovel, minding the mixer, and pushing the heavy wheelbarrow were almost pleasant.

The masons were second and third generation immigrants and hardly spoke Spanish. "How much are you making, Pancho?"

"A fortune," Mario said. "You call me Mario, or I'll call you Speedy Gonzalez."

The fraudulent Mexican grinned. "I'm making twice what you do, and work's easy to find for a mason. After this, we'll build a school in Oklahoma City. Government work, Señor Mario. It never ends."

Mario didn't want to argue. "You're lucky, amigo."

A quarter of a mile down the road, a dozen barns gleamed in the sun, and Mario expected to see hogs in pasture. But Raul explained that, like the chickens raised in Arkansas, these animals were never allowed outside. "And the owners are fussy about it. Last week I tried to go near one of the buildings, and a man came running. They are afraid of disease, he said. These pigs are clones and very delicate."

"I've never heard of a delicate pig," Mario said. Like a bunion predicting rain, his stub of a toe twinged. Maybe he was allergic to hogs.

"It's true. You could have a head cold, one of the pigs would catch it, and they'd all die. That's what the man told me."

"And they're *not* clones."

"They shoot them with a needle, thirty or forty sows, twelve hundred hogs. Doesn't that make them clones?"

"You're saying they're artificially inseminated, but they still need boars. To make a clone, they'd have to do something with the hog egg."

"Hogs laying eggs, my friend? You think I believe that?"

Mario sighed. A little of Raul went a long way. And he'd have left at noon, with or without pay, but Raul's back gave out. Mario covered for him, leaving the older man to shovel sand and mix mortar while he ran the wheelbarrow up a ramp onto a pallet held by the forklift. Like an elevator, the forklift boosted him high enough to reach the scaffolds, where he shoveled mortar to the masons even as a man on the outside, on another forklift, hoisted up cinder blocks.

The wind shifted, and the smell from the invisible hogs settled on them. It was an ammonia smell similar to chicken manure, but more lethal. Mario's father had raised pigs, and they smelled bad sometimes, but this was like the dead man in Maribel's Cadillac. Yes, Mario thought, holding a scrap of towel over his nose. He smelled death.

The masons were fast workers and, upon the arrival of the hog smell, worked even faster, finishing by three. Mario thought they were done for the day and that he could reach the highway with daylight remaining, but the boss had one more task for his day laborers.

Because it was built on a grade, the hog house needed special shoring on its downhill side. As they built the wall, the masons had mortared in pilaster sections, each a foot tall and a yard square, piled twenty-four feet high—and anchored even deeper with rebar and prestressed concrete. Now the pilasters had to be filled.

You stepped on a pallet and the forklift raised you as far as it could, then maneuvered near the pilaster. The mixer backed up from outside the wall, and you guided the auger and bucket over the high hole.

"Can you do it?" Mario asked.

"Sure," Raul said. "It's the last thing, and the bus will be warm."

Mercifully, the death smell had shifted toward the lake. But the kid running the forklift couldn't position them precisely, and the gusting wind, rocking the pallet, made their footing tricky. Nor could the mixer operator pivot his bucket with perfect accuracy or slowly enough. You had to grab the bucket and somehow hold it still despite its momentum. It meant reaching into space, trying to balance. A wrong step and you'd fall to the cement floor twenty-five feet below.

"It ain't the best conditions," the boss called up. "But the truck's here, an' paid for. We don't get this shit poured tonight, it screws up the en-*tire* day tomorrow. Pay you double-time, how's that?"

It was fine, but they couldn't find a workable routine, a rhythm. After the second pilaster, Mario instructed the kid to put them directly opposite the bucket's path, so that he stopped it with brute force. If it knocked him down, at least he'd fall back onto the pallet. And the third pilaster went well enough, but on the fourth, Mario grabbed the bucket too high, so that it tilted and belted him in the stomach. He reeled, steadied the bucket over the hole, and a river of cement ran down his arms. "¡Jesuchristo!"

"What is it, my friend?" asked Raul.

"Cold! Cold!"

Raul peeled off his gloves and his heavy shirt.

"What about you?"

"You're doing all the work, my friend. And I have this sweater."

On the fifth pilaster, the operator couldn't negotiate the grade outside the wall and had to back around from the opposite direction. Mario and Raul shifted to compensate, but it was almost dark, and Mario sensed, rather than saw, where the bucket appeared. He stepped back to button Raul's shirt, and Raul stepped forward. Otherwise, Mario thought later, it couldn't have happened.

Raul took the full impact of the bucket straight in his face and fell down the pilaster neatly, almost comically, as if he were trying to sit. He grasped the pilaster lip, but couldn't hold on. "I don't think—" he said, and slipped away. The bucket stabilized exactly where it needed to be, and the cement poured out.

Mario choked. "¡Basta ya! ¡Basta ya!" he cried, but not loudly, and then he thought, ¡inglés, inglés!

"Stop!" he screamed. "He's down there! Raul! Stop! Stop!"

The shadowy operator finally understood and jerked back the still emptying bucket. Engines throttled down, and Mario shouted again, and someone went for an extension ladder. Mario reached, but couldn't see. He called, "Raul! Raul?" into the hole.

And then he sat in a big Dodge truck drinking coffee, while generators ran and bright lights flared. The Highway Patrol had arrived with their red lights and a rural, volunteer fire department with its old yellow truck. Red and yellow, fluttering over him. Lacking other tools, the firemen were going after the pilaster with sledge hammers.

"Jesus, I never had nothin' like this happen, I jest don't know," the boss said. He handed Mario a sack full of hamburgers. He'd bought them for the emergency crews, but they'd shaken him off. "Dead! I mean, he's gotta be. Dead! He your buddy?"

"I hardly knew him."

"What about his family?"

"He had a sister, but she's dead now."

"What am I gonna do?"

"I don't know, sir. Find a priest, perhaps."

"Oh. Yeah. That's good." The man brought out his billfold. "You take this."

He tucked a wad of bills into Mario's shirt pocket and went away somewhere, to lose himself in the blinking lights. Chewing a cold hamburger, Mario stared through the windshield at a band of stars. Lights jiggled downhill, along the rough lane. That's the bus, some part of him announced. It's time to go.

First, he'd climb down from the truck. Next, he'd walk across the turning area, avoiding the deep ruts. He'd step onto the bus and find a seat in the back, in darkness. That was all he had to do.

Once, he'd watched as a soldier reached out for a bottle

of beer, then fell into the water, where a propeller killed him. A man laughed, not understanding. But after you'd talked it through, after you'd explained it and written a report, you still couldn't understand. Laugh, cry, it was all the same.

The gringo driver pointed toward the nearby train station, and talked in slow English, as if Mario were some stupid immigrant. "This is Plano," he said. "You can ride downtown."

What was he doing in Plano? Wasn't he headed for Arkansas? He hadn't noticed where the bus went, hadn't cared. *Playno. Plah*-no. The train ran to Dallas, deep into its evil canyons where you couldn't find a safe place to sleep. In Plano, he could eat and rent a room. Maybe when he woke he'd be alive.

He hadn't slept in thirty-six hours and had trouble focusing. He found himself walking along Highway 75 because the sign at an on-ramp pointed toward Oklahoma. He had to pass through Oklahoma in order to reach the chicken country of Arkansas, where there was always work.

Four lanes of traffic zipped by at 80 miles per hour. Scowling down at him from the high banks were McDonald's, Papa John's, Pet Palace, Walmart, Manny's Chiquita, Paesano's, Mattress Land, Home Depot, Kroger's, Baptist Church, Culver's, Bank of America, Albertson's, FedEx, Hampton Inn, WhataBurger, Wendy's, Jack in the Box, Dickey's, and then it began again, the same stores and seemingly the same automobiles. He ran to the median, blinded by the headlights, horns blaring at him in a discordant song. He ran to the opposite side, holding his hands to his ears, and staggered up the bank, amid agave and crepe myrtle and Japanese pines.

He crawled to an overpass. Facing south rather than north, he read the same signs: Lowe's, First Bank, Second Baptist, Dickey's, WhataBurger. Now the lights streaked below him, the trucks roaring implacably, the cars sleek and indifferent. Dallas was one great highway, with islands for sleeping, eating, pissing. So much gasoline, so much pork and chicken and potatoes and sugar, so much coal to bring the electricity, and it only went in circles.

He walked. He couldn't find the name of the street. The same signs glared at him, though here also were walled-off neighborhoods, rich pockets of silence. Shifting his shoulders, he grew conscious of his backpack and drew into a hedge near a tall, magnificent house. Dogs barked while he counted his money. It was all that he had.

Nine thousand. Still there.

He remembered the money in his shirt pocket. He counted it, another $460, though of more interest was the envelope beside it. For a moment, he didn't understand. He wore Raul's shirt. And the papers proved to the world that Raul was legal.

New papers. Never used. Raul wore a gray beard in the photo, and Mario's own beard, if he allowed it to grow, would come in gray. Their noses had the same crook. One, two, three, four, five, six men had died, and he was legal. Permanently, he surmised, but he might have stood above the great highway and allowed the papers, and his $9,460 dollars, to flutter away. He didn't care. About anything.

It doesn't matter how you get it, only that you have it.

It doesn't matter that you have it, only how you got it.

He walked on. He'd been awake for thirty-nine hours but hadn't found a motel. What time was it? Dawn. What day? *Domingo.* He kept walking. He counted cadence.

At a stoplight he heard a familiar voice. A friend sang on the radio: Randy DePaul, last heard from as he broke a young woman's heart in El Paso. Now, after endless hardship, after seeking comfort in a bottle and finding only despair, he'd come to Jesus. And it was as though DePaul provided a soundtrack for life, because now a cross beckoned to Mario. He'd seen it somewhere, on a brochure, perhaps, or in a dream. No, late-night TV: a canned sermon for the sleepless. An ethereal blue, electric cross pointed skyward, while beneath it a neon sign read, "Brighter Day Fellowship."

Press one, hours of worship. Press two —

The cross floated in the strengthening light, calling early worshippers, a beacon to the lost. The cross was eerie and affecting, but the church itself might have been a Walmart. Everything was flat, squared-off, relentlessly efficient. On the roof, mimicking Walmart, massive air-conditioners exhaled the stink of humankind.

Inside, the music also reminded him of Walmart. The voices were too sweet to be believed, the lyrics without cohesion. They had no high points, no lows, no changes. Still, the drone of the music calmed him, and he felt the tensions in his gut relax.

A thought: Walmart sold everything. If you couldn't buy

it at Walmart, you didn't need it, but Walmart had no church. Brighter Day franchises could be sandwiched between the nail parlor, the bank, and McDonald's. Randy DePaul could belt out testimony. A funny idea, but he had no one to share it with. He couldn't laugh anyhow. He was too sad.

He stretched out on a bench. He'd die here in this gringo church, listening to the bland music. He heard voices, a child asking about him. "Who *is* he?"

"Shhh," her mother said.

He staggered down the hall as it slowly circled the massive auditorium. The faithful came in numbers now, flowing around him, laughing, ascending stairways. Afar were bright lights, and as he neared them, he thought he entered a tunnel. The walls around him dropped away in the fearful light, and he believed he might see God—and Amanda, and Boss, and his dead captain.

The brightness fell to dimness, and he saw only a small office. Inside, a woman with long dark hair typed steadily. He knew who she was. Anyhow, he couldn't walk any farther and dropped into a chair inside her door.

Maribel turned. Over her shoulder, light broke through a window, casting her profile in shadow but brightening her face. She could be, he thought, an angel. He grinned stupidly.

"Hola, Mario," she said.

- 10 -

The General's Wife

She handed him strong, sugared coffee and then sat on a straight-back chair directly facing him, her hands folded on her skirt, her legs tightly together. She plucked at his rumpled shirt and laughed. "Mario, I believe you've been wandering in the wilderness."

After so long without sleep, his judgment was frayed, and he broke down. He buried his face in his hands and wept. He told her about Raul—so close to peace on earth, dying so grimly.

"You know of a pleasant way?"

He swallowed and fought to understand. She was right, of course. No pleasant way existed. "But God—if there is a God—"

"Doesn't send hurricanes, either," she said. She laid a hand on his arm. "We cannot blame God simply because we encounter adversity. What *is* this life on earth, Mario, when *He* can come at any time? I am sorry for your friend's death, and we can pray that he'd found redemption. That's all that we can do."

Her reaction seemed strange. Perhaps in his recollections he'd idealized the pretty woman, the woman he'd rescued, forgetting she was an evangelista. What he'd tried to say, forgetting his audience, was that Raul Zamora, after a hard life, had almost come into his reward. Then God promptly snuffed him out. But Mario had decided not to blame God when the wild boar tore off half his toe, and he had to limp through purgatory; he couldn't blame Him for Raul's death, either.

The point was, an attractive woman whose religion answered her every question sat across from him, concerned for his well-being. Composing himself, he sat back to study her. At least she made a good cup of coffee.

He didn't know much about clothing, but could tell that her dark blue suit was expensive. She might have worn it to a funeral, except for the tight fit and the lowcut blouse. Dignity, status, looking good meant a lot to her, he guessed, though her eyes, glowing with the little vanity of her point, somewhat betrayed her regal composure. Yes, and somewhere in the mix was the memory of what had passed between them in Ciudad Acuña. Her eyes grew softer as he met them, and sympathetic. Had his breakdown been a ploy, it was the right one. She'd try to save him.

He told her of the deal gone wrong on Lake Amistad, pausing politely for her to draw a moral, but she averted her eyes. So, as he continued, he experimented with her reactions. An obvious indiscretion, such as his robbery of snacks and water at the Judge Roy Bean Museum, caused her lips to part, and she drew a sharp breath. No matter his desperation: he'd *stolen.*

He edited his sins, presenting moments when he thought he'd behaved well. When he described how hard he'd worked at the junkyard, she seemed interested.

He described Boss's suicide, trying to shock her. She waved her hand impatiently; the death of infidels did not move her. She wanted Dallas, he saw. She was suspicious of his resume in the city. As well she might be, and then he understood that whatever thoughts he'd had of her were fantasies merely, and even that he couldn't quite trust her. Two days in Mexico had bonded them, yes, but they remained strangers.

"You're missing your sermon," he said, managing a smile.

She laughed. "Oh, it's over by now. And I think it's the Lord's work to put you in bed."

Silently, she gathered her purse and coat, locked the door, and walked slowly beside him out of the church and across the acres of asphalt. He sank into the black leather seat of a black Cadillac and stretched his legs in the immaculate space. As she turned the wheel, he was mesmerized by her long, red fingernails, contrasting neatly, almost mathematically, with her light brown skin. "I'm thirty four," he said, and she threw him one flirtatious glance.

He fell asleep, and woke to an almost imperceptible shuddering as the Cadillac purred to a stop. He stared at a tennis ball hanging before the windshield, unable to comprehend its purpose, and then the door opened, and Maribel guided him out of the garage like a failing old person. Drearily, his eyes took in a great brick house with a thick privacy hedge, ten feet high, around the yard. She opened a gate and he stumbled on the stone steps.

"Why didn't you call me?" she whispered.

His legs buckled, and he flopped back on the grass. She knelt, alarmed, but he shook his head. Like a homeless man producing the torn clipping that proved he once partook of greatness, he found the note she'd tucked into his pocket at the Rio Grande.

"Oh, dear Lord," she said. "I gave you my maiden name."

She held out her hands and he climbed to his feet. He couldn't comprehend where he was, and yet it seemed familiar. Perhaps he'd come here with Roberto, replacing an air-conditioner or stealing one. The yard sloped down through live oaks, past a swimming pool, and then onto a baseball diamond with a sagging backstop. She led him into a long, rectangular building made of blue steel. She turned on a bank of lights, and he looked out upon a small auditorium.

"Mickey's Prayer Warriors met here," she whispered.

He nodded as if he understood. She patted a door marked "Men," and this struck him as funny somehow, and he laughed maniacally. She snapped a pull chain and pointed to a cot hanging at the end of a long narrow room with shelves of canned goods. She might have intended he move the cot somewhere less claustrophobic, but he pulled it from its hook, snapped the braces in place, and dropped.

"My last name is Akins," she said. "I'm *so* sorry. But who'd have thought—?"

He couldn't keep his eyes open.

"See you in the morning," she whispered, and turned off the light.

Mario sat up on the cot, disoriented. Light streamed from under the door, and slowly he recalled where he was. Above him stood shelves of plastic cups and utensils; cans of chili beans, salsa, and fruit punch; a mammoth coffee pot; and kettles for making soup. Maribel's pantry.

"Oh!" a woman cried.

He'd heard the same voice in Ciudad Acuña, at Las Palmas. He padded to the door and quietly entered the kitchen.

Over the counter he could see a blonde with cartoonishly large breasts—but with pretty legs. Presumably *those* were real.

The woman was on top of her lover now, crying "Oh! Oh! Oh!" in time with his grunting, and jerking up and down in fake intercourse. Mario laughed softly.

A gasp escaped from the auditorium, and Mario realized that someone lay on the couch beyond the kitchen counter. The blonde, shuddering in ecstasy, dissolved into a shot of two men fishing on a lake, and then the lights came on. A young man danced about among the folding chairs, hitching up his pants, his eyes searching desperately, while, over his shoulder, one of the fishermen landed what looked like a bass.

"Hola," Mario managed.

"You, you—" said the angry young man.

Mario tried his best. "I heard voices—"

Who was this boy? Some neighborhood kid? He was a teenager with unformed features, and scruffy white fuzz on his chin. He grew his hair long, not unlike that of the white Jesus in the hall. He was crying, and Mario wished he could help. Once upon a time, he too had been young, his every movement a study in doubt.

The kid slid back the drapes, letting in sunshine, and stumbled outside. Mario followed, but what could he say? The boy ran across the baseball diamond and around the pool to the driveway. He yanked open the door of a red Mustang coupe, climbed in, and promptly killed the engine. He started it again and roared away.

Maribel's son, Mario thought. He understood so little.

She gave him a tour of the house, which, years after her husband's death, remained a shrine to him. And to Mickey Mantle.

She'd married Lieutenant General Mickey Akins, born in Oklahoma like Mantle and also known as "the Mick." The general attended college in Joplin, Missouri, and played centerfield at Joe Becker Stadium, where Mantle had made a stop on his way to fame. Though no one confused their talents, some old-timer said Akins resembled Mantle, and the general never got over it.

"He looked exactly like him," Maribel said.

Along one wall were photographs of Mantle in his prime and in late middle age at a book signing. Studying the general's gigantic portrait in the hall—in his beribboned greens, with the American flag behind him and holding a Bible over his lapels— Mario had to agree. If Mantle had been a general, he'd have looked like Akins.

The general died in Iraq when his Apache helicopter went down. Staggering from the flames, blood in his eyes, he was still able to hold off the insurgents with his nine millimeter pistol. When the rescue team arrived, he insisted they attend to his men first, and because of his actions several lives were saved. But his disregard for his own personal safety caused the general to succumb to his wounds.

"Yes, of course. What general died a coward's death?"

"He was a very great man," Maribel said, and Mario nodded agreeably. It was Maribel's house. Rather, it was the Mick's house, and Maribel had inherited a small empire because of him.

"I never understood how you met."

"The Prayer Warriors built a church in our village. I taught in the school—I knew some English. I came to Jesus because of him, Mario. I renounced the Pope and those Catholic idols! I remember him standing in our humble little church, the rain falling on the tin roof, and his big voice calling out, 'What a joy is the Lord's work!' And, and—his wife was divorcing him. Mario, he was so sad—a *good* man—and I did what I could to comfort him. We fell in love."

"He was quite a bit older, wasn't he?"

"That never mattered. We had eight wonderful years and could have had another twenty."

Mario smiled sympathetically. "And the auditorium—"

"That's where he trained his prayer warriors. Carpenters, plumbers, masons—he was a developer, so he knew all those people. He knew everyone! And they went all over Mexico and Honduras, building churches for the campesinos."

Another wall showed happy peasants standing before their cinder block churches.

"But how could he be in the army—"

"National Guard." She sighed. "He could have stayed home, Mario, but he did three tours! Three! I said, 'Mick, you're already a hero to me!' A lot was going on in our business—oh, how the Lord blessed us! But he *believed*, Mario."

Behind the auditorium Mario had explored an immaculate,

splendidly-organized workshop full of expensive tools. "A contracting business?"

"Yes. He built half of Frisco."

"He was a reserve general who made his living building houses. And then he volunteered for active service," Mario said. "A warrior not just of prayer."

On yet another wall was the photo of a fierce-looking Iraqi rebel whom apparently the general's men had captured. The quotation attributed to the general read, "He said Allah would protect him, but we proved whose God was real. Wake up, guys! It's about *Satan.*"

Something turned over in Mario's memory, and he saw again the CNN story about a general who liked to preach in churches throughout the American South. Trouble was, he preached in the same dress greens of his portrait, giving the impression that General Mick's beliefs were also the American government's. "I remember him! They . . . they made him stop preaching."

"What was the harm?" Maribel asked. "Those churches *invited* him."

Mario tried to think of an officer he'd known quite as eccentric, and the closest he came was one Colonel Ibáñez, who liked to hunt tigrillos. Tigrillos were endangered, or nearly so, but their scarcity increased the challenge. When you reported to the colonel's office, you found yourself surrounded by the little tigers pegged to his walls, their glass eyes staring down.

Colonel Ibáñez hadn't thought himself a nut, and neither had General Mickey Mantle. Or whatever his name was. "A contractor, a missionary, *and* a general," Mario said. "A great man. But no matter how great he was, such a bad war, don't you think?"

She eyed him strangely. "He thought it was the end times."

"The what?"

"The last days. Look around you! Legalized drugs! Marriage between men! And a government that does nothing. Your *own* life, Mario! Every day, Satan battles for dominion—"

Enough of this, he thought, and bent to kiss her.

She turned her head, then kissed him primly on the cheek and pushed him away. "I'm a widow. A recent widow."

"Five years? Six?"

"And Mario, I'm a . . . "

He recalled her in the motel room, not so assured, vulnerable, but still Maribel. "You're a prayer warrior. Carrying out the general's mission."

"Yes! And Mario, you, I think you—"

"I'm an incrédulo."

"A fine man, you saved my life, Mario, but . . . an unbeliever."

To his mind, their encounter had reached a satisfactory resolution. He'd enjoyed fourteen hours of sleep and regained his bearings. Clearly Maribel and he had nothing in common except for a few atypical adventures in a border town; whatever debt she owed him was paid. That she wasn't remotely similar to the woman he'd filed in his memory was testament only to the fact that fantasies were fantasies. In the end, he wasn't drawn to her and hadn't been in the motel. He was *lonely*. What else was new? He should strap on his back pack full of cash and catch a bus to Arkansas.

He rose. "I will go then, Maribel. I thank you very much for your . . . Christian charity."

"No!" she said, and he sat again, puzzled. Her voice had pain in it, as if she were a lover, and he, dense as any other man, didn't understand her delicate point of view.

"Let me fix you breakfast," she said, and turned down the hall. He studied her slender ankles, her full breasts under her sleeveless white blouse, and sat in the dining room, his ill- advised penis rising as she glided around the grand teakwood table.

"It seats fourteen," she said, beaming.

Swiping at imaginary dust, she leaned far toward the middle, revealing the high secrets of her thighs, and the odd scar that he'd thought in Mexico must have resulted from a burn. Now he wanted her. He'd throw her on the general's thick carpet and make glad, guileless love. He reached for her arm.

She turned, the surprise in her face real? feigned?—and dropped into his lap. Still holding her dust cloth, she clasped her hands behind his neck while holding her body far back. Then she kissed his cheek quick and hard as a bird pecks at grain, and his penis died its little death.

She said, "I might have work for you."

Now he understood: Maribel was a businesswoman. Whatever job she'd offer had been her design from the first; she'd seen his attempt to leave as a negotiating ploy. She'd kissed him to raise the ante ever so slightly. She might raise it again.

Maybe he wanted her work, if it were steady and honest. He had no true destination, and possibly the police were looking for him. If so, they wouldn't think of affluent Plano. Possibly Maribel would exploit him, but he might leave one night without a goodbye. Who'd use whom?

She bustled about the kitchen, talking of myriad guests the general and she had entertained, the clergy, the Christian athletes and singers, the politicians. "The governor was here," she said. And they'd had wonderful meals, elaborate Mexican meals, a fiesta every evening.

Yet with all her energy, what she set before him was a short glass of orange juice and two blueberry Pop-Tarts. No bacon and eggs, the gringo meal he'd grown to love, at least when Amanda served it. No juevos rancheros. Was she joking?

Nothing in her face said so. He wondered if she *had* a sense of humor.

He smiled as he munched on industrial blueberry bits, and she smiled, too. He wondered if, as part of his job, he might pretend to convert. Pretending would satisfy her, he thought, even if she saw through him. She'd pretend not to.

Plano was one of Dallas's richest suburbs, but it had a wrong side: Old Plano, a remnant of the farm town that once had been—a remnant, too, of the Old South in which blacks were relegated to separate communities. Maribel owned six houses there, and wanted to rehab and sell them.

"This is so difficult for me," she said, clenching the steering wheel and looking up at Mario desperately. "I'm going to take a terrible loss."

Mario didn't agree. He'd lived in Dallas long enough to know where the poor people lived, and in his opinion what they needed was not six-bedroom mansions made of waferboard and plastic, such as Roberto and he carried air-conditioners to, but cheap houses in safe neighborhoods. Kill the termites, seal the leaks, paint every surface, fix the plumbing and install central air, and Maribel's houses could easily be worth a million even in—or especially in—a market trolling the bottom.

Three houses stood vacant. The other three were filled with the general's charity cases—destitute people who came begging to the church. Long before Mario finished with the vacant houses, Maribel said, they'd move on.

"The Mick was so kind to them," she said, daubing at her eyes with a tissue. "He'd bring them groceries and drive them to services."

"He was a great man," Mario recited.

They sat beneath a magnolia across the street from the Ramirez house. It needed a new roof, and the porch sagged so dramatically, it probably should be ripped off.

"I remember when Mrs. Ramirez—oh, she's a good woman, Mario; she's Catholic, but that doesn't mean she's not *good*— when her washer broke. Water all over the floor! Well, it was seven in the evening, but the Mick—they'd been pouring concrete in Frisco, and he was tired. But he knew that Mrs. Ramirez had six children—*I* come from a big family, and believe me, Mario, I know. I said, 'Mick, sweetie, you just want to go to bed, of course you do. But our Lord commands this!' The Mick had another washer, it was almost new, out in the Prayer Barn, and we came over and installed it, and then we ordered pizza for all the kids. Oh, it was a time of great rejoicing!"

"Where will they go? Señora Ramirez and her six children?"

"Back to Mexico." Maribel studied his face. "She can't pay her rent—I'll give them money to go, Mario. It's the kindest thing."

"Where's Señor Ramirez?"

She shrugged. "He lost his job last winter—I couldn't say where he is. I don't think *she* can say. Mario, I am *one woman*. The general, he had so many interests, I can't do it by myself."

He nodded. "How did your husband come to own all these properties?"

"He heard that Walmart was planning an outlet here, and he bought them over several years time. Then petitions circulated, and the city made things difficult, and Walmart never came."

"He turned the properties into charities?"

"He wanted to sell them to the church, but—"

"The church was not so easily fooled."

She eyed him as if he were an infestation of termites and hit the accelerator hard, so that the big Cadillac lunged onto the street. Quickly, she cut her speed and taxied.

Control, Mario thought. *In her DNA.*

"This was *charity,*" she said. "This was . . . *walking in His steps.* You don't understand, Mario, who the Mick was."

Mario sighed. He might have been talking to Captain Luis Tejón. "He was a very great man."

The next tenants were "white trash"—Maribel crept up on the term, whispering it, lamenting that it was so. As in the Ramirez house, children were everywhere, and Maribel grieved for them, because they were dirty and ran about without supervision. They couldn't be blamed. The husband was in prison for manufacturing methamphetamine. The mother was still present, but addicted to the drug, and Family Services would soon take her children away.

"My heart breaks for them," she said. "But how can you help people who refuse to be helped?"

To underscore her point, she told of a visit the general and she made to San Francisco. The homeless were everywhere, and at first they'd tried to help by giving a dollar to each they saw. Later, when they bought sandwiches and sat to watch the ships on the bay, the same homeless materialized, demanding more money. "This is *my* bench," one said.

"Ah," Mario said. "They had a union."

"They were . . . menacing. One of them lit a big cigar and blew smoke at us. Another insisted we buy his silly newspaper. We couldn't eat our sandwiches!"

Mario laughed. "It should be a law. If you're homeless, you're required to be pleasant about it."

In the last house lived Abraham Potts, a bald, irritable black man bound to a wheelchair. At first he didn't answer the door, yielding only when Maribel cried out, "Potts, I know you're in there."

The door opened slowly, and Potts wheeled backward from them, glaring. "What you want?"

Maribel ignored him, slipping past his chair to point out the curled-up linoleum in the bathroom and the stained toilet, but the path wasn't easy. Potts had piled his mysterious possessions, in boxes and paper sacks, to the ceiling, leaving wheelchair-wide paths from the bathroom to the bed to the TV.

In the kitchen most of the plaster had fallen away, exposing the lath.

"Been that way," Potts said. "Leaks."

Maribel wouldn't speak to Potts, which embarrassed Mario. He said, "It's a beautiful day, sir."

Potts snarled at him. "What about the rats?"

Now Maribel turned, bristling. "I called the exterminator—"

"Yes, yes, that's what you are. An exterminator. Like that

military man you was married to, over in I-raq, gettin' them boys exterminated."

"Mr. Potts, I don't have to listen to this. You were lucky to have this place. My husband treated you fairly."

"What about the rats?"

Maribel shook a finger, as though at a bad child. "We can't just throw poison everywhere; it will take more than that. If you'd keep your trash picked up—"

"They dump! Them Mexicans, they think my yard's a motherfuckin'—"

"Mr. Potts, please," Maribel said.

"A damn landfill! I'm a disabled veteran! How am I sposed to move that motherfuckin' couch?"

"I'll move it for you, sir," Mario said. "I'm a veteran, too. What war were you in?"

"Vietnam!"

"That was a hard one."

Potts stared incredulously, turned his head, and spat.

They fled to the Cadillac, and Maribel rolled up the windows to the man's screams. "You see what I mean? Some people just can't be helped. I have found a place, where others of his—"

"A veterans home?"

She turned her head. "Something like that."

He sank back, closing his eyes. Maribel had no desire to be a slumlord, he concluded, and was looking for a way out. And he was grateful for her offer of work, much of which he'd enjoy. Still, Abraham Potts depressed him. The man had the same blind defiance, and helplessness, as Boss Carter.

They ate lunch at a Mexican restaurant where the pretty Latino waitress addressed them in English. Somehow this added to Mario's depression: it was as if the three of them were trying to be gringos even when no gringos were present to witness. If you kept company with a rich suburban woman such as Maribel, a gringa in every way but her skin, how could you be Mexican?

Mexicans dumped garbage in your yard.

He smiled at the waitress. She probably couldn't even speak Spanish. Who was he to judge? Señor Abraham Potts had reasons to be angry, but that didn't make him wise.

And anyhow, this wasn't Mexico.

"What do you think?" Maribel asked.

"I think you are like a gringa lady who believes every Mexican man comes out of the womb holding a hammer and saw."

Her smile was almost sincere. At least it was ironic. "Didn't you?"

"I can do the work," he said. "Wages?"

He watched as something like indignation fluttered across her face, but he knew it was only a tactic. "Mickey operated at a loss, Mario. Surely you can see that."

"How then did he make his money?"

"He was a contractor, a big one. He made money, no question. The Lord wants us to prosper, Mario. But these old houses, he rented them almost at cost just to help these poor people. He made very little."

"A write-off. Isn't that what the gringos call it? I will take six hundred a week in cash, if I may stay in the Prayer Barn."

"Six hundred may be reasonable—how would I know such things?—but this is church work." Her eyes implored him, and she lowered her voice. "And you cannot stay there, my—my friend. People would talk."

"Charity is a fine thing, but I am an incrédulo. If I must factor in rent, then the fee will be thirteen hundred a week."

"Three hundred, and you can stay in whatever house you're working on."

"Seven hundred. I'll have utilities."

"Five, and I'll pay the utilities."

It was fair enough. They both knew that she was exploiting an illegal, but on the other hand, she hadn't blinked at the notion of paying in cash. "There's the question of permits—"

"I'll take care of them. And establish an account for you. Mickey's partners bought out the contracting business, but his tools are still in the Prayer Barn. I don't know what to do about a truck."

He consulted his memory of Roberto's Tacoma. "I know where I can rent one."

Her eyes narrowed. "How much?"

"Fifty a month." Roberto was a source for air-conditioners, too. And perhaps electrical work. Maybe he could begin turning both of them toward the straight and narrow. In any case he welcomed an excuse to contact Roberto, his only friend. What they'd done was their shared tragedy, born of desperation. All a man could do was get on with life. "It will need tires, but otherwise, I believe it's in working order."

"Bueno," she said, with a rare lapse into Spanish. She seemed uninterested, suddenly. "I'll buy you some tires."

Was that the agreement, then? No fine print? If so, he was cautiously optimistic. Possibly, working some few months for Maribel, he could incubate his own business. At the right juncture, he'd cease to be Mario and become Raul Zamora, the contractor with his very own green card.

"One more thing," Maribel said. "Next summer, you'll have a helper. Young Mickey, my . . . son."

"Oh," he said, and made a note. There would always be one more condition.

Stepson, she meant, the kid who liked pornography. Well, she couldn't be blamed for trying to put the boy to work. "A fine young man," he said. "We met this morning."

- 11 -

Life among the Evangelicals

February, and instead of cold, rainy days, heat descended. Toward evening, spent, Mario and Roberto bought salsa, chips, and a twelve-pack of Budweiser and parked under a bald cypress at Roberto's college. The cold beer was the Fountain of Youth, soothing their sore muscles. They rolled down the windows and watched the girls go by dressed in their summer clothes.

"How can so many exist?" Mario asked. "Is this the factory where they make them?"

Roberto smiled, but seemed sad.

"Roberto! You're an electrician now, and engaged to a . . . goddess."

A woman so compelling, in fact, that Mario often ducked his opportunities to meet her. The way she looked at him might be the way she looked at every man, but he didn't think so. He didn't trust himself.

Roberto shrugged and turned on the radio to a ranchera station. They listened to a woeful ballad about a farm boy who'd ended up in the San Antonio city jail for assaulting his gringo boss. "Martín" had a hauntingly familiar melody, and slowly, listening to the verses reserved for Martín's novia, he realized the song was meant as a sort of companion to "Felicia." Sure enough, Randy DePaul's song followed, and Mario settled back and closed his eyes. He'd come to love the song.

"I'm worried about the police," Roberto said.

"Your inside man—?"

"He was questioned, but they didn't suspect him above any others."

"They were convinced by the busted locks. That was genius, my friend."

"They have film. Two guys in masks."

"I think we're safe. The police are busy with their drug busts and harassing the homeless."

"This was a murder, have you forgotten?"

"I will never forget. But it was manslaughter, as I understand it, not murder. And does anyone really care about those men? Have you even heard their names?"

"Perhaps you're right."

"What of the goods?"

"The large items have been fenced. The wire I'm holding back. No one is building anything, and if I must sell it as scrap, I want the price to go up. As for your cut, I'm a little short of cash because of Rosa's project—"

"Ah, the picketing of my favorite stores."

"They aren't so cooperative."

"Can't you just arrive with your signs?"

"Not on their property. So we are across the road at one place, on a side street at another. Even then, Rosa has had to talk to all these little city governments and buy their parade permits."

"Not such a free country, after all."

"You can have all the freedom you want, if you pay their fees." Roberto sighed and opened another Budweiser. "Life is hard work, Mario. I'm thirty-three, you're thirty-five, and we're like old men with our aches and pains."

"You're almost there, amigo!"

"I wonder where is 'there' in this country. A McMansion in Frisco? And it's the *almost* that concerns me. A man is hungry and hurt and almost out of strength, but ahead he sees the great fence along the border and a hole he can duck through. He picks up his feet and runs the last little distance—even as the wolves pounce."

"You are philosophical today. What I think, Roberto, is that this country provides ways to *escape* the wolf." Mario lit a cigar and let out smoke luxuriously, dousing the prickly aftertaste with beer. Another pretty girl neared, languorously lifted her eyes, and smiled. "Here we are in your fine truck, drinking gabacho beer as the sun sets and pretty girls go dancing by. How could life be better?"

Roberto turned up the volume for the old saloon singer Lydia Mendoza, whose bitter lament of a faithless man was tempered with her brisk twelve-string. He sighed heavily. "You're right, amigo. Life couldn't be better."

Mario saw young Mickey from time to time, but the kid always dropped his eyes, mumbled something, and slipped away. At spring break, when Mario had proposed introducing him to roofing and carpentry, Mickey, his Mustang, and several of his Christian school pals left before dawn for a week on Padre Island.

He returned on a Sunday night at three A.M., but Maribel snapped awake, as she told it, and crept into his room to steal his car keys and repossess his credit card. Mickey's introduction to the hard, cruel world was at hand. He'd be working every Saturday until school was out and every day but Sunday after that.

He'd need to, if he expected Maribel to make any more car payments, and shell out for insurance, and slip him a fifty now and then for incidentals. *And what about college in the fall, young man?* Oh, she was happy to pay for it. The general would have wanted her to, but he had a saying: "There's no free rides in this man's army."

On the first Saturday in May, at 9:30, Mickey presented himself in what once had been the Ramirez living room.

"Our day begins at six," Mario told him. "That's so we can deal with the heat. Where have you been?"

"I got lost."

Mario put him to scraping the last stubborn bits of linoleum from the bathroom floor. The surface had to be smooth before they could lay tile. A boring job, punishing to the hands and wrists, but a steady hour would dispense with it. The kid seemed to settle down, scraping in time with the music in his earphones. Mario returned to the living room, where he dug out the rotten places in two wooden sashes and filled them with Bondo. Leaving them to set up, he painted the ceiling and fitted a light fixture, and at last remembered Mickey. He returned to the bathroom, but the kid had vanished.

Mario sat on the rickety back landing. Treated lumber would repair the steps, he thought, and he'd build a railing. He might do it in late afternoon when the backyard was shaded. This heat was a beast to contend with. Yesterday reached 109.

A sweet smell came from the old barn on the alley, and for an instant he stood again on the cliffs above the Rio Grande. Probably half his soldiers smoked marijuana. When the army disciplined them, they deserted. He himself had smoked it, finally swearing off because it made you too stupid to read, but he'd done so reluctantly. When your days were infinitely dull, stupidity had some appeal.

He threw open the sun-bleached, sagging barn door and called into the darkness, "Mickey! Let's go for lunch." A silence followed and then a rustling, like rats, as the kid stumbled into the sunlight. "Sorry, man. I was lookin' for a better scraper."

A frontal attack wouldn't do, Mario thought. Mickey's sullen eyes announced that he was used to that. Thinking of the pornographic movie, he almost began, "I seem always to be catching you—"

That wouldn't do, either. He drove them down the alley, turned uphill, and parked on the crest. "All of that was pasture," he said, pointing down on a dozen houses.

"Huh?"

Mario swept an arm across the horizon. "The house we're working in was a farmhouse. These other houses came later, with the city. See the wood line? Just behind is the creek where they watered their cattle."

"So?"

"So why not learn the history of a place?" He reached for a cigar. "Is Wendy's all right?"

The kid shrugged.

They ate silently. In a day-old newspaper, Mario read of thieves who had stolen antique copper guttering from an old Presbyterian church. The guttering was worth perhaps one hundred dollars as junk, but to replace it cost thousands. The article went on that so many copper thefts had been committed recently that every recycler in Dallas was under investigation. You couldn't sell an automobile radiator, for instance, without producing the title.

I didn't steal the church guttering, he thought. Maribel was a demanding employer in some ways, but at least the work was honest.

Mickey paced in the foyer, trying to make a phone call. When he finally got through, his face grew steadily more red. At last he snapped the phone shut and returned to their table. "Shouldn't we get back?"

"You're on the clock?"

"No, but—"

Mario smiled amiably. "You're a spy for your mother."

"Shit! She's not my mother. And I'm not. . . " He looked away and twisted his hands nervously.

"She has a mother's authority."

The kid stared angrily. "I do what I want. What business is it of yours?"

"Bueno," Mario said. "It's not my business, except that we're working together and your mother—"

"Stop calling her my mother!"

"Maribel, my *employer,* has asked me to supervise you through the summer ahead. If you're able to do what you want—a wonderful ambition, which I have yet to see anyone achieve—then why work on this house? Why not drive to the beach in your pretty car?"

The kid stared. "I have to do what she wants until June. When I'm eighteen and out of school."

"Then?"

"Then, if I work with you all summer, she'll pay for college in the fall and give me gas money in-between."

"Do you want to go to college?"

The kid shrugged.

"Church work?"

He stuck out his tongue.

"Maybe the army, like your father?"

Now the kid stared intently. "Maybe."

"Do you hate carpentry work?"

"No, sir."

Mario acknowledged the "sir" with a nod. "But you don't like your stepmother ordering you around."

"She can go fuck herself."

Mario frowned. "That's harsh. What if she paid you wages?"

"Yeah! It's like she makes me beg."

"I'll say that for a man's work you should be paid a man's wages. I'll tell her you plan to save every dollar for school. That's right, isn't it?"

Mickey laughed. "Sure, Mario."

At first he felt like the head vaquero, come to the grand hacienda to report on the thoroughbred breeding program, but as the work progressed, Maribel dropped some of her façade and was occasionally playful. With a serious face, she set out blueberry Pop-Tarts and ketchup—a reference to their first morning together. When he stared, she punched him sharply in the shoulder. "It's a joke," she said. "Ketchup on Pop-Tarts? Please laugh."

Not much of a joke, but then she poured powerful, Mexican coffee and set out a tray of mango and pineapple slices, tomato juice, and toast. It was a fair match of his bachelor tastes.

And he admired her discipline. Perhaps, if he'd come on a Tuesday instead of the Mondays they'd agreed upon, she'd still have been in her housecoat, her face set in its unadorned, slightly bulldoggish middle-age. But on Mondays she wore her professional clothes, her professional face. Often he caught her in an office chair, whirling between computer and calculator.

She supported the idea of paying young Mickey wages, but he braced himself. He'd learned that when she agreed to something quickly, she exacted a price. First came the moral.

"It's so important for our young men to be men!"

"What else can they be?"

"I mean strong men. Godly, masculine men like the Mick. Not weak men. Not . . . *homosexuals.*"

"Mickey likes girls," Mario said. "Soon, he'll find one who likes him, too."

"Not that it's their fault. A generation of absent fathers and worldly women who think only of themselves—what can we expect? But Mickey has a unique burden, Mario—a legacy, his father, that *no one* could live up to. And then his father died. Died a hero, and Mickey loved him. Do you see, Mario?"

He sighed. "He resents you, perhaps."

"You don't know how hard I've tried with him, how hard I've prayed, but I'm just one woman."

"His mother?"

Something of the bulldog showed itself. "She left the church."

"And so—"

Maribel frowned and wouldn't offer more. "My point is that you're a man. A good man, Mario. You're a role model for Mickey!"

At least if we disregard the felonies, Mario thought. Longing for a cigar, he bit down on the last remnant of toast.

"And I think you are closer to the Lord than you know." She reached across the table and took his callused hand. Her eyes were moist. "Will you come to church with me, Mario?"

He swallowed the strong coffee. "Where you wave your hands in the air and roll about on the floor?"

"Mario, the incrédulo." She laughed. "And with such a miraculous story! Why can't you see? Our Lord, his forty days and nights in the desert—that's you. The wild boar that bit you, wasn't that Satan, testing you? And you were strong, Mario! But do you really think you did it alone? God was with you."

If God has been helping me, he thought, *then God help me.*

"Will you do this for me? For *you?*"

He leaned back. "I'll do it for a kiss," he said.

On Sundays they always arrived separately, though she watched for him. As they mingled with the crowd, he slipped his arm around her waist, and she looked up at him with luminous eyes.

In the great auditorium, they stood with five thousand others to sing songs projected on a screen:

> Jesus, Jesus,
> He loves me, loves me.
> Jesus, Jesus,
> He died on the cross.
> Oh, he died on the cross,
> Because he loves me, loves me.

The congregation sang many such songs, punctuating them with pleas for sick people needing prayer, a call to join an adventure to the Dominican Republic that a men's group was undertaking, and a report on the blessings God had bestowed on a couples ministry called "The Bible-First Marriage." Song lyrics at last dissolved to a transmission from the foggy baptismal chamber, where a lieutenant in the army of assistant pastors waded forward and doused a middle-aged man and then a frightened teenaged girl.

> Oh, he died on the cross,
> Because he loves me, loves me.

Now the five thousand rose to pray, and not like the Catholics of his youth, not so well-rehearsed or assured that any slightest variation was heresy. For these Texas believers, it was as if God had revealed their liturgy as they were eating breakfast. They were timorous and at the same time feverish, as if they were about to undergo a collective breakdown. Meanwhile, the band—two guitars, two trumpets, a drummer, keyboards, and a xylophone—brought up a soft, plaintive tune, while yet another assistant pastor moaned like a lead singer: "Praise Jesus, praise *Jesus.*"

Maribel's hand shot up. Mario glanced about to see a score of women with their hands up—single women, if their naked fingers were a guide, and uniformly pretty. They had all taken strategic locations around the great, half-round dais, so that the television lights bathed them in an angelic aura. Eyes closed, they looked toward heaven and held up their trembling arms as if to say, "Call on *me*, Lord!"

Then the lights dimmed in the auditorium, and the pretty women fell back as if spent. Reverend Tom Malone walked confidently into the spotlight, wearing white pants and the colorful shirt of a surfer taking his ease.

"We can lay all our cares upon the Lord," Reverend Tom said. "And no question, life will throw us some curves. No question, Satan has his snares. But I'm not here, brothers and sisters, to beat that old horse of negativity!"

Reverend Tom spun about between the cameras, striking an imaginary horse. The auditorium flowed with laughter.

"That old horse of evil!"

He beat some more, and the laughter rose defiantly.

"That horse of *sin*, brothers and sisters!"

The laughter fell away, and Reverend Tom paused so long that Mario began to wonder if something were wrong. Then the Reverend spoke quietly, earnestly, as if his words were manna dropping from Heaven. "Do you really think that God doesn't care about your dreams? Do you really think that God wants his followers here on earth—that He wants man born of woman—to be of few days and full of trouble? Of course, He doesn't! Even poor Job was rewarded in the end."

Reverend Tom stepped forward with his arms open. The sounds of sobbing, of joyous praise, ebbed from the congregation, but the Reverend was addressing the cameras, positioned all around the dais. Many more than the five thousand had come for the good news and watched in adjacent rooms on big screens. The word went out on Dallas TV as well and via satellite to hungry souls in Mexico, Panama, and the Caribbean.

"Like many of you, I grew up in a church environment with a fixation on suffering—on *sin!* But my god is a god of love! He is a positive god, not a punishing one. And His son brought a new message. 'I have come that they may have life,' He said, 'and have it more abundantly.'

"*Abundantly!* Sisters and brothers in Christ, Jesus wants you to prosper. Does that mean He wants us to love mammon? Of course not! But what better witness for his kingdom than happy, prosperous Christians? Does God want us to lie and cheat, and prosper at the expense of those less fortunate? Of course not! He said, *abundantly!* His riches are infinite!

"So pray for that automobile, if that's what you want! Don't be ashamed. Don't fall into the trap of thinking—as some well-meaning folks do—oh, not *me*, Lord, I'm not worthy. Because when you believe upon Him, *hallelujah!* you *are* worthy. Let us pray."

Wiping at her tears, Maribel caught Mario's arm, and they stepped into the aisle and joined the crowd in front of the dais. She will want to discuss these lessons in prosperity, he thought, but for the moment she busied herself chatting with friends and shaking a dozen hands. He made his way to the lobby without her and stood in the cool air looking out upon the parking lot, where answered prayers basked in the Texas sun.

A woman sauntered proudly by with her two children following, a husband bringing up the rear. The woman smiled at Mario, proving that she welcomed to the fold Mexicans who were reverent and well-dressed. Or perhaps she was simply proud of her family, Mario thought, smiling in return.

The woman herself was not merely pretty, but perfect like a proud white goose, leading her goslings. She had perfect, modest curves. She had lovely legs, modestly revealed. She had perfect, simply styled hair and flawless, pale rose nails. Her face was perfectly chiseled, with high cheekbones and well-trained eyebrows, a narrow—but not too narrow—nose, and thin, pale rose, perfect lips. She wore a black and rose, shimmery, expensive polyester dress, but Jesus wanted her to express her Christian prosperity; she was His ambassador even when she visited

Walmart. Her one indulgence—that Jesus, proud as He was of her prosperity, might have questioned, at least if He could have worked up the nerve—was a gleaming diamond ring the size of Texas.

The immaculate, smiling children looked as though they'd been plucked from a TV show featuring immaculate, smiling children.

And the husband! He was slight, almost emaciated, and his expression of joy seemed counterfeit, as if he'd practiced it in a mirror until he was mostly convinced. He looked as if he didn't quite believe he was the father of his children or hadn't had sex since the younger one was conceived.

Ah, well. Who wasn't counterfeiting something? Roberto, pretending to be a respectable tradesman to win the love of Rosa, the counterfeit revolutionary. Maribel, counterfeiting a gringa. And Mario himself, pretending he belonged in the United States. Pretending he belonged in this church. Pretending to be like that weak husband, in fact, in a strong woman's shadow.

He knew he couldn't keep it up much longer—but false or true, didn't a part of him long for that perfect woman? And know he'd never find her? That he could work all his life, even grow rich, and still be an unworthy Mexican? He remembered the fat señora at Guadalupe Cathedral, with her worn dress and disheveled hair, imploring her scrawny husband to give a dollar to the Virgin. She wasn't counterfeiting anything.

By the time Mario had attended three Sunday services, the novelty had worn off. This morning he'd been especially restless, enduring Reverend Tom's prattle from the pulpit by imagining what he'd do with his afternoon. Read a book. Eat at Pancho's Buffet. Get drunk. He hadn't counted on Maribel taking over his free time, too.

When the general was in Iraq, Maribel assumed a project of his called "The King's English," to help immigrants. For this she was paid a small stipend and given the title, "Outreach Minister." The idea was to establish a comfort zone for the newly arrived where they could learn about their adopted country and practice their English. At first Maribel drew only one group, consisting of Asians, Africans, and Mexicans.

"But I hit upon a need," Maribel said. "We talk about how

to order in a restaurant and where to buy ethnic food, how to ask directions and deal with officials, how to prepare a resume. All of a sudden, the Lord has blessed this project *miraculously*, and instead of ten in the group, or fifty, I have a hundred! I need help, Mario."

"You want me to be a discussion leader?"

She smiled. "Your story is as dramatic as any of theirs. You're college educated, and you speak English like you were born here."

He laughed. "I'm a role model."

"In many ways," she said, throwing him a flirtatious glance and squeezing his arm.

Well, he was curious. Such a group might have helped him when he first came to Dallas; it would have been worth swearing allegiance to Jesus if he could have found somewhere to stay other than the Heavenly Nights Motel. Besides, Maribel said, he needn't preach. If a fallow soul presented itself, he'd turn it over to her.

He took the four o'clock session, and only three showed up. They were more nervous than he, all new to the program, hardly a month in the United States among them. They included a Kenyan slightly older than Mario, a tall, grave man wearing a narrow blue tie and a black coat; a newly married Ukrainian woman wearing a bright red sweater over her ample breasts; and a young Chinese woman with a pageboy haircut.

Mario had barely got them to introduce themselves when Maribel burst into the room with her cart of punch and cookies, smiling and exuberant. "Quo vadis!" she said, as if fire had erupted inside the church. "Quo vadis!"

The four looked at one another in alarm. The Kenyan rose as if to flee.

"That's the King's *Latin* for 'Where are you going?' My friends, where are we—where are *you*—going? Well—" Maribel looked toward the ceiling. "I'm full of joy today, because I know where *I'm* going."

All four tried to smile.

"Heaven!" Maribel proclaimed.

My employer is crazy, Mario thought, as he passed around the cookies.

"Jesus," the Kenyan said, nodding soberly as Maribel smiled her way out the door. "Jesus Christ."

"Yes," Mario said. "But your story, sir. We're here to tell our stories."

The Kenyan nodded as if he understood. The Ukrainian looked disgusted and glanced at her watch.

"Teacher," the Chinese woman said.

"No, no," he said. "We speak English here, but this is not a class. I'm not a teacher."

The Ukrainian said, "I thought—a *class*. This was."

The Chinese brought up her purse. "I pay," she said. "Teacher—"

"No, please," he said, holding up a hand. "Your *story*. How did you come to Texas?"

Her name was May Wong. Her uncle, who ran a restaurant, had sponsored her, and she'd crossed over from Vancouver with a car full of Chinese Americans.

"They gave me paper."

"Documents," Mario said. Now he forgot Maribel and the task she'd set him, and lost himself in May Wong's woeful tale, difficult to piece out because of her halting English, but enough like his own story that he was spellbound. In moments she spoke only to him, her big eyes tearful and brave, full of the mysteries of an exotic land.

At fourteen her father had pulled her from school to "stay with the pigs," but the chance had come for factory work in Guangdong Province. All day she painted toy cars in the basement of an office building that was hot and poorly ventilated. The cars were for American children, or at least children anywhere but China. She worked twelve hours, ate, slept, and worked another twelve hours.

She lived with five other girls in an abandoned army barracks and had no place to put her clothes. They weren't allowed to go to the disco down the street. They had no radio or anything to read. All the girls sent so much money home they were rendered penniless, and none knew where they'd find a husband.

The last assertion brought a laugh from the Ukrainian and briefly returned Mario to earth. May Wong was sweet, but he was "Teacher" and shouldn't even notice that she was an attractive young woman.

Why not?

Because Maribel would find out. And because the cultural

barrier was unfathomable. The Chinese were at least as family oriented as Mexicans, and their families large; he might offend people all the way to Guangdong Province. He tore his eyes away, embarrassed by how much he was drawn to May Wong.

And then his eyes drifted thoughtlessly back. The girl wore an obvious hand-me-down: a beltless, knee-length orange dress with buttons the size of quarters. She'd missed one above her navel, or the button itself was gone. Nothing was exposed, but the cloth made a bubble there. His eyes traced the outline of her belly beneath down to her crossed legs. Somehow the hem of her dress had crept ten inches above her knees.

The Kenyan nodded at everything May Wong said. He was enrolled at the Dallas Theological Seminary and lonely. He wondered if other Kenyans lived in the city. Mario instructed the group to continue talking and, keeping his eyes averted from May Wong, went off to find Maribel, who had a contact for Kenyans at SMU. Her eyes shone as she handed him the number, but he scarcely noticed.

The Ukrainian was a mail-order bride, though that wasn't how she described herself. She'd been working in a department store where she earned almost nothing. She still lived with her parents. Then she met Jim on the Internet, and he flew to Kiev to woo her. She showed his picture. He looked to be sixty.

The top button of May Wong's dress had come undone. She leaned forward, exposing half a breast, as the Ukrainian talked. She looked up at Mario innocently. *May Wong* must be Chinese for trouble.

Maribel rapped on the window and pointed to her watch. Mario stood and said goodbye cordially. The Ukrainian's stare announced that she thought of him as some sort of American pervert—how odd, that these people thought of him as *American*—and that she'd never return. The Kenyan pumped his hand, thanking him for all that he had done. May Wong, eyes downcast, slipped by without a word.

He spied Maribel at the end of the hall, talking to Reverend Tom. He recalled she'd said something about dinner before the evening service. One could admire the stamina of these Plano folks, but he'd had his religious fix. Time remained to get drunk.

"Mañana," he called out, waving.

"Mario! You're not *leaving*? Please, come and meet our pastor!"

He counterfeited a smile even as he envisioned that tall bottle of rum.

Reverend Tom stuck out his hand. "So glad to have you with us today!"

May Wong must have brought something infectious into the country. The second button of the preacher's shirt was unfastened, revealing a wisp of black hair. "So glad to be here," Mario muttered.

"Sister Maribel's a real breath of fresh air for us. What an innovative program!"

"A real service to the immigrant community," Mario said, quoting Maribel's brochure.

"The Mick's idea originally, of course."

"He was a great man."

"Truly he was. A real asset to the church."

"And to his country."

"And to his country, you're absolutely right, Brother Mario."

Their positive assessments could have gone on all night. At last Mario freed himself, pulling himself almost forcefully from Maribel's imploring, then doubtful, eyes. As he moved toward the door, he tried not to run.

In Plano you could buy beer and wine only—damn Texas with its mishmash of liquor laws—but wine would do if it were stout enough. He turned into a supermarket parking lot, and rain began to fall. He fully understood the Kenyan's loneliness.

Down the aisles he found a wine called Texas Red that was 14 percent alcohol. He bought the half-gallon size and in the parking lot discovered it came with a cork. He made do with a screwdriver and drank a quarter of the bottle, spitting out bits of cork, then lighting a cigar in a nauseated daze. He didn't feel better, but the point was *not* to feel.

Jesuchristo, how he hated that church!

The rain fell steadily as he drove. He passed the church again, where the parking lot slowly filled for the evening service. Maribel or no Maribel, job or no job, he couldn't go there anymore.

A mile onward he spotted a kid walking. Oh, that poor girl, he thought. He braked and backed up, swerving not too wildly. "May Wong!"

She kept walking, but he drove ahead and threw open the passenger door. "May Wong, let me give you a ride."

She turned round and round on the sidewalk. "I walk everywhere."

"It's raining! I'll take you home."

She crawled in, not looking at him. He produced some clean shop rags from behind the seat, and she dried her short hair, threw it forward, dried it again, much like Amanda used to. They came to a stoplight, and he stared at her breasts, precisely outlined in the wet dress.

Her directions took them to a dark, seemingly vacant store in a strip mall. She probably had a cot in some dusty corner. He was overcome with pity for her, because he'd lived in such a place only months before. He reached for his billfold and produced two twenties. "You first get here, it's hard," he said. "You can make mistakes."

May Wong grabbed the twenties. "Thank you, Teacher."

"Bueno. You were walking in the rain, I couldn't just—"

"Suck blow," she said.

"What?"

"Suck blow." She leaned across and began working on his belt, and he pushed her back. "May Wong, in America—"

But what did he know of America? It was a land far across the sea, full of evangelicos who prayed for automobiles.

"You look at me." She climbed into his lap, banging his chin with an elbow, arching her back against the steering wheel. "You like?"

Well, yes. But how could he explain, with so little language between them, that the two twenties weren't to pay for her services, but just to help? That the last thing he needed was sex with her, right under his employer's eyes? And most of all, that he didn't want another waif, another Amanda, in his head? The twenties truly were Christian charity. How could he explain that?

A car turned into the parking lot, and lights flashed over them, but then it pulled onto the street again. He opened his door, dropped a leg to the pavement, and carefully brought them both to their feet. "Come," he said, and drew her toward the long porch along the strip mall. She lagged, then ran ahead of him and fumbled for a key. He came forward slowly, prepared now for that last difficult bit of conversation, where he established his missionary bona fides, but then the lock clicked and May Wong slipped into the darkness within. She faced him briefly, eyes downcast, and closed the door.

He stood in the rain. He detected no signs of life in the strip mall, but at the end, tucked between a pin oak and a privacy fence, a big Cadillac rested. He couldn't determine the color. He walked the length of the porch, peered at the car, and decided it *could* be Maribel's, but wasn't. Cadillacs abounded in Plano.

He sat in the pickup, drinking wine and listening to the rain. He tried to take satisfaction from having done a good deed, though admittedly May Wong hadn't seemed grateful. Anyhow, he'd finished with the Brighter Day church. It was no better than the slippery wet streets for determining right from wrong.

- 12 -

Viva la Revolución

He still reported to the hacienda on Mondays, and Maribel still made coffee and put out shortbread cookies. Perhaps they both looked forward to the meetings and prolonged them before attending to their day's business. Sometimes their conversations were edgy, as if they'd truly been lovers and had gone through a break-up. But in the end she was his boss, he her employee, and they needed each other.

In July, Mickey and he finished painting the Ramirez house, and Maribel sold it after eight days on the market. With such results, Mario thought, she'd have put up with the devil himself.

Roberto had joined an electrical workers union, and he, too, was making money. One hot Friday, he drove from Grapevine to overhaul the air-conditioning in house number two.

Mario had to ask. "That compressor is legitimate?"

"I'll show you the invoice."

Roberto wanted to go boozing afterwards, with his first stop a festival of conjunto music in Oak Cliff. Mario thought about it.

Before Rosa and Roberto announced their engagement, wine and song were guiding principles, as the two friends trolled for women at the community college. Mario was nearly twice the age of some of them. He didn't understand their music, and none seemed to have read anything. They drank and took drugs as if tonight's supply were the last on earth, as if they were sailing on the Titanic and had missed the lottery for lifeboats.

"Not tonight, my friend," he said. "I need to go over to the Prayer Barn and machine a bushing for the garage opener."

"Buy a new one," Roberto said. "Your woman can afford it. It's your night off! Are you her slave?"

Mario shrugged. "She has kept our bargain. I try to save her money."

"Let him be, Roberto," Mickey chimed in. "He's an old man." He sat on the hood of his Mustang, drinking a Budweiser. "*I'll* go."

"You want to be a Mexican tonight? You're brown enough."

True. Even though they'd restricted their roofing hours to early mornings—if you used composite shingles, they became like hot tar, and easily tore; if you used tin, it grew too hot to touch—Mickey's skin had gone from pasty white to a deep tan. "I'd love it!"

"That red car of yours," Roberto said. "It's a . . . a chica. . . "

"A chick magnet?" Mickey laughed. "Not so's you'd notice!"

"Your luck changes tonight, amigo," Roberto said.

"You know what conjunto is?" Mario asked. "Stupid dance music. A lot of old people at the veterans' hall."

"Don't be so sure," Roberto said. "It's still quinceañera time, *amigo*. Pretty women everywhere."

Mario shrugged. "Go to Walmart. Pretty women everywhere."

"He *is* an old man," Mickey said.

"Poor Mario," Roberto said. "Come with us, we'll find you a *mature* woman."

But he waved them off and drove slowly across town, skipping all the Mexican places because he wasn't feeling Mexican. He hardly felt alive, but a small Vietnamese restaurant had some appeal, and he sat for an hour over *pho* with its strange but tasty meatballs, reading Louis L'Amour's *Hondo* and studying his map of Arkansas.

To fix the garage door opener, he needed a thick washer with a fourteen millimeter hole, and the dead general's Prayer Barn workshop hadn't failed him yet. The Mick's wood screws, metal screws, bolts, nuts, lock, and flat washers were sorted by sizes, and neatly labeled in drawers and clear plastic bottles. One day, Mario thought, he'd have his own shop, just as well organized. He found an oversized washer and clamped it onto the drill press, bored his hole, cut the lights, and entered the auditorium.

A party went on at the hacienda, and he was surprised at the curiosity it evoked in him, perhaps even the jealousy. He walked onto the baseball diamond for a better view. The party was evangelical, and therefore quiet, but a score of smiling heads bobbed in the windows: Reverend Tom, Maribel and the other assistant pastors, half a dozen plump women probably part of some discrete group—all of them done up formally, jollying about Maribel's massive teakwood table.

He sensed a sea change. Not that he'd have desired an invitation, but Maribel had held open a door to her world, and now moved on. He wondered if that mysterious Cadillac hadn't been hers, after all.

Back in the Prayer Barn, he pulled the heavy drapes so his own lights were blocked. Maribel wouldn't object to his presence, but for Mario, solitude had always been medication with which he doctored his soul to ward off full depression.

He made himself a pot of black tea and settled back with ¡Ahora!—Rosa's newsletter, passed on to him from Roberto. It seemed to hark back to the days of the Chicano movement. He read an article on the growing restiveness in New Mexico: gangs in Albuquerque demanding tolls to pass through their territory, and a sort of pony express that ran ATVs packed with drugs 400 miles north of the border. You had to admire the nerve of such an operation, but it was too audacious. Pretty soon, the police, maybe even the army, would muster out to smash it.

Mario visualized Rosa, closed his eyes, shuddered with a fearful pleasure. Ah, but she was naïve. Her demonstration would go nowhere. That fellow Ricardo was right: the gringos would put up with Mexicans only as long as it profited them. As they lost their jobs, they'd turn on those still worse off. By now Mario knew fully the pain of being dead in his own country and a nonentity in the one he'd adopted.

The article also mentioned the "Cíbolistas," tentatively linking them with the bank robbers in New Mexico—the "Las Cruces Seven." Somewhere in the north of vast New Mexico, the article claimed, the Cíbolistas had discovered a source of water, some fertile ground, and steadily carved out a colonia. Disaffected teachers had set up schools, and even adults had to attend literacy classes and learn about computers. Quietly, the governing authority—which seemed to be a sort of city council—bought up failed ranches surrounding the area, so to foil any legal maneuverings from the xenophobic state.

The author of the article could not—or would not—say exactly where Cíbola was. All you'd see there in any case, she claimed, was house trailers and ramshackle adobes. Nonetheless, out-of-work legals and illegals alike trickled in, claiming their trailers and plots of land, preferring utopia over slicing artichokes in California or returning to jobless Mexico.

Mario shook his head. The Spaniards found no gold in Cíbola. Utopia wasn't possible if it involved men and women. Some big dog would always emerge to grab the biggest chunk of meat. He sighed. Musing on great issues only brought home how insignificant he was. How did it matter what he thought?

Was he depressed because Maribel hadn't invited him to her party? No. He admired her, but never could get past her fervency. The time drew near to seek out that—utopian—farm in Arkansas. He felt bound to finish Maribel's houses—at least a year's work. But posing as Raul Zamora, he could buy land, couldn't he? And look for a tractor at a good price. Arkansas was three hundred miles away; he could make the drive on Saturday evenings.

A plan, he thought drowsily, sprawling on the couch, pulling an afghan over his legs. He flipped on the big screen to the Rangers playing Seattle. The Prayer Barn was exquisitely cool. Give me a taste of the kind of utopia that money buys, he thought, the air-conditioning, the soft couch, before I brave the impoverished world again.

He woke to a banging and hollering as Roberto and young Mickey came in through the shop, carrying pizzas, taco chips, and two cases of beer.

"We met many pretty girls," Roberto announced. "What was her name . . . Mickey?"

"Rebecca."

"Roberto," Mario said. "You didn't—"

"He is *old*, Mickey, you're right." Roberto said. "We had fun, that's all. Fun for the entire family!"

Mickey quickly agreed. "They *line dance*, Mario, that's all it is. We did it in junior high."

"And you met beautiful Rebecca."

"Rebecca Bareiro," he said. "She's going to UNT, and I—"

"It was the red Mustang," Roberto said. "All the young girls, they were crowding around us, trying to tear off our clothing."

"But he was a responsible adult," Mickey said, nodding and nodding. "A role model."

The kid was drunk, Mario thought, but what was the harm? If ever someone needed to loosen up, Mickey did. Weaving, jolly, the kid headed off for the bathroom.

Roberto handed Mario an envelope. "I met someone tonight," he said. "While Mickey was dancing."

Mario lifted the flap: ninety one hundred dollar bills. He had to sit. "My God, man. I can buy land."

"One-quarter for you, one-quarter for our helper. I took half."

"It's—"

"Over," Roberto said, staring at the carpet. "The thing is done."

Mario lowered his voice. "Amigo, I will join your demonstration on Monday. You'll be in Carrollton?"

"I thought you didn't care about such things."

"I care about you and . . . Rosa."

Mickey returned, holding up a DVD. "Movie time!"

Mario glanced at him nervously, and quickly Mickey added, *"High Plains Drifter."*

"Clint Eastwood! I haven't seen that one."

"We had an argument," said Roberto. "I told him the best Eastwood movie is *The Good, the Bad, and the Ugly* because it also has Lee Van Cleef."

"And Eli Wallach," Mario said.

"And Eli Wallach. 'That's a good one,' Mickey said. 'But *High Plains Drifter* is the best because—'"

"Because Eastwood is the Devil," Mickey said. "Except maybe he's *God*. He comes into this town, the place is absolute evil, and it's like, you know, Judgment Day."

"You evangélicos," Mario said. "You see the Devil under the kitchen sink."

Roberto brought down the lights, and they sat back to watch Eastwood on the magnificent Prayer Warrior screen. They drank beer, wolfed the pizza, and ate the chips with salsa so hot you wanted to bawl. The process called for a great quantity of beer, but they lived in America, the land of plenty. Somewhere out in the night, the world was ending, but Mario could have cried, he was so happy.

Then the movie was over, but Mickey also had *The Outlaw*

Josey Wales, which he said was almost as good as *High Plains Drifter,* maybe even better because it wasn't so metaphysical, depending on your point of view, of course. Because the chips were gone, Mario went treasure hunting in the pantry and found a jar of popcorn and a skillet with a lid. He filled a great bowl, and when he returned Roberto had lit a cigar.

You couldn't hide cigar smoke. Oh, perhaps you could, with a fan as big as Dallas and a carload of air fresheners. If not, he'd explain it somehow. To hell with that prissy woman, he thought, and lit one himself. If this wasn't a time to celebrate, when was? Mother of God, he had $9,000 in his backpack and, under the name of Raul Zamora, another $16,000 in the bank. He *loved* this country.

The movie was fine, but it turned out that everyone had seen it. Roberto and Mickey staged a fast draw, and both fell dead like little kids. Mario told them to behave themselves, they'd wake the neighbors, and so they watched *Pale Rider* for a while, even though Mickey said it was a rip-off of *Shane.* Roberto tossed a Budweiser can from twenty feet out and made the tall wire basket, and then quickly made another. Mario missed four, banging them off the wall, before hitting one.

Someone pounded on the glass door. Roberto glanced quickly at Mario, and took a step toward the shop.

"Plano Police Department!"

Roberto stood, shoulders hunched forward, eyes jumping about.

"Easy. Easy," Mario said, the lieutenant inside willing him calm and trying to will him sober as well. He'd only drunk beer. It took Texas Red wine for him to go chasing after Chinese girls.

"This is the Plano Police Department, we've had a—"

He slid back the drapes and the door, where a policeman held up a long flashlight. Maribel stood behind the officer, eyes wide and frightened—then horrified.

"Were we a little loud?" Mario asked. "We were having a party . . . end of the week. Just watching Westerns. Officer—Maribel—"

"I know them," she said.

The policeman dropped back a step and lowered his flashlight. "We'll need to file a report, ma'am."

"You knew the Mick."

The policeman cleared his throat. "Everyone knew the Mick, ma'am."

"I'm just a nervous . . . widow, and I over-reacted." She smiled sweetly. "My silly mistake, Officer. It's a family matter."

"Of course, ma'am. Have a good rest of the evening."

When he'd gone, Maribel ducked her head inside and threw a murderous look at Roberto.

"Roberto Figueroa," Mario said.

Roberto pointed a finger, smirking rather like Mr. Eastwood. "Mucho gusto."

"We didn't do anything," young Mickey said. "We were just watching the movie, and having pizza, and maybe we got kinda loud. Roberto and I were coming back from the *conjunto* festival—"

"In Oak Cliff, you mean?"

"It was amazing. And then we decided—because old Mario was all by himself and feelin' kinda blue—we decided—"

"Go to your room. You're drunk."

Mickey hesitated. He was too old to be talked to in this fashion, and his face worked angrily as he struggled to react. "I have to take Roberto back. He left his truck—"

"Go to the house! You're *drunk.*"

He swallowed and looked at both men. "Sorry, guys," he said, and stepped through the door, lifting his knees high over the threshold, then stumbling, not from alcohol so much as uncertain youth.

"See you Monday," Mario called out.

Maribel motioned, and he walked with her toward the baseball diamond, in and out of shadows.

"Mario, I don't know what to say. You do excellent work. You know I like you." She drew her head back into darkness. "At one time I thought we might even . . . have something. But *drinking* and . . . *smoking* in the *Prayer Barn!* The Mick, I owe him. I owe his son—"

"Were Mickey's Warriors always so serious? Did they never kick back, have a beer or two, and laugh like hyenas?"

"I don't know what you're talking about."

Her party was over, and she'd already gone to bed, he thought. He saw her without makeup, and she looked . . . not old, exactly. Worried. Lonely. "Letting that innocent boy, that Christian boy, go with that . . . *man.*"

"Roberto is my friend. They went to a street carnival, that's all. Ate some tacos."

"In Oak Cliff! Where—"

"Where Mexicans live. Maribel, *you're* a Mexican."

She glanced from Mario to Roberto, who had come to the sliding door and tried to look sympathetic. But the idiot still smoked his cigar.

Maribel struck across the diamond toward the swimming pool. "We'll talk about it on Monday," she called back.

On Monday she had a new look. She wore three-inch, open-toed, suede pumps to display her new pedicure. Her navy professional outfit had been replaced with crisp tan pants and a white, long-sleeved blouse with narrow strips of lace at the cuffs. It was buttoned to her neck, but the lace lapping the buttons softened the prim effect, as did the satiny blouse, which with its loose fit suggested, more than tightness would have, her breasts and flat stomach.

Her hair was no longer black turning gray, but brownish-black, with blonde highlights. Somehow her skin seemed different as well—almost rosy despite her south-of-the-border tan.

"I'll get your pay," she whispered, announcing without words that he should remain at the door, but he didn't understand. He followed her authoritative heels across the marble tiles, feeling rather like he'd joined a column of troops.

"Good morning to you, Brother Mario!"

Reverend Tom sat at the teakwood table, hoisting a coffee cup. "Just been visiting with your employer here. It's hard to leave, when you run into a hostess like Sister Maribel!" He rubbed his stomach. "She fixed me an authentic Mexican breakfast!"

"Blueberry Pop-Tarts?"

"Goodness. What did she call it? Huevos con cor—"

"Con chorizo? Chorizo con huevos?"

The reverend smiled. "Sí."

Maribel came clicking back from her study, holding Mario's pay envelope.

"I like bacon and eggs," Mario said. "Over easy. Rye toast and grits."

"Well!" Pastor Tom said. "Me, too, and isn't that what it's all about? Diversity!"

Mario turned toward the door. "Good to see you, Reverend."

"Good to see you, too! Sister Maribel says you're doing just *wonderful* work with the Mick's old houses!"

Mario smiled. He enjoyed this silly man. "With God's help, Reverend."

"Oh, of course. Hasn't it been just an incredible year?"

"Incredible."

"We all need to pause now and then, and count our blessings."

He'd have left without another word, but Maribel followed, ducking her head out the storm door as he stood on the walk. Down the long hall behind her he could see Reverend Tom, grinning and waving. He wouldn't be impossible for a clever woman to seduce, Mario thought. He was a man alone, under enormous pressure. He must be lonely. Sometimes, passions ignited even among the workers in the vineyard. And the man had qualifications a general couldn't match, though you had to wonder about his skill with a hammer.

In the sun Maribel's hair looked almost blonde, and as she bobbed from sunlight to shadow, she seemed younger. "Mickey and I had a talk," she said, dropping her eyes.

He wondered if he could throw her off guard. "You're very beautiful today, Maribel."

She sighed. She *was* beautiful, if she took time to pose. "You were beautiful in the desert," he said, and she *had* been, without time to pose.

She closed the storm door and stepped outside. "I need to ask your forgiveness, Mario. I jumped to conclusions. Mickey said they barged in on you, that you were working on something for the houses. On your own time. You're a fine man, Mario."

He laughed. "For an incrédulo."

Her eyes moistened. "But I can't have—I can't let down the Mick in this way—I can't have his son, well, walking the wild side. It's how it looks, Mario. What if my guests had still been there—all the important people in the church?

"I have my network—Mick's friends, my friends. I spent Saturday morning on the phone. Your friend, Roberto, is under suspicion for some pretty awful crimes. I'm not saying he's guilty. I don't judge, but think of Mickey! I know he's your friend, but Roberto has a record, breaking and entry—from several years ago. Just an accessory, but—"

No doubt. Roberto had never been completely forthcoming about why he'd left Dallas for Podunk San Angelo, casting his lot with Boss's lowly junk business. "You turned him in?"

She looked up through her tears. "Yes."

"*You*. A Mexican."

She lifted her chin. "I'm an *American*, Mario."

"Why don't you turn *me* in? I'm illegal."

"Through no fault of your own. And you're not a criminal."

"How do you know?"

She daubed at her eyes with a tissue. "I know because I know you. I trust you. I—"

He took in the tenderness in her eyes, even as he panicked. He envisioned Roberto trapped in an alley, like a scrawny in-documentado he and his men had run down in Piedras Negras once upon a time.

"Do you know about the Walmarts?"

"Well, of course. Haven't they done everything they could to publicize it? All over the TV? I just didn't know that Roberto was one of those radicals, too."

"You turned him in and you fingered him," he said, trying mightily, and quickly, to understand. "How did you . . . how did you . . . Mickey?"

"Mickey tried to defend Roberto." She drew near him, and her perfume was so sweet, her dark eyes so alluring, that he almost embraced her. She was as lovely as the well-groomed roses blooming to either side of her. She could be standing in a layout for a home and garden magazine. Yes, and he'd play the gardener in the side panel, lifting his rake, doffing his sombrero—grinning like Reverend Tom.

"I'd better get to work," he said, as neutrally as he could manage.

"I know—right now—how all this must hurt. I just didn't have any choice." She smiled bravely. "Can we talk some more, Mario? Tonight?"

He walked deliberately toward the Tacoma. Roberto might still have a chance; he couldn't tip off what he meant to do.

"Mario," she called out. "We miss you in King's English."

He turned, showing nothing in his face.

"Jimiyu misses you." He was the fellow from Kenya. "And I think that little Chinese girl has a crush on you. What did you say to her, Mario? I'm jealous!"

He shrugged. "Can you drop by this afternoon? We need to work out how you want that sink installed."

She stared for a long time. He thought she wouldn't answer. "I'll be there," she said at last, listlessly, and turned toward her house.

He'd met Rosa several times again, though he tried to avoid it. Every time he looked into her eyes, he fell deeper. She knew it. She looked off, as though surprised, and looked back, and then they chatted superficially, in collusion to fool Roberto.

Yet when she talked about her demonstrations, sobriety returned to him, and he thought, pretty rich girl, prattling on about the downtrodden. He supposed if she'd been his girl, he'd have tried just as hard as Roberto to please her. Maybe not, but with deliberation, he hadn't scribbled down her phone number. Now he called Roberto, but got no answer.

They'd scaled back Rosa's first plan from some seventy-odd Walmarts and Sam's Clubs to five. The one where Rosa and Roberto would be was about twenty miles away, and because he'd planned on attending, he knew precisely where to go.

He hadn't planned on a race. He hit every light, but five miles north of his destination drew up beside a Border Patrol paddy wagon. Perhaps it meant nothing. They might be bound for the airport to pick up a prisoner. But he turned into the center lane, increased his speed, and ran two yellow lights.

Near a drainage ditch behind an Arby's, men in black vests unloaded wooden barricades. He knew their uniforms from watching TV. Once he'd had a nightmare about them. They were ICE—Immigration and Customs Enforcement—agents.

Two highway patrol cars crept up the side street. Border Patrol, ICE, and the Texas Rangers! And by the liquor store, a TV crew with a dish atop their truck. A live broadcast.

Maribel couldn't have called down all this. It had been carefully set up in parallel with Rosa's hard-won publicity. To find locations, schedules, all they had to do was check her website. The media was here, so that the public could see how tough federal policies were and how well government agencies worked together. The entire operation was going to be instructional, like those raids on meat-packing plants in Colorado and the Panhandle.

Still, he was a few minutes ahead of them. He made a slow turn, and ICE dropped barriers right behind him.

He parked the truck and grabbed his backpack with its $9,000—he hadn't had time to go to the bank. The demonstration was in what only months before had been a pasture, perhaps three hundred feet from the store itself. A few Latinos—and a few gringos—paced in the heat, while Rosa stood atop a stage to introduce a white-haired man wearing a coat and tie. She looked farm-laborish in jeans and tee shirt and baseball cap. The sweat beading on her cheeks only made her lovelier.

She looked like *Maribel*—younger, of course, but like Maribel intent on her cause to the exclusion of all else. Still, her serious brown eyes, dropping briefly to meet Mario's, couldn't perfectly camouflage her flirtatiousness. That, too, was like Maribel. Perhaps those eyes explained why Roberto had waded in over his depth—and why Mario had never reached Arkansas. Both had hoped for love where logically it had no place.

Roberto sat beneath an awning, where you could stop for brochures and iced tea. The demonstration was absurdly peaceful, Mario thought, as bland as a poor kid's birthday party and no better attended. He grabbed paper towels to wipe the sweat from his neck and ran toward his friend.

"It just gets hotter and hotter," Roberto said. "If we had any sense—"

"You know what's happening, my friend?"

He shrugged. "They called from Fort Worth. Twenty were arrested."

"And you're not running?"

"It's over, my friend." He pointed.

ICE moved up its vehicles quickly—and efficiently, as though they'd drilled the procedure. In several minutes they blocked every street exit but one, where they stopped exiting customers, then waved them through. In the field behind the podium, an olive drab bus stopped, and twenty men in riot gear took up positions, blocking the last possible escape route. They'd look quite fierce on the evening news.

"Can this be real?" Mario asked.

"Real enough for you and me."

The picketers stopped. Rosa ran among them, pointing to the TV truck; perhaps she thought good publicity resulted from serving themselves up as victims. Shots of government thugs hauling away attractive college students was precisely the thing to get a movement going.

Fine for her, Mario thought. She was born here. "Maribel turned you in."

Roberto chuckled. "Was it the cigar, you think? Those damned Te-Amos of yours."

"She *fingered* you. She said an old charge existed."

"Fuck it, man! They planned this for months."

"Roberto—"

"I almost made it, Mario, that's my sad story. We had some good times, huh? Go!"

"Go where?" ICE had formed a shock-line ahead of them. A young woman screamed as Rosa's little band huddled. Bravely, Rosa thrust herself toward the cameras. Mario's leg muscles tensed. He wanted to run to her side.

"Maybe you can hide in the store. Anyhow, we shouldn't be linked."

"My friend—"

"You came to warn me, amigo. I will never forget." Roberto reached awkwardly to pat Mario's shoulder, and his eyes glistened. "Maybe that religious bitch did me a favor. They know about the old charge going in, they won't keep looking, huh? For our little adventure? The worst they will do is deport me."

"And then?"

Roberto hung his head. "Then we'll see how much Rosa loves me."

Mario gulped and turned away, but he dared not walk directly toward the enemy with tears in his eyes. He veered left, piercing a hole ICE hadn't quite closed, and strode for the Walmart's front door. Inside, he passed through the knotted, panicky crowd—the angry gringos, subjected to such indignities, already threatening to sue; and the Latinos, with "legal" or "illegal" written on their faces. He walked straight toward the back of the store, then through the associates' door into the great warehouse behind. It was deserted. Every employee had gone to the front.

He knew the bathrooms wouldn't suffice, and he couldn't squeeze inside an employee locker. He found an empty box a big screen TV had arrived in, but didn't trust it. The box might be adequate to hide from a casual search, but these feds would be thorough.

He saw the trailer truck and hardly paused to think. He found a cap and a Walmart shirt thrown across a file cabinet and stepped up to the cab. The keys were in the ignition. The manifest lay on the seat. He couldn't have backed the truck into its stall, but it pointed outward and had an automatic transmission. He just needed to start the engine, slip on those sunglasses, and go.

By now ICE had closed in everywhere. But they hadn't reckoned on commercial traffic in the narrow lane through which they allowed exits. He drove straight for two Border Patrol wagons, parked grill to grill. The agents were startled, but he smiled, lowered his window, and pointed toward the highway. He rode the brakes, and air hissed dramatically.

One of the border patrolmen neared, frowning. Mario rehearsed his speech: "What a mess, huh?" He'd tap his watch and say, "Got to get to Wichita Falls." But he didn't speak, instead holding up the manifest as if to pass it down.

Then the two vehicles split apart, and the officer jerked a thumb. Breathing deeply, Mario jerked up a thumb too, hit the button for the window again, and taxied toward the highway, turning toward Wichita Falls as the manifest suggested. He glanced once toward Rosa's demonstration, but could see only a milling crowd.

How long before Walmart deduced that one of its trucks had gone missing? The governor would probably call out the National Guard. Stealing something so large from America's true church mattered more than a few Mexicans trying to find the good life.

He timed the first light perfectly. Now he could cry.

- 13 -

A Little Corner of Hell

He wore a neatly-trimmed beard with streaks of white in it, and his name, just as his drivers license and green card said, was Raul Zamora.

He found a trailer park where he could rent by the week. It was a trashy place but quiet, because many of the residents had moved on. "Welcome to our little corner of hell," the manager said with a crooked smile.

He meant Dalhart, not the trailer park. The appellation was the parting gift of singer Randy DePaul, who'd collapsed on stage while performing his comic cowboy hit, "Choctaw Bob," at the XIT Rodeo. A heat stroke, and DePaul wasn't gracious about it. "This place is hail," he pronounced. "A little corner of hail."

It was Dalhart's hottest summer ever. So far, ten old people had been found dead when their air-conditioners failed. Only late at night, when the air cooled enough for the town to catch its breath, was life bearable. Raul took long walks then, down to the supermarket to buy TV dinners, cigars, and rum.

It had also been the driest summer, following nine years of drought. The city was forced to ration water. Out in the county, wells went dry, and grass turned brown because it hadn't rained since December.

Raul had no plans to remain. But maybe Dalhart, tucked into the farthest northwest corner of the Panhandle—not quite to New Mexico, Oklahoma, or Colorado—was a good place to find his bearings. If Dalhart were hell, who would follow him?

He bought a Ford F-150 pickup from a rancher done in by the drought. "My tanks is all dry and I cain't afford the gas to pump water," the rancher said. "Reminds me of the Fifties. We'd get them dry storms, and you couldn't see the danged ole *barn.*"

With the truck, Raul planned to make his way to the rainy hill country of Arkansas. If he were stopped, he could show a legal title and his green card. He'd say that he'd been doing farm work in Dalhart, but on the day he planned to leave, the truck blew a head gasket, and so he paid another week's rent and bought a manual on F-150s.

Unbolting the head wasn't so simple. A sequence of systems had to be disengaged. You needed a torque wrench. Raul was a good carpenter, but he'd never claimed to be a mechanic. His friend, Roberto, could have unbolted a head blindfolded, but Raul plodded through every step as if it were a philosophical question.

The manager told him that a mechanic lived at Lot 17-A, but when Raul knocked on the door, the man's wife said he'd gone to Iowa to look for work. He'd return on the weekend and perhaps could install the new gasket then. Raul called the Ford dealership, and they charged fifty dollars merely to tow the truck and couldn't schedule the job before the middle of next week. Raul decided to wait on his neighbor.

He visited the library daily, reading for hours to wait out the worst of the heat and using the Internet connection. Whenever he entered, the three librarians ceased their chatter. They were unhappy women with pinched faces. Why were they unhappy, working with books in an air-conditioned place and able to sit most of the time, eating their cheap chocolates?

He was forced to conclude that they were afraid of Mexicans. New Mexico, where all manner of protests and attacks were going on, and where the police regularly rounded up illegals, wasn't far down the road. His beard probably added to their fears: he'd lock the doors and hold them at knifepoint until his revolutionary demands were met.

The suspicious librarians brought to mind Dallas, where so many libraries existed—and so many cultures—that you were always anonymous. That was the great thing Dallas offered: it didn't care.

Revolution had precisely the appeal of an old movie. It

needed a beautiful co-star, like Rosa. He could drive the truck due west and within one hundred miles, disappear in Cíbola—if it existed. No, he thought, enough of the desert. Give me green country.

In any case, he had business to conduct. The money he'd tried to send his mother through Western Union hadn't reached her. Finally, after almost three years, he e-mailed her. How could he have waited so long?

> July 2
> Mama,
> It seems so stupid and sad to tell you I'm not dead, but I'm not. I have been trying to make my way in this strange country. I wanted many times to write you. Perhaps I was waiting until all was well. Perhaps I thought that one day I could return home and we'd be a family again.
>
> I can only hope that you'll forgive me. I've had a difficult time of it and can offer some excuses if you'd care to hear them.
>
> How are you? The last time I wrote, you and Silvio had a big melon crop. Cold melons would sell very well where I am now in Texas. I've never seen such a dry, hot place.
>
> I believe I'll be able to buy a piece of land soon. And I can wire you some money, too, if you'll send me your account number. They told me here that the old account is no longer active.
>
> Hoping to hear from you, and begging your forgiveness,
>
> Mario

He haunted the library, breaking through the gauntlet of librarians to check his e-mail several times a day. After a week, still without a reply, he attempted to e-mail the hotel where his mother had worked, but the message bounced back. His last option was to contact his sister Inez, but she had no phone, and all he could think to do was send her a letter, providing his cell phone number and e-mail address.

And what about Roberto? He didn't have Rosa's e-mail address, but he found her organization's website. He read through some defiant talk about lawsuits. At last he found half a page concerning the ICE raid on Dallas Walmarts. Citing violations of the parade permit, city police had arrested some ninety protesters. Eighty-eight of them had been released by midnight the same day, with no charges filed. No names were given.

He e-mailed the "Contact Us" address, asking for Rosa. He found a phone number. He went out into the heat and punched it in, but the service had been discontinued. He stepped back inside, and the librarians looked up suspiciously. Maybe they thought he'd just made a drug deal. He sighed. This was tiresome.

Five people waited to get onto the Internet, so he walked downtown and bought a box of chocolates. The clerk showed him the cheap ones, but he opted for the expensive variety. He deposited the chocolates on the circulation desk, smiled, and waved a hand grandly. "For being so helpful," he said.

The librarians crowded around the box, each taking just one.

"That's what we're here for," said the oldest, a tall, slender woman with shrunken cheeks, wispy gray hair, and a smile so faint it was as though she had to retrieve it from a file.

The mechanic, Amado, returned from his travels in a good mood, because he'd found work at an ethanol plant in Iowa.

"I thought the corn had become too precious," Mario said. "And that you produce less fuel than goes in."

"They are trying to use cellulose now. Corn stalks and truckloads of crap I couldn't even recognize." Ernesto pointed at all the empty trailers. "You should leave, too, amigo. This place has no water."

"It will rain sometime even here in hell."

"It could rain all year and it wouldn't be enough. They have been pumping water from very deep to grow their corn and cotton and pumpkins. They are using up their aquifer. And with this heat, the water just goes into the air."

"You're probably right," Raul said. "I want to go to the chicken country of Arkansas."

Ernesto nodded. "I know it. The rivers are pretty, but the ground is rocky."

"I'm from Jalisco. The land is rocky, but you can pick out the rocks."

"In Iowa they have no rocks, and the topsoil is ten feet deep!"

He handed the mechanic a cold Budweiser, and they walked

toward the F-150. "Then you have made a good choice, Amado. Your family will prosper."

Amado sipped his beer and eyed the Ford as if he were a doctor contemplating a cure. At last he propped up the hood and ran a finger along the valve cover. "Coolant in the oil?"

"No."

Amado spat. "It's a simple job. You could do it yourself, amigo."

"Yes, but I'm slow. When I heard that an expert—"

"I'll tell you what. We'll push the truck to my place on Saturday. Some friends are coming over and there will be lots of food. Meanwhile, you can buy a new gasket."

Raul stuck out his hand. "And I will bring a tub full of beer as well."

He checked out a novel called *The Invisible Man,* which he thought was the science fiction tale he'd read back in school, but this one was about an American Negro growing up in the segregationist South. The man was in some ways privileged, though his path in life seemed prearranged. He could never quite be himself, or find a way to exist that was productive and satisfying, because he was black in a white world and could not escape into simple—what would you call it?—personhood. His blackness, paradoxically, made him invisible. Raul believed he understood: as Raul or Mario, he was just a Mexican. Wasn't that how the librarians saw him?

You could break through. You could offer chocolates.

Maybe then they saw him as a *nice* Mexican, an exception but still invisible, still deportable. He returned the book without finishing it, depressed by Ellison's metaphor. It was too intellectual and hopeless. Don Quixote's heroism was more appealing, and he settled in for an hour with the addled knight.

After Amado finished with the F-150, he drove a distance into the baked, juniper-covered highlands of New Mexico, and gradually it occurred to him that he was looking for Cíbola. Why not look for it, if you had nothing else to do, and—he laughed to himself—were invisible?

He stopped for fuel and cigars at a town called Sedan, a hamlet surrounded by crop circles. The crop circles were brown. Farmers couldn't pump enough water to keep them alive, he surmised, or every well had failed.

He drove on into the dry grassland, all of it fenced but with not an animal in sight; he pulled over to study his map. A great, orange, roadless area stretched two inches across the page, but if he looked up at the real world, a dirt road struck out to the southwest and a sign pointed to "Solano." Yet according to the map, the only route to Solano would have him loop around, traveling a good hundred miles farther.

Perhaps the sign could not be trusted. He of all soldiers knew how treacherous the desert could be, but his truck was full of gas, he had water and a little food. The Cíbola of myth lay far south, near Gallup, but from what he'd read, the new Cíbola lay somewhere between where he sat and Solano.

He smiled. Like the good knight, he searched for what did not exist.

For a long time the road ran due south. In patches it ran as rough as the road north of Langtry, and he slowed to fifteen but made it up to forty as the road curved slowly toward low, parched mountains, colored almost orange. Ochre, he thought; that was the word in inglés. He passed through a large ranch and waded milling cattle, indifferent to him as if he were a boulder. Now the road bent westward toward a range of ochre mountains, and in the bright, shimmery air he spied a dozen adobe structures nestling beneath a high outcropping of sandstone. A side road carried him toward them; in the red sand, he nearly buried his rear wheels down to the axle, but bulled through, until he reached rising ground, and small, orange rocks crackled under his tires. Here he parked and looked down on a village, but even without binoculars he could tell no one had lived there for a long time. Another of those frontier windmills still turned, squawking. Perhaps even it pumped water, because below it, the ground was stained with rust.

Back on the dirt road, he came to a T, with no signs of any sort. If you were out this far, you should know where you were going.

He cut the engine and lit a Grenadier. To his right, the road climbed over the low mountains, in a direction he thought to be northwest; a snow-capped peak sat at the crest, where the road disappeared into a dreamy horizon perhaps one hundred miles away. If the road were paved, that would provide a clue that civilization, as represented by Solano, was near, but the road was orange dirt, no different than the one he'd passed over.

To the left, the road meandered southwest, toward more low mountains, cutting through the endless sagebrush and juniper and brown grass.

He turned left, but without confidence. Even when he reached Solano, he'd find nothing of interest and face a journey of almost three hundred miles back to Dalhart. And yet there was nothing to do but plunge onward, over stretches of bumpy road, down through a washed-out arroyo where he could barely find a passage and feared for his tires. The sun fell, burning orange in what he'd thought to be the southern sky. He was down to a quarter tank as he plunged into the shadow of a mountain, and when he emerged, from a cold valley, over a rise, he faced the moon—an old man, bobbing along the fenceposts, grinning toothlessly. At last he saw lights.

He'd reached Solano! If it were large enough for a motel, he'd spend the night. Maybe he'd find Mexican food, but a hamburger would do. Or a can of cold beans.

The road became a street, unpaved but graded, and looked familiar. He spied a post office, built in the same practical style as the one in Sedan.

He reached the highway. The post office was *exactly* like the one in Sedan, because he'd traveled in a 200-mile circle and reached a point about 500 feet from where he'd turned toward Solano.

He screamed. And laughed—at his navigational skills, at the very idea of Cíbola. He turned toward Texas.

- 14 -

Cíbola

A dust storm blew the day he found out about his mother. He ran the windshield washer several times and couldn't see well even with his headlights. He'd been driving about town, gathering supplies for his journey to Arkansas. The library was his last stop.

The librarians were glad to see him now. "What did you bring us today, Raul?"

The two younger ones, single and grossly overweight, always found subjects to chat about: Texas football, the unrelenting heat, all the people out of work, how Dalhart wasn't what it used to be. The old tall one who ran the place smiled wistfully, and when she looked at Raul, kindness lit her eyes.

Mario,

I'm so sorry to be the one to tell you this. You've had so much trouble in your life and none of it of your making. You were always the best person in our family and even Papa said so before he died.

You know, I learned only a long time afterward that you went into the army to help pay my medical bills. When Mama said God had provided for me I wanted to shake her even though I loved her with all my heart. It was not God but Mario, I wanted to say.

Mario, our mother is dead. You know she had grown heavy and her legs were weak. She slipped on the floor at the hotel—I think the floor was wet from mopping—and broke her leg. The account you had for her, we took the money from that, and she got the very best care, Mario! But she was cut, also, when she fell, and her blood turned to poison before they understood.

She's buried on the hill above Boca de Tomatlán beside Papa. Father Reyes gave a beautiful talk. Everyone from the hotel came, and Papa's old friends, too.

The lights flickered, and he looked toward the windows. It was mid-morning, but the air was so full of dust that it seemed like night had come.

Inez went on to ask for money. Her husband and she had experienced great hardships, and money was so easily made in the United States. *And so forth,* he thought. *And so forth.* He printed off her message and tucked it into a pocket. Maybe he'd send her something. Not today.

A new priest. Old Father Barojas had at last drunk himself to death.

His sister could sell the family acreage. Not worth much, but Raul wished he could take it over. And transport it to Arkansas.

"He's very bitter."

One of the librarians, Cathy, was talking about her uncle. The librarians didn't trouble to keep their personal lives from him anymore. They sat talking at the service desk as they did over lunch.

"Well, they transferred him. He used to drive around and around the fences, all night long. You know that place is *huge.* Then—"

"They're afraid of break-ins? Way out there?"

"Those animal activists. But Denny says he never saw anything but sage brush and coyotes. Feral hogs, sometimes. Then they pulled him back and made him haul out the dead pigs. Sometimes ten or fifteen hogs died over night, and he didn't have anybody to help him—"

"But to *fire* him like that. I—"

"It was an ambush. They're cutting back; they may even close the place. You know, he lived out there?"

"I couldn't stand the smell."

"Oh, yeah. Yeah. It's poison. But the Mexicans, they have a trailer park there, what's the word for it—?"

"Colonia?"

"Colonia. He lived there because it was so cheap. You know, just a bachelor. Never even had a girlfriend, so far as I know. They came around and woke him up—to his trailer house. They said he was sleepin' on the job."

"He was off. His shift was over."

"I don't know. They were just lookin' for an excuse, that's what I think. After ten years!"

"You can't count on anything anymore. There's *no* job security."

Raul stood abruptly, knocking back his chair, startling the two women. He had no moorings. He'd go out in the storm and blow away, because nothing remained to bind him to the earth. Nothing in Mexico. Nothing in Texas.

He'd tried to keep his sights on Arkansas, at least the Arkansas that the previous owner of his name had described, but he doubted the place was Shangri-La. It wasn't Cíbola. If Dalhart were hell—well, at least the town had a library. Also two Mexican restaurants, a movie theater, and a Walmart.

He smiled, even as he visualized his mother, lying on the soapy floor, stabbed by something dull and rusty. "Where is this place?" he asked the women. "Where the man was fired?"

And because they were librarians, trained to answer questions even though no one ever asked them anything, they offered anecdotes, Xeroxed an article, and printed off a map.

American Family Farms, High Plains Division, was twenty-five miles northwest, almost to Colorado, on land that at first seemed flat until you climbed something and looked over it. Then you saw ravines, dry creeks, and small escarpments lying dull and brown like wadded cardboard; you saw stretches of sand and, toward New Mexico, great sweeps of mesquite and juniper. And flat places as well, covered with a burnt brown grass that stretched to eternity.

He'd read about this place at the library. It was the *llano estacado*, where Coronado and his men wandered as they looked for the seven cities of Cíbola. The sky and horizon seemed the same in the brutal sun, and the Spaniards lost their way.

He drove past the farm before he saw the driveway, a long gravel road that bumped up over railroad tracks and climbed through the sage and dusty buffalo grass to a paved parking

175

area with a truck scales, a small metal office, and a guard station. He turned around and yielded for a little Honda on his way back. He followed the car to the guard station, where the driver, a big, broad-shouldered man, got out, and greeted the guard.

The guard wore a uniform and indeed the place suggested an obscure military post. A big sign discouraged visitors, but seemed ironic. Who'd want to visit?

Only an invisible man. Beyond the guard shack, the road struck due west, tilting slowly toward a settlement at the base of a long escarpment. He could make out dusty streets, trailers, a water tower—the colonia, he realized. And a bizarre thought occurred to him. American Family Farms, High Plains Division, was Cíbola!

He laughed. Cíbola was where you found it.

Far to the north, a pickup truck drove slowly along the metal fence. The fence ran as far as he could see—at the library he'd read the ranch occupied over 40,000 acres, stretching into New Mexico. A ranch so big and wild you could get lost in the middle. He'd like that job, driving all night. Raul Zamora, Border Patrol!

On the other hand, he could head onward to Oklahoma in his Ford truck. It hardly mattered, but as he drew to a stop, God gave a sign. That's how his mother, much on his mind, would have characterized it. The high black dust turned gray, and all at once rain stabbed the earth.

Men ran from the office. "Jesus Christ!" one yelled.

"Ah!" said another. "Ah!" He sat in a puddle and pooled the water in his hands.

Raul walked up slowly, holding his hands high in the steamy rain that washed the big trucks and ran blood-red on the pavement. The men stared at Raul as if he were a prophet walking out of the desert.

He pointed. "The grain."

They turned, not understanding. And then they did understand: the semis piled with sacks of feed and supplement, the big dump trucks full of shelled corn. One man backed the semi under a shelter, while Raul and another man fought the wind, securing tarps over the corn.

Then all of them ran into the office, laughing like kids. They stared at the rain, marveling at how it ran in gullies.

176

"Gonna settle down that dust."

"Might plant *wheat* this fall."

Raul's co-worker took off his wet cap and shook his hair. But Raul was startled to see that he wasn't a he. She was a tall woman with the muscles of a man—a rough gringa woman, and he stared at the oddity of her. Yes, a woman, not so bad-looking but . . . he realized his rudeness even as she tore her eyes away.

A smaller man sat studying Raul. At last he stuck out a hand. "Thanks for the help, amigo," he said. "Me . . . llamo . . . Bill. Only most folks call me 'Bud.' Bud Varner."

Raul opened his wallet to his green card. "My name's Raul, Bud," he said, smiling. "And I'm looking for work."

III. The Panhandle

- 15 -

Romeo, Romeo

They chugged up the hill toward the farrowing barns and what Bud Varner called "Hog Heaven," stopping by a new concrete pad. Varner told Raul to lay a line of cinder blocks for the wall of an incinerator; mortar and trowels were in the truck.

A sort of job interview.

Varner struck for the office, leaving Raul at the edge of the desert, if he faced west, with a sea of stinking hogs behind him, to his east. They nosed against the wire with their insatiable curiosity, at the very end of a barn much like the one he'd worked on by Lake Texoma. He studied a pilaster for a moment, marveling how an accident had brought him to this place. His life was nothing but strung-together accidents.

Was everyone's? The evangelicals didn't think so. They thought God's design was in everything.

A mile to the west stood the escarpment, maybe three hundred feet high, a barrier to mysterious land Raul longed to explore. Was there some sort of crop up above? Irrigated, miraculous corn?

So, he thought, drawing a bucket of water. *If only for that, for the mystery, I will lay some bricks. If only because today is accidental.* If only because the weather was cool, the work moderately challenging, and he liked this man Varner. He swept clean the pad and proceeded to mix mortar.

An hour later, Varner nodded shortly at Raul's line of cinder blocks, which were straight and level—all that the world required of cinder blocks. He said, have you ever dressed out a deer, and yes, Raul had, with a pocketknife, and a kind of amazement crept over Varner's wrinkled face. He said, can you run a lathe? Do you know how to weld? Sweat a fitting? He put Raul on a John Deere and told him to spear a big round bale of wheat straw—and then he hired him, and not just as a laborer or strung-out night watchman. As Head of Maintenance, at roughly twice Maribel's wages.

Raul thanked him and afterwards couldn't speak, for fear that Varner would change his mind. He sank back in the old truck—a plateless, three-quarter-ton GMC that you might have seen on a ranch in Sonora.

Under the mud and alkali, the truck was green or red—it depended on your vantage point, because sun and sandstorms had reduced the paint to primer. 1951? 1954? He identified with the truck. He *was* the truck, anonymous, a tool like a pipe wrench. Pretty soon, before winter when snow blew level before you in that eternal Panhandle wind, the truck would chug into the dusty warehouse and park in its snug stall.

Me, too. I'll rest for a little.

Never before had he hit upon such blind, dumb luck. God's handiwork? An accident? Statistically speaking, you couldn't avoid some good luck here and there.

Maybe it wasn't luck—or God's work, either. He had experience with, maybe even he'd trained himself in, every skill Varner required. Just maybe, he was the right man for the job, and Varner, just maybe, saw past skin color and accent to do his company's bidding and get the work done. It was ordinary work, after all, to be done by ordinary men.

In mid-afternoon, Varner drove him up on the escarpment, where two great pumps supplied water for two crop circles. Sometimes, he said, Raul's job would be to haul up a tank filled with liquid manure and connect it to an irrigation assembly. The corn was an almost unnaturally deep, forest green, with no brown edges despite the dry air. "What about the land in-between?" Raul asked.

"Where the crick is? Ain't no fish in there, Raul. Runs dry by June."

"Could I use it for—for—?"

Varner laughed. "A truck farm?"

"Yes."

Varner shrugged. "Try it if you want, Raul. On your own

time. And this is dry country. Ain't meant for growin' carrots and peas."

Raul pointed at the circles. "Not meant for corn, either."

Varner laughed again. "True enough. And you'll get some runoff."

Cheap housing came with the job, and as the day ended, Varner dropped him off in the colonia. It was a company town, complete with a laundry, a tienda, and a desiccated, treeless playground with a soccer field and one sad-looking basketball goal.

But company housing had its advantages. You didn't have to commute from Dalhart, burning all that over-priced gasoline. You could pull electricity from off the grid, generated from hog manure, and pump pure water from the Ogallala Aquifer. You could have a vegetable garden if you wanted.

Varner pointed toward the designated trailer. "It ain't much. It ain't required, neither, and I gotta tell you, you smell that pig shit when the wind shifts. Gets in your closets, the women say, and all your clothes stink no matter what. Except, you're half a mile from the barns here, and it'll go weeks, sometimes, with the wind blowin' toward Oklahoma. I'd live here, if I was a single man. That way you don't have to shower in, shower out, be changin' your blues all the time."

Varner said nothing of another advantage, but Raul quickly deduced it. Many of the families were illegal, and this farm was as remote as you could be east of the Rockies, north of the border.

He also deduced that Varner had offered him the fired man's trailer—possibly the worst-looking trailer in the entire colonia. Still, as Varner suggested, it was good enough for a frugal bachelor. Better than Roberto's place or Maribel's fixer uppers.

Varner handed him a key, drove back up the hill to dispense with the GMC, and Raul walked the perimeter. There were vacant lots to either side of the trailer, grown up in weeds, and in his mind's eye he laid out rows for melons and beans. A lawn mower protruded from a broken place in the skirting; perhaps it ran. And he'd inherit a small outbuilding with a door off its hinges—he could run out a light and make a workshop.

Not quite rationally, he pounded on the door. Then he turned the lock, opened the door slightly—and reeled from the stench. The dead man in Maribel's Cadillac flashed in his thoughts, but this was not the smell of death, not a pig smell, but simply something rotting. He went out to his truck for a shoprag and held it to his nose, as he felt down the wall for the switch. As he was about to flip on the light, he heard a low growl, a swishing, and instinctively yanked back his hand, even as teeth nearly closed on his wrist.

"¡Mierda!" he cried, and fell back on the steps. The worst trailer in the park, and a cross dog guarded it! So much for his run of good luck.

He jumped in the F-150 and caught Varner at the guard gate, turning toward Dalhart. "Dog!" said Varner. "Woolsey left his dog? In that shut trailer?"

"And the place is full of garbage."

"Ah huh." Varner nodded thoughtfully. "I apologize, Raul. First month is free?" He paused, waiting for Raul's nod. "You need to see Carrie Kreider."

"Who?"

"Carrie Kreider. The hog whisperer."

"What?"

"It's a joke. You never seen that movie? With Robert Redford?"

"I have seen *every* movie. *The Horse Whisperer,* you mean."

"Well, Carrie kinda talks to 'em. And they listen, I swear they do, I seen it myself. She don't work the barns; she's doin' research. Kinda our vetinary."

"A scientist?"

"You could say. She'll take care a' your dog."

So Raul, bemused, again thinking this was his lucky day, sought out the trailer of Carrie Kreider, hog scientist, fourteen lots to his east. He stalked up on her screened-in shelter and stood a long moment. His boots were clean, inexpensive but relatively new. Same with his shirt and trousers. He took off his baseball cap and stood holding it in both hands, as if it were a sombrero. He thumbed the bill nervously.

A woman came to the door—he might have thought her a man, she was so broad-shouldered, but then he smiled, recognizing the woman from the guard station. Off-duty, her ragged hair came to her shoulders, and she wore shorts and flip-flops. She was big, all right, but her legs weren't flabby. More like logs.

Behind her played the version of Star Trek, *Voyager,* that featured a gringa mother for its captain. They should have called her Ma Janeway. But also, Raul remembered, the series co-starred a dominatrix blonde who played an alien. He'd lusted after her in Deep Ellum, as he stripped copper wire. "My name is Raul Zamora. This is my first day. And they gave me—here in the colonia—the trailer of the man who left."

Her eyes registered recognition, but his presence clearly puzzled her, and she stiffened. She was as tall as he. "Dennis Woolsey. He was fired for—"

Raul was curious, not wanting to repeat Mr. Woolsey's mistakes. "Sleeping on the job? Drugs?"

"He was abusing the animals. How can I help you, Mr. Zamora?"

"I don't have much to move in, but I wanted to turn on the air-conditioning. Except—there's a big dog."

"Yes, he had a dog," she said, understanding slowly coming to her eyes. Now she stared at him almost longingly. Kindly eyes, he thought, a little wild. He sensed the big woman's loneliness, and she was not unattractive, exactly. He might have to revise his idea of womanhood. She seemed so plain and practical that the idea of attraction—of pheromones, of silly men standing on their heads—didn't apply. No more Maribels, thank you very much, but how novel the thought of friendship! How superior to romance, with its endless affronts and redresses!

The woman still stared, and Raul smiled awkwardly. "You are Carrie Kreider?"

"Yes!"

"Mr. Varner said you are the one to see about animal problems."

"Oh! Of course." She stepped back to her dinette table for a scuffed leather bag—his glance took in an antiseptic aerosol, various salves and ointments and packets, and some tools as well. Needle nose pliers. Duct tape.

"I thought he would take my hand off," Raul said, as they walked toward the trailer. It was evening, the sun had dropped over the escarpment, and the desert began to lose its heat.

"How do you know it's a boy dog?"

"The neighbor called him 'Romeo.'"

Carrie pushed wide the door. With the air off, Raul thought, it was a wonder the dog hadn't died. They stood an instant in the darkness, fighting for breath, and to see, in the rank heat. Then Raul found the living room light, which revealed a psychotic mess of broken furniture, piled-up dishes and spoiled food, and bright blue bags of trash.

He slowly smiled. "The first month is free."

Already several steps down the hall, Carrie turned, and smiled, too. He caught up in the bathroom, where the dog lay, a big, black mongrel with a big scrotum. Blood had caked in his nostrils, and he panted heavily. The two big bodies overwhelmed the little space.

Carrie gently probed him up and down. "I think he's just weak. No food and the terrible heat." She wet a washcloth in the sink and daubed at the wounded nose. Romeo whimpered and pulled his head back. "A *lot* of life left," she said.

Raul went through the trailer opening windows and found a fan. He tossed several of the garbage bags out the door. Then he ducked his head into the bathroom again. Romeo growled and tensed, but calmed as Carrie stroked his ribs and gulped at the bowl of water she held out.

"You have a touch," Raul said. "Will I need to . . . take him to the back of the farm?"

"Shoot him?" she asked. "Oh, no. I'll take care of him."

"That's good," he said. "I don't believe he likes me."

"Right now he thinks you're another Dennis Woolsey, whom no one liked. He'll get used to you. Buy him a package of bologna sometime."

Raul laughed. "I wish that were all it took with human beings."

Carrie stared up at him as she stroked Romeo. "Me, too."

- 16 -

The Hog Whisperer

Carrie Kreider was famous. She'd just returned from Kansas City, where she received the American Family Farms Employee of the Year Award. The company maintained operations in South Carolina, Oklahoma, Arkansas, Missouri, Nebraska, Iowa—and Texas, with over five thousand employees. An impressive award, Raul thought.

But what for? Raul asked Manny DeJesus and Refugio Martín, the two men of his crew. What did she do? Whisper to hogs? Talk to them about their cruel mothers?

Maybe she invented something. They didn't really know, though they liked Carrie well enough, the big woman in her blue uniforms, rubber boots, and prescription goggles to keep her eyes from watering. "I worked here two months before I knew she was a *she*," Manny said.

Refugio joined in. "One time, I saw her pick up a tire from the John Deere and throw it in a truck."

Her strength so impressed them that their doubts about a woman doing such rough work—a gringa, at that—were assuaged. Her job didn't compete with them. She studied things.

"Something to do with the pig shit," Manny said, laughing.

"Make it smell like a rose, man!" said Refugio.

Yes. American Family used wave machines to wash out the barns every two hours, pushing water under the slatted floors of the pens and keeping flies and rats, and thus diseases, to a minimum. Raul was amazed by this—by the profit-minded thinking that would crowd so many hogs into such small spaces, first of all. But if this were your method, the result was manure, so much you had to wash it away or soon it would rise taller than pigs, taller than you. Manny shook his head. "Taller than—"

"¡Pico de Orizaba!" said Raul.

"¡Sí! ¡Sí!" both men said, laughing. "Mountains of shit!"

The valley operation alone produced more than the city of Dalhart. You could spread some through your irrigation assemblies, absorbing it in corn and alfalfa, in effect feeding it back again, but the root systems of your crops, and the soil itself, rebelled from too much nitrogen, too many phosphates. Though it might not show up for ten years—until it percolated down—eventually such quantities of manure poisoned the aquifer.

The aquifer was drying up anyhow, a direct result of all the big livestock operations and all the irrigated crops required to keep them going. Again, who thought this way? The logic must be that if you mined Ogallala water to the last extractable drop, then abandoned the High Plains, it didn't matter if strata two hundred feet down were besotted with nitrates. No one would remain to yell, "Pollution!"

This was not so much a farm, Raul thought, as a mine.

Lagoons, the industry solution, worked to a point, but not fast enough to accommodate American Family's volume. They stank and drew vermin. And they seeped, no matter what company engineers told the state, the weak county authority, and irate citizens—who, after American Family's lawyers invaded Austin, didn't even have the right to sue.

And no matter where you disposed manure, flies gathered and bred, endless flies, clots and gobs of flies, flies like thick black paint. At last Raul ran across a summary of Carrie's work, in an illustrated company document boldly stamped, "Proprietary":

1) Pump the hog water into a digester;

AKA, a septic tank.

2) Let the solids settle;

3) Recirculate the water to the scrub system;

Otherwise, wells couldn't keep up with the demand. And, not least, you'd be flooded with foul water.

4) Heat up your solids, mixing in ammonia-eating polymers;

Chemistry wasn't Raul's strong point, but he knew that "polymer" was just a catch-all term meaning the lengthy, repetitive combination of molecules. What kind of molecules? Some sort of carbon, and it had to be organic, or bacteria wouldn't go to work. Bacteria that fed on ammonia, but wouldn't your biproduct be some other form of nitrogen? Apparently, a less objectionable form. Anyhow, this was where Carrie got rid of odor, by attacking the ammonia.

5) Bleed off the methane, and run your generators;

Granted, hogs—chickens, turkeys—shouldn't be raised like this, but corporate folk saw their animals as moving parts in a long assembly line. They were the raw materials of "product." From the factory's point of view, burning off your methane, producing the farm's and the colonia's electricity, was sheer genius.

6) Aerate the sludge;

Turn on a fan?

7) Heat it slightly again and run it through a coarse sieve, making grub-sized pellets, and

8) Bag it—now odorless, black as buckyballs, and benign—as suburban fertilizer.

This explained why Carrie became employee of the year. She solved the volume problem by diluting it—hauling it to the four corners, marketing it to Ace Hardwares and Walmarts. Maybe the stuff would sell, maybe it wouldn't, but Raul knew one thing: Carrie was a very smart woman.

He also figured out—from Manny, a witness, and later from Carrie herself—how Dennis Woolsey lost his job.

The man worked for several years as the night patrolman, driving round and round the farm's 40,000 acres, night vision binoculars and shotgun handy. It was easy duty compared to what the barn crews went through. And it was a perfect job for a schizophrenic—which Woolsey probably was—because you zoned out for hours, and no one knew. But, Raul was sorry to learn, the company was cutting back everywhere. And the first to go were the patrol jobs.

They were created in the first place after the animal rights organization, PETA, made one of its famous raids, not on the Dalhart farm but up in South Dakota. Secretly, they filmed men much like Woolsey, torturing hogs. The film sent shock waves through the industry—Raul got this much from the Internet—but the animal rights people had since moved on to other issues. Also, costs were running high at the High Plains operation, because of scarce water and competition for corn on the world market.

Woolsey was offered the dead wagon run down in the valley—those thirteen 1200-head barns nearest the highway where shoats were finished into 250-pound hogs. The process took five months, but here was the thing, the reason Woolsey got himself fired. You could expect two to four percent mortality, as hogs went limp on the concrete slats of their cages, or developed tumors which their brothers and sisters worried with their teeth. Eventually, the "technician" spotted the downers and wrestled them, dead or alive, onto the long center aisle.

Some downers burrowed into a corner like dogs, closed their eyes, and gulped at the steamy air as they awaited the end. Others squealed as the executioner neared, swinging his captive-bolt gun.

Did they remember their mothers, from which they'd been weaned at twenty-one days?

"I don't think so," Carrie told Raul. Hogs felt pain and knew fear, anticipated being fed and grunted pleasantly if they liked you, but she didn't believe they remembered much. It was mostly the change in their routine that frightened downers, and that they couldn't stand up anymore. She didn't believe they understood that they'd been moved to death row.

But Woolsey! All he was supposed to do was touch the captive-bolt gun to the downer's forehead, or eye, or ear, and pull the trigger. It was instant. It cut the hog off mid-squeal. Shoot the bolt, drag out the hog: nothing more to it than that. If it was near its market weight, you could find someone to help or tip the carcass into a wheelbarrow. Not a pleasant job, but not impossible. Something you grinned and bore perhaps ten times a day. Better than no job at all.

Then you drove out to the compost pits, where the flies fought the buzzards which fought the coyotes, and dropped your load. It was a good place to smoke a joint if that was your persuasion. (That's what they said about Woolsey. They said he was a pothead, and lately had been using meth as well.)

Did meth make you more cruel? It certainly made you more neglectful: witness the trailer and Romeo.

"Fucking pig!" Woolsey screamed, and kicked the hog in the ribs. It squealed in agony, and he kicked it again. "You like that? You like that? I'll show you!" Now Woolsey hammered on the downer's snout with a two-foot length of pipe. It tried to stand, making two quivering steps, and then it hunched forward on its knees. Its squeal was more like a scream now. An almost human scream.

Why do such a thing? What possibly could be accomplished? Who was impressed?

Maybe the other hogs. *They* were screaming now, in shrill protest.

Here's where Manny came in, carrying a tool box, on his way to repair a dripping faucet.

Carrie, watching from the end of the barn, could only conclude that Woolsey was a mad man who should be put away.

"Didn't you think . . . *I am a woman alone. . .* ?" Raul asked her, long after.

"No," she said.

Because she was no prairie flower. She was six feet tall, strong as the Ukrainian Mennonites she descended from, and could swing a post mall if required. She grabbed Woolsey and spun him around. His unsubtle face crowded with amazement and outrage. His eyes were blood-red. "You . . . *bitch. . .* " he managed, and stopped. Carrie was bigger than he was and in much better condition.

Manny stood transfixed. But it didn't occur to him to rush to Carrie's aid. Despite Woolsey's meth-addled bluster, he was over-matched.

Carrie reached to grab the pipe. "If I *ever* see you treat an animal—"

Woolsey shot the captive bolt, and the downer shuddered to its death. Then he yanked up the steel pipe, causing Carrie to stumble backward. He laughed at her. He threw down the pipe and brought a rope from his pocket. He bound the hog's hind legs. Then he produced mason's gloves and drew on the rope, pulling the hog toward the far end and the faithful GMC.

Carrie sighed. "I'm going to report him," she announced, speaking aloud as if to a companion. Raul imagined it: Carrie turning about, as twelve hundred pairs of eyes fastened on her, from up and down the aisle.

"That Woolsey, he's crazy, man," Manny said.

Because of Manny, word leaped from barn to barn, and even down to the colonia, that a man was being fired for animal abuse. Of course, some of the men despised the foul-smelling lives they led, and drank too much, and took their woes out on their wives with their fists. Such men found the concept of animal abuse a tricky one. Where was the line between abuse and good husbandry? Did such thinking have any place on a factory farm? Sometimes, you had to use prods when hogs knotted up at a narrow exit; sometimes, you kicked at them if they bit your knee or exposed hand. Was this abuse?

Relief passed among them when they learned that the abuser was Woolsey, a gringo and a crazy man. If it had come to a matter of testimony, they'd all have taken Carrie's side. Anyhow, ten hours later, more because Carrie had requested it than because of the downer's inalienable rights, Varner fired Dennis Woolsey. And five days later, as the fateful rain fell, he hired Raul Zamora.

Carrie's trailer, among the newest and largest, had been installed on a grade, and its downhill side, shored up with cinder blocks, rose five feet above the ground. In his first several days, Raul enclosed the area with wafer board, fit an old sash to allow in light, and ran a line to an automatic pig waterer. He made a door Romeo could nose open. Inside, he raked the dirt level and laid indoor/outdoor carpeting. Carrie tested the dog lair herself, drawing in two worn blankets and sprawling in the darkness like some kid with a hiding place in the barn.

"Thank you, Mr. Zamora," she said.

"Please. Call me Raul."

He couldn't come up on Romeo quickly, or the dog shrank and bared his teeth. But Raul took Carrie's advice, offered the dog bits of meat from time to time, and spoke in a low, consoling tone. Romeo still growled at most men, but grew tolerant of Raul.

Still, he was Carrie's dog. "I'm right here, boy," she said. "Things are gonna be all right. See what the nice man did? He built you a dog *spa.*"

Carrie left him tied to her clothesline through the day, from which he could reach his spa, but he knew when she was due home and greeted her wagging his tail. "Did I have a good day today?" Carrie asked. "Well, yes, I did. And look what I brought home for you." She fed him piglet testicles, and by late fall, his coat glowed from such fine fare.

A little kindness, Raul thought. The world was so full of indifference that a little kindness was more powerful than the unleashed atom. Despite the affair of the downer, Raul didn't believe Carrie was a do-gooder, but she was kind. Instinctively kind, and he thought of her kindly, as the other men did. As men, they were bound to protect her, whether or not she needed it. Often, after dark, another long day behind him, he drove by her trailer. When he saw Carrie and Romeo's profile in the darkness, sitting upright on the couch, with Captain Ma Janeway between them, he thought he had a part in making the universe safe.

Winter blew in early and hard, and Raul spent long hours clearing snow, weather-stripping windows, keeping generators and well pumps maintained. On Christmas Day, his crew had to thaw out one of the wave systems and replace burst plastic pipes; working conditions—with shit misting in their faces, and slushy brown water underfoot—were almost too much to bear. But his crew busted up pallets, built a great bonfire, and took turns diving in.

Then there were those days when they finished their rounds and retreated to the machine shed, where they changed oil in the tractors and repaired tools as that awful wind blew. One day in January, waiting for the snow to stop, they played poker for twelve hours, with players dropping in and out as they had money or work called them away; even Varner sat in for several hands.

Occasionally, like an afterthought, he saw Carrie, stalking toward Hog Heaven in her bulky long coat, gloves, and goggles, with scarves and stocking hats covering every inch of skin. She waved at him clumsily.

On a clear day late in January, Varner dispatched him to Amarillo to pick up air freight from Kansas City, and just as Raul shifted the company car to Drive, Carrie pounded on the passenger door and climbed in beside him.

"FrankenCarl's semen," she said, and looked away.

He had no idea of her meaning, but smiled agreeably. What a guileless woman! She was embarrassed by the word "semen."

"Pig semen," he said, sympathetically.

She drew a breath. "It's a—in Kansas City. I used to work at headquarters in Kansas City. For FrankenCarl, that's what they call him. I—"

"Another scientist," Raul said gently.

She swallowed and patted her breast. How isolated had she

been, in this desolate place, the only woman on a crew of over a hundred? And, in the colonia, the only gringa? "They sent me out here to work on commercial fertilizer. You've seen the green plastic bags?"

His crew had sealed and shipped the first ten pallets of Carrie's black pellets just the week before. The bag she spoke of featured a green, smiling pig in overalls, skipping down a yellow road lined with sunflowers and marigolds. An army of happy children trailed behind. "A big success," Raul said, smiling a little.

"We'll see," she said. "Carl Franken, that's really his name— he's the biotech guru. The semen, it's for the new banties."

Raul did not perfectly understand. The banties were small, experimental pigs—named after a miniature breed of chickens. "With your big project done, you will be leaving us soon?"

She shook her head. Her eyes lit up, and for an instant she was almost pretty. Certainly she was pleasant, and he liked the job of putting her at ease. He sighed. Nothing was more difficult than to be friends with a woman, to admire and enjoy her, but with no sex in the prognosis—even as you talked about pig semen. He kept his eyes on the road.

"Nervous little pigs," he said.

She was silent, leaning her head against the window and looking across the snow.

They picked up tractor parts and FrankenCarl's semen, packed in dry ice, at the FedEx office, then stopped for lunch at a cramped Vietnamese place. Sitting across from Carrie, whose broad upper body hulked over the little table, he saw she'd done something with her hair, though he didn't remember exactly how it looked before. Ragged, he thought. You couldn't work at these rough jobs and suddenly turn glamorous, but even so her hair was neat today, and blonde. Was she blonde two weeks ago? And she wore one of those Western blouses like dancers in country shows. All dressed up for the big city of Amarillo! "How many generations of banties?"

"The fourth. Carl claims this batch of semen will be perfect."

Damn, he liked this. To be included in something that required a brain. Never an idea out of Maribel: just that relentless, evangelical pounding. And all Rosa talked about were the poor illegals—such as himself. "What does that mean?"

Carrie frowned. "There's a sugar, a basic sugar, that causes the human body to reject pig organs. A transplanted pig kidney will start dripping urine, but then stop and turn black. He's found a way, using human DNA, to defeat the sugar. It works in chimpanzees, but people trials—"

"Shouldn't all of this be out before the public? Is it even legal—human DNA? Why don't you write it up?"

She stared. "It's proprietary."

Everything was proprietary. The company even staked a claim on shit. "Put it on the Internet."

She seemed to consider, but shook her head."I'd lose my job, Raul."

On a proper farm, the way Raul's father would have proceeded, you erected a stout steel fence between your young boars and gilts, letting them nose each other through the wire until an adolescent daze overcame them. Suddenly, the virgins were in estrus, the swains crazed with lust. Then you put them together. Natural hog love-making wasn't prolonged or tender, but it was ninety percent effective.

Artificial insemination, Carrie said, was a different matter. Look moon-eyed at a cow, she was pregnant, whether from a penis or a needle. Not so sows, prolific as they almost always turned out to be. And these little GM hogs, bred for leanness and, well, their human qualities, were nervous twits. They grew fast and were healthy for the most part, but they were skittish about sex. Prudish, almost.

After weaning they'd never seen a barrow, much less a relentless old boar, and Carrie maintained that keeping a few boars around, stoutly penned, could provide inspiration. Ordinarily, Bud Varner indulged her, but what she suggested was rather mystical, in his West Texas estimation.

"And they'd eat a lot of corn," Raul put in.

"Oh, yes."

The banties weren't even hogs, in a way. They were a hybrid, possibly explaining why they had difficulty reproducing. Anyhow, Carrie was faced with the task of impregnating three hundred virgins with no interest in sex. And it wasn't as though she could sit out in the middle of the barn for story-time and tell them how boys and girls were different. They weren't *that* smart.

As they'd grown, she'd made sure that her crew performed

the traumatic tasks such as cutting wolf teeth and vaccinating for pseudo-rabies. And she never raised her voice, except in the mornings when she greeted them with a bracing, "Sooo-ooo, piggies!"

After that, she whispered.

Perhaps she looked for evidence, but in some hard-to-iden-tify, way the banties did indeed seem, if not human, then not quite hoggish. When she entered the end of the barn, donned her "blues," and swung open the tight-fitting door, heads lifted not entirely in unison, as you grew used to with normal hogs. That is, some banties were interested, some were bored, while some seemed to feign boredom until she herself showed interest.

"Like a teacher," Raul said. "When she enters a class."

"That's right!"

Some kept eating. Some lifted their heads in expectation, but didn't commit, while others pushed at the bars containing them, and raised their snouts in greeting. They knew her. They liked her. She almost expected to hear "Hey!" and "How are ya?" and "Good morning to *you*."

She climbed into the pens to pat backs and scratch ears, and then her young ladies milled around her legs like cats expecting milk.

She was the hog whisperer.

When the virgins were eight months old and almost at their full, genetically-inhibited weight of two hundred pounds, Car-rie cleaned out a stall and scattered several hay bales. Confined hogs didn't know about hay, but quickly learned to root in it, settle in a nest, and chew barbs of timothy. She brought in the gilts one at a time.

Though she discouraged spectators, workers passed in the office and work area at the front of the barn, and watched her. Varner, her nominal supervisor, stood by like a proud papa.

"Hey, baby," she said, and waited a moment to see if the gilt seemed suspicious, but most trusted her. And this was Diana, after the late English princess. Even Carrie had a hard time tell-ing the banties apart, but a gene must have slipped past Fran-kenCarl, because Diana had the droopy ears of a Chester White, and Carrie could pick her out from the other end of the barn.

Diana was different in other ways. She'd stand in a shaft of light, head held high, as if . . . what? She was studying the dust motes? Carrie eased forward, patting Diana, rubbing her, checking her vulva to see if she was ready. Often, she got lucky.

In one hand she held the big needle—more like a small pump—and in the other, corn meal laced with cocoa. Hogs liked chocolate as much as she did.

She murmured, "Soo-oo, Diana," and "It's OK, baby, it's OK," as the gilt licked her hand, grunting contentedly. Then she lifted a leg over the young sow's back and sat lightly on her spine. Some men sat with all their weight, which was all right with a large sow, but these banties required finesse. Just the right pressure.

Diana hunched beneath her, adjusting her legs. She was "standing for the boar," as breeders put it. She was wet, and no problem at all. Carrie slipped in the needle, shot the dose of semen, and knew it would take, making eight or nine pigs for Carl. Nine pigs, each one-tenth homo sapiens; did this mean she'd created a human baby, too?

Of course not, but the thought kept coming to her.

She looked up. She had another spectator: Raul had come in from the outside, a banty gilt under each arm.

Varner had moved him to the farrowing operation in Hog Heaven. He'd offered some terrible news, at least if you liked your work, which Raul very much did. Gilts and barrows the company had formerly finished in the valley would be trucked to Iowa now, and when the sows were four years old, they'd be taken to slaughter. Nothing would remain on American Family's 40,000 acres but FrankenCarl's banties.

Raul was as startled as Carrie. "You're good," he said at last, nodding to Diana.

Carrie patted the gilt and let it through the gate. She pursed her lips, but couldn't speak. She looked up at Raul like a wild thing, terrified.

-17-

Trials of a Goddess

Three weeks before Christmas, Rosa called to say she was driving to Denver for a rally and that she'd stopped in Dalhart, which happened to be halfway. "I have news of Roberto," she said. "Lunch?"

Rosa was part of his old life, Mario's life, and for an instant Raul had difficulty placing her. In his new life, he was again a sort of lieutenant, and he was proud of how far he'd risen, but his status wasn't anything he could brag about to the likes of Rosa. "I'm working," he said, and tucked the cell phone between his cheek and shoulder, so that he could turn his screw driver. He tightened a clamp on a fluorescent light housing he'd installed at the far end of the barn. "Dinner?"

The hogs were near market weight and milled about his step ladder, their big snouts uplifted as if to offer advice. Looking down the length of the barn, you saw nothing but heads and white backs. So crowded, hogs grew collectively nervous and somewhat dangerous; you learned to move slowly among them, as if you were wading through high water.

And the air was bad. Up by the ceiling joists, it was so full of dust, particulate, and the heavy, hot smell of meat that instinctively Raul held his breath, but then he'd exhale and breathe the stuff. His mask helped, but he'd left it by his tool box.

He almost hadn't answered the phone, but sometimes Bud Varner called him with a work order. No one else.

He detected a hesitancy in Rosa's voice. "I'm across from a place called La Española."

Now he grasped the phone properly, even as he stepped

carefully down from the ladder and waved to Refugio, at the front end of the barn, to flip the breaker.

"I know it. Maybe 7:30?"

"I can't imagine your work."

He suppressed a laugh. No, pretty Rosa couldn't imagine it.

"I mean, how dirty it must be. And when summer comes, how hot. Listen, do you want to take a swim at the motel? If you don't have a suit you could buy one at your favorite store."

Walmart, she meant. The reference was almost intimate, and he envisioned Rosa's long legs in the heated pool. He gave a thumb's up to Refugio when the light fluttered on, folded the ladder under an arm, and began swimming through hogs.

"It will be wonderful to see you, Rosa."

He arrived before her, expecting her to be late, remembering that she liked to make an entrance. He grew engrossed in an article from *Popular Science*, which was arriving by mistake at the farm's office, addressed to a public relations officer who'd long since moved on. The article described a group of climate change scientists who thought they could control the weather from space. Rosa's soft voice startled him, and also her use of his name, "Mario."

And because he was startled, he couldn't control the leap of appreciation in his eyes, for her plain blue blouse and short jeans skirt, and for her Mexican-made brown boots, plain also but with a fringe of fleece outturned at their tops. A simple girl, her outfit announced, who'd spent a lot of money on being simple.

She kissed his cheek, her long hair brushed his neck, and he was a goner. Maybe he'd been a goner all along, since that evening she broke the piñata and fell into his arms.

The news of Roberto was grim. "All that stolen money," she said. "For *me.*"

His enchiladas arrived; she'd ordered a bowl of menudo and a salad with those anemic, gringo tomatoes. Two things you couldn't find in the United States: real bread and real tomatoes. The idea came to him that he could grow tomatillos up on the escarpment. A patch fifty feet by fifty would feed the colonia.

"What are you thinking?" Rosa asked.

He met her eyes. "Of poor Roberto. And of how odd it is that you and I are sitting here."

A smile broke through her tears. "How is it odd?"

"If we were in Mexico City, and I was, let us say, now a major in the Mexican army and keeping company with a woman so exquisite, it would be my great good fortune."

"Mario—" she began, almost reproachfully.

"Here, I find some contentment in being no one. I have ambitions to be a farmer, only that, while you want to change the world. And you are—still you are—Roberto's girl."

Her eyes widened, and she slid back her chair. "Excuse me."

She spent fifteen minutes in the women's room, long enough for him to pass through regret for his frankness and to decide that Rosa was fabricating another entrance. He brought out his article so that he could pretend to read, and as he reached for his coffee, she reappeared.

She stood leaning back, with her arms pulled back, too, palms grasping a railing for the handicapped wound with red and green foil. Her naked elbows turned inward, following the curve of her body, and one leg pushed forward out of the jeans skirt, as if she were about to be summoned. Her head was slightly bowed, she smiled faintly, and her wild, almost Asian eyes studied him like an atlas.

The pose haunted him for years, as somehow the single most expressive of what it was to be Rosa: simultaneously aggressive and demure. But at the moment, his eyes fell helplessly to her breasts, thrusting against her tight blouse.

He lay down money for the meal and went to her, and she glided forward as if to kiss him, but then just took his arm.

"You brought something to swim in?" she whispered.

He nodded, and they drove to the motel without speaking, she seated far opposite him, her pretty legs crossed but turned away, one Mexican boot dancing. When he cut the ignition, she stepped out quickly and walked around to his door.

"Mario," she said, taking his hand, rubbing it against her cheek. "I'm tired. I've got a long drive tomorrow."

The warm water, he thought, massaging his aches, cleansing him at last. Afterwards, the cool air in her room, and Rosa beneath the cool sheets. "You—"

"Mario knows the way to Dallas," she said, laughing.

He took Friday off and drove all day, fighting rush hour and arriving after six at the grand house where Rosa and Roberto had announced their Walmart campaign. He parked his truck between a Mercedes and Rosa's Hyundai, ducked the cascade from a sprinkler, and walked across the lush grass, around to the rear. He spied the two-story cottage house, itself finer than half the houses in the city. Rosa's mother had lived there for years, like her husband not caring much for the big house—and not caring much for her husband, either.

The mansion was for show, often featured in city magazines, and used otherwise for parties and business retreats. Rosa's father lived in the mansion, but he cared for little but business and just as often slept at his office in one of the downtown towers.

The cottage house door flew open. "I'm *so* glad to see you," Rosa said. She kissed him lightly on the lips and tugged him inside by the shirt sleeves. "Your clothes are on the couch," she said, and then hurried upstairs to her living quarters.

What? He'd driven five hundred miles, keeping awake with thoughts of Rosa's naked body. Now he felt like the FedEx man.

By "clothes" she meant a suit he recognized as Roberto's. He was surprised to find that it fit, because he was bigger than the Salvadoran; she must have gauged his sizes somehow and had everything altered. Or she'd bought an identical suit in his size. He almost went out the door again. Then he put on the suit, selecting the tie on top.

The downstairs was given over to a work room, where Rosa composed her newsletter on the plight of illegals. On three long tables stood a computer, reams of colored paper, a copying machine, stacks of printed sheets awaiting collation, and a long-armed stapler.

He sat reading the latest issue, which featured an article that attempted to track the origins of Randy DePaul's song, "Felicia." Did a real-life Felicia exist, slaving in the onion fields of Uvalde? Did it matter, if the song was true to its theme? Should white Americans try to take the point of view of Latinos? Well, yes; *more* should. Perhaps DePaul had some of his details wrong, but his song had brought a great deal of sympathy to illegals.

And to onions, Raul thought. Rosa emerged wearing heels, black pants, and a fitted white blouse with puffed long sleeves, set off with a Santa Claus pin. She achieved the exact slinky, professional look that Maribel took to church, and once again, he was struck with how much she resembled Maribel. Of course, they were opposites: Rosa the American girl, striving to be Mexican; Maribel the Mexican woman, American as money.

"I apologize for springing this on you," she said, pressing the keys to her Hyundai into his hands. "It's not fair."

He smiled agreeably. Maybe he was a hired hand, but *she* was stunning. And what else would he have done this weekend? Knocked down a bottle of rum. Slept.

"We *have* to go. The Awards Banquet. Everybody will be there."

He liked her little car and concentrated on driving, as she prattled on about how important the occasion was.

"If we're going to have any *future*—" she said, looking up at him with that perfect, precise nose and those slightly astigmatic—slightly insane—eyes.

"Yes?"

"Latinos have *got* to engage the business community, brown and black and white. So they know that we aren't just waiters and gardeners."

"And hog farmers," he murmured.

"You don't belong there, Mario," she said, patting his hand.

He handed over the car to a Latino valet, doing his best to act as though he came to this hotel every day; and as they made their way through the crowd, he smiled distantly, and hardly spoke. He shook twenty hands and said, "I'm in agriculture," until he'd worn out the phrase. "I'm with FedEx," he said, and elicited the same smiles.

Rosa hustled him into the banquet room, where "God Rest Ye Merry Gentlemen" played and where braised chicken, a vegetable medley, a white-bread roll, and chocolate mousse awaited. The coffee wasn't bad, though he longed for a cigar.

The lights came down and important people spoke, exactly as when, back in Mexico City, they'd mustered out the cadets to provide an audience for doddering General Jiménez, who received a medal for something or other. Tonight many generals displayed themselves, and colonels and proud enlisted men. All were outstanding and deserved an award. Rosa herself received an award, and he stood loyally, applauding.

It was over. Those who hadn't received awards headed for the doors, while the awarded crisscrossed the room. Rosa, acquainted with everyone, laughing her merry laugh, flashing those wild eyes, talked and drank. Raul spotted her father, tall and grave, also an award winner, and the old man threw him one hard stare.

She changed into slacks and a sloppy sweatshirt, he got out of the suit, and she mixed margaritas in a blender until she achieved a pink slush. She was already drunk and happy. Apparently what he'd done at the banquet, which was nothing, had sufficed.

She dipped the lips of their glasses into salt, just so, and put out sliced limes.

"Nice," he said. He took a sip and kissed her, but she turned her head. He moved from the couch to the chair opposite.

"It was sweet of you to come, Mario," she said.

He studied a light fixture through the prism of his margarita. "Think nothing of it," he said, grandly waving a hand.

"I talked to Tim Irwin tonight."

He'd be a while understanding the pace of this. She treated him like a gringo husband, and he knew what they were like only from watching television. Bumbling, though assertive fools, always outsmarted by their wives. "That's good," he said, affecting a supportive tone and as if he knew the distinguished Mr. Irwin from their many business dealings.

"He's going to send me the forms for the Marshall Fellowship."

"Really!" The girl certainly knew how to make margaritas. "What's the Marshall Fellowship?"

"An all-expenses sabbatical in Belgium. To learn about international relations and diplomacy. Tim says they're right up on the deadline but he thinks I have a good chance."

He'd forgotten she was a student. "You're studying. . . ?"

"Latin American studies and political science," she said, sighing. "Next year, I have to come up with a doctoral thesis."

"Something about illegals," he suggested.

"Yes!" She smiled admiringly. "Maybe you can help me."

"I'll be part of your data." He rose and brought over the pitcher of margaritas. "These are *very* good, Rosa."

"My father taught me." Shoulders slumping, she looked up at him, and he bent from dizzying heights to kiss her. Then he dropped besides her, and they kissed for a long time. He began pulling up her sweatshirt.

She caught his hand. "You're not *macho*, that's what I like about you."

"Not like Roberto."

She hung her head. "I feel so guilty."

"We can be sorry for him in the prison, we could even send him money, but he'll never be back."

Crying, she marched unsteadily to the downstairs bathroom, and when she returned she'd combed down her hair, pulled on a long tee shirt, and was barefooted. Her feet were narrow and small.

"I came after you," she whispered.

"Very American," he said, kissing her.

She pushed him back. "I'm a proud Latina, Mario!"

"You wouldn't like it much in Mexico. Few opportunities exist for women—"

"I know!"

"Or for men."

"Oh," she whispered. "You've had such a hard life."

He held her soft face in his rough hands—gently, as if he might cut her. He turned her head as if to achieve a more divine pose. He raised her arms and pulled up her tee shirt.

She unbuckled his belt, and in moments, he stood naked, too, his erection poking at her belly. She bent to taste him, but he was quickly losing control and caught her in his arms and carried her up the stairs, reeling backward once.

She offered a ritual fight, beating lightly at his arms and kissing his chest simultaneously. He pushed open her bedroom door with a knee and lay her on the bed like an offering to the gods.

"Under the sheets," she whispered.

And he rolled her to the side and pulled down the bedspread. She lay before him, long brown legs pulled chastely together. She opened her eyes and wouldn't let him go, and he could do no more than enter her and explode.

In the middle of the night, he said, "What do you want with me, Rosa?"

And she said, "What do you want with *me?*"

"What is our future? I am illegal, while you—you are going to be an ambassador."

"You think so!"

"The future, Rosa."

"Already, he's so *serious.* I'll introduce you to my father tomorrow. He'll—"

"Shoot me on the spot."

She slipped under the sheet, said, "*This* is the future, Mario," and took his penis in her mouth.

She slipped him inside her and leaned forward to kiss him, rolling her breasts over his chest. Afterwards, he slept. But even at breakfast, when they tried to sit up like normal folks, like the Latino middle class, like suburbanites, they were bad children. He crawled under the table, parted her legs, teased her with his tongue. They hurried up the stairs, pawing at each other, and fucked, and laughed, and then went out somewhere to eat, and in the movies necked like teenagers. Sleepless, sore, they fucked, and made burritos, and watched television. Birds sang in the trees, the sprinklers came on and went off, and her father's diesel Mercedes chugged throatily to life.

Mario, too, had to work, had to call to explain his lateness, had to resume being Raul. Still, she pulled at him, unwilling to give him up, because if their idyll ended it could never quite be resumed. That was worth everything, wasn't it, to find bliss amid sorrow and know that you'd found it?

He got off early but only by working a twelve-hour Thursday, loading hogs from the dwindling valley operation. He was so weary on the drive he napped for a while in a Walmart parking lot.

The truck's starter was going out. The Bendix caught the flywheel three times, then missed it for two, whirring in space, but with so many trips to Dallas, he had no time for an overhaul. He didn't dare cut the engine except on a grade. Then he pushed the truck until he had some speed, jumped in, and popped the clutch in second.

Even if the truck were in perfect repair, gasoline gulped down his wages. Refugio said, "Run with your tailgate down," but after two trips he couldn't measure an improvement, or the one-fourth mile per gallon he calculated had, finally, to be attributed to a tail wind. He over-inflated his tires and picked up 1.5 mpg, and then reluctantly, but relentlessly, dropped his speed to fifty-five. His mileage improved from sixteen to twenty-three, saving about $20 a trip.

His poverty bled into the dread he felt, each time he drew near to Highland Park. He didn't belong in such a neighborhood. He betrayed not only Roberto, but the other Raul.

Then came that night in January when the feeble Dallas winter heated up, and he could almost turn on the air-   conditioning. The truck had failed to start twice, both times in awkward places to give it a push. Such incidents always proved solvable, but they left him apprehensive about being stranded.

All the fans in her house ran. It was only eight, but Rosa had turned the lights low; when he called, she didn't answer. Maybe he could mix a rum and coke, and pass out on her thick carpet.

He walked to the easy chair to retrieve the remote and saw Rosa on the couch, wearing her jeans skirt and those dazzling Mexican boots. She crossed and re-crossed her legs, and drew a blanket over them. She stared with such hatred he fell back.

"How'd you get in?" she hissed.

His head throbbed. "The key you gave me."

"Roberto's here."

"Roberto!"

"He went to his old place to get a gun. I told him you raped me."

"Rosa, what are you saying? Roberto, poor Roberto, he's—"

She rose quickly and slapped him. "Raped me."

"He can't be here. But if he is—"

"He'll kill you." She ran to the stairs as if he were chasing her and turned. "I'll call the police. I'll turn you in."

Her excitement failed to transfer. He felt more like an estranged father than a lover, and studied her overwrought face for doubt, for signs of delusion. "Are you high on something, Rosa?"

She took three steps up the stairs. "Don't you come after me!"

He wasn't going to. It was time to call it quits, if she had to resort to a rape fantasy to be excited. He went out the door. All that sex, the nectar and decay of it, the spell it cast, was slavery. And he was going to be free. Free of those agonizing drives. Free of Rosa, the divine.

He turned the key, and the Bendix whirred in air.

"Mario!" Rosa came running across the green grass, and he rolled down his window.

"I was in a play like that, you're so—so *stiff*, sometimes. It was a *joke*."

"A poor one, to involve Roberto, our friend in jail. Rape?"

"I'm *sorry*."

She climbed into the truck, and he was too weary, and yet too proud, to tell her about his unreliable starter. He turned the key, and the engine shuddered to life.

"Mierda!" he said. He didn't want to go anywhere but drove anyway. Rosa sulked, but she was at fault, and he had nothing to say. He pulled off in Richardson at Pancho's Buffet and cut the engine. Behind them, along bloody Highway 75, the traffic roared past Papa John's, Pet Palace, Walmart, and Mattress Land.

"They're *closed*," Rosa said.

"I'm sick of your fancy restaurants," he said. "We'll come here tomorrow."

"You can come by yourself."

He lit a cigar, which she hated as much as Maribel had. "Roberto brought me here when I was near to suicide."

She shrieked. At the cigar? At mention of Roberto? She cried inconsolably, but he remained unconvinced. He turned the key, and the starter clicked like a gathering of crickets and failed to engage the flywheel.

"Oh, great," Rosa said, instantly recovering. "You could *buy* a new truck. Roberto said you had enough stashed to buy Plano, but oh no, not Mario. Mario, the frugal. Mario, the monk."

"There isn't a grade here," he said neutrally. "I have to push. I yell, you release the clutch—"

"I've done it," she said. "I had a Volkswagen once, the same fucking thing."

They started the truck, and he climbed in on the passenger's side because he couldn't stay awake anymore. She looked at him, prepared for more battle, but he closed his eyes.

And then they were in the cottage house again, and she made him a drink and took off his shoes, and they talked like the old friends they were. She promised never to try such a stunt again. She pulled a bag of marijuana from a cookie jar and passed him the joint. When she went to the door for the pizza she'd ordered, she floated like a goddess.

He slept on her Persian carpet, and at three in the morning, stumbled up to her bedroom, and she pulled herself close. The sweet haze of love permeated everything, and he forgot that, long ago, he'd wanted to be free.

Of course, she had to visit the farm. She stayed for two weeks, this God-sent girlfriend, and it was like a honeymoon.

She donned old clothes and strolled between the trailers in the colonia. To be among the people! Even the word "colonia" spoke to her, reserved as it often was for squatters' settlements around onion feeds and pecan orchards, with their shifting populations of legals and illegals. Colonia implied that workers had a right to their territory, that they'd taken back a piece of Texas.

She donned blues one day and walked down the aisle of a hog barn—or tried to. Quickly, the gassy stench overcame her, and she fled outside and popped out her contacts. But she observed through the windows, took extensive notes. She interviewed workers, recording them and working up their histories.

"For your doctorate?" he asked.

"What an opportunity—what a rich *world*—you've shown me, Mario."

No matter how she dressed down—hair subdued under a scarf, pretty feet encased in engineer's boots, and legs hidden under baggy jeans—she still seemed like a goddess. The last thing Rosa wanted was to appear to be slumming it, and yet that's what everyone thought.

They liked her, though. The shy señoras pointed her out to their daughters as an example of who they might become. They humored her as she burped their babies and folded their laundry, and listened good-humoredly to her health tips and pointers about government benefits. As for the men—

"You are one lucky bastard, amigo," said Refugio.

"Quite a gal, Raul," Bud Varner said. "Ain't you a little outta your league?"

He couldn't do much about the condition of his trailer, but he bought a new mattress—bringing it in after dark, to escape the catcalls—and bedding to go with it. On Friday nights while she drove to Dalhart, he mopped the floor, swabbed the toilet, and prayed that the smell of hydrogen sulfide blew toward Oklahoma. She arrived at midnight, dragged her little airline suitcase into the bedroom, and related her struggles—the struggles, he sometimes thought, of a heroine in a novel—through the week. She claimed she wouldn't be any fun tonight because she was so worn out. He said, take your bath, Rosa, and you'll feel better. And then they made love all night.

But he saw it coming. He couldn't blame her, anymore than you could hold a javalina responsible for not being an iguana. In

just three weeks, she could no longer find any charm in the colonia. And by February, they exhausted such entertainments as
Dalhart offered—and Amarillo, for that matter, where he drove
them night after sleepy night and cruised until Rosa found the
perfect restaurant.

She said that if he loved her, he'd quit his dreadful job and
move in with her.

"What would I *do*?"

"Maybe what you were doing for that religious woman, you
know, the handy man stuff. Daddy owns a lot of old houses."

Her father was forbidding, but Mario did good work; perhaps he could win the man over. Yes, her plan had merit if in the
bargain they were married and the problem of his being illegal
were on its way to a solution. Still, they never quite had that
should-we-get-married talk.

Every trip to Dallas, he thought, *I'll propose*, but always she'd
forgotten to talk to her father about the job. *Ask* him, he said.

I will. Mario, I *will*.

On her next-to-last visit, Rosa saw Carrie. Dusk neared, and
they'd thought about driving to Dalhart and getting a room because, though he'd closed every window, it was one of those
days when the smell of hog manure descended on the colonia.
Rosa stood by the window at the end of the trailer, where a
bay window bulged over the hitch. He sat at the formica table,
stunned by her perfection. How possibly could such a creature
have ended up here, in this beat-up trailer house, in his little
corner of hell?

"Who *is* that woman?"

Perhaps he'd been too receptive to Carrie, but she seemed so
lonely. And she was a relief from Rosa, so effortless to be with,
like an extension of himself. Slowly, it came to him that Rosa
was suspicous, and . . . jealous? Of Carrie? She was a friend,
hardly "another woman." And how could another woman
tempt you when a goddess stood at your side?

"Is she your playmate? Look at her, on that bicycle."

He wrapped his arms around Rosa and tried to draw her
back. "She's a supervisor. A scientist—very intelligent. Really—"

"Look at her. Something's *wrong* with her."

He sighed. "She's awkward, sometimes, but—" Now he saw
her, turning the bike around in jerky motions, peddling slowly
away. She was too large for the bike, for any bike; her broad

shoulders, draped in a sweater big as a barrel, overwhelmed it. Still, he knew why she'd bought it. She'd seen him riding toward the back of the farm and wanted to join him. Maybe, as Rosa surmised, Carrie was more than a friend. How did women know these things?

"She's got muscles," Rosa said. "Somebody should buy her some clothes. Poor thing."

He nodded miserably and remained silent. Coming to Carrie's defense trapped him inside Rosa's jealousy, which wasn't jealousy anyhow, but her desire for him to return to Dallas. In that moment he knew, like Roberto who'd gone to jail for her, that he wasn't man enough for Rosa.

He heard her throwing things around the bathroom, but did not rise to comfort her. He mixed a rum and Coke. He couldn't reason with her, so always he gave in, and then the sex was glorious. Wild, delirious, maybe spiritual sex, but slowly she'd begin her assault again, her illogic a battalion mounted against a tired old soldier.

No, he couldn't return to Dallas. At the same time, she couldn't move to Dalhart; what would she do? Yes! Yes! He understood. Why couldn't she understand that in Dallas he was nothing? Lord, he'd die for her, but he'd already played step-and-fetch-it to a strong woman. He didn't like the role.

He mixed another drink as she came busily down the hall, banging her rolling suitcase against the paper-thin paneling. She didn't have to go yet. She was making a point about the horrid trailer, the stench of the colonia, his inscrutable choices. He was supposed to rush forward with regret and passion—but too much passion; that was Rosa. Even if he *could* go to Dallas—

He didn't turn at the precise, optimally dramatic moment, when she faced him. He let her crash out the door. He came to the window, but didn't chase after her. He heard the yowling of coyotes far back on the farm, then the *ding! ding! ding!* when she opened her car door, and then an affected "Mierda! Mierda!" Her skills in Spanish were one of her vanities, but she wasn't very fluent.

In a burst—roaring to the right in reverse and screeching away—she was gone. He carried his drink to the front steps and placed his cell phone near. He didn't suppose the affair was done, but sorrow swept over him. Wasn't there something in life besides love? Religion, he thought, laughing softly.

She called, and they talked until two, and he made that interminable drive once more. At least he'd had time to fix his starter.

All Saturday he helped compose and print her newsletter. A piece she'd been expecting didn't materialize, and he wrote without stopping how his mother had worked for years to support the family when his father couldn't sell his crops anymore.

It was because of the laws the capitalist pigs had passed, she said.

"Put that in, too?"

"Yes!" she said, and then shook her head. "No, you can't say that anymore. We've struggled and struggled to nail down a few ads. Business is our future. No."

He called the piece, "Mi madre santa." Rosa said it was the finest, purest thing she'd ever run. She translated his words, running the Spanish side-by-side to the English, and they finished the entire newsletter a day before deadline—punching it up on her website as well. They made love, and next day enjoyed a sleepy farewell lunch at their new favorite restaurant, Pancho's Buffet.

Back in Dalhart he wrote to say that he loved her, but wasn't her equal. What nonsense, she replied, you're a wonderful man. But she didn't make the drive west, and two weeks passed. It was over, he thought, a three-month affair. Amanda lasted longer.

Winter wasn't over, but he had no time to lose. South of Dalhart, he bought a grey market tractor, a three-cylinder Yanmar diesel without a roll bar. He hauled it atop the escarpment, and far back on the farm, at an abandoned hacienda, he found a rusting, four-bottom disc. He bathed the disc in oil, and still it squawked when he pulled it, left the ground imperfectly cultivated, had no effect on the mesquite and huisache. He'd have no end of hoeing and spade work.

He was on the escarpment on a sunny Saturday afternoon when Rosa came bumping along in her little car. Perhaps she'd called—he'd left his phone in the trailer. She wore that jeans skirt again, and the boots he loved. She held up a basket. "We can have a picnic," she said.

She didn't ask about his tractor. He supposed she hardly saw it. He jammed his shovel under a huisache stump, finally

busting through. Huisache roots didn't grow as deeply as mesquite, but even so, they wore him out. He pulled at the stump
and fell back, out of breath, angry. He was angry at all huisache
trees and didn't want to see Rosa. "My work may seem quaint
to you—"

A look crossed her face that surprised him. It was almost
fear. "You could say hello!"

"Hello? Yes, yes, I'm sorry. But this will be a little farm,
Rosa. My experiment. For years I have wanted—"

"What will you grow?"

"Who knows?" He threw up his hands. "Maybe pumpkins."

"I'll buy them from you."

He snarled. "From your token illegal? Your Roberto re-
placement?"

"You *know* that's not true." Her face twisted in agony, and
she dropped to her knees beside him. For an instant she had the
look of a prayerful Madonna—not just beautiful, but ethereal.
"I will buy them for Guadalupe Arts. We have a children's program, Latino kids—any kid; every year they carve pumpkins.
They—pumpkins—are expensive in Dallas. You could make a
good profit, and still we'd save money. I want to—to make you
happy, Mario. Why can I never make you *happy*?"

He held her close. Oh, it just couldn't be, but he knew she
was sincere, and guilt flooded his soul. "You *do* make me happy.
How could any man be so lucky? Rosa, you're a—"

"Don't say it," she said. "Oh, *please* don't say it."

So he didn't tell her she was a goddess, though he'd called
her that in bed often enough. He kissed her wet cheeks and
stroked her hair, and said, "I know where we can go."

He drove them far back on the place to the ruined hacienda, where he'd found the disc and where there was another
of those old windmills, with ponderous blades, slowly turning
like a forgotten clock. He found a patch of grass that was almost green. He spread out her blanket, and they sat looking
toward the golden mountains of New Mexico as they ate her
sandwiches. They were good, of course. She'd found a perfect
German deli on her way from Dallas.

"Let's join the rebels, Mario. The Cíbolistas."

"They exist?"

"Who knows for sure? Things get blown up. The *Cíbolistas*
get blamed."

He stared, but didn't believe she knew what Roberto and he had done. "They were the ones who robbed the bank."

"Maybe. I'd love to do an article."

"And took over Columbus."

"Yes, they idolize Pancho Villa because of his raid. I heard a man speak in Dallas. He says they are five thousand strong."

He said softly, "I wanted to think of them as utopians. Not as an army."

"Of course. But if you have nothing, if the system is fixed so that all you'll ever have is nothing, then maybe blowing it all up—"

"I've read some history, Rosa. I understand."

"That would be us among the rebels, Mario—with nothing. Starting over. You could be an officer again." Her voice faltered. "And I wouldn't have to be a. . . "

"You'd be a goddess anywhere," he whispered, and he couldn't bear it anymore, her beauty, her good intentions, how mismatched they were. He set the basket aside and drew her to him. Slowly, he bent her back onto the blanket.

"I won the Marshall Fellowship," she whispered.

"I knew you would."

"It was all very last minute. I go to Belgium next week. I bought a ticket, and I . . . thought about you."

"Try to get *me* through security." He rolled from her and studied the wispy clouds. "I will grow some pumpkins, Rosa. For your children." His next speech came harder. "My . . . *support* for what you do. And I—Rosa, I believe that—we should stop seeing each other."

He thought she agreed. They needn't go down the checklist of all the reasons they should part. She nestled close to him and whispered something he couldn't decipher. And then, with the windmill's shadows crisscrossing them, they made love in the late winter sun. It wasn't an act of mutual desperation, but two friends saying goodbye. As always, it was sweet. It was the only thing they were any good at.

-18-

The Farmer

Roberto once said to him, as if speculating whether it would rain, that the best way to get over a woman was to seek out another. In the end he couldn't follow his own advice. Rosa did him in.

Roberto had also said, about Amanda, that she'd be easy to get rid of. The man was a barbarian.

Mario had brought things to their only logical conclusion, and if he hadn't, Rosa would have. Yes, but love wasn't logical. If it were, if A led to B, then surely C would be celibacy. Just the opposite of Roberto's theorum: cut out Rosa, not like a cancer, but because she was sweet—and beyond his reach. Put her out of your head, soldier. Get to work.

She wasn't so sweet. She was ambitious and manipulative.

She was what every man wanted.

Correction: she was what every man lusted after. You could not drink enough of her, and years from now, when he was old and bent, he'd still summon images of her, in the bathroom brushing her teeth, in his arms beneath the windmill.

Logically, he should be able to clear his mind of thoughts that wasted his time and depressed him; he should make lists in the morning and carry them rigorously through; he should will his mind to focus on machinery, on seeds and live plants and scientific articles and—well, the meaning of life.

Rosa was the meaning, and he'd missed out. Rosa was the ultimate lesson in how, if you were illegal, you'd always miss out. Hiding yourself away, doing lowly work because nothing else was available, that was the meaning of life. His life.

He tore up her phone number—and looked it up again. He burned his photographs of her. Dully, he realized that *she* hadn't called or e-mailed. He'd freed himself of her, but she also of him.

She never introduced me to her father or any of her college friends. I was a fantasy!

He wasn't a fantasy, but *her* attempt to find meaning. When he couldn't provide it, she went back to her life of causes. The immigration issue and Belgium. A Ph.D. And then perhaps another poor fellow without documents.

Now it was April, and he was falling behind on the escarpment. Two rains had fallen, and the creek flowed full; he might not have such luck in another year.

How he despised being lovesick!

He remembered a woman in the trailer park. She worked at Dollar General and had given him the eye more than once. All the señoras disapproved of her without saying why, but he knew; everyone knew.

He had two drinks and drove to town. He parked behind the old Camaro that sat in the same spot when Ernesto fixed the F-150. Here was the point, ordinarily, where he'd lose his nerve, but not tonight. Used, meaningless, he knocked on her door. She stood before him, her legs plump silhouettes under her house coat, not bad-looking except for the false eyebrows. Later, he tried to remember what he said to her, but it didn't matter. She dropped her eyes, took a step backward, and handed him a beer. Her name was Marta or Marfa or Felicia.

They sat on her couch, and he counted out one hundred dollars. The fee guaranteed that he wouldn't have to see her again.

American Family maintained four crop circles, two atop the escarpment, two directly below. A creek ran down the middle, forming a thin waterfall as it fell over the escarpment, and dropped into a murky pond.

He worked furiously, mostly with a shovel, pike, and axe. The ground was moist now, the sun merciful late in the day, but Bud Varner told him that the spring would dry up by July—by June, in some years. So he dug and ditched, and channeled the little creek under a rock shelf, forming a pool; and he dug down below, too, shoring up the pond with railroad ties and dirt, to keep what remained of the creek from disappearing on the dry desert floor. Here his tractor helped; he borrowed a blade from the company.

He wore out three pairs of gloves, and his hands were cracked and calloused and pierced from huisache thorns, but still he had ditches to dig. Even though the circles had been laser-leveled, they tilted slightly toward the creek, and he ditched the run-off and the puddles that formed around the big pumps, channeling water toward the creek. Using pumps, siphons, and drip lines looped around stems, he figured he could nurse his crops through August if just one or two rains fell to help, and if the creek held up even through June.

After a dozen passes with the disc, he had half an acre under control. The soil was rocky and thin, but certainly he could mix in manure; all he needed was water. That's what farming was: water.

He made coldframes from window sashes and started tomatillos and five kinds of peppers, then in plastic pots he planted cucumbers and honeydews. He worked until dark, cutting out rows, stretching drip lines, and planting radishes, kohlrabi, onion sets, and cabbage. Always before he quit, with his last energy, he propped up a lantern and grubbed out another mesquite root.

Their circumference was larger underground than above, and they reached so deep a bulldozer couldn't uproot them, but he wrapped a chain around one and goosed the tractor. The front wheels lifted up, he almost turned over, but other than skinning off bark, he had no effect. So he clawed his way two feet down with pick and shovel, then attacked the root with a chainsaw and axe, until the monster's head fell off. By then he was so exhausted, he didn't think about Rosa or need rum to sleep.

He had the two acres on top under control by mid-May and planted his cucumbers and peppers. Then he hauled the disc down to the colonia and up the valley past Hog Heaven, to the other crop circles. Nothing grew in the uncultivated land but stands of prickly pear and a tall wild flower called Apache plume. He ran the disc in wide circles, nibbling at the stuff, and then crisscrossed in bolder strokes, bringing his feet to the steering wheel so he wouldn't be speared with needles. Thankfully, cactus didn't grow as tall in the Panhandle as in Coahuila.

Jack rabbits, packrats, and two mule deer ran ahead of him. Swallows that nested in the escarpment face dive-bombed him, snatching up insects. Soon enough, green cactus blood mixed with the red earth in an acrid slush, and he sat back, cut the engine, and lit a Grenadier.

"Sweet corn," he announced to the stars.

In June, when his sweet corn was ankle-high and he wondered if it would ever rain again, he began to see Carrie, climbing the old Kiowa trail along the waterfall, as cooler air dropped with the sun. She waved and kept walking. Sometimes, she brought her camera to shoot road runners and hawks, Apache Plume and evening primrose, and even the prickly pear in its various stages of bloom. Raul looked for her every evening and was disappointed when she didn't come. Already, he'd sold radishes, leaf lettuce, and kohlrabi.

One evening Romeo ran ahead of her and threw himself in the pool, while she climbed a boulder above the creek and watched Raul work. After a while, she came down to his makeshift shed and grabbed another hoe. "This is amazing," she called out. "The *work* you did!"

He grinned. Gardening—farming—was full of little triumphs and reversals, and he enjoyed sharing them with anyone who cared.

"What's this new plot going to be?"

He hesitated. "Pumpkins."

"They take just buckets of water. August will be hard. You'll drip them?"

"Yes. Everything."

They hoed his onions, potatoes, and honeydews, all growing fast now. They could barely make out the plants in the moonlight, and the drip line, like a long black snake, was still harder to see. They both stopped simultaneously, knowing it was long past time to quit.

"It's wonderful," she said. "It's *smart.*"

He shrugged, but she'd found the only thing he was vain about. "It might not work. And next year, maybe I'll have even less water to work with. But it's what I've always wanted to do."

"Really?"

"Since I was a kid. My father had a place, not even this big, though water wasn't such a problem." He stared at her. "I'll sell what I raise in the colonia."

"*Very* smart. The women won't have to drive all the way to town for that crap at Walmart. Make sure you give some to Alejandro in the tienda, so he doesn't get mad at you."

He nodded. "That is wise, Carrie. I hadn't thought of that."

"How will you kill the weeds? You can't keep hoeing all this."

"Well, in country so dry, if you just drip the vegetables, you starve out the weeds."

"Not all of them. Not the stubborn ones. Listen, there's an old roto-tiller in the yellow barn. I think it still runs. Then maybe you could put down black plastic. Grass clippings would be better, but I don't know where you'd get them. Used to be you could in Dalhart, but it's so dry nobody mows anymore."

He stared, but couldn't read her face in the waning light. "You're right, Carrie. I could use a roto-tiller."

"Maybe I could help you. With hoeing? Setting up a stand?"

"Oh, no—" Why would she want to help? He thought all the way back to the day they'd rescued Romeo, how she'd looked up at him, innocent, yearning—lonely. He'd been so dazzled by Rosa he hadn't proved much of a friend.

"It's what *I've* always wanted to do," she went on. "You don't have to pay me. Except in tomatoes, maybe."

"It's fun tonight, in the moonlight." He laughed. "We'll see what your attitude is in July, when it's 110 out here."

They both turned toward the creek, where a black shape raced toward them.

"What is it?" Raul asked. "Carrie, get in the truck, I'll—"

She laughed. "Romeo!"

He ran up between them and shook himself, raining all over them. Before Carrie could scold him, he barked once and jumped into Raul's pickup bed—at last showing some manners.

Raul covered his tractor with a tarp, and they slid into his pickup and jostled along the company road in second gear.

Carrie yawned and stretched her arms, almost filling the cab. "Sometimes, Dad and I would come in from the field late. If he was in a good mood, he'd take me to the Dairy Queen."

"What about your mother, Carrie?"

"Oh, she left us."

"You were raised by your father?"

"More or less. You?"

"No, both my parents were there. Your father is still on the farm?"

"He cleared out last summer. He's up in Canada."

"Canada!"

"Yes, he thinks . . . where are we going?"

"You said you wanted ice cream. Payment for your work tonight."

She hit him with a fist, and it hurt a little. "I wasn't hinting. It's just a good memory, that's all. We don't need to—"

"Oh, Romeo needs a ride."

They hadn't much to say, suddenly, and briefly he felt the same guilt he used to with Rosa, showing the lady a town that had been mundane in the best of times and now was full of boarded-up businesses and desiccated parks. But Dalhart was Carrie's town, too, and he wasn't courting her; they were just pals. They went through the drive-up, and he ordered a Peanut Buster parfait, she a banana split, and awkwardly came up with exact change between them. Yes, he might have done this with Rosa. She might have enjoyed it.

"Did you see my new bicycle, Raul?"

"Looks like a good one."

"It's a big, strong bike. I ride it up to Hog Heaven."

He finished the sundae and longed to light a cigar.

"You want to go riding sometime?"

"Sure, Carrie."

"Back on the farm? Whereever it is you go with that girl."

He didn't respond. He felt cornered.

"She's really pretty."

He started the engine and slowly backed out.

"I'm sorry," she said. "I just noticed—I walk by your place, sometimes—"

"She's gone, Carrie. Four months now."

"I'm sorry! I'm an idiot!"

They turned off for the farm before he spoke again. "Some Sunday soon," he said. "Before it gets too hot."

She sighed. And he could have sworn she giggled. "An adventure!"

"You may be surprised."

-19-

Feral

They peddled and coasted for several miles along the perimeter road that the hog patrols had driven but that might have been one hundred years old. Carrie couldn't keep up with Raul, and on a slow grade, where freezes had buckled the gravel, she had to dismount and push. When she caught up, he was leaning against a high limestone boulder, smooth and concave from eons of scaling, streaked black from leaching manganese. Five miles from the farm, you entered a wilderness.

He smoked a cigar, studying her, coming slowly to the realization that she hated the smell. He held it up. He loved the things, but if you escaped the stench of hogs, you ought to revel in fresh air—desert air notably, with intermittent odors of sage and juniper, and their harsh purity.

She stopped at a flat place in the road. "You look like Clint Eastwood."

"Thank you, Señorita." He laughed and stepped onto his bike again. "It isn't much farther."

She climbed slowly to her feet. "Down?"

"Down and up, Carrie. Are you truly worn out?"

"I just—can't—go on," she said, shoulders slumped, eyes downcast, and then with a giggle she pushed down hard and vaulted past him over the grade. The rock face twisted sharply, and then the road followed a smooth, slow grade downhill for half a mile, onto an ancient flood plain. Before them stretched rock-and-juniper strewn New Mexico, stretching to yellowish low mountains that hunkered like crowns. Carrie hit the sandy basin in fourth gear, twisting crazily around bumps, not looking back, while Raul fell behind. Inhaling the heavy scent of honey mesquite, he pushed hard and gained again on Carrie, who had to shift down. By the new crest, she was in low gear, standing up, and it looked as though each push was her last. Raul passed her again.

He dismounted and stepped from boulder to boulder up a dry, precipitous creek bed. "Watch for rattlesnakes," he called back, and veered into the mesquite branches along a deer trace, through yucca and gray buffalo grass that rasped in the wind, and toward the low summit.

The trail grew easier, and he waited. When she came into view, he signaled her to drop to the ground. They crawled through the dry grass into a stand of bristly junipers, where the grade dropped down a pebbly plain into a valley. The valley itself ended at a low mesa below which cottonwoods grew, with squat oaks beneath them. Somewhere along the base of the mesa, a spring seeped.

He settled on his elbows, focused his binoculars, and then handed them across. "Under the cottonwoods."

She saw them immediately along a dark pool. "Wild hogs. That boar—"

"The old black one?"

"He's the king. A Russian boar."

He laughed. "Not Mexican? Australian?"

"His lineage, Raul. Maybe a hundred years ago, a man in New Jersey brought in Russian boars for a hunting preserve, and some of them escaped."

"So far west?"

"Some say the Spanish brought black ones, too. Anyhow, he's the kind trophy hunters go after." She returned the binoculars. "See his tusks?"

"I've been thinking about shooting him."

"He'd be good to eat. The sows, too, if they're not too old, with plenty of barbecue sauce. They're not so far from domestic."

"How many, you think?"

She took the glasses again. "More than thirty, that I can see, and several litters. Lots more in all that brush. I'd say at least two hundred. How'd you find them?"

"Something tore up my potatoes, and I followed the trail."

"They're like rats. No license, no limit. You can shoot a dozen if you want, and the State of Texas will give you a medal."

"A barbecue is what I had in mind. For the Day of the Dead."

"You mean Halloween? In October?"

"Close enough. Will they still be here?"

"This is Hog Central. They've got water. And lots of little pigs, Raul. They won't go anywhere."

"Then maybe four of those sows. And the old boar."

"A fiesta! We could hire one of those Mexican bands like they have at weddings. You know what I mean?"

He shrugged. "Sí, Señorita."

She rolled over on her back and closed her eyes. "Of course, you do. Listen, can you shoot?"

He reached out and touched her nose, startling her. "I was in the army, Carrie, in Mexico. I was the best marksman in my company."

"Oh." The sky was a pale blue, the clouds white like a new tee shirt. The air was suffused with the camphorous smell of junipers. "I have a thirty-aught-six with a telescopic sight."

He nodded. "A deer rifle. You're really something, Carrie."

"Thank you." She closed her eyes, concentrating. "You'll need help butchering."

"I can get Manny and Refugio," he said. "Mr. Varner, too."

"And me." She sat up. "My dad and I—sometimes, I was all the help he had. I know how to make fresh sausage, too."

He nodded without commitment, crawled backwards twenty feet, and walked ahead of her down the deer trace. Her voice drifted down: "We used hickory back home. To smoke the meat? Here, they use mesquite."

He caught her eyes as she burst from the brush, and she wouldn't stop looking at him. He sat on his bike, eying her steadily as well.

"I've been cleaning out barns in the valley all week. How does it go with your banties?"

She seemed relieved. "Fifty-two percent."

"I'm sorry?"

"Pregnant. We'll run the others through again this week."

"They are odd little hogs. Mr. Varner says they're unnatural. I mean, they have that human DNA—"

"So do baboons, or we have *their* DNA; it's just that no one inserted it." She sighed. "Sometimes, they're almost like children. Almost intelligent, you know?"

"Yes, I have felt that. I'm not sure such experiments should be made. Have you talked to your supervisor, the one in the East, about this?"

"Kansas City, Raul. It's hardly the East."

"I've only seen Texas." He paused. "And Oklahoma once. I'm thinking this job will not last much longer, and I'll go to a place called Arkansas."

"They get rain there." She went silent for a moment. "To answer your question, I did bring it up; I asked about publishing—all the stuff we talked about. Carl just cares about the pregnancy rate. 'You can teach them to fetch if you want, as long as they're healthy,' he says. He thinks he'll have his results, and people will say, it's cheap, it solves a big problem, it *works*. Then I'll be publishing all over the place."

Raul shrugged. Mutant hogs didn't concern him, suddenly. They turned their bikes around and looked over New Mexico. Massive clouds marched northward, casting shadows on the red land.

"I have some errands in Dalhart," he said at last. "We could get something to eat."

"Right now?"

"If you are available."

"A date?"

His nostrils flared in a tiny ripple of pride. Just for a moment, she was playing hard-to-get. Yes, he supposed it was a "date." He had no words.

"Your hair's turning gray," she said.

He threw out his chest in mock-outrage. "You think I'm too *old?*"

She kept her eyes low, as if considering. She shook her head slowly, and then her smile formed, but still she didn't lift her eyes. "I love you," she said.

IV. Another Country

-20-

The Hunt

In August, coons got into Raul's sweet corn. They preferred it to American Family's field corn. He set out a trap, a cage with a plate on the bottom that, when the coon stepped on it, tripped the door. He baited it with a can of cat food, but the damn things were so smart they could walk into the cage, steal the bait, and never disturb the plate. Bud Varner told him to bore a hole in the can, and attach it to the cage with baling wire, on the theory that the coon would abandon caution in its struggle with the can.

Next day, he caught a mangy old rascal that stank of carrion and snarled as Raul approached. When he shot it, holding the barrel an inch from its brain, it thrashed about for almost a minute. The old fellow had big, callused feet, and claws worthy of a bear. Raul went about spilling its blood, and the scent kept coons away thereafter.

Except for one more, a foolish youngster, and it didn't snarl as Raul approached. It just looked at him. Those eyes! They weren't innocent exactly. They were resigned. Like a downer, the coon knew it was dead. Raul shot it and scolded himself for feeling regretful: either he killed coons or lost his corn. Then he understood. In the animal's wild, sad eyes he glimpsed Carrie.

It grieved him to hurt her feelings, because truly he liked her. Admired her. But love? Love was confusing and risky. What *was* love? Still he popped awake, thinking of Rosa—was that love? If so, as all the stupid songs told you, and the stupid movies, and the stupid books, love was misery.

.

He knew when Carrie went to work and made a point of arriving earlier or later. He detoured her trailer when he drove to town. Still, they ran into each other accidentally—or, it almost seemed, as if some force beyond his understanding drew them together. Was guileless Carrie suddenly calculating, deducing where he was likely to be, and creating an errand? Perhaps not. She threw him terrified looks and hurried past.

He was overwhelmed—blessed—with work. The maintenance crew pitched in to load hogs for slaughter, then cleaned and fumigated barns that wouldn't be used again.

His crops kept him running until midnight. He overwhelmed the tienda with his sweet corn and hauled thirty truckloads to town, not just on weekends but in the evenings, too, selling it on the square or the Walmart parking lot. It fetched a good price, because no one else had any. He'd drained his pond bringing it in.

Up above, he hauled ten barrels of water a night. The creek was dry, nothing remained of his pool but cracked clay, and he'd abandoned his tomatillos, but by September his pumpkin vines stretched out twenty feet and more, and some of the fruits already weighed fifty pounds. Despite his mulch, the massive leaves collapsed in the sun, so dramatically it seemed emotional, as if this were the day they died. Then he gave each vine 25 gallons, and the leaves puffed up magnificently under the moonlight.

The desert was no place to grow big balls of water. He'd never try it again, but it was just about the last thing he'd said to Rosa, that he'd bring pumpkins for her kids. He was a softhearted fool—Rosa was in Europe. Why drive to Dallas again, revisit the pain of it?

At last, in October, he asked Carrie to dinner, but their date didn't go well. At the restaurant, he heard himself ranting against the company that had treated him so well, at least in the person of Bud Varner. American Family configured their farrowing cages so that sows had enough room to lie on their sides, allowing piglets to nurse through the rebar, but not enough room they could roll over and kill their offspring. It was an ingenious solution to an age-old problem, but the sows couldn't nose their pigs away; they couldn't *stop* nursing. Those raccoons had awakened something. How cruel, he said.

Carrie stared at him mournfully, as if this exploitation of

sows were her fault. But if he'd held such high moral attitudes about corporate hog farming, why had he continued at the job? Could he, a lowly, illegal man, do anything about it? This is *Carrie,* he thought, who not so long ago declared that she loved you. Why are you off on this tangent?

But that was the crux of it: love. What man wouldn't be taken aback by Carrie's outburst? Was life a Western, where the drifter found what he'd always been looking for in the hog farmer's daughter and never again visited that saucy saloon girl named Rosa? She *loves* me, he thought, but couldn't understand. Was he supposed to say, "I love you, too!" He didn't. He *liked* her.

Two hours before daylight, Raul backed his F-150 into a rocky draw where the danger of his fire spreading was slight, then dragged up two cedar logs and a long-dead, desiccated barrel cactus for kindling. As the fire settled, he read by flashlight from *Don Quixote* and reached the scene where the good knight threw off all his clothes to prove he'd gone mad, even though he hadn't.

Except that he *had,* if he was so deluded by chivalric romances that he'd venture naked into the prickly wilderness. Raul closed the book and studied the stars, wondering what sense the scene made. Maybe the point was that you must bare your soul to arrive at the truth.

But unlike the knight, unlike any woman he'd known, Carrie had no artifice. Her soul was right there to see.

Sometimes when he was alone, and miles of emptiness stretched in every direction, he brooded over those drug addicts he'd condemned to death in Dallas and on how the man whose identity he'd stolen had died. He was a criminal, different from others in volition, perhaps, and because he hadn't been caught, but still a criminal. Thoughts of Carrie soothed him and pointed him toward something—it was a forgotten idea—*wholesome.* A thing couldn't be evil if Carrie were part of it. He opened the book again, wondering if she were too good for a weary man to measure up to.

Streaks of gray dropped into the canyon, receded, and came back a fluttering red, and a slight wind rose out of New Mexico, rattling the brown, brittle oak leaves. Raul set Romeo free for a morning prowl and started breakfast. Bud Varner arrived with Carrie, Refugio, Manny, and a tall, thin man with a pock-marked face, named George, who spoke only to say hello.

"George is a real hog-killer," Varner said.

They all stood around the fire in their bulky coats, talking in low tones, eating Raul's slapdash, bacon-and-fried-potato burritos, and drinking his strong coffee. Roaming Romeo must have smelled the cooking. He rustled against Carrie, and she slipped him a slice of bacon.

She'd turned up her collar, battened down the flaps of her woolen cap, and wore those aviator goggles. If a stranger had come upon the group, he wouldn't have known she was a woman. Still, as the morning light slipped into the draw and Raul caught her eyes, she seemed all right to him. He smiled tentatively.

She'd put their bad evening away. Some words needed to be exchanged, but just now he sensed her determination to be a good soldier, to eat the rations he provided, and take orders. Falling into old habits, he gave them, even to Romeo, whom he tied to the truck despite the dog's betrayed look. He dispatched Bud Varner and George the Hog Killer along the ridge above the scrub woods where the wild hogs lay sleeping. While they moved into position, he motioned to his squad and dropped to his knees, and now and again his belly, in the thin blue stem grass, to avoid any chance of being seen as they crawled forward. In ten minutes, they reached a knoll across from the shallow pool, half-covered in scummy green ice, along which he expected the hogs to run. Carrie, Manny, and Refugio took up positions farther along the knoll, twenty feet apart.

A wind rose, but it blew the musky hog-smell toward them, rather than informed the hogs of their presence.

They waited. The sun broke across the valley, reflecting off the pool and the undersides of cottonwood leaves. Refugio took off his coat. From above the cottonwoods, 500 hundred meters away, Varner waved a red rag, and shouted.

Noise no longer mattered.

Again Raul motioned, and squad members brought up their rifles in a likely aim. At this distance, if you couldn't drop your target, you were no marksman at all. Raul positioned the venerable Marlin .30-30 Varner loaned him—not a match for Carrie's .30-06, but powerful enough. He liked the lever action and the heft of the octagonal barrel.

Varner and George the Hog Killer fired straight down into the brush, on the theory the hogs would run in fear, though you never knew. Varner and Raul had discussed simply driving up the narrow valley in a pickup, honking, but they feared this might risk putting the truck in a crossfire if hogs bolted unpredictably, which they were known to do.

At intervals, Varner and George fired twenty rounds, but nothing happened. Then George threw a stick off the ridge— and the stick exploded in air. This wasn't part of the plan, and Raul sat up straight.

"What did he do?" Carrie asked.

"Texas fishing," Raul murmured. That's what Boss Carter had called it, an unsporting technique, to say the least, and not confined to Texas. When he was a boy, Raul had seen men throwing dynamite in the sea coves near Boca de Tomatlán, netting a week's catch in an hour.

But dynamiting wild hogs? Well, even though some hunters valued them as trophy animals, they were nothing but pests. They were devouring rodents, worse than coons.

George missed with another stick, but had found his range, and dropped five more in succession. And at last one hog flushed. It ran straight from the brush, then staggered, almost danced, sideways. Carrie fired, it dropped, and then a score came out at once, some already bloodied. Everyone fired, dropping sows and shoats and one small, black-and-white boar that looked like a domestic Hampshire.

"This isn't hunting," Carrie said, glancing up at him with disgust.

"Ever watch your dad shoot a hog on butchering day?"

"Between the eyes and an inch above. Even a .22 will drop them if you hit that spot."

"The merciful way. But not pretty, even so."

Manny and Refugio began firing again, but now the hogs came in a wave, swerving left and right. Still, several hogs dropped as they rushed toward the knoll. For an instant, it seemed as though Raul and his squad were being charged, and everyone stopped shooting. Manny raised his rifle skyward as if to affix a bayonet.

Then the horde broke in two, swirling toward opposite ends of the valley and kicking up so much dust that it was hard to aim. Like a good lieutenant, the black boar came last, nipping and nosing a band of sows and their piglets.

A strategy? The boar had a strategy?

Raul drew a bead on the boar, aiming slightly in front of an eye, but the boar veered left, now fending for itself and driving through the terrified piglets. Raul aimed behind the shoulder, then down slightly, to cut through both lungs. Old hogs developed a thick skin in the wild, almost like armor, and sometimes took a round that would have felled a mule deer, and lived another decade. But Raul could have pinpointed two rounds into the boar's soft place. He didn't fire.

Carrie drew near and put an arm around him. He felt her warmth through the bulky coat and was grateful. She was comfortable, he thought.

They watched as the men moved slowly down the knoll onto the plain of slaughter. Varner and George shouted from above and fell from view.

"You *had* that boar," she whispered.

They'd killed thirteen hogs with their rifles, and when they combed the brush, found another seven dead from blast waves. Raul looked with a new respect upon Varner. "That's some technique George has."

Varner shrugged. "See how sporting *you* are, after they've ruined your corn. Boars get into your sows, you'll have nothin' but runts and throwbacks to sell. I had one tear up two dogs of mine once. They're *rats*, Raul. Big ole Texas-style rats."

They drove the two trucks into the valley and loaded them with pork, but Raul's chain hoist went unused. Skinning and evisceration took too long when you were presented with such bounty. Refugio field dressed a 150-pound sow, which he planned to process properly back at his trailer, but otherwise the men just bled the hogs and chain sawed hams and shoulders, leaving bloody stumps everywhere, with glassy-eyed heads still attached.

Romeo ran from carcass to carcass, growling, crazed, finally dragging a piglet under some sage brush and tearing open its stomach.

If you stepped back three hundred feet, the dismembered hogs looked like soldiers fallen in an artillery barrage. Mario found the scene disturbing and had to keep reminding himself that wild hogs were pests. You didn't show any mercy to a colony of cockroaches.

"Like a buffalo hunt," Carrie said, staring across the valley at the men lifting their saws.

-21-

Fiesta

Next morning he returned with Carrie's rifle. Buzzards, crows, and one eagle had found the killing field. Some eyed him warily and kept feasting. Some flew up, their beaks bloody, as he neared; they flapped quickly back as he passed, like gigantic flies. He followed hog tracks out of the valley and shot a gilt that had dropped behind the herd, wounded, but still strong enough to snap at buzzards. Then, on hard ground, the tracks grew less distinct, finally disappearing over rocks. At mid-day he stood atop a mesa looking into New Mexico, trying to pinpoint what was bothering him.

Had the blood-letting disturbed him because it reminded him of his mortality? Of Boss Carter, who'd put away many a pig in his time and died like one? Life was short and brutish; ask any hog. You'd better snatch what you could, and Carrie, in her simplicity, knew that.

But even May Wong hadn't been so direct. In a wife, once you grew accustomed to it, such directness could be fine. Carrie wasn't wily like Maribel—or Rosa, for that matter. She hadn't much of a sense of humor, but neither was she sardonic. He appreciated her intelligence, her knowledge of farming, the fact they saw the world in much the same way and perhaps shared the same goals. Wasn't that the idea? Wasn't that "love," the sum of irresistible parts, greater than the whole? He admired her. She was comfortable.

By contrast, Rosa was dynamite, dropping on you as you curled up in the weeds, wriggling your ears in a spot of sun.

He tried to imagine going to bed with Carrie. She was a big woman. Muscular, even, while Rosa—

Well, as he and Rosa had demonstrated, sex wasn't everything.

As he mused, he walked and tracked an intermittent set of hoof prints. It took a more skilled tracker than he to discern between hog prints and deer, and he didn't know what he was looking for anyhow. Irrationally, he'd associated the sagacious boar of the hunt with the one that had bitten off part of his toe, but of course the Langtry boar ranged more than five hundred miles to the south. He was curious about the boar. He admired an animal fierce and smart enough to survive in so inhospitable a place as the Panhandle, and he regretted the slaughter. But the boar wasn't Moby Dick.

He'd wandered deeper into the farm than he ever had, paying little attention to landmarks. Five hundred acres had been turned into a hog factory, but the remaining 39,500 were, in effect, a nature preserve; without a compass, it was possible to get lost. Then atop another rise, he sighted those golden mountains and oriented himself to the west again. The perimeter road couldn't be more than a mile ahead, and he'd have perhaps a three-mile walk back to his truck. He'd be just in time to clean up for the barbecue.

And say what to Carrie? That he *liked* her. And that—and that—

Great clouds rose over New Mexico, and he recalled Varner's tales of sudden blizzards in the Panhandle, of men and horses growing disoriented on the staked plains. But it was too warm to snow, and what struck him now was what a tinder box he walked through. He wondered if the ground contained enough moisture even to plant his crops in April.

He spotted the perimeter road and, tucked behind a rise, the windmill where he'd taken Rosa back in February. And though he was tired, he made a detour. The windmill, still turning after a century, reassured him somehow. It still pumped water, though the metal stock tank below had rusted through. Water trickled twenty feet and disappeared into the gravelly red soil. Raul bent to drink, then turned quickly at a sound behind him, unconsciously leveling his rifle.

"Don't shoot, Señor!"

The speaker was a thin, bedraggled Mexican. He staggered out of the adobe-walled ruins of the hacienda, overlooking a spread that must have extended toward the mountains. He raised his hands high, then dropped one to shield his eyes from the sun.

Raul lowered the rifle. "You are indocumentado?"

The man looked miserably around him as if for a place to run. But it was three hundred feet to good cover, and Raul could have shot him down like a hog. The man sighed. "I am from far south, in Jalisco state."

"You know a town called Tomatlán?"

"That's on the Pacific. I've heard it's a beautiful place. Señor, I'm no trouble for you; I only stopped for the water. And to rest a little."

"It's all right; I'm illegal myself." Raul reached deep into his coat and produced a chocolate bar. "Here."

The man squatted and wolfed the candy without saying thanks. Then he licked the wrapper.

Just a hog, Mario thought. A feral man. "Where are you going, amigo?"

"I do not know where it is. Somewhere east of Santa Fe."

"Cíbola? It doesn't exist."

"A friend of mine . . . he said they give you land there."

Raul shook his head in disbelief. "Well, you're as far north as you can go in New Mexico, almost to Colorado. A thousand kilometers from Dallas, nearly that far from Santa Fe."

"I walked and walked, through the country of oil wells, and towns, many towns. Everywhere they chased me. I was shot at twice."

"Border Patrol? Army?"

"I don't know what they are, but they have uniforms and they are gringos. They killed a drug runner, and I took off on his four-wheeler." He motioned. "It's back there a little ways, out of gas. I saw the windmill and thought there might be water. Just some water, Señor! I want no trouble."

Promising food and five gallons of gasoline, Raul overcame the man's apprehension, and they walked together to the F-150. Despite himself, Raul was curious what the man had heard about Cíbola, but it seemed he'd ventured north in blind faith, assuming anywhere would be an improvement over the bloody borderlands. As they crested the escarpment and looked down on the colonia, Raul had a strange insight.

The colonia had been a good place to live. Everyone got along, there wasn't any crime, and behind his trailer stretched

40,000 wild acres. He could hunt and grow his crops. He lacked only a woman by his side—and perhaps, at that, he didn't lack her. Like the stranger, he had chased across the desert, tilting at windmills. Whimsically, he'd called the hog farm Cíbola, and it had been.

The few who remained in the colonia couldn't eat so much food, nor could the gringo guests account for it. Smelling powerfully of sweet mesquite, basted with Bud Varner's famous sauce, hams and shoulders lay on the tables with cornbread, tamales, and mixiote—or shredded pork, steamed over cactus paddles with onions and chilies. The mound of potatoes—Raul's potatoes, dug a few weeks before—would have satisfied a battalion. And Refugio's wife had made creamy mole, a chocolate sauce with chilies and—she explained, beaming—pine nuts rather than peanuts.

At the end of the table was a seventy-four pound pumpkin, his largest, which the six remaining colonia children had carved into a devil, driving hog teeth into the mouth. Still more of his pumpkins were carved in ghoulish visages, adorned with hog hair, and strung in the air.

But Raul had lost his enthusiasm. Did slaughterhouse workers go home to pork roasts? He piled his plate with potatoes, spreading mole over it. Then he poured a cup of stout coffee and sat eating by one of the fires, casting his eyes over the shadows, looking for Carrie.

The band—the fellow with an accordion from Dalhart, the other three, a guitar, a trumpet, and a fiddle, from the colonia—played slow numbers, conjunto and country and western. It was sweet, sad music, good for old folks to dance to, good for a lonely man to drink to. He lit a cigar, closed his eyes, and heard the plucking of a guitar string.

"You play, my friend?"

Bud Varner frowned. He wore a Stetson and a fancy white shirt with a string tie. "Yeah. Ran around with Bob Wills and Lefty Frizzell."

"Bob Wills I have heard of. He—"

"Oh, that's a joke, Raul. I'm not *that* old. We had a band, sure we did, *good* band. Some of us county boys, we got back from Vietnam, lookin' at the hind end of a heifer just didn't have no appeal."

"Texas swing?"

"Little bit. Little bitta Mex-Tex, little bitta Creedence, whole buncha ZZ Top. Played the gas fields in New Mexico, over to Fort Stockton, played San Antone, up to Amarillo, down to San Angelo, never got to Dallas. The gals, they fell in your arms, only we never made no money. Elvis got his start in Texas, you know that? *He* played Dallas."

Raul spotted Carrie, blonde hair down, bobbing among the women by one of the fires. No goggles tonight, he thought, and smiled at Varner. "Elvis Presley. I am somewhat familiar with his music. 'Hound Dog.'"

Varner laughed easily. "Listen, I wanta apologize for yesterday."

Raul shrugged. "The food is very good."

Varner spat. "George—he was in the band, see—and he's had some hard luck. What we thought was bad times, they turned out to be the good ole days. Anyways, that was a bloody mess, Raul. We shouldna killed them wild hogs that way in the first, and then we shouldna wasted all that meat. The old Indian thing. Even a mean old wild hog has a spirit."

Raul nodded, watching as a boy dressed in a toreador costume kicked out his boots in fancy steps, while a girl wearing a black veil wove a delicate path around him. Hovering over them both was a devil-woman in curlers, a mock chaperone who kept coming between the fledgling couple, shaking her fist. The band did its best to provide pratfall music with a drum and flatulent trumpet, and everyone laughed.

Gringo and Latino couples, old, middle-aged, came out of the darkness and danced across the dry red earth, their breath steaming as the fires blazed higher and the moon climbed high. Raul stared across at Carrie, whose eyes he couldn't catch.

"Buena suerte."

Raul turned. Varner hadn't meant "good luck," as in "Hope that girl will dance with you." He meant good luck in life.

Raul nodded. "Everything is changing, my friend."

She came to him. Old friends, they didn't trouble with excuses such as "I can't dance." Neither could. Nor could the workers around them. And maybe the band couldn't play, but Varner could sing, his raspy old voice unwavering through "Miles and Miles of Texas," "Faded Love," and the hillbilly number, "Ida Red."

Bob Wills was a puzzle to the band. But they came together with "San Antonio Rose," and Carrie and Raul drifted lazily, shivering, hugging.

When a request came for Randy DePaul's "Felicia," Varner laughed, and the band huddled in crisis. At last they requested Maria, Manny's wife, to sing the part of the onion field worker, torn from the arms of her cowboy lover by the cruel border patrol.

"Me?" Maria asked, as if everyone didn't know she had a fine voice. Two women dragged her from her chair, and then she took the mike and cast a spell under the fluttering lights.

Raul pushed Carrie back by the shoulders. It was disconcerting, still, that to look at her he must lift his head a little. He said, "I *like* you."

She giggled.

"You're an amazing woman." Talking to college girls was so much easier. He could say anything because not a word was true. "I'm driving to Dallas tonight."

Her eyes glistened in the firelight. "Why? To see that girl—?"

"No, no. Rosa's long gone. In Europe." He wished he had more to say, but he was getting there the best he could. "I made a promise. I'm taking some pumpkins to poor children. But soon—"

Now her eyes, fires in them, were almost sly. "Soon what, Raul?"

He looked away in desperation. "We'll talk."

-22-

Hog Heaven

February brought wind. Ashes swirled in it, apparently from a fire in Utah that had smoldered all winter and now coursed toward Zion, and of course the black dirt of the High Plains, which scoured your skin like sand. All in the colonia wore masks and goggles, and covered their heads as they marched up to Hog Heaven. It was easy to lose the path.

The storm hung on for three days, ending with a gentle, night-long rain, inspiring those intrepid souls who'd planted wheat the previous fall. And then the rain fell regularly, even filling some of the ponds.

"Is the drought over?" Raul asked.

Bud Varner shrugged.

The plains and mesas and arroyos were covered with flowers. Prickly pear and wild plums bloomed and set on fruit, as in Coahuila. Raul planted his truck crops relying only on rain, but afterwards spent a week shoveling out the oozing silt, dense as apple butter, from his irrigation ditches.

Forests burned in Colorado and Arizona, according to the news; he stood atop the escarpment as if he could smell smoke from seven hundred miles. His bones told him that drought was coming, that his spring, always unreliable, would run dry by the first of June. He asked Bud Varner if he could borrow American Family's bulldozer.

"You still tryin' to be a dirt farmer, Raul? You know this ain't the country for it."

"I succeeded last year."

"But we ain't raisin' corn no more. You won't get no more runoff."

He nodded. The two wells, where Raul tapped his runoff water, weren't completely dry, but no longer could sustain the pull—twelve hundred gallons per minute—made by the big Chrysler engines. Casing couldn't be sunk any deeper because it would only punch through gravel into the shale that sealed the aquifer's bottom. The failed wells—and eight others in similar decline—had doomed hog production in the valley, and it was nearly finished in Hog Heaven as well.

"That's why I need the bulldozer. With so much rain falling, I could build a dam up on top."

"If you want my opinion, and I know you don't, it won't work." Varner laughed. "But I'll dig it for you, what the hell. Ground's soft; won't take no time atall."

Varner cut out the dam in an afternoon and in three weeks big storms filled it, giving Raul an acre of water fifteen feet deep at its center.

The storms were violent. Lightning crackled across the flat land stretching toward Oklahoma and struck one of the vacant barns, leaving a black patch on the roof where the paint burned. One Sunday afternoon the temperature dropped twenty degrees, and Carrie shouted, "Hail." Raul hardly knew what the stuff was.

But he followed as the big woman vaulted down the tomato rows, covering plants with buckets and coffee cans. They saved the tomatoes, but lost the sweet corn and Raul's fledgling melons. Over one long weekend he replanted everything, but again he stood atop the escarpment, looking west and north, and felt doomed. Even if he brought in his crops, most of the workers living in the colonia had moved away to the promised lands of Missouri and Iowa. He'd have to drive to Dalhart and devote every evening to selling out of his truck.

The dust storms began in earnest. Carrie had seen a few in her life, and Varner remembered them well from the Fifties.

"One of those cycles," he said. "Comes along every ten, fifteen years."

"Like the Dust Bowl?"

"I hope not that bad, but the weather's pretty bizarre everywhere. In Houston it won't *stop* rainin'. But like the Dust Bowl, yes, or maybe like the 1890s in New Mexico, where the sodbusters turned over the tall grass and done just fine until it stopped rainin'. Which it's always gonna do in this country."

But Varner was surprised by the ferocity of the storms and also their duration. The first blew for six days. They'd had eight inches of rain; where was the dust coming from? At sixty mph, it scoured the paint off Raul's tractor in one afternoon, and he had to replace the air cleaner and drain his fouled diesel fuel. He couldn't work outdoors because he couldn't see. Or breathe.

Masks became an article of clothing. Walking up to Hog Heaven from the colonia, Carrie and he clasped hands and bent low, yet sometimes gusts pushed them off the path, so that they learned to crawl over the rises. Twenty feet apart, they had to shout to be heard above the strafing wind. The inside of the banty house hardly seemed a refuge: jets of dust shot through the roof and siding; the stillness itself seemed to tremble.

On the 20th of June, the winds ceased and the sun emerged as if seeking vengeance for the easy time they'd had. Temperatures crested at 112, but the sun was an improvement on the dust. It lay everywhere. With a broom, a rake, and shovels, Raul uncovered his rows of plants, but the winds had not just deposited dust, they'd blown it away. Some of his corn, now knee-high, was buried, while the rest scarcely stood upright, its wiry roots undercut.

Another storm blew. It lasted only two days, but he abandoned the high plot for his two acres of tomatoes and melons down below. The dust here made lone curling drifts, but the escarpment had created some shelter. A week passed, and again the only weather to contend with was the merciless sun.

He sat for several hours in a patch of shade, sipping water and staring up at the imperturbable escarpment. Melons and tomatoes were fragile; they thrived in heat, even the 112 that the Panhandle subjected them to, but quickly withered without water. The pond below was almost dry, but he could clean out his irrigation ditches one more time and siphon water from the dam. The water was silty, and the sun evaporated an inch a day, but he still might manage a crop.

Farming was always a gamble, and you learned to minimize losses and maximize gains. You also had to know when you'd lost.

So he gathered his favorite hoes and shovels and returned to the nearly deserted colonia, broke out a bottle of rum, and lay on his couch to watch the Kansas City Royals playing on green grass. He'd been almost two years in this place, holding down a tough job fit only for a pariah's pariah. He'd enjoyed it, grown into it, and saved a lot of money. Now, as he'd promised himself a hundred times, he could head down the road toward Arkansas.

As if to underscore his decision, the wind rose yet again. Dust sifted through his jalousie windows and found its way around the doors, even though he'd duct-taped every crack. You couldn't stop it.

Drunk, he threw open the front door, which the wind immediately slammed against the trailer. "Blow!" he screamed. "Blow!"

He might as well have whispered.

On the weekend, three tractor-trailers arrived at the guard station, but one immediately died, at least until help could arrive from Amarillo; the diesel engine had sucked in too much dust. The solution might have been as simple as replacing the fuel, but every source in Dalhart had closed or awaited resupply, and the farm's reserves were dangerously low. Varner sent for another truck.

Hearing the news, Raul ran his pickup out of the dust and into a utility barn. He filled the tank with company gas and then stood looking out over the dust swirling high and the half-covered road north. He wanted to leave, but the farm was shutting down in any case, and he knew he couldn't abandon Carrie. He'd see things through.

He followed behind as the two serviceable trucks chugged up the road to Hog Heaven, a tractor with a blade clearing dust before them. The drivers found something to eat and slept, while what remained of the barn crew loaded sows. At dawn, during another lull in the wind, the drivers hosed down the squealing hogs, switched on their headlights, and turned toward the slaughter house in Oklahoma, one hundred miles northeast.

A phone call from Kansas City authorized the workers for another week's work, cleaning and shutting down the empty sow barns, but next morning they were gone. That left Raul, Carrie, and Bud Varner at the banty barn. And Romeo, who paced and howled at the wind, until at last they shut him in the utility room with water and a can of mackerel.

Now neither cell phones nor land lines worked reliably, but at last Carrie got through to FrankenCarl with an e-mail.

"He's sending a truck," she announced. "They'll haul them all the way to Iowa."

They spent the afternoon drinking coffee and playing hearts, glancing up now and again at the quaking tin roof. Varner was as restless as Romeo. He tried to call his wife, at last throwing the phone down and smashing it with a boot heel.

"I gotta take care of my horses," he announced.

"How far is your ranch?" Raul asked.

"Twenty miles. We just wasn't expectin' to feed *hay*, Raul, not in the summertime. When's this thing gonna end?"

"What will you do?"

"I'll take 'em to my brother's place in Corpus. If I can get through the damn flood down there. You believe it?"

"Go, Bud," Carrie said. "We'll be all right."

He shook Raul's hand and gave Carrie a hug. "I'm sorry," he said. "We had a damn good run."

The electric grid, fueled by methane, went out sometime over night. But by then they'd abandoned the colonia for cots in the banty barn's tidy office, where the gasoline generator kicked in with hardly a flutter of the lights. They even had air conditioning.

They cooked oatmeal and made coffee in an approximation of breakfast.

Almost unconsciously, under stress because of the perils facing the farm, Raul and Carrie had become companions. They ate together, and often he fell asleep on her couch, watching television. Even as the world fell down around him, his spirits lifted when he was with her.

"Where will you go, Carrie?"

"Back to Kansas City, I suppose. They'll reassign me. You?"

"I've wanted for a long time to go to Arkansas. And buy a farm."

"You have money?"

He stared.

"Because I could loan you some. Because you're a *friend*."

In the afternoon, from Hog Heaven's high advantage, the air cleared enough that they could see the highway ten miles away, where a few trucks slogged along. To the west, dust churned before the escarpment, rays of sunshine containing it, seemingly, in massive cones, mystically illuminating the dense centers.

Through a brisk wind he drove the old GMC across to the sow barns, where he loaded sacks of supplement. To access the liquid feed, he'd have needed electricity, unless he broke the vats with an axe and caught what he could in buckets. It might come to that.

He pointed to the sky as they unloaded the sacks. "Carrie, it's coming again."

She laughed nervously. "I *have* to stay. The banties, Raul. You can go if you want."

He shook his head.

"The truck'll come," she said, with a sweet smile.

Odds were that it would, though the phones and computers had failed utterly, and they had no way to confirm the truck's progress. The generator had failed as well, out of gas, but he found ten gallons in the sow barns and started it again.

It was three in the afternoon and dark. The generator powered only half the lights in the barn, but the dimness seemed to calm the banties, and they lay about in huddles, snoring like a barracks full of men. Carrie walked among them with her flashlight, looking for trouble.

At what his watch told him was evening, when the wind seemed to have abated slightly, he said, "We don't have enough water to get the banties through the night. I need to go to the tower."

"All the pumps are out."

"There's a hose for filling trucks; it just works with gravity. I should be back in an hour."

"No, no. I'll go with you, Raul."

The road into the valley was mostly passable, though they bumped their way through several drifts. He stopped at Carrie's trailer. "You should pack."

She nodded, silently stepped out, and walked up her deck, while he taxied toward the tower. The colonia was a ravaged town—doors thrown open, windows broken, skirting blown away, antennas and satellite dishes and electric lines dangling. Trash cans lay scattered, but now he saw that this wasn't entirely from the wind. In his headlights familiar shapes scurried. Dogs. Why had people abandoned their dogs?

Wild hogs. Two stood fearlessly in his headlights. Six more joined them. He backed the truck up for three hundred feet, almost blindly, aiming between the hulks of trailers. He honked.

"I need your rifle," he called.

She returned with it quickly. "Don't you get *hurt*, Raul."

"Keep your door closed."

He drove straight for the gathering horde, accelerating, and they parted at the last instant. He found the lane by the laundry building and accelerated until he'd left the colonia proper, then crawled up the hill a quarter mile farther and backed the GMC beneath the tower. Then he wrapped his head with a towel and climbed onto the bed, laying the rifle and his light on the cab. He brought the hose over. A gust of wind nearly knocked him down.

He supposed he could do this several more times if the truck for the banties failed to arrive, but in another day they'd need to go canvassing for hog rations as well, not to mention human rations. He had a few items in his trailer, and Carrie in hers. If they went from trailer to trailer, even if they had to break locks—

Lightning flashed in a grand arc, touching ground by the highway. He topped off one barrel, shifted the hose to the other, and lightning struck down the company road by the guard station. He saw wild hogs everywhere, running along the colonia paths, and they milled at his wheels. He fired the rifle, but he shot at shadows.

He lifted the hose from the second barrel and opened the valve full, which yielded enough pressure that the hose was hard to hold onto. He shot water at the hogs, and they scurried, and for the first time, began squealing. They sounded like any other hogs, but more anxious. Panicked. Crazy.

They were *thirsty*.

He aimed over the truck cab toward a dark depression where he remembered that water pooled after a rain. He held the hose steadily for ten minutes. Shapes came running from everywhere in the colonia, ducking into the stream, falling down. The old black boar stood in his headlights momentarily, feet apart as if to withstand the wind, before joining the party.

Raul closed the valve until only a dribble escaped. With fifty thousand gallons to draw on, the hose might run for a month. Time enough for the dust to stop blowing and rain to fall *somewhere*.

Cradling the rifle carefully, he eased off the bed and quickly jumped into the cab, but the wild horde was interested only in the water. He shone his light to confirm his amazement: on the far side of his shallow pool, coyotes, deer, jack rabbits, raccoons, owls, and pack rats had gathered. The old boar lifted its head.

"Adios," Raul said.

Carrie threw four suitcases onto the truck bed and crawled into the cab, holding a bundle the size of a baby, swaddled in layer upon layer of plastic.

"Meatloaf," she said.

"You had time to cook a meatloaf?"

"It's frozen. I was gonna invite you over one night, but you were with that *girl.*"

He sighed. "Carrie, she's long ago."

"I just have to zap it the microwave. Do you like meatloaf?"

The wind had strengthened and threw up so much grit he had to drop to first gear and crawl along at five miles per hour in order to make out the road to Hog Heaven.

"Who doesn't like meatloaf?" he said at last.

She ran inside while he siphoned the water into five-   gallon buckets and replenished the waterers. The banties crowded around him in the flickering light, snorted water, and looked up at him as if trying to formulate questions.

"I don't *know* what's happening," he said, and they snorted among themselves.

"There's a truck coming for you, but—"

They turned away, retreating to their dim corners.

"Not to the slaughter house," he called out, and waited an instant, as if he expected replies.

He checked on Romeo's water as well, and let him out into the work area between the feed room and the hog pen. Raul stepped into the office and took a long breath of dust-free, cool air. Carrie had her meatloaf on the table, with carrots and potatoes; she'd set paper plates and plastic utensils to either side. And she had a bottle.

"Rum!"

He didn't know if he'd ever had an authentic gringo meatloaf, but anyhow, he was ravenous as a pig. Between them they finished it quickly, and half the rum, too. The room grew hazy. And though he heard the rising of the wind, the pounding of debris on the roof, he'd done all he could for one day.

He stood, stumbling, and she rose as if alarmed. They kissed awkwardly. They couldn't speak, but lay blankets and pillows on the floor as if they'd practiced it.

She had big breasts, wide hips, thick legs, and was probably stronger than he. She fell to giggling and couldn't stop, and he lay a finger on her lips and kissed her breasts. Unaccountably, she grew rigid, and he kissed her again and laid his body along the length of her, stroking her until she relaxed and grasped his penis with her big fist.

Then it was easy. She wasn't, as he'd feared, a virgin. Maybe the alcohol helped, but she dropped her head on a pillow, threw her arms around his neck, and they rocked like a chair. When he slowed, filled with joy because of the joy he saw in her face, she dug her heels into the back of his thighs and urged him on.

"You're beautiful, Carrie," he murmured.

"You say that to all the girls. Girls, girls, *girls!*" she said, laughing until she choked. "I'm your girl, Raul!"

He rose to find her a glass of water and held it to her lips.

"My name isn't Raul," he said. "I took the name from a dead man. I'm Mario Oliveros."

-23-

Flight

He awoke next to the big woman, snoring amiably beside him. For an instant, he couldn't remember where he was, even what country. He heard the wind howling and imagined a great explosion, fire coursing through the floors of an abandoned factory, men awakening in agony.

He staggered out of the office to the side door and took a few steps into the darkness. They'd been living inside a roar so long that calm would have seemed unnatural. The dust was so thick he held a hand over his nose. He shuffled to the corner and peered east. According to his watch, it was seven A.M., but he could see no hint of the sun. Is the world ending? he asked himself.

The generator throbbed steadily, reminding him he'd have to find more gasoline. Romeo came up from behind, and Mario scratched his ears. "What?" he said, as Romeo tugged at his trousers.

Then he saw. Both sides of the barn had torn away in the night, while Carrie and he lay in their meatloaf-and-rum induced stupor. Eerily, the lights were still on.

Perhaps a hundred banties lay dead, huddled in a great pile. Hogs were like chickens that way. Frightened, they piled on one another, smothering those on the bottom. But a number must have scattered in the storm.

He let Romeo into the office and gave him the meatloaf crumbs while he made coffee. He knelt and kissed Carrie.

"*Mario.*"

"Lovely Carrie," he said, handing her a mug of coffee. "It's morning, as if you could tell. The banties are gone."

244

She rose laboriously and staggered out of the office. He heard her scream.

Her Civic wouldn't start, and the plateless GMC seemed to have died at last. They loaded everything into the F-150—nothing of his but clothing, his books, and a few tools, and nothing of hers but the suitcases, her DVD player, and all her *Star Trek* episodes. They made a place for Romeo among the suitcases and stood the rifle between them behind the gearshift.

Mario took a detour to the water tower, showing Carrie the gathering of animals by the waterhole he'd made. The banties seemed to have melded with the wild hogs, and Carrie thought she saw Diana, the pregnant banty with floppy ears.

"They're too delicate," she said. "They won't survive."

"Some of them might." He shook his head. "All those fancy genes."

They drove north toward Oklahoma, meeting three vehicles in one hundred miles, stopping several times to shovel their way through drifts. Forty miles from the state line, the storm blew itself out, and the orange, westering sun emerged.

The highway stood bare in spots, had drifted over in others, so that he could hardly distinguish it from the bright-white, infinitely flat landscape. Mario continually ran onto the shoulder, and yanked the wheel toward the center. They'd hoped to reach Guymon by nightfall, but Mario was seldom out of second gear. It was all he could do to stay awake. He tried the radio, but even the strongest signals had dissolved into static.

"Where are we going, Carrie?" he asked. "Kansas City?"

"To my dad's place. Near McPherson."

"Will I meet your father?"

She glanced sideways. "Sometime, maybe."

"Tell me about him. And your mother. How you grew up."

"It's boring."

"We won't make Guymon before midnight. I want your entire life history."

She's laughed. "It's crazy."

Neither Pete nor Debbie Kreider ever offered Carrie a coherent account of their marriage, so she assembled her history from misplaced letters, stray remarks, and eavesdropping on Pete's friends.

Debbie, from a suburb of Kansas City called Overland Park, had gone off to the university in Lawrence, where she majored in English and sex and fancied herself a radical. She met Pete in a poetry class. He was just back from Vietnam, and his ravings about corporate America seemed original and prescient. He seemed elemental and liberating.

"He was a soldier," Mario said.

"Not much of one. A draftee."

He remembered the black man, Abraham Potts. "It was a bad war."

They married, and for a time Pete straightened up and flew right. Together they took courses in history and literature, and made plans to immigrate to Australia as teachers, because, Pete thought, the United States was corrupt beyond saving. But then the family farm, in central Kansas, unexpectedly became Pete's, and it seemed as though they'd won the lottery. It was rolling land, half of it untillable or in timber, but with some fertile fields and an artesian well that supplied a pretty stream.

Here was an opportunity to strike a blow against "chemical agriculture," as Pete called it, which was closely allied with the military-industrial complex that had sent him off to defoliate trees, burn villages, and try every stimulant ever devised. They moved to the drafty farmhouse and raised organic fruits and vegetables. Rather, they tried.

Maybe Pete gathered his demons in Vietnam, or maybe his hillbilly DNA just couldn't be overcome. Anyhow, when the organic idea fell to defeat from codling moths, squash bugs, and tobacco mosaic, not to mention Mennonite gardeners who'd been at it for decades, Pete got into hogs.

"Who are these Mennonite people?"

"They came from the Ukraine. The Germans pushed them out because they refused to baptize their babies."

"Catholics? Who cares one way or the other?"

"Not me, Mario. But it was their guiding light, and they were persecuted because of it. They fled into the Ukraine because the czar knew they were good farmers, and he told them they'd never have to serve in the military."

"They were pacifists?"

"Yes. Then the czar went back on his word—"

"What a surprise."

"And they emmigrated to Kansas. That's how we got winter wheat. This doesn't have much to do with my parents, Mario—"

"But you are a Mennonite."

"Vaguely. Mom's Methodist. My grandparents were Mennonites, but there were some scoundrels on Grandma's side, and the Church shunned them. Anyhow, Dad isn't really anything. That is, he's not religious."

"We have gone twelve miles since you began talking."

"Sleepy? Want me to drive?"

"I'm fine. Just keep talking."

Pete shored up the barn, erected stout fences, and contracted with all the local schools and restaurants to haul away their garbage. He raised hogs on the swill, at one point reaching three hundred sows and marketing four or five thousand feeder pigs a year.

It was the nearest thing to genius Pete ever demonstrated, but Debbie was appalled. By then she'd finished her degree and begun teaching high school in McPherson. She learned anew that her husband and his family, going back at least as far as their bootlegging enterprise during Prohibition, were disreputable. Garbage hogs were only the latest manifestation.

She feared she could never achieve respectability saddled with a husband she couldn't coax out of his Lee overalls even for a funeral, and who always, always smelled of hogs. Smells became an obsession with her, and she went everywhere armed with air fresheners and cans of deodorant. She grew depressed. She tried Librium and Valium. She liked the Valium.

She rented an upstairs apartment in McPherson, and drove to Overland Park on weekends. Carrie suspected she had some affairs. Pete, in a gesture of reform, began showering and driving into town periodically, to claim his conjugal rights. Sometime during this period, Carrie deduced, she was conceived.

"I have no idea what was happening when *I* was conceived," Mario said. "I don't believe my mother was working at the hotel yet."

"You have brothers, sisters?"

"A younger sister."

"You should call her sometime. Where are we?"
"Oklahoma."

Before long, the state of Kansas began harassing Pete over his garbage hogs. They tested for cholera, found none, but made him cook his garbage. For a time the fires of hell burned under a big cast iron cauldron, because Pete, warring with the military-industrial complex, took delight in using discarded tires for fuel. Foul black clouds rolled toward McPherson, insulting Debbie's—and McPherson's and every hard-working Kansan's—sense of propriety still more.

The people of Kansas sent an inspector every day to check the temperature of Pete's simmering gruel. Containment farming was just coming into its own then, and Pete grew convinced that big corporations, bribing legislators who fingered health officials, were to blame for his woes. You couldn't come in under corporate costs unless you had an edge, and feeding garbage was definitely an edge. Either the corporations wanted to eliminate him, or Pete was paranoid about corporations.

"What do *you* think, Carrie?"
"The company's treated me well, all in all."
"Not so well in Kansas City. And in Dalhart, they forgot about you until your breakthrough."
"That was people, not the company."
"Mmmm. Wouldn't you rather be on your own?"
"Yes. But I'm not sure you can make a living growing vegetables, Mario."

It seemed as though some person, or some agency, had fostered the rumor that Pete's feeder pigs weren't healthy. You couldn't fight such a thing. His pigs looked healthy, but maybe they weren't. If they didn't have cholera, maybe they carried trichinosis. Anyhow, he could still sell his feeder pigs, but he had to undercut the going rate. And when he did this, and still turned a profit, the tax audits began.

Pete knew he was doomed and developed an exit strategy. He called his old college buddies and organized a monthly rock concert up on the hill. "Woodstock comes to McPherson," read the teaser, and handbills popped up in Tulsa and Kansas City and Omaha.

He stopped raising hogs in any significant way, though he

kept a few for his smokehouse, and sometimes he had one or two pasture hogs, finished on garden surplus and corn, to take to the auction.

That's when Debbie, pregnant with Carrie, came home.

What happened after that was vague to Carrie. She knew that the neighbors hated the rock concerts—the hippies and druggies and motorcycle punks crowding the roads—and that soon Pete got out of that business, too. But then he got into the marijuana business, growing patches in rocky corners of the farm, deep in the woods, and on the fertile plot of a collapsed barn. The beauty of it was that he never sold any of his crop locally. The concert trade had given him dozens of contacts with rock groups. It was great weed, they said. Organic.

"A drug dealer?"

"Still want to meet my father?"

He laughed. "Oh, once I would have cared."

"You nearly died."

"Doesn't matter. I'm just trying to imagine this fellow."

Pete also planted corn and wheat like Kansas farmers were supposed to. He ran some Black Angus. And dressed better and didn't smell so bad. Still, Debbie wondered how he could afford his new truck and seemed always to have cash. Soon enough, she overheard one of his late-night conversations.

Carrie's birth filled Debbie with sadness. Breast feeding saddened her still more. Was she a sow? She couldn't even hold the baby without breaking into tears. Clinical depression, as it came to be called.

"How do you even know all this, Carrie?"

"Dad. Letters I shouldn't have read."

Debbie's principal needed a summer school teacher, and she said yes immediately. Only when she put on nice clothes, only when she went out into the world, could she hold her sadness at bay.

Thus Pete was both Mom and Dad from the first. He took Carrie everywhere. Feed dealers, hardwares, the library. He'd lift her to the service counters, pick her up to burp her, change her in the pickup seat. He'd take her out to the strawberry patch and let her crawl.

"I understand," Mario said, "where you get your kindness."

At first Debbie lobbied to sell the farm and move to Overland Park, where she thought, without quite expressing it, that she could convert her family into a facsimile of normal. But Pete was as happy as she was sad. He was happy getting stoned and hoeing his marijuana plants, getting stoned and listening to Pink Floyd while he cooked dinner, getting stoned and running errands in his fine truck. And all that off-the-books cash was making him rich.

Carrie cried when Debbie came home and tried to pick her up. When she learned to walk, she walked away from her mother. When her mother bawled, she hid.

Carrie's first word was "Dad," which she pronounced clearly but attenuated: "Da-a-ad." Next she said "frog," because Pete found one for her, and she held it and jabbered at it. And then she said "bad" and "pig" when she held up a barely weaned gilt, and it squealed and kicked her in the face. "Bad. Pig."

"A difficult child?"
"They thought I was retarded. But yes, difficult."
"I was cooperative, I think. Well behaved. Never gave anybody any trouble."
"To this day, Mario," she said, patting his hand.
"¿Es verdad?"
"Sometimes."

Then little Carrie stopped talking. She spoke a few words, but not in sentences anyone could make sense of. She'd stand on a hay bale and step in and out of the sun. "Sun. Cold," she'd say, a hundred times if Pete allowed it.

The local doctor said, "She'll come along. She's slow, but she'll come along. You say she used to talk?"

They tried a specialist in Kansas City, but he wasn't much more helpful. "She may never talk," he said.

"You bet she will," Pete said.

Through it all, when she woke in the night, Carrie wanted her dad. She'd scream if Debbie even touched her.

Debbie left for good. Left the drug-dealing hillbilly who'd

stolen away her daughter. Left the strange daughter she couldn't talk to or touch—who ran from her sight. She stayed with her folks for a while, in her old room, and cried.

There was a final incident. Pete drove to her parents' house, ostensibly to talk things through, but first off Jobeth, Debbie's mom, opened the garage door and motioned for Pete to pull inside. "You can't park in the driveway."

"Why not?"

"You can't, that's all. It's a truck."

Pete nodded agreeably and pulled inside. He had dinner with the wife and mother-in-law, and told several of his more entertaining yarns. Jobeth failed to laugh, and Debbie sat looking up through her tears. "Excuse me," Pete said, and stepped into the garage, where he opened the door, drove twenty feet backward, and shoveled two hundred pounds of hog manure onto the driveway. Then he made a broad turn across the yard, taking out a blue spruce and a "We support our troops" placard. The sign angered Pete. What did these women know about "troops"?

Jobeth, showing admirable restraint, didn't file charges. Debbie filed for divorce but not for custody. She faithfully paid child support for fourteen years, until Carrie left for K-State.

A bank thermometer registered 94, the wind scarcely could be felt, but Guymon seemed unnaturally quiet even for the witching hour. Only a few lights were on. No dogs barked; no owls hooted. Maybe the dust over everything blanketed sound, but Mario suspected almost no one remained. One gas station was open, with a line twenty pickup trucks long, each piled high with family belongings, some hauling horse trailers. As Mario pulled in line, Carrie hurried inside, but the store was out of food and bottled water, and the restrooms had closed. People used buckets in the lot behind.

By eleven-thirty, they'd filled with gas. Carrie knew the town, so she took the wheel and drove them to the Walmart, where the parking lot had filled with army vehicles.

"Jesuchristo," Mario said. "Let's get out of here."

"No, no," Carrie said, pointing down an aisle left open for traffic. "I think the store's open."

Mario peered hard, and though the shelves inside looked depleted and dim, he thought he saw several customers and at least two clerks. "I don't like it."

She stroked his hand. "We need water, sweetheart. And food."

Sweetheart.

They tied Romeo to the truck bumper and walked forward, holding hands, past the troop trucks and the men sleeping on the pavement, their gear strewn about them.

"Rescue," Mario said. "National Guard."

In the parking lot lights, the soldiers seemed gray, rather than green, and Mario realized that they were covered with dust. A lieutenant moved among them, offering quiet encouragement and pointing to a field shower that had been set up inside the gardening center and a station beyond that where ghostly, naked men pulled on fresh fatigues.

Lights flashed behind them, and they moved to one side of the traffic aisle as an Oklahoma patrol car slowly passed, and the dusty lieutenant went to meet it. As they drew abreast, Mario realized that the policeman had sprung a trap. Still seated in the car, the trooper turned a spotlight on them both, while the lieutenant took several steps backward and gripped his pistol.

"Where you from, folks?"

"Dalhart," Mario said, taking a long, dry breath.

"*God.* That town'll never come back. Where you headed?"

Carrie glanced sideways at Mario. "Kansas City."

"Smart. Road gets better over in Kansas. Reason I stopped you folks, that dog of yours is *hot*. Lying there with his tongue out—"

"We're out of water, sir," Mario said. "That's why we stopped."

"Well, I don't think Lieutenant Cain would mind a bit if you took your dog up to that shower they rigged up and gave him a bath while the lady does the shopping."

"That's nice," Carrie said. "Isn't that nice, Mario?"

"You don't know how many dead dogs I seen, ma'am. This thing, this wrath of God that's come down on us, has been awful hard on animals."

As the trooper promised, the going in Kansas was easier. Drifts filled the ditches and topped fence posts, but the road remained clear. The temperature was not much above 90, and in the headlights he could see where farmers had been working, cutting their withered corn for silage. Mario wondered if they'd return another year.

Carrie, so near to home, drove slowly eastward, while Mario slept. He woke at four A.M. to find she'd turned off at a roadside stop and lay sleeping atop a picnic table, a sweater pulled over her face. A harsh wind blew from the west—grasshoppers zigzagging before it, bouncing off his legs, clinging to parched weeds. Lightning quaked in the east. He let out Romeo and yanked him toward a freeze hydrant that he doubted would work. But water gushed forth, and Romeo stuck his muzzle in it, shook himself, and ran into a field of stunted soy beans, barking maniacally. Mario bathed his face in the cold water and carried a cloth and basin to Carrie.

He took over the driving again, while Carrie slept. She woke as they passed McPherson College. Simultaneously, the sun rose, quickly to be drawn in by dark clouds to which it gave an orange outline. She directed him down blacktops toward her father's farm. In another time, another country, Mario might have felt like an interloper, an alien invading Carrie's girlhood haunts. But Pete was gone, his farm would soon be auctioned, and nowhere was home.

Carrie fumbled with her key and managed a call to turn on the electricity, and then they threw down a mattress on the living room floor and slept through the day. They woke to a radio blaring, and water gushing in the kitchen sink.

Her father hadn't left much food, and they drove to town for supplies, not speaking, lost in thought. Ordinary chores—buying gasoline and groceries—felt exotic. They returned to the farm, filled the refrigerator, made coffee. Carrie began to cry.

"What, Carrie?"

"I've never been here when you couldn't hear the hogs banging on their feeders, and the cattle bawling, and the chickens—"

A rooster crowed, and they broke into laughter. They ran to the barn, where Carrie threw a bank of lights. Two black Australorps hens squawked and flew from their perches on an old stanchion up into the mow.

"Your father didn't find them all."

"Oh, they were always half-wild." She turned, looking older and serious. "Mario, do you want to be together?"

He drew near and stroked her cheek. "I do."

He left her and walked along the woodline, listening to whippoorwills and smoking a cigar. No wind here, and the great moon, with a golden circle around it, announced that rain drew near. He walked by the failed spring, and dry pond below. What a beautiful farm this was, he thought.

And then they sat with coffee at the kitchen table, fans pointed on them from two directions, and Carrie found a pencil and notebook.

"You like to make lists," he said, smiling.

"I do," she whispered, and began to lay out their options.

-24-

Another Country

1) Buy a Farm in Arkansas.

They drove to Bentonville, the industrious home of Wal-mart, and sat for a while on the old square, in front of the museum that had been Sam Walton's first store. Bentonville was the county seat, and, as they discussed buying land somewhere to the east, a plain-looking, scrubbed-up couple went into the courthouse, beaming.

"Getting married," Mario said.

Carrie snuggled close to Mario and said, "I love you."

Love, again. It was all mixed up with the movies, and then with sex, and he wasn't sure if it had staying power. He believed himself quite original in thinking that if in the morning you had "like," you stood a chance. Love was flimsy. He wanted things to last with Carrie. "You're a fine woman, Carrie, very intelligent."

She frowned and moved away from him.

"And I believe—I *know*—we have a future together."

"I won't win any beauty contests, Mario, but that's—"

"You *are* beautiful. In your *soul,* Carrie."

"—Sweet," she finished, and bent to kiss him.

He sighed. "You would be . . . Mrs. Zamora."

"You're *Mario.* I want to be Mrs. Oliveros, not Mrs. Identity Theft."

"I would have to return to Mexico. Years have passed. Perhaps I *could*—"

She stood. "You didn't do anything wrong!"

"I've done much that was wrong." He hung his head. "But

let us say we get married in Mexico, and I apply to become a permanent resident as Señor Oliveros. The CIA checks the applications now, and it takes them years. A military record is obvious—they'd find that much, at least, that I am not dead! But we'd face a long delay and many fees to lawyers, though we would be married and could live together in Mexico. We could even start a farm. Do you want to live in Mexico, Carrie?"

She looked away. "No."

They walked down the courthouse halls in silence, past the ornate door where you'd buy a marriage license. The scribbed-up couple came out, laughing.

Mario looked at Carrie sheepishly. No matter what he said, it would be wrong.

He thought he heard the echo of a song bouncing off the vaulted ceilings and feigned a conspicuous interest just to change the mood. But he *was* interested. He took Carrie's hand, and they descended a worn marble stairway, and now he made out the words to . . . "Felicia"?

Mario saw no obvious exit, but there was an unmarked door, and he put his shoulder to it. Immediately, a man shoved him against the courthouse's limestone wall, and immediately Mario struck the man in the nose. "Quiet. Quiet," the man hissed, holding his nose, staring down in disbelief and hurt.

They'd come out of the basement through a seldom-used door the crew failed to secure, to the side of the grand limestone entrance—and stepped into a movie. Mario met Carrie's bewildered eyes, smothered a laugh, and they both fell silent.

From the sidelines, parallel to the nearest camera, Mario spotted a signboard that said, "The Randy DePaul Story." Starring DePaul, apparently, marrying a real-life Felicia, a lovely Latina now coming down the steps, the long train of her wedding dress sweeping the stone. DePaul played himself, to the tune of his most famous song, piped squawkily over tall loud speakers for the benefit of the real crowd—perhaps one hundred people.

DePaul was all dressed up in a red suit, with rhinestones and yellow zigzag embroidery all over it. The movie guy Mario had slugged handed them both cups of rice, and, part of the movie crowd, Mario and Carrie peppered the famous singer and laughed merrily, on cue, not on cue. The second camera panned to their right and caught the big white limo. The beautiful girl playing Felicia—it could have been Rosa—slipped inside the car, while DePaul flipped up his wraparound sunglasses and grinned like the good old boy, the Arkansas boy, everybody knew him to be.

They left Bentonville—that holiest of holy places in America's practical heart—unmarried. They'd been upstaged by hillbilly glamor.

Mario drove east into a region called the Ozarks, a hilly, green country filled with abandoned mines, abandoned farms, and small cattle operations. Finally, he drew up by a two-story house made of native stone, with a new metal barn, and a pasture sloping upward into a range of hickory-covered hills. A river came out of those hills, he knew, because he'd seen it curving toward the town.

The place was for sale. But he couldn't persuade Carrie even to leave the truck, and somehow the farm, pretty as it was, didn't feel right to him, either. Maybe *that* was love, he thought, when you wouldn't proceed without your partner's support. He'd reached Arkansas, and it was as green as promised, but if Carrie didn't want it, neither did he.

2) Take over Pete Kreider's Farm.

Pete had sold his livestock and planted no crops, because he was putting his energies into his place in Manitoba. The farm appeared abandoned, and no question, the failed artesian well—the place's unique asset—was ominous. But the farm was east of the High Plains and had received enough rainfall for winter wheat even in this dry year. Raul walked the land carefully, mapping out where ponds could be dug to sustain a cattle herd. Even so, at only three hundred acres, the farm wasn't large enough to support a family—at least not in the gringo style that was his now, too—without another income source.

"A beautiful place to grow up," Mario said. "Though you weren't a happy child."

"I was," Carrie said. "But I was . . . strange."

"We're all strange."

At four Carrie still didn't speak, though she'd grin, almost nod, when Pete asked her questions, and he knew she understood him. And she threw tantrums—Lord, such tantrums! The time Pete didn't put raisins in her oatmeal, for instance. She pointed at the oatmeal and screamed.

"I forgot to buy raisins, all right?"

She screamed some more and beat on the table.

"If you can say, 'raisin,' we'll drive to town right this minute and buy you some."

Carrie threw her bowl on the floor.

"Let's make that, 'I want some raisins, please,'" Pete said.

He'd placed her on the hay bale because he knew she liked to study dust motes. He did, too, when he was stoned. Perhaps that explained why he understood her so well. Pot slowed things down, and Pete studied her. The dust motes tumbled in the long shafts of light that poked through the siding up high. Carrie's eyes seized on a tiny speck and watched it sail. It fell toward her and she reached out, but it lifted again. She could watch the dust motes all day. They were tiny creatures: grasshoppers and birds and winged pigs.

She became aware that something was wrong in the pen ahead of her. She rose, and without realizing it—without resisting it—she cried out, "Dad!" As Pete came running, she tried to climb into the pen.

"Pig hurt!" she cried.

The old sow—too big for motherhood, but unusually wily whenever Pete tried to load her for market—had rolled over on her litter. Carrie never forgot the high-pitched, terrified squeals, as the wounded pigs piled on each other, and the grief-stricken sow growled out her own agony.

"You can't go in there!" Pete yelled, grabbing her from the boards of the pen. "She's crazy now."

The sow ran in circles and banged so hard against the barn siding that she bludgeoned through into the hog lot.

"She killed the babies," Carrie said.

"Shh," Pete said, picking her up, stroking her.

Then Carrie subsided into moans and sobbing, and Pete took her to the house and gave her—of course—a box of raisins. Losing four pigs didn't mean much in the scheme of things, because Carrie had spoken—and in full sentences, as if she'd been listening to what adults said ever since she went silent. She even knew what death was.

"The hog whisperer!" Mario said. "And you weren't re-tarded, you were advanced. Already a brilliant young woman."

"Only Dad understood," she said.

"Yes. A strange man, but just the right father. Still. I have no room to talk, but it's a wonder he isn't in prison."

"Oh, he's rich, Mario. He bought 1500 acres up there."

Carrie drove to Manhattan, where K-State was located, to inquire of old professors about teaching some agriculture courses. The department met on her behalf to hear of her adventures in the Texas Panhandle. She commanded respect and could sit on a task force to confront the future of farming on the High Plains.

"As if *that* will help," she told Mario. And she hadn't scavenged a job, at least not for another year; academia didn't work that fast.

"Still," Mario said. "Promising."

"Promising," she said. "And we have money, Mario."

He nodded. "Quite a lot of money."

"We could buy good machinery. We could rent more land. Grain prices are good. Cattle are selling high, and we could raise a lot of our feed. Still—"

He sighed. "What are you getting at, Carrie?"

"Well, Dad thinks the place is doomed. He thinks—lots of people do—that we're in for hot, dry summers from now on. And there's no room to expand. But—*we* have a future, sweetheart. Somewhere! I love you. You love me—at least, I *think* you do. Let's get married."

He knelt before her. "Where's my *ring?*"

Giggling, she reached behind her, and removed the wire fastener from a loaf of sliced bread. She fashioned it in the shape of a ring and held it out; with mock solemnity, he slipped it on his finger. "Don't you want to plan it, Carrie? Invite your friends in Kansas City? What about your mother?"

"I never have *understood* all that. Beyond wanting someone, I never had . . . those dreams. I was always a loner—on this farm, even, I never had any friends but the animals. Mom—my mom—"

Carrie had begun to cry, and he pulled her close. "I should meet your mother."

"We'll have a nice dinner," she said, smoothing his hair. "Then maybe we can go to the Holiday Inn. We'll take a few pictures, too. That's enough. That's wonderful!"

"And the last name?"

She laughed. "Zamora is fine with me. We'll *both* be illegal."

3) Return to the Company.

In Kansas City, they made a nervous visit to Carrie's mother, Debbie—at least, Carrie was nervous. Mario sympathized with Debbie, a conventional woman who, when the breezes of youth blew on past, had at last understood just how conventional she was. And yet she couldn't rise to the most conventional duty of all: motherhood.

She was a failure, but then most people were. Debbie was overweight, always suffering from one malady or another, always behind on her bills, and her jobs—posts he didn't perfectly understand, but having to do with school administration—were forever being eliminated. In his opinion, a lot of her unhappiness was endemic to urban life, but, on the other hand, his experiences had to do with Mexico and Dallas, and he was biased toward open spaces. He fixed a tricky light switch for Debbie, replaced a fascia board, and reattached some guttering, but he didn't figure he'd have much to do with her in the future. The way he saw it, his main task was to establish that he didn't have two heads.

"You didn't tell me he was so handsome," Debbie said, in a tone that meant nothing. It was how people talked when they didn't know what to say. "You didn't tell me *anything*. Just, suddenly, you're married. I mean, I'm overjoyed, Carrie, but—"

"We didn't want a lot of fuss, Mom."

Mario sat thumbing through twenty-year-old *National Geographics*. Logically, Carrie's strained relationship with her mother made little sense. Yes, Debbie had been an inadequate mother, but all of that was long ago, and Carrie had far surpassed her in education, accomplishments, and salary. Perhaps not, however, in confidence or emotional stability. While, logically, it would be best just to take Debbie as she presented herself and not stew over the past—no, he didn't suppose you could do that. He himself, when he pictured his mother, was always about thirteen.

Anyhow, Debbie didn't have two heads, either. Certainly, she wasn't filled with hatred and did not seem conniving. He heard crying followed by silence and ducked his head into the kitchen again. "Mrs. Kreider—"

"It's Burns, Raul," Carrie said quickly. "Mom went back to her maiden name."

"Call me Debbie, please," she said.

"Would you mind if I watched your television, Debbie?"

"No, of course not."

"And do you suppose I could have some tea?"

"Oh, yes. I have Earl Grey and some wonderful Darjeeling a male friend of mine brought back from India."

Male friend. Another lonely soul, and he understood loneliness. "That sounds wonderful."

There. He'd given them something to do. His intrusion seemed to break their mood, and they scurried about the house, gathering trinkets that Debbie thought useful in a new marriage. Mario stretched out on the couch to the Atlanta Braves, who'd won their division and now were battling the Padres for the National League championship. October, and winter nipped the air.

He woke. Carrie sat near, panting, overwrought, and he stroked her back repeatedly. "Are you all right?"

"We're going to dinner," she said. She tried to smile. "Another buffet."

"We don't have to," he said. "If you're—"

"I'll make it," she whispered.

Hard to say where Bud Varner had gone, or Refugio, or Manny. Without Carrie, he'd have remained just as obscure, but tales of their last stand in the Panhandle had turned them into heroes, and for a while they had to act the part. Carrie could deliver a technical presentation, relying heavily on Power Point, but she had no knack for boosterish speeches, and certainly he did not. Nonetheless, they drove into work every day and appeared on task forces, as they awaited their new assignments.

Several weeks after their return, the company sent a stretch Lincoln to Debbie's little house. "You're going to the Savoy?" Debbie asked. "That's the fanciest place in town!"

It seemed that Roy Jarvis, American Family's CEO, thought that a celebration was in order for something or other. Carrie and Raul hadn't saved the farm, but they'd come doggone near to going down with the ship.

"*So* glad to see you, Carrie," Roy Jarvis said, from the seat across. The phoniness in his voice was so ingrained it was genuine. He reminded Mario of Maribel's pastor—what was his name?—Tom Malone. "Let me just say, Carrie—and you, Raul—before we go ten feet more down this great road of life together, let me just say: you guys are heroes in my book. I mean, it was the Alamo out there. In the Great State of Texas!"

The young woman beside Jarvis leaned forward. "American heroes, both of you. I just wish we could get the kind of publicity you guys *deserve*. It's always the celebrities, you know? And they don't do a thing, really."

Carrie knew this pair because of the Employee of the Year award. "Roy Jarvis," she said, and Mario, FedEx man, shook hands. "And Melanie Grundy, Director of Information."

Mario shook her hand, too, with care. Melanie's eyes lingered just an instant too long on Mario, his face, the length of him, but he surmised that she was exactly like Jarvis, doing business rather than flirting. She might even be Jarvis's mistress. He couldn't say. It took him a while to fathom strange gringos. And the Americans had lots of rules about office romances, didn't they?

"I've—I've worked very hard on my speech," Carrie managed.

"Oh, absolutely!" Jarvis said. "Can't wait."

"I just have so much admiration for you, Carrie," Melanie said. "Working so far away? All by yourself except for those men? You're a pioneer, Carrie."

"The Iowa Pork Queen," Jarvis said, winking at Mario.

Melanie punched his shoulder. "Pork *Ambassador*. I mean, if ever an industry had an image problem, *you* know what I mean, don't you, Carrie? That's a pretty blouse."

Carrie swallowed. "Thank you. I don't think about such things, usually. I just work."

"Wish we had a dozen more like you two," Jarvis put in, though really he just talked to Carrie. "Frankly speaking. Front office people—Melanie and me—we're just pretty faces."

Melanie slapped his shoulder again. "Speak for yourself!"

Not exactly sure if it was appropriate, Mario laughed.

"Carrie, Raul, wouldn't want you to get the wrong idea here in the big city. It ain't Sodom and Gomorrah, not Kansas City, no doggoned way. But it *is* Friday night, and we kinda let down our hair. Darn it, we're all just *farm* people. Like you, Raul! And I wanta say, I'm not a chauvinistic pig, and believe me nobody works harder than Melanie, but I like to kid her, you know? That's who I *am*. Get up with the chickens, go to bed with the sheep—"

"Oh, you're the salt of the earth," said Melanie. They were crossing the river now, and the bright lights of downtown shone in her eyes.

"I saw your picture in the *National Hog Farmer,*" Carrie said. "Several years ago?"

Melanie smiled sadly. "Yes. I'm not sure they're going to continue with the pageant. Girls just don't want to be 'Miss Pork' anymore, which shows you how ignorant people are."

"I know what you mean," Carrie said, throwing Mario a bewildered glance.

"Children now, they're divorced from the land. They think milk is something you mix up. They don't know that French fries come from potatoes, and whether potatoes grow on trees. And they *sure* don't understand all the work that good, hard-working people do to bring them their meat. I'm talking about tradition—farm families, farm communities—"

"Excuse me for putting this in, just the male point of view-- who cares about *that* anymore, right? I just think, if they're not doing the beauty contest, we go out and find this very clean-cut young man, some Marine from Nebraska, maybe he lost an arm or something in Afghanistan. And we call him, you know, *Mister* Pork."

Mario didn't suppose that the Reverend Malone ever took a drink, but he began to understand Jarvis. The man preached pigs. In an alternative universe.

"Mr. Pork Council *Ambassador.*"

"It doesn't really matter what you call him—"

"Roy, we've been *through* this, he's not going to like the riding around in convertibles part, showing off his legs—"

"Melanie, I think you exaggerate--"

"Or the being groped by men part."

"Here we are, Carrie." Jarvis jumped from the car, pressed a tip into a valet's hand, and then held Carrie's door. "Ever been to the Savoy?"

He took her arm, and gorgeous Melanie hung on to Mario, and the four marched through the foyer of a very old restaurant, with quaint booths lined with green tile like something you might see in Mexico City. Along one wall stretched a mural of Conestoga wagons on the Santa Fe Trail.

Melanie guided him to the New Century room, dropped crawdads and catfish and cole slaw on his plate, and brushed ever so lightly against him, before fading away like a beautiful mirage. Mario sat amid strangers, looking toward the little stage, as laughter broke out from some story Roy Jarvis told. He introduced Carrie, Employee of the Year, company hero. Carrie blushed and stepped to the microphone.

Mario was sweating. This was rather like the banquet Rosa dragged him to. He couldn't follow, but didn't need to. God help him if he ever had to make a speech. A waiter held out wine, but he asked for a rum and Coke.

"As I don't have to tell you," Carrie said, into the microphone, and a shrill tone echoed. Melanie slipped forward and made an adjustment. Carrie looked miserable, but stumbled on: "Containment hog farming has been a victim of its own success. That is, the more lean and nutritious hogs we bring to market, the more hog manure we produce, and we can't build a farm far enough away that somebody won't smell it."

Carrie had run this by him at Debbie's house, theorizing that laughter would break out at this point, but the audience was silent. And it seemed she wasn't even supposed to speak. Somehow, effortlessly, with no air of offense, Melanie stepped again to the microphone, clapping, saying "Thank you," and "So gracious, Carrie," and everyone applauded, because Melanie, as the gringo next to him murmured, was easy on the eyes. Yes, indeed. Mario watched her as if she were television. The girl was very good at the almost-nothing she did.

Jarvis returned to tell more jokes and talked about the Alamo and how American Family would rise again in the Panhandle. Carrie stepped down the hallway to talk to a sober-looking little fellow who turned out to be, she told him later, Carl Franken, biotech guru and father to American Family's banty pigs. She joined Mario, finally, after he'd downed a second rum and Coke, and the room whirled, and the talk around him seemed like white noise. He knew he shouldn't drink so much at a company function, but his commanding officer, General Roy Jarvis, salt of the earth, didn't provide much of an example.

The banquet ended their purgatory. Next day, Jarvis summoned them and laid out their choices, while the comely Miss Grundy, wearing glasses today, typed the news release that would appear on the company website.

Two jobs, either of them a promotion, awaited Raul: return
to the Panhandle over winter to direct a salvage operation and
a foreman's job in northern Missouri. Or he could finish the
Panhandle job first, then move to Missouri. The new banty operation, Carrie's project, would be brought into operation near
Ames, Iowa, about two hundred miles north of the farm where
Raul would work. Raises were due them both.

Land was hilly but relatively cheap near the Missouri lo-
cation, and Mario could build up their own place over several
years. Alternatively, he might quit the company; they could
buy a farm in Iowa and plant corn right up to the back door.
They'd live on Carrie's salary while Mario developed the farm,
but land prices were almost prohibitive in Iowa, and even with
their substantial savings, capitalization would put them heavily in debt.

They returned to McPherson. Carrie went silent, and Mario
thought how strange it was, that a job he'd have been delighted
with only a year before seemed such a dreary prospect. As they
pulled into the driveway, Carrie turned in the darkness and
said, "Do you want us to begin by living apart?"

"Maybe it's all we can do for a while. In Mexico, men are always leaving, and women, too—going all the way to the United
States to make a living."

"But you don't *want* to."

"No, Carrie," he said, kissing her. "Of course I don't want
us to live apart."

His pronouncement seemed to complete an equation: they
could live apart as long as they didn't want to.

4) Another Country.

Pete Kreider called. Of course, he knew almost nothing
about Mario, while Mario knew a great deal about him, but
you'd have thought he'd congratulate them on their marriage.
Instead he launched immediately into his new business scheme.
The feeder pig market was growing fast across the Canadian
prairies. They grew corn in Manitoba now. With the changing
climate, Winnipeg was the new Minneapolis. Who could pre-
dict, but for the forseeable future, the exchange rate made it
profitable for Canadian producers to sell in Minnesota and the
Dakotas.

Carrie put her father on speaker-phone. "And Iowa?" she
asked.

"Why not Iowa?"

The farm he'd bought had three old turkey barns. They needed to be transformed to accept hogs, and he planned to build four new barns.

"Yes, I've done that kind of work," Mario said. He kept thinking about the term, "forseeable future." He'd never been able to see past Wednesday.

Additionally, Pete said, he'd need to secure boars and sows whose offspring were acceptable to the big American producers.

"You need a liaison," Mario said.

"That's the word," Pete said. "Far as labor's concerned, I been usin' a couple a' Amish fellas. They're real good, but if we was to move quick on this, well, there's a Mexican community in Brandon."

"I understand, sir. When do you want to begin?"

"Spring. Winter here is a thing to contend with."

"Carrie and I will discuss it."

Carrie broke in. "It'll work, Dad. I can go to Roy Jarvis; I *know* it'll work. He'll smell money."

Pete laughed. "Hey, congratulations to you guys!"

"Thanks, Dad. You'll *like* Raul."

"Thank you, sir," Raul said. "It's a fine idea."

"Call me Pete."

They sat at the kitchen table, discussing their new plan. First, Raul would undertake the salvage operation in the Panhandle. Carrie would begin work in Ames, but also attempt to negotiate a contract between American Family and her father.

"I will be illegal in still another country," Raul said.

"How long before you're an American citizen?"

"The laws have been reformed, but Mario is still a criminal. You are supposed to come forward as in an evangelical church, but Mario could never become legal. For Raul, who is doubly illegal but has a green card—well, I don't see how they could ever know the truth. So, married to you, maybe just a year or two. Or—"

"Or what?"

"If I were Mario again, in Canada, maybe I could start fresh. Become a landed immigrant like your father."

"How would you account for all the time you were Raul?"

"I don't think I'd need to. Your father would be sponsoring me, he has money, he employs people—"

She smiled. "So we aren't married, after all?"

"Of course we are!"

"Well, I'll drive up there as much as I can, sweetheart. Maybe we'll . . . buy our own farm." She came up behind him and massaged his shoulders. "It'll work out. If we *love* each other, Mario."

The previous summer, Pete had moved those tools he couldn't bear to relinquish to Manitoba. His sturdy furniture had long since gone to Debbie, but Mario and Carrie hauled away her own bed, a dresser that had belonged to her grandmother, and various kitchen utensils, including a pressure cooker which Carrie wanted for cooking beans. "Frijoles," she said.

February had been so warm that forsythia and wild plums bloomed, but the weather turned cold and drizzly for the auction. Mario drove in from the Panhandle in Carrie's revived Civic, and Carrie came down from Iowa in their new, natural-gas-powered truck. Buyers huddled near the wood stove in the house, reluctant to venture toward the barn. At last the Kubota tractor sold, the one-man baler, the hand tools, and all the sundries of the household; and as the buyers scattered with their prizes the land itself sold to a Colorado cattle corporation for more than Carrie believed it was worth.

She came through it all right. It's business, she told Mario, a matter of shifting numbers between banks. When it was done, she climbed the hill a last time and joined her husband.

Mario, finding no useful thing to do, had fled to the springhouse, where he built a fire and read from *Don Quixote*. He found the failed artesian well depressing. Something had changed in the land that couldn't be changed back. From this hill, atop Kansas, you could see far west and contemplate how high and wide the country had been, how rolling and boundless and bountiful. Oh, to be a young man one hundred years ago!

"Do you think the world is ending?" he asked Carrie.

She shrugged. "It's changing. But people—"

"They'll *die*. In the cities, places like Dallas, where they imagine they are producing something by typing on their computers, while all they truly do is suck up electricity—"

"The world will stumble along, Mario. People will adapt."

He fell silent. He was a lucky man.

She kissed him. "*We* will."

The road he followed was gravel, thus he could see a vehicle kicking up dust from far off. In a way the road was similar to the one he'd followed north of Langtry, except that it pierced a green country, boringly productive with its fields of soy beans and sunflowers.

According to the research they'd done at the Ames Public Library, Romeo, and even the crate of Australorps chickens, weren't a problem at the border. Mario, transformed to Raul, and perhaps back again to Mario, wasn't exactly contraband, but he balked at presenting his green card to border police. Married to an American citizen and holding down a respectable job with an American corporation, perhaps he was too cautious. But the United States was full of paranoia, and he thought it wise not to expose himself to some overly zealous official, Canadian or American.

Which meant that if he visited Carrie in Ames, he'd need to follow this underground path yet again. Of course, Carrie could come to him. As for the company, his e-mail reports on his progress with the barns would suffice most of the time, and his paychecks would drop into Carrie's and his account. In not much longer, Carrie and he would move freely, or as freely as one could in this overcrowded world. They'd provide a good life for their children. He'd work long days, drink a little, and fall asleep watching baseball.

Maybe he'd buy a telescope.

Something inside him expected a river and a golden horizon beyond. But all he saw were tractors working the fields and the road headed north. He heard meadowlarks and twice flushed pheasants. A deer stood staring at him, ran a few feet, turned, stared again. The road ended, and grass lanes teed east and west. He crawled under a metal fence with four strands of barbed wire, and he'd entered Manitoba.

Perhaps airplanes patrolled the area, but as far he could tell, surveillance here consisted of three curious cows. He looked in all directions, not for border police, but with the suspicion the pasture contained a bull.

His destination was a hamlet named Lena, five miles to his northwest. He crossed the pasture and found a gravel road, which led to a paved highway that ran due north. He spied a grain elevator just as a feed truck came over the horizon, and he hurried off the road. He lay in a hay field with its new grass. When the truck had passed, he jogged up the highway to a stand of trees several hundred meters from a farmhouse and crawled under a pine. Wind whistled above. The air was cool. He scooped a place for himself and slept.

He woke slowly, as if his sleep were his old life. He sat in an air-conditioned café with Captain Pérez. They overlooked the plaza, where indocumentados, trying to look casual but unable to hide their hunger, mingled with the souvenir vendors, the tourists, and the prostitutes. Mario knew he dreamed, but chose not to wake himself. Perez would speak to him as a prophet.

"Was it you that night?" Mario asked. "Were you the one who killed me?"

He woke. Waking or dreaming, the question would never be answered.

As the sun dropped into the west, he took to the highway again, walking toward the red light atop the grain elevator. Soon he walked in the town's shadows and at last stumbled across railroad tracks. He followed them west to a scrap yard where old augers and combines pointed their broken parts skyward. He slept again.

At eleven, a van drew up and flashed its lights.

"Mario," she whispered, and reached from the back seat to squeeze his shoulder. He kissed her hand.

"This is my dad," she said. "Pete."

The man stuck out a hand even as he pulled onto the road north to Brandon. "Happy to meet you," he said, and then drove steadily, never exceeding the speed limit.

An awkward silence built, as even Carrie fell silent. Though he couldn't see her face clearly, he thought she'd been crying. Her father might well have expressed doubts about her marriage. How long have you known this man? He's Mexican? Is he, is he . . . *legal?*

But they were a family now, and things simply *had* to gel. Mario, shy as Pete, undertook a mighty effort. "I look forward to working with you, Pete."

"Well, that's fine," Pete said. "I never thought—"

Mario couldn't let it go. "What's that, sir?"

"Aw, never thought I'd join up with a corporation, that's all. Few years, I'm gonna *be* one. With Carrie and you."

"They—they—"

"They're *there*. It's the American Way."

"And the Canadian." The sparkling northern sky lit the highway, and Mario settled back and breathed deeply the fine air. Borders, armies, corporations; they meant nothing to him. You just kept looking for Cíbola. He said, "I love your daughter very much, sir."

From the back seat, Carrie shrieked. She threw her arms around his neck and kissed his cheek. "You never told me," she said.

Mario was embarrassed. "I did."

"No. *No.*"

Mario turned the best he could, to kiss his wife. Was *that* why she'd been crying? Because he hadn't said the silly words? "I *love* you," he told her. "I like you; I *love* you. You're what I've been looking for, Carrie. I *love* you."

"Well," said Pete, laughing. "Well."